Searching for Ami

By John O'Keeffe

Many

Best wishes

SEARCHING FOR AMI

BY JOHN O'KEEFE
First published 2012
Red Rock Press

Claremont Road

Howth

Dublin 13

Ireland

redrockpress@eircom.net

www.redrockpress.ie

This edition published 2012 © John O'Keefe
The moral right of the author has
been asserted.
A catalogue record for this book is available from the British Library.
ISBN:978-0-9548653-9-9
Printing
Imprint Digital
Printing liaison
Hugh Stancliffe.

For Yvonne, Amelia and Ivan

About the author

John O'Keeffe is a doctor working as a General Practitioner in Dublin.
He is married to Yvonne – they have two children.
This is his first novel.

'Battle not with monsters, lest you become a monster, and if you gaze into the abyss, the abyss gazes also into you.'
Friedrich Nietzche

'After the first death there is no other.'
Dylan Thomas

Prologue

Switzerland

Harry Katz moved to the balcony to take the call. Far below, drifting into sight through scattered wisps of valley mist, a small alpine village awakened. Tendrils of white smoke rose from chimneys silhouetted in the weak dawn sun. He looked at the screen of his iPhone. It registered 972 2 – familiar Israel and Jerusalem prefixes – followed by a landline number. He pressed the active button.

'With you in a second,' he muttered in German. He laid the phone on the white marble parapet, damp with dew, and beside it placed a delicate blue china cup with its matching saucer, half filled with his strong coffee. He glanced down at the view: the old wooden houses of the village, surrounded by green pastures and darker woods. Restless spirits live in those trees, an old man had told him and Uri in the hotel bar last night. Uri had laughed and walked away, but Harry had listened.

He picked up the mobile.

'Sorry for keeping you,' he said.

'It's Eshan. Don't cut me off – you'll regret it.' A harsh authoritative voice, speaking in Hebrew.

Harry's body stiffened as his mind raced. Eshan Bercovic! How had he found this number? Could Eshan even know he was in Switzerland?

'What do you want?'

'Can't talk over a cellphone, it's not secure. It's about your daughter Ami. Call me from a landline – you should have my number there.'

'It's here.' He held the phone away. Every instinct shrieked at him to press the 'end call' button, to dispatch Eshan Bercovic back into cyberspace, but three words overcame. "Your daughter Ami".He decided. 'Okay. Give me ten minutes.'

Harry clutched the parapet to steady himself, as a cold sweat appeared first on his brow then on his back. He shivered, shook his head and turned around. A faint haze had crept across the hotel veranda, and the guests taking break-fast outside were rising from their tables, moving inside to the warmth. Uri remained, sitting quietly at his table, a flicker of concern crossing his face as he stared across. Harry put the phone back into his pocket as he moved over to his boss.

'What's up?' asked Uri.

'That was Eshan Bercovic.'

'Bercovic!' Uri's placid face contorted. 'Hope you told him to go fuck himself.'

'No, I have to call him back.'

Harry turned away without waiting for a reply. Hurrying along the corridors towards his room, questions raced through his mind. What was happening? Why had Eshan called him now? What did this phone call mean? Were all the nightmares from his past about to engulf him again?

Part One

Tiberias, Israel

September 1997

1

—

Ami careered into Harry, screaming with delight at seeing her father. He managed to drop the flowers he was carrying onto a table and kick the apartment door shut before lifting his excited daughter. Sixteen months old and a bundle of energy, Ami's masses of blond curls were tied with small yellow ribbons and she wore a dress of the same colour. Her hair smelt of fresh shampoo. She had a green glass-beaded necklace, the same colour as her eyes, looped around her neck. Laughing loudly, she rattled her jewellery in his face before demanding to be put back on the floor, from where she dragged Harry into the kitchen by his trouser leg as he picked up the flowers.

Rachel stood beside the window, iron in hand, a jumbled pile of clothes in a basket at her feet. Barefoot and wearing a loose white T-shirt and black leggings, his wife looked tired. As always, she had music playing, a soft piano piece Harry thought he recognised. Her initial smile of greeting altered to one of mild surprise as she looked at the white lilies and yellow roses in Harry's arms. She turned down the CD player and stood expectantly, waiting for Harry to speak.

'That French guy, Eric Satie?' asked Harry. 'Right?'

'Don't be a smart ass. What's with those flowers?'

'Three years to the day,' he smiled, 'anniversary time. Sorry I'm so late home.'

Rachel's face lit with pleasure. She took the flowers and laid them beside the sink, pushing aside some of the clutter to make room. Putting her arms around her husband's waist she lifted herself up onto her toes to kiss him on the lips.

'Jeez, I totally forgot. Okay, full marks.'

Harry was about to reply but was interrupted by Ami, who tugged at his leg then ran over and clambered onto a chair beside the dining table. Among the scattered toys was her special candle, which Harry always lit when he came home in the evening. Babbling excitedly, Ami pointed. Harry reluctantly disengaged from Rachel, gave her another quick kiss, walked over and lit the stump. Rachel picked up two vases and began to arrange the flowers, loudly singing while Harry chased Ami around the apartment. Her New York accent sounded even more pronounced whenever she sang.

'Choose them yourself, did you?' Rachel kidded as she smelt a rose, smiling broadly as she turned towards her husband.

'Well, the florist did help,' admitted Harry with a sheepish grin, but there was no need to tell his wife that deciding on flowers had been the least of his problems. His unit had been alerted about a suicide bomber in Nazareth. The youth had been identified and disarmed, but at the moment of his arrest he had glanced at a teenage girl standing nearby. One of Harry's colleagues made the immediate decision to approach her, and as she had ignored his strident commands to keep her hands raised high, instead reaching inside her tunic, he had shot her twice in the head. She had died instantly, and a major disturbance had been averted when the officers opened her tunic to reveal multiple sticks of explosive strapped to her chest. It was nearly five o'clock before Harry could leave, and he had arrived at their local shopping centre in Tiberias just after its closing time. The security guard at the mall entrance had wanted to search the car, but Harry had intimidated him with his ID and been allowed through. Luckily the florist, an American compatriot of Rachel's, had waited for him.

'Can you mind Ami?' Rachel called over to Harry. 'I need a shower and I'm running late.'

'Still going?'

'I promised them I would.' A hint of regret in her voice, then a change of expression. 'No, it's our anniversary. I'll call and make an excuse.'

'Thanks,' Harry stood up, walked over and gave her a hug, 'but no. Go on, you need to get out.'

As Rachel had so often remarked, the "moms club" had been the saving of her sanity. A chance meeting in a supermarket with a young Irish woman, who had a baby the same age as Ami, had introduced her into a group of English-speaking expatriate mothers. Two American, one Irish and one British, they had become firm friends. In addition to the frequent meetings with their children they now got together one evening a month without family or husbands.

'Where tonight?' asked Harry.

'Margaret's house, so it'll probably be a bit boozy. I'll walk there and get a taxi home.'

'Okay, but don't stay too long. I've an early start tomorrow.'

Harry grinned, knowing full well Rachel would be late.

'C'mon Harry, I'm always first to leave.'

'Yeah, sure. Not want me to drive you over?'

'No, I can do with the walk, and Ami hasn't seen ya all day.'

As Rachel was leaving the room she turned around, her smile fading and a look of concern appearing.

'Did I hear something on the radio about a bomb in Nazareth?' A statement, not a question, its meaning all too clear to Harry. Yes, Rachel and he loved each other unconditionally. Yes, his wife was happy in their new apartment, felt secure in Tiberias, and had begun to learn Hebrew. However, she worried about her husband's safety and the effects were beginning to show. She knew only too well the nature of Harry's work. Although Rachel repeatedly insisted Israel and not New York was her home, he knew, he just knew this was coming to an end. It was asking too much of her, and if their relationship was to progress they would have to move to the States.

'It was all under control,' said Harry. 'Stop worrying, Nazareth is totally safe.'

'Okay, then.' A pregnant pause between the two words.

Harry had no chance to respond as his daughter demanded his attention by wrapping herself around his leg and bouncing up and down noisily. They moved to the play corner and Harry lowered himself onto the ground to commence her current favourite game – watching her father assemble a pile of coloured bricks before she careered into them with a loud shriek. Time passed. He was barely aware of Rachel getting ready to leave until she came over and kissed them both goodbye. She looked lovely. She had tied her hair with a black velvet ribbon, making her appear much younger than her twenty-five years. Her makeup seemed different. It reminded him of when he first knew her – dark eye shadow and a dusky red, almost gothic lipstick which emphasised the clustered brown freckles on her nose and cheeks. She wore a short maroon dress and flat shoes of the same colour.

'Don't get up,' said Rachel. 'Thanks for the flowers, and sorry about tonight. I'll make it up to you later.'

'That a promise?'

'For sure. There's a pizza in the freezer,' added Rachel as she moved towards the door. 'You should be able to manage fish fingers and rice for Ami.'

'Thanks.' Harry had married his wife for many reasons, but her cooking was not one of them.

Ami awoke her father just before dawn. They were assembling a large blue hippopotamus on the living room table when Rachel stumbled past, muttering that she needed a Tylenol. Returning from the bathroom she moved behind Harry, twined her arms around his neck and leaned her head on his shoulder.

'Couldn't wait up for me, could you, lover boy?' she chuckled as she flicked her tongue along his earlobe. 'I heard you snoring from the corridor.'

'Should have woken me,' Harry replied, reaching backwards and stroking her thigh. She purred in response, and then lightly cuffed him on the shoulder. 'Double the fun tonight then.'

Rachel moved around to the other side of the table and picked up Ami, who had her arms outstretched in anticipation. While cuddling her daughter she looked towards Harry.

'Did you remember about today?'

'Today?'

'I need your jeep to visit Beth.'

'Shit,' Harry grimaced, 'I'd forgotten all about it.'

He stood up and walked to the door.

'Take it then. I'm not going to argue,' he called from the bathroom.

Having shaved and dressed in silence, he came back to the living room. He gave Ami a warm hug and Rachel a token peck on the cheek before slamming the apartment door behind him. Moments later he returned in a worse humour, as he realised he had taken the wrong car keys.

Outside the air was oppressively warm, humid and calm – unusual weather for early September. To the east, above Lake Galilee and the distant Golan Heights, the dawn sky was a vivid and angry red, reflecting on the lake below like a stain of blood. To the west the heavens merged into darkness, the hills of Lower Galilee huddling under the shadows of the towering clouds. Distant flashes split this gloom, lighting up an otherwise invisible horizon. He heard a faint roll of thunder.

In his wife's small Peugeot Harry drove towards the gathering storm. Half way to Nazareth he had to slow to a crawl as four trundling flatbeds – each silhouetted with the outline of a Merkava main battle tank – pulled onto the road in grey clouds of dust, giving him no option but to follow. Now with time to think he forced himself to breath slowly and deeply. To calm down and rationalise why he became so angry and upset whenever Rachel visited her sister.

Beth was always welcome at their home in Tiberias – indeed Harry greatly enjoyed her company – but he strongly objected to his family going to visit her. His wife's twin lived in a Jewish settlement in the Israeli occupied Golan Heights of Syria. Harry liked Beth, but he considered her naïve to a fault. She could see no wrong in assisting in appropriating land "promised to the Jewish people". In Harry's four years of working for the Shin Bet, Israel's internal security service, the degree of anger and frustration caused to Palestinian Arabs by the illegal Jewish settlements was a fundamental issue. He had to deal with its violent consequences on a daily basis.

The flatbeds turned away heading north, probably towards Lebanon. Harry's annoyance gave way to regret. In his three years with Rachel this was the only matter they ever seriously argued about, and he always felt terrible afterwards. He resolved to phone her as soon as he arrived at work, to apologise and make up.

His office was located in the shabbier part of Nazaret Illit, the Jewish section of Nazareth. Previously an Arab town, Nazareth was now one third Jewish, but both communities lived in very separate neighbourhoods. The building itself, an ageing nondescript concrete and glass slab, had no sign indicating its purpose but on its roof clustered a complex of communication aerials. Harry opened the gate with an infrared beam, grateful he had remembered to put a unit on the spare key ring. He parked, strolled across to the battered metal door and inserted his card, looking up at the surveillance camera to show his face. Inside he walked over to the lift but cursed when he saw the peeling note that it had still not been repaired. He kicked aside a cluster of empty cans, food cartons and cigarette packs. Maintenance and Cleaning had been on strike for over three weeks, and the effects showed.

He worked on the fourth floor, at the top of steep and echoing concrete stairs. As he opened the door into his department he noticed other sections were as busy as usual, with the sounds of voices, phones and electronic beeps. There were at least eight Uzis stacked in the communal rack, along with a couple of AKs. Everywhere smelt of stale cigarettes.

His own office was empty. A small room, it was crammed with four desks, green metal filing cabinets, Apple Macs and printers. Maps were taped to the walls, and balls of crumpled paper littered the floor. He went to the coffee percolator in the main office and poured a cup. Going back inside he sat at his desk beside the window, picked up his desk phone and called home, only to hear an engaged tone. Turning his chair around to the grimy window he gazed out over a familiar dreary urban landscape of jumbled grey roofs, washing lines and television aerials. An old woman hurriedly gathered in the white sheets on her washing line, looking anxiously upwards at the approaching gloom. Harry picked up a framed photograph from the windowsill. Spinning back to his desk he redialled, but his home phone was still in use. He smiled as he looked at the photograph.

The family Katz, taken by Beth on the evening of Ami's first birthday.

Harry was standing, holding Ami in one arm, his other over Rachel's shoulder. Rachel's head leaned gently against his chest. The picture presented an amalgam of contrasts. Harry was tall, over one eighty-two centimetres in height, thin and dark skinned with straight black hair just covering his ears, framing an eager, almost boyish face. Although an Ashkenazi, or European Israeli, he looked far more like a Sephardi, or Oriental. Ironically this almost Arab appearance, allied with his fluency in Arabic, had facilitated his participation in some of his organisation's more dangerous assignments. Next to him Rachel looked tiny. Over twenty centimetres smaller – "I'm five feet bloody nothing and I don't care what that is in centimetres" – she had long wavy brown hair and a face covered in freckles from the early summer sun. She too was slender, but physically strong to an extent that far belied her appearance. Ami, in contrast to her parents, possessed long blond curly hair that already reached nearly to her shoulders. In the photograph she was ignoring her aunt, insisting on being put on the ground where her teddy bear had fallen.

Harry put the photograph back and dialled again. He exhaled in relief as Rachel answered immediately.

'I'm sorry about this morning,' Harry began, but Rachel's simultaneous apology interrupted him. He could hear the happy sounds of Ami playing in the background. 'You know it's not you, it's just you going over there.'

'I'm sorry as well.' Rachel sounded upset. 'Hate arguing with you.'

'There's a storm coming. Don't go if it hits Tiberias.'

'No, I won't.'

'Okay.' Harry's mood rose. 'Drive carefully, and remember it gets dark about six-thirty.'

'I promise. Can you get supper ready for us?'

'Sure.' Harry noticed the office door opening, and then closing. 'Someone's coming, I'll have to go!'

'Wait a second; I'll hold the phone to Ami.'

Harry heard a clear 'Daddy' before a loud clunk as the phone fell, followed by a resounding laugh from Ami.

'Did you hear that?' Rachel exclaimed. 'She's never said that before.'

Harry grinned with delight. 'Give her a huge hug,' he said, 'and tell her she's the cleverest girl in the world.'

'Will do. See you later. Love you!'

'Love you.'

Hanging up the phone his mood altered as all his concerns resurfaced. Rationally he knew the Golan, now fully incorporated into Israel itself, was safe. He regretted he had ever told Rachel, as she used it to justify her going there. Knowing he worked for the Shin Bet she trusted he would tell her of any security fears. There were no current alarms, but he still worried.

Minutes later he looked up from his mail to see his colleague Eshan standing in front of him. Harry had long stopped wondering how Eshan managed to silently glide into any space. Slightly older and smaller than Harry, Eshan was thin and wiry, with close-cropped black hair. His dark eyes, almost sunken in a lined and weary face pitted with acne scars seemed rarely to blink, never to relax. Constantly scanning, when they fixed upon a person they did so with an intimidating intensity. He seldom smiled, and never made small talk. As usual he carried a weapon – a Glock semi-automatic in a shoulder holster – and a mobile phone in a loop on his belt.

He reached across, took and lit one of Harry's cigarettes. As Harry grunted a greeting he remarked Harry's car was missing. Before Harry had a chance to reply, Eshan picked up something from his own desk and left as quietly as he had come. Harry looked out the window at the continuing gloom.

He called Weather Ops in Haifa, but they predicted the storm would miss

Tiberias and had already begun moving away. He considered driving home and taking back his jeep. Rachel could not get to the settlement in her small Peugeot, and he could always invent a terrorist scare. There would be the mother of all rows, but their marriage would survive.

He decided to check on the security situation in the Golan, walking down the corridor to Current Status. Surprisingly quiet, it had only one operative, a young blond woman whom Harry had never seen before. She looked up from her computer and beamed at Harry, only for any warmth in her smile to diminish as she noticed his badge.

'Can I help you?' Her voice was polite, formal.

'Are you in charge here?' Harry asked.

'That's me.'

'I need security status for the Southern Golan.'

She reached for a small pile of faxes and leafed through them.

'Nothing there. I'll log on to Jerusalem.'

She fiddled with her computer, then sat back in her chair, took out an emery board and began filing her nails.

'Takes a few minutes,' she said. 'Why do you want to know about the Golan anyway?' The implication was clear. Harry's section dealt with fraud in grimy industrial zones, not important or interesting theatres like the Lebanese border or the Golan.

'Just do it!' he snapped.

He moved to the window and looked outside in silence. It had become darker, but no rain had appeared. The cars on the street below needed their full beams.

'That's it,' she said eventually. 'No warnings for the Southern Golan, or anywhere at all in the Golan. It's quiet there.'

Harry turned to leave, as she inspected her nails.

'There's a maximum alert for the Shebba area, but that's not what you asked about,' she called after him, a triumphant hint to her voice.

Harry kept walking, but his relief was tempered by annoyance. Still, he was reassured, and explained why those Merkavas were going north. There would be no need for a row with Rachel, but this would be the last time his wife and daughter would ever visit that settlement.

2

Harry picked up two coffees from the communal dispenser, booted his computer and had just begun tapping into it when Eshan returned. Without acknowledging the coffee, Eshan picked up the cup and sat at his desk. The men ignored each other, as they had being doing for most of the six months since Eshan had arrived. Their relationship had not progressed beyond colleagues forced to cooperate together. Little warmth or friendship existed, and barely any interest. Eshan seemed to have no emotional attachments. Harry had never heard any mention of a girlfriend, partner or family, but a colleague had once remarked Eshan had acquired a considerable reputation among the female staff of the organisation.

Eshan had bitterly resented being relocated from active service to an administrative department and had made little secret of this. Both Harry and he knew his stay would be temporary – he was too ambitious to remain in this provincial backwater, this dumping ground for disgraced or disabled Shin Bet agents. He had simply run out of luck, being implicated in a botched operation in Jordan which had attracted the full glare of hostile media attention. His fall from grace had been considered political, not institutional – the politicians had needed a scapegoat and he was sacrificed. Powerful patrons and admirers in the higher ranks of the Shin Bet were biding their time until the opportunity presented itself for his rehabilitation.

Eshan's phone rang and Harry listened to a sycophantic conversation, peppered with intermittent use of "I appreciate that" and "thanks for your support", and repeated use of the name "Amihai". From the first day he had come to the office, Eshan had repeatedly reminded his colleagues of his close relationship with Amihai Ayalon, now Director General of the Shin Bet. In contrast, Harry had only met Ayalon once, an occasion burnt into his memory.

Harry had been called to headquarters in Jerusalem, under no illusions about the nature of the summons. When he submitted his detailed report of the atrocities he had witnessed in Khiam Prison in Lebanon he suspected his career would be threa ened, and anticipated some degree of fallout. His meeting with the Director General, a large muscular man about fifty years of age with an unlined face framed with receding straight black hair, had been short. Even now Harry shuddered as he remembered how his boss had leaned back in his chair, smiling thinly.

'Congratulations are in order for your report,' Ayalon had said in a monotone. 'I've recommended, no, ordered your promotion to major. As of now.'

Harry had waited in silence as Ayalon's thin smile weakened.

'I am transferring you from your present position,' he continued. 'You will be moving to admin in Nazareth, concentrating on fraud and espionage in our main industrial sectors. I wish you well there.'

'Thank you,' Harry had replied. He stood, ignored the offered handshake and walked out the door into professional exile. To the department of the pariahs. He did not care, did not hurt. His priorities had fundamentally altered. His family now mattered above all, and the relative lack of any physical danger in this new placement took on a welcome significance.

Mid afternoon: The storm had abated, and the sun shone brightly. As Harry stood up to stretch his legs his pager bleeped. He saw a message to phone a number, which he recognized from the prefix to be in the Golan. His call was answered immediately.

'Kibbutz Meitzar,' spoke a familiar sounding voice.

'Harry Katz. Someone paged me.'

'Hiya Harry. It's Rollie Herzog.'

Harry knew Rollie from their army days, but had not seen him for some years. A large and cheerful man, famous for his unending expletives, Rollie had been the goalkeeper in the battalion soccer team. Harry had always liked him.

'Yeah, how's it going Rollie? What you want me for?'

'I've just driven back from those idiots up at the settlement. They wanted me to fix a motor, but turns out it's yours.' Rollie coughed and continued. 'That piece of Yankee crap hit a hole and has a broken axle. I can fix it, but can't get the parts till tomorrow. I told the assholes to get stuffed, but then find out the driver's your wife!'

'Are they all right?' interrupted Harry.

'Sure, sure, they're cool. I can fix it easily. Says she and the kid are fine in her sister's caravan. They'll be home by midday tomorrow.'

'You are absolutely definite?' Harry persisted, his voice rising.

'Stop worrying Harry!' Rollie laughed. 'They're only up there for the night. I'll radio up and tell them I spoke to you. Next time you're here why don't you visit? You know our kibbutz?'

'Sure. Okay.'

'Look, I have been here for years and nothing ever happens,' Rollie emphasised. 'Call me later if you want, since I can't phone you. Bloody spooks all have pagers. See you sometime.'

'Thanks Rollie! I owe you one.'

Harry paced around the office for a few moments, lost in thought. Why had he not gone with his instincts and driven home? He sat down, lit a cigarette and gave Eshan a brief account.

'Where's this settlement?' asked Eshan.

'Southern Golan, near a kibbutz called Meitzar.' Harry moved over to a large map on the wall and pointed with his cigarette.

'I didn't realise there were any settlements in that area,' Eshan said, walking over and looking for himself. 'There's nothing marked.'

'I'd never heard of it either until Beth moved there,' Harry said as he sat down. 'It's tiny, about ten adults and no kids. Mixture of Yanks and South Africans.'

'Security?'

'I've only been there once, but it seemed okay.' Harry gestured again to the map. 'It's right on the Syrian border, but that's quiet now.'

'So, you trust this guy's assessment?'

'Yeah, totally. Rollie could repair anything, so if he says he can fix the car he will.' Harry relaxed slightly. 'I just don't like Rachel and Ami being there at night.'

'Well, I'd planned to work late,' Eshan replied. 'Do you want to stay and help if you're doing nothing better?'

Harry sat silently, drumming the desk with his fingertips.

'Why don't you phone your wife if you're concerned?' Eshan injected.

'It's not so simple.' Harry looked up. 'There's no phone line to the settlement, and no mobile coverage. They radio to the kibbutz, and if Rachel needs to contact Beth she has to phone there. No, Rollie's right. I'll stay on here.'

Later that afternoon, Eshan brought a sheet of paper over to Harry's desk.

'Saw a fax you may be interested in. It's a satellite report about something going on at the Syrian border in the Golan. I'll call army headquarters in Tel Aviv and see what it's about.'

Harry scanned the fax, which was a bulletin from the Intelligence section of the IDF – the Israeli Army.

'Thanks.'

Harry listened as Eshan chased up the report, eventually finding the person who had sent out the faxed communication, discussing and questioning it.

'What's that all about?' he asked as Eshan hung up.

'They got images at the end of the visual window,' Eshan gestured towards the map. 'Some activity at the border. There shouldn't be anybody there, but Tel Aviv seems unconcerned. They've only given their Grade Five – that's the fax and no alert to the IDF or local militia.'

'Where exactly is it?' asked Harry, as he moved towards the map on the wall.

'About twelve K north of your settlement,' Eshan replied, 'near a kibbutz called Ramat Magshim. Can you see it?'

'Yeah. It's right on the border, but looks like more like fifteen K away from the settlement. Nothing in between, just scrubland.'

'So it would take them a week to get there,' Eshan shrugged in dismissal. 'Sorry I troubled you!'

But Harry was worried. A pain had appeared in his stomach and a sweat on his brow. Something rankled, but he couldn't put a finger on it. He lit another cigarette and paced around, then turned to Eshan.

'No, it's not enough,' he said. 'Bear with me. Something's wrong, but I don't know what. Let's get these images here. How long does it take?'

Eshan called Tel Aviv.

'Few minutes. They're sending them to Current Status.'

The same officer was still on duty. She had been about to leave, but reluctantly agreed to reboot her computer and check for their information.

There were three pictures, all with different detail. The first hazy satellite image showed a group of four men standing close together, their faces hidden by peaked caps. They appeared to be young, casually dressed in T-shirts and jeans. The second, focused back, showed the same four men, now smaller, with the border fence and its protective sand strip visible beside them. An attached message indicated the strip and the fence looked undisturbed. The last image showed the group, now as dots in a barren landscape of rocks and scanty scrub. The line of the fence and sand strip could be still made out, but Harry noticed what appeared to be a white taxi on a dirt road nearby. Another message said the men were standing approximately three hundred metres from the car. Each screen had been imprinted with the time of the image.

'They drove up in a taxi!' Harry exclaimed. 'All right, let's analyse. Hats on – I don't like it. Four of them – that's a bad number. So, what are they up to? No weapons, but there could be anything under those bushes. Do they know we're watching them?'

The duty officer moved behind them to view the screen, placing her hand on Eshan's shoulder and leaning her elbow across his upper back. Harry smelt a faint perfume, a musky tea scent.

'We always assume they know our satellite times,' she interrupted, 'but they repositioned this one yesterday and it makes its last sweep seven minutes later. Maybe they didn't know.'

'No, I don't buy it,' Eshan said. 'The Syrians always keep their guys in touch. Two possibilities. One is they are clean – surveyors or something, especially with that obvious taxi.'

'And the other?' asked the woman.

'They want to be seen,' Harry said. 'Oldest trick in the book – create a diversion. We chase up there and they hit us elsewhere.'

'Well, the army doesn't agree with you,' said the woman, 'they only gave it a Grade Five. Anyway, why are you so concerned about the Golan?'

Harry turned on her, his face flushed.

'Just go and paint your bloody nails,' he snapped.

Eshan took him firmly by the arm and returned him to his own office. Harry picked up his phone. 'I'm calling Tel Aviv to tell them to upgrade their warning. Can I take your jeep? I'm going up there, but my car wouldn't make it.'

'I'll come with you,' Eshan replied immediately, reaching into a desk drawer and removing a spare clip for his gun. 'You'll need a hand.'

Harry turned to him in surprise.

'It's okay. I only want the car. I'm fine on my own.'

'Look, I'm bored shitless sitting here behind a bloody desk. I'm coming.'

'If you insist.'

Harry connected to IDF headquarters in Tel Aviv, but nobody was prepared to sanction a costly security alert. Harry slammed down the phone.

3

Coming out of his apartment, his Uzi in one hand and Ami's teddy bear in the other, Harry bumped into an elderly neighbour. She wished him a pleasant evening. Harry tossed the weapon on the rear seat of Eshan's car and directed him out of Tiberias.

'I know the road as far as Deganya,' said Eshan. 'You'll have to show me after that.'

'It's easy.'

'There's a radio there,' said Eshan. 'Do you have the frequency of this settlement?'

'No, but it's no use anyway. They're surrounded by ridges and can barely get through to the kibbutz at Meitzar.' He thumped the dashboard in frustration. 'Shit! I should have phoned the bloody kibbutz. I'll call them now, the number's still on my pager.'

He took his mobile from his pocket and punched in the number, only to grimace with disappointment.

'Useless bloody Cellcom – no signal strength. Who are you with?'

'I'm the same. We can try later.'

They drove in silence. It was a cloudless evening, and dusk became darkness as they left Tiberias along the busy highway south. A slim crescent moon cast little light on the waters of Lake Galilee beside them. They passed through the small town of Kinneret and stopped to fuel the car, noticing a warm southerly wind had suddenly sprung up, raising white horses on the lake's surface visible in the town's lights. A problem arose as Harry went to pay for the petrol. The young attendant had an attitude, and refused to speak Hebrew, pretending he could speak only Arabic. Eshan tensed, prepared for a confrontation, but Harry stood between them.

'Not now,' Harry insisted. 'Come back later if you want.'

Eshan shrugged and walked out. Harry paid the bill hurriedly. Back in the car Eshan sat in seething silence. Just outside the town Harry pointed to his left.

'There's a beach down there,' he said, instantly regretting he had spoken, but with no choice but to continue. 'You can't see it now, but it's where we had Ami's birthday party. Just us and an Irish couple with their baby.'

'Irish?' Eshan managed to load a one word question with menace.

'Yeah.' Harry did not care. Eshan could think whatever he wanted. 'Rachel's best friend is Irish. Her husband's with UNIFIL.'

'I presume you registered that?' asked Eshan coldly. Relationships between the Israeli military and the Irish troops in UNIFIL, the United Nations peace-keeping force in Lebanon, were at an all time low. Any contact, even social, between a Shin Bet agent and a member of UNIFIL had to be reported.

'Of course I did.'

Eshan raised his eyebrows in disbelief but Harry turned away. He tried the mobile again, but the signal strength had not improved. Ten minutes later they reached Deganya, one of the pioneer kibbutzim. Traffic was still heavy, unusual for a Tuesday evening. Beyond Deganya Harry instructed Eshan to take a turnoff to the left, along the southern shores of the lake towards the well signposted resort complex of Hamat Gader. They exited the busy highway, inter-mittently lit with huge advertising billboards, onto a quieter secondary road. Although they had now left Israel proper they saw little evidence they had entered what was technically a foreign country, an area captured from Syria in the 1967 war and still subject to bitter dispute. Darkness surrounded them, as few people lived outside the fortified kibbutzim or settlements.

'That's it with the traffic,' Harry pointed to a small sign, 'and with the mobiles. No coverage at all here – we're in the Golan. It's a crappy road from now.'

'Don't know what you're complaining about, this is easy,' Eshan said.

'It's all right now, but wait till we get to Hamat Gader. Then you'll know what I'm talking about.'

It was eerily quiet, and few cars passed them in either direction. As they approached the bright lights of Hamat Gader, Harry instructed Eshan to take another turnoff left, and their route immediately deteriorated to a bumpy narrow road.

'I've only driven this in the daylight,' stressed Harry, 'and it scared the shit out of me then. Do you want me to drive, I know it?'

'I can manage.'

They drove up a seemingly endless series of tortuous bends. After ten nervous kilometres, which took more than forty minutes, they emerged onto a plateau, still in total blackness and silence. Three kilometres farther bright lights appeared.

'That it?' asked Eshan.

'No, it's another kibbutz. Keep an eye out for a small turn to the right.'

Harry noticed two sets of vehicle lights rapidly approaching from the side road.

'Something's coming. Better slow down!'

Eshan halted and two jeeps full of soldiers screeched onto the main road and sped away into the distance.

'What's that about?'

'No idea. Just keep going.'

They turned onto the minor road, but around the second corner their car lights illuminated a darkened IDF transporter with three soldiers on it, all smoking. Eshan stopped beside the vehicle. The soldiers stepped out of the beam of the car lights and approached suspiciously. They were young, definitely army conscripts. Harry opened his door, getting out with his hands elevated. Eshan did the same on the other side.

'What are you guys doing?' demanded one soldier – a small youth wearing spectacles and an oversize helmet.

'Who's in charge?' Harry ignored the question. He was only too aware of the threats posed by heavily armed youngsters with no senior officer in sight.

'I am,' came a voice from the bushes on the left as an IDF sergeant appeared, fastening his trousers. 'Go for a shit, and two assholes appear.' He laughed. 'What's up?'

'I'm getting my ID,' replied Harry, as he reached into his pocket and took out his card. The sergeant examined it and looked at the two men with new respect. The young soldiers put down their weapons as Harry explained about the satellite images.

'That fits,' said the sergeant. 'Those guys in the jeeps are civilians from the Golan militia. They've been called to the kibbutz at Ramat Magshim – apparently somebody has attacked there. Most of the militia are from Kibbutz

Meitzar, but three are from your settlement.'

Harry turned, his face reddened and contorted.

'What! They've left the settlement?'

'Looks like it,' shrugged the sergeant.

Harry could barely contain himself as he and Eshan rushed back to their car.

'What's the frequency of the settlement?' Harry called out to the sergeant as Eshan prepared to drive away.

'Don't know, but I have the kibbutz's.'

'Give it to me.'

The soldier shouted it out as both vehicles passed each other and drove off in opposite directions.

'They didn't seem too worried,' Eshan said.

'Fucking idiots! There's only three in the settlement with any training and they've all just pissed off. Hand me that radio.'

Harry raised the kibbutz and passed on the details of his conversation with the soldiers.

'Call the settlement and warn them about the diversion. And tell them we're coming. Give me their frequency and I'll try as well.'

'Sure.'

'How far is it from here?'

'Roughly thirty minutes,' the kibbutznik estimated. 'Be careful of the track, it's terrible.'

'I know.'

'Leave your lights on and blow the horn a few times,' she continued. 'The gate's always locked, but they'll hear you. We'd send someone up but a lot of our guys have gone with the militia. Sorry.'

'Not your fault. Thanks.'

Fifteen tense minutes later Harry pointed out an even narrower track, barely visible just before the gate of Kibbutz Meitzar. As they turned onto the hard packed dirt road Eshan engaged the four-wheel drive.

'What a crappy road! How did they get a caravan up here?'

'Don't know, but I saw four there.'

As Eshan negotiated the rutted and winding stony trail Harry repeatedly attempted to contact the settlement, but there was no answer. He was close to panic as he called the kibbutz again.

'Any reply?'

'No, but I'll keep on trying.'

Eshan stopped the car thirty metres from the settlement gate and cut the engine, leaving the lights on. All was silent except for the moan of the wind. A head high wire fence ringed the settlement, and they could just about make out the outlines of caravans and low buildings. There were no visible lights in the settlement, and all around was darkness.

'I'm not happy about this!' Harry's voice trembled with worry. 'There's no light, and I can't hear the generator.'

'The wind could be carrying the sound away,' Eshan whispered, 'or maybe they turn it off at night. I'll drive up to the gate and sound the horn.'

'I'm not happy about that either, but I can't think of anything better.'

Eshan restarted the engine and moved slowly to the locked gate, a simple four barred structure attached to the wire fence on either side. He sounded the horn repeatedly, but there was no response. He beeped once more.

'Let's go,' interrupted Harry. 'Now. Quickly.'

'I've a flashlight somewhere.' Eshan had a hurried look, and then cursed. 'Shit, can't find it. Did you bring one?'

'No. Come on. I'll go first – they know me. Leave the car lights on.'

Without waiting for a reply Harry left the car and began to climb over the gate into the silent settlement.

4

They saw the first body less than twenty metres from the gate – two legs sprawled on the edge of the track, with the rest of the corpse barely visible, arching back into a shallow ditch on the right. Both men stood transfixed, like rabbits caught in a beam. Eshan reacted first, grasping Harry and pushing him out of the car lights into the ditch. Harry let out a groan as his head hit a rock, momentarily disorientating him. He looked in dread at the body. It was a young woman, her white T-shirt covered with blood. Not Rachel or Beth. Her eyes gazed upwards, unseeingly. Harry tried to stand, only to be dragged down by

Eshan. Blood was pouring from his forehead and into his left eye. He took a tissue from his pocket and held it against the cut, in an effort to stop the flow.

'We're sitting ducks in that light!' Eshan hissed. He reached into his jacket, took out his gun and shoved it into Harry's free hand. 'Cover me. I'm going back to the car.'

Harry turned in pain to see Eshan run to the fence, and then emerge into the car light as he vaulted over the gate. No reaction came from the darkness of the settlement as he moved to cover Eshan, the Glock semi-automatic firmly in his hand. The car lights extinguished. Moments later Eshan's outline appeared beside the gate before vaulting back into the settlement and hurrying over.

'Got the guns and I found the flashlight,' he whispered, as he passed Harry his own Uzi. 'Anything happening?'

'Nothing in front. You go first; I've only one arm free. I'll cover you.'

In the faint moonlight they could see the outline of the caravans. A large object, possibly a cement mixer, stood halfway. Harry pointed. 'Wait there.'

Eshan sprang from the ditch, ran in a crouch to the mixer and lay directly behind it. Harry got up, and ignoring his own unsteadiness ran to Eshan. The only sound was the wind. They stayed motionless for a minute.

'That one on the right is Beth's caravan.'

'Okay. I'll go first, you follow,' Eshan instructed.

Without waiting for a reply, he ran the thirty metres to the side of the caravan. Harry followed more slowly, pausing to regain his breath. The door of the caravan was lying open.

'Give me the light.'

Eshan passed it over, while Harry exchanged his Uzi. Holding his forehead with his left hand he shuffled up the two steps to be met by the smell of fresh blood. He turned on the flashlight. The beam shone upon two people slumped in embrace. Harry looked upon the faces of his wife and his sister-in-law, both with dark bullet wounds in their foreheads. They looked almost serene. Rachel's open eyes gave no hint of suffering, her left arm protectively draped over her twin's shoulder, the right around her waist. Beth's eyes were closed. She appeared to have ended her life in the way she had lived it, being comforted by her sister.

Harry grasped the door to steady himself. He took bigger and bigger and deeper and deeper breaths as he swung the torch to his left. The jumping beam shone upon the child safety seat from his car, with Ami's blanket thrown across it, sitting on a low table. He lifted the blanket, but the seat was empty! Heart thumping, he directed the light along that end of the caravan, pushing heaps of clothing off the table and the chair beside it on to the floor, but there was no sign of Ami. He whirled around, the light rushing past the sisters. Sprawled on the floor at the other end of the caravan was the body of a young woman, with an enormous red gash where her throat should have been. Terrified at the thought of what he might find, he hurtled everything aside as he searched the rest of the interior, but there was no child. He staggered to the door and vomited onto the ground.

Eshan, who had remained outside covering the position grabbed the lighted torch from Harry and shone it around the interior. Ignoring the sisters he bent down to the dead woman on the floor and felt her blood.

'This happened about half an hour ago. They must be gone.'

'But where's Ami? I've got to look for her.'

'No. Stay right here and cover me. I'm going back to the car to radio. And don't fucking argue.'

Harry stood in the darkness, but after a few seconds started walking around the open ground between the caravans, calling out. 'Ami, Ami, where are you? Ami, daddy's here?'

'I don't know what you think you're doing,' Eshan hissed when he returned, 'but they're gone if you survived that. Let's check the other caravans.'

The second caravan was empty and undisturbed, as was the third, but outside the fourth lay the body of a man. Inside they found two women and two men, all with small-bore bullet holes in their foreheads, but no sign of Ami. They had no worries about making noise, and Eshan joined Harry in walking around the compound calling out her name. Harry's cut had stopped bleeding, and he had two hands free. The last body, that of a woman, was just outside the hen house.

Then they heard rapidly approaching engines, and moments later two jeeps drew up beside Eshan's, carrying a group of heavily armed civilians – five men and two women. Rollie from the kibbutz was in charge. He was deadly serious, totally concentrated. Harry, horror edging his voice, told what they had found.

'You're sure they're gone?' asked Rollie.

'Sure.'

'Okay. We need light. I'll turn the generator on. Two minutes. Everybody get some cover.'

The Israelis went into silent concealment as the area flooded with light, but nothing happened. They methodically searched the settlement, but with no success. Harry returned to Beth's caravan, checking it from top to bottom before collapsing beside his dead wife. He detached her body from her twin and cradled her fiercely in his arms, rocking her while crying bitterly and incoherently. Eshan stood guard outside. He refused to let anyone enter. Finally Harry stood up, wiped his face and came to the door. 'They must have taken Ami. I'm going after them.' He picked up his Uzi and started to move towards the rear of the compound, in the direction of the Syrian border, but was physically restrained by Rollie and Eshan.

'You can't, Harry,' Rollie's voice was sympathetic. 'It's too dark. We'd kill ourselves or they'll do it for us. We'll have to wait for the army.'

His voice was drowned by a thumping noise as two large helicopters roared into view from the south, powerful searchlights lighting all below them. A kibbutznik lit a flare, to indicate the wind direction, and the first helicopter landed in a cloud of dust. The other prowled around above as guard, cannons sweeping in constant awareness. Eshan ran over and explained to the pilot what had happened. The gunship took off again, joined its fellow, and headed away in a searching pattern towards the nearby Syrian border. Within minutes the radio operator on the ground, beside Harry, received a message.

'They can see a hole in the border wire, and tracks going in and out,' she said to Harry and Eshan. 'No sign of anything between here and the fence. They're going to keep on looking.'

Harry snatched the microphone from the woman.

'They have my child,' he shouted. 'Go after them. Don't let them get away.'

'Syrian radar has lit us up.' The pilot sounded worried. 'I'm not starting a war over a baby. We'll keep looking for the body here.'

'They can't cross into Syria.' Eshan shook Harry. 'It's not their fault. She may still be in here. Come on, we'll keep looking.'

The helicopters and the others on the ground kept up their search for the next twenty minutes until the pilot radioed down that they had to return to base, adding he could see some IDF vehicles approaching. By this stage someone had broken the gate lock and the three vehicles had been moved into the compound. Nobody seemed sure what to do. The arrival of two army personnel carriers and a jeep, with a major in command, added another fifteen or so soldiers to the crowd. Eshan told Harry to wait as he had a conversation with the IDF officer.

The major called Harry over. A grey haired man in his late forties, he introduced himself as Samuel, sympathised with Harry's loss, but stated firmly any farther searching outside the settlement would have to wait until morning. He shone a torch onto Harry's pale and bloody face.

'You're forehead's a mess. I'll get someone to look after it.'

Samuel called over the unit's medic, who ordered Harry to sit while she sutured the gash on his forehead. Noting his suffering she cleared it with her superior to give Harry an injection. Harry protested, but the major insisted, and she gave him a needle in the arm.

As the medication took effect Harry started to feel drowsy, but in one last moment of clarity asked the officer if he had access to tracker dogs. Samuel nodded a 'yes'. As Harry began to sway, Eshan steered him over to one of the empty caravans and made him lie down.

'You'll have to sleep. I'll tell you if anything happens.'

'Wake me before dawn. Promise.'

'Just shut up.'

Tears streaming down his face, Harry desperately fought sleep, but the combined effects of the morphine and diazepam won the battle and he passed into a troubled unconsciousness.

5

Rachel and Beth's bodies lay sprawled among the dead as Ami played in the rubble. Harry crouched, desperately calling for air support, when he felt a hand on his shoulder and a voice speaking his name. He turned in confusion. Above him stood a worried and exhausted looking Eshan, silhouetted by the caravan light.

'It's all right.' Harry shook his head to banish one nightmare. The other returned as the full horrors came tumbling back. 'I'm awake. Any sign of Ami?'

'No. Nothing.'

As Harry tried to sit he moaned and grasped his forehead, a spasm of pain creasing his face.

'The medic gave me some painkillers,' said Eshan, handing him two pills and a plastic water bottle. Harry drank eagerly.

'What's happening?'

'It's almost dawn. The army has taken over, but you've to decide what's to happen to Rachel and Beth.'

'What do you mean?'

'Where to take their bodies.'

Harry struggled to his feet and made his way to the caravan door. It wasn't yet dawn and the light outside came from the settlement's lamps. There was a faint chilly mist – the wind having abated. Army vehicles were scattered around the compound, with silent groups of soldiers huddled together. To his left was a military field ambulance. 'Is that where they are?'

'Yes. Both of them.'

Harry looked at the ambulance, but the realisation his murdered wife lay there was far too painful to assimilate. 'Can they be taken to Tiberias?'

'Sure.' Eshan's voice was almost sympathetic. 'I'll get the army guys to look after it.' He motioned in the other direction. 'I managed to get dogs from Palat.'

An unmarked green van was parked in the middle of the settlement. Two men in the grey uniform of the Israeli army's elite Palat Search and Rescue Unit emerged, stretching their limbs and looking around curiously. One of them opened the back of their van and out jumped two eager Mallanois dogs. These large brown Belgian hounds were reputedly the most efficient tracker dogs in the world. The handler came across, spoke to Eshan whom he seemed to know, and then moved over to Harry. Older than Harry, probably in his early thirties, he had a lined, worn face.

'Name's Luke,' he said, making no attempt to shake hands. 'You the father of the kid?'

'Yes.'

'I'll need a scent for the dogs. Do you have any of her clothes?'

'I'm not sure, I don't think so. Would her car seat do?'

'Car seats are perfect.' Luke looked around. 'Where is it?'

'In that caravan.' Harry pointed. 'I'll get it for you.'

'No, don't touch it. Leave it to me.'

Luke emerged from the caravan with the car seat, which he placed on the ground. He led one of the dogs over to scent it, and then nodded in satisfaction.

'That's enough for her to go on. Don't allow anyone out the back until I've searched it. My colleague will check the settlement and I'll try the trail to the border. Follow behind if you want.'

Eshan organised a group of four – two army men and two women – to accompany them. They shook hands briefly with Harry, muttering their condolences, avoiding his eyes. Harry and Eshan followed the handler to the rear of the compound, via the caravan to collect their weapons. They passed the ambulance with the bodies of the sisters inside. At the rear of the compound they saw the hole in the wire fence where the intruders had entered. Harry shook his head in disgust. 'That fence is a joke. A child could get through!'

The dog handler took the lead as the group filed through the gap and into the cleared fields behind, usually grazed by the settlement's sheep.

'Stop where you are now, and when I find the scent stay at least twenty metres behind,' ordered Luke. 'Keep a sharp eye out. It's unlikely there's any traps, but watch where you put your feet. If you see any movement, shoot first and ask questions afterwards.'

'I'll lead,' Harry turned to the soldiers, 'and you follow behind. It's my daughter, so don't get too trigger happy.'

The sun had not yet risen, and in a faint and silent dawn mist there was a surreal beauty to the rocky and scrubbed terrain around the cleared land. The painkillers Harry had taken had begun to work, and as his adrenaline kicked in he became less conscious of his throbbing headache. Luke and his dog walked straight across the pasture, and Luke shouted again to the others to remain where they were as he and his dog crossed into the scrub beyond. They made their way for about fifty metres, with no response from the dog.

'Nothing this direction,' shouted Luke as he turned the dog around. 'Don't move until I try the other way.'

They retraced their steps, and thirty metres farther Luke called out that the dog had begun to smell something.

'What is it?' shouted Harry.

'Not the scent from the car seat. There's a track going that way in the right direction. I'd say we are wasting our time. The kid will be found in the settlement.'

'Just keep looking,' snapped Harry.

Luke progressed slowly but purposefully in a straight line along a faint track, following the scent being picked up by the dog, the others filing behind. They walked uneventfully for approximately a kilometre, as the trail led into rockier and more uneven ground, but the dog seemed to be following a definite lead. Soon they saw in the distance the wire security fence and sand strip of the Syrian border, with empty rocky wasteland in between. Two hundred metres farther the handler called that he could see a narrow but deep wadi in front, and to be careful. Luke and the dog disappeared from view, but as the others approached there was an excited yell from Luke.

'She's going mad. It's a definite contact. Don't come down. Leave it to me.'

They hurried forward, crowding together at the lip of the wadi to see the dog circling and pawing at the earth of a small clearing between three large rocks.

'Are you sure?' Harry could not contain himself.

'Of course I'm sure.' Luke shot him a look of disdain. 'This is a positive. That kid's been here. Radio back and get the other dog, and tell them to bring the seat to confirm it.'

'Okay.'

'Well, there's no sign of any kid here, but she's been on that ground. I'd stake my life on it.' Luke seemed more helpful. 'We'll follow on and see what happens.' He dragged his reluctant dog onwards in the direction of the border, and the animal recommenced following the faint trail. 'They must have put the kid on the ground there and picked her up again, that's why her scent has diminished.' Luke shouted back over his shoulder.

While one of the soldiers radioed to the settlement, the others followed into the wadi and climbed up the other side. The ground sloped gently downwards towards the border fence. The pale dawn sun had cleared the low hills of Syria and shone directly into their eyes. Harry took the lead and stopped at the edge of the flat sandy security strip on the Israeli side of the border. There were clearly visible tracks across the strip to a jagged hole in the border fence.

'They must have known the positions of the mines,' said one of the soldiers. Harry nodded. The border fence would have been relatively easy to bypass, but the mines buried in the sand remained the principal deterrent.

'That's for sure,' said Eshan. 'Knew exactly what they were doing. Satellite diversion and now this.' He looked at Harry, who shrugged in sad agreement.

'What now?' asked Luke.

'Can you confirm with the other dog?'

'Sure. And sorry for what I said earlier. Turns out you're right, but they don't take kids. I don't understand it.'

As Luke and his dog retraced their steps, one of the IDF women took a video camera from her backpack and began to record the scene. The other radioed back to the settlement.Harry and Eshan stood in silence until eventually Eshan spoke. 'I don't understand it either. If Luke is right Ami must be alive. But why?'

'She survived.' Harry felt a surge of relief – one faint light in so much darkness. 'She's over there somewhere, I know it.'

Across the border a distant low rumbling became louder, and two Syrian armoured personnel carriers trundled into view, pulling up alongside the break in the fence. A group of fifteen or so soldiers emerged and milled around, looking at the hole in the fence, chortling and laughing. As some stared down the group of Israelis fifty metres away, others started to take photos, only to be shouted at by an officer. Hurriedly they put their cameras away. The officer walked over to his radioman, took the microphone and began to speak.

'Do you want to talk to him?' the Israeli radio operator asked Eshan.

'Put me on.'

The Syrian and Eshan had a heated exchange. Eshan turned to Harry.

'He knows what happened. Says it's nothing to do with the Syrians. They must have come from Lebanon, he says, and they are looking everywhere for them. Do you want to waste your time speaking to this pig?'

'I'll do it.'

He took the microphone.

'I'm a civilian, not a settler or army.' Harry spoke in Arabic, in his strong Nazareth accent. 'Are you a father, do you have children?'

'Why do you ask?' The officer looked at Harry, a faint puzzlement in his voice.

'They have stolen my baby from the settlement, and she's over there somewhere.'

'You must be mistaken, they never take children, but if happens to be true then we in the Syrian army will do everything in our power to get your child back. I will let my superiors know.' He passed the microphone back to his operator and barked orders to his men.

Harry put down his microphone, and turned to Eshan.

'He's full of shit, but what do you expect.'

'Nothing more we can do here,' said Eshan. 'Let's see what's happening with the other dog.'

Harry took a last despairing look across into Syria, for a second harboring a fleeting thought that this was all a terrible nightmare and Ami would suddenly appear. They left the four soldiers, measuring and recording evidence of the incursion, and retraced their steps. As they approached the wadi Luke came scrambling up with his dog. 'The other dog confirmed it – it's now a definite,' he said. He shook hands with Harry and walked away.

Harry climbed slowly down the wadi wall and retrieved the car seat. Together he and Eshan walked back to the settlement. The dog teams were leaving, the ambulance had departed, and only a few soldiers, a group of army photographers, and a police forensic team remained. Rollie walked over to them, wiping his hands.

'Did the best I could do. I got the parts and fixed the jeep. Some of the army guys helped me, and it seems okay now.'

'Thanks, I appreciate it.'

'That's not all. I've all sorts of messages for you, but first some food.' He indicated a table in the shade beside a caravan. Harry drank strong black coffee from a white foam cup as Eshan, crumbs spilling from his mouth, chewed a bread roll.

'The Syrians know nothing,' said Eshan. 'Not they would have helped anyway.'

'I'm afraid I agree,' said Rollie. Reaching into his pocket he removed a small business card which he passed to Harry. 'I almost forgot about this. The army guy asked me to give it to you. It's the number of the Chevra Chadishe burial agency in Tiberias. They'll organise everything. Call them as soon as you get home.'

'They've taken Rachel there?'

Rollie nodded and moved away. Harry walked over to Beth's caravan, stood at the door for a moment deep in thought, then turned and went to his own car. Automatically he began to open the rear door, to put the child's car seat inside, but instead he opened the boot where he placed it and his Uzi. His voice steady, he thanked Eshan for his assistance. Then, picking up Ami's teddy bear, he placed it gently on the passenger seat and muttered a quiet 'shalom'. Without a backward glance he drove slowly past the army checkpoint at the gate.

6

Outside the settlement gate a television crew was arranging their satellite aerial. Harry barely noticed them and drove carefully along the rutted track from the settlement, grateful for the silence. Reaching the turnoff to the paved road beside the kibbutz he met another army checkpoint, but the soldiers just waved him through. Beyond stood a noisy cluster of television crews, all with trucks and satellite antennae. Ignoring attempts to stop him, he accelerated away.

As the road leveled out he began to think more clearly. Two intertwining sets of images kept jostling through his mind. One, the memory of his wife and her twin sister embraced together in death, a picture of devastation and sadness. The other, the vision of the dog handler as he found the spot where Ami had been placed upon the ground, was one of hope. Not a faint hope, in spite of what everybody else told him, but firm proof Ami had survived. This thought was replaced by guilt at the realization that he could so easily have prevented all this. He should have acted on his instincts and driven home. He could have protected his daughter but he had failed her. Had she seen her mother and aunt murdered? Were they abusing her? Even torturing her?

Stop this, he told himself. Self-flagellation will not help, but his mind kept going back to the image of Rachel. He slowed the car to a crawl, reached into the glove box and took out a tape – Keith Jarret's "Koln Concert", a soft jazz piano piece.

He drove along, numbly listening to the music, quietly promising his dead wife he would find her daughter.

Harry retraced the remainder of the previous night's journey, to his apartment block, to a virtually empty car park. He stopped at his door, then returned to the car and removed Ami's teddy bear. Inside, the first thing he did was go to

Ami's room and put the toy into her cot.

'I will find you,' he said quietly. 'I promise. I will never ever abandon you. But first I must look after your mother.'

The normality of the apartment was eerie. It was silent, with neither music, which Rachel always played in the background, nor the babbling and laughing of Ami to be heard. It looked its usual mess. Rachel had always been untidy to a fault, leaving all her and Ami's clothes, toys, books, newspapers and anything else scattered everywhere. She tidied up once a week when Harry, the exact opposite of her relaxed attitude to tidiness, had endured enough. It had been approaching clean-up time, and confusion reigned throughout the apartment. Harry did acknowledge that he was probably a little over-organised – a product of his military training allied with his somewhat obsessive personality. But he had been coming around, albeit slowly, to accepting that Rachel would never change, and that babies and overly fussy organisation could not co-exist. The domestic chaos impacted on the pathos of his current situation in a way which he had not considered possible.

'Don't even think, just do it,' he spoke again, aloud, to himself.

He went into the kitchen, made a pot of coffee, gulped a bowl of cereal and sat at the phone with his drink. On the table stood a formal family photograph, taken by a professional photographer just two weeks ago. Rachel standing beside Harry, he holding Ami on his knee while seated. Ami, face framed by her golden curls, this time smiling broadly at the photographer, her new front teeth clearly visible, wearing an embroidered white dress given to her by Beth.

He turned the photograph over, too upset to continue looking at it, and with extreme difficulty focused his attentions. First he took out the card Rollie had given him and phoned the Chevra Chadishe, the Jewish Burial Society. A woman, who sounded both efficient and compassionate, calmly explained to Harry what the process entailed. Harry had been to many funerals, often of comrades, but never had organised one before.

'I know it should be today,' Harry said, 'but Rachel's parents don't know what has happened. They live in New York. The twins are their only children, so it will have to be tomorrow. That's not an option.'

'I understand. We are allowed postpone if necessary. I'll arrange it for early afternoon tomorrow.'

Ignoring the incessant flashing of the telephone answering machine Harry took out Rachel's address book and phoned her parents. He looked at his watch. It was ten-thirty, but before he could estimate New York time Rachel's mother Anna answered.

'Harry. It's you, thank goodness.' There was desperation in her voice. 'It's all over the news here. I've been phoning and phoning. It's Beth's settlement, isn't it? Oh God, Harry, do you know anything? Is she all right?'

Harry took a deep breath.

'Rachel and Ami were there as well.'

'What! Rachel and Ami? Oh my God, Harry!'

He heard the phone being dropped and the sound of crying in the background.

'Roy! Rachel was there too.'

Rachel's father came on the line.

'Harry.' Roy's voice sounded steadier.

'Roy, they are both dead,' Harry forced the words out. 'I'm so sorry.'

'And Ami?'

'She was there too, but she's still alive. They took her with them into Syria.'

'She was stolen?'

'We are searching for her. The funeral is arranged for tomorrow afternoon, that's the only definite thing I can tell you.'

'We'll be there as soon as possible. I can't speak any more.'

Roy hung up. Harry exhaled slowly. He slumped in despair, with his head in his hands, then sat up and dialed his own mother's number in Haifa. She answered immediately.

'I'm coming straight over,' she said.

'Please do.'

Without allowing himself to feel anything, he proceeded to his next task. He looked through Rachel's book of numbers until he found the phone number of her Irish friend. Margaret Farrell answered; almost breaking down when she heard what had happened, but through loud sobs said yes, she would ask her husband to call to Harry immediately. Brian had the day off. He had gone for a run and had left his phone behind, but she would take the car and go look for him.

Harry sipped his coffee in quiet despair. The most urgent calls had been made, and he could plan. Barely ten minutes later the doorbell rang. Brian

Farrell stood outside drenched in sweat, wearing a green football shirt with "Ireland" written in white across the front, white shorts and running shoes. He was a heavily built man, with short brown hair and a youthful freckled face. Slightly shorter than Harry, he was about the same age. He wiped his sweaty hand on his shorts and shook Harry's hand firmly. Brian drank a glass of cold water and Harry lit a cigarette.

'You haven't called me over for my sympathy,' Brian said. 'So. How can I help?'

'We are presuming whoever did this came from Lebanon. You know the story – you guys have different contacts there than we do. If you hear anything about a kidnapped child, would you get involved?'

Brian nodded.

'The next bit is more difficult. In Israel we never pay a ransom for kidnappings, but could you let it be known that, in this case, it could be discussed.'

'Could be big trouble for you.' Brian looked concerned.

'What would you do if Alice was taken?' Harry studied Brian carefully as he asked, seeing a flicker of agreement. 'Unfortunately I don't think a ransom is likely, since Ami wasn't supposed to be there.'

'I agree, and they probably did come from Lebanon. I'll go straight to HQ in Naquora and get on to it.'

Harry gave Brian his pager details, but did not offer his mobile number. As Brian was leaving the phone rang. It was Eshan. Harry gestured towards the phone and put his finger to his lips. Brian nodded silently and left.

'Heard anything?'

'Nothing of any help. The satellites saw those tracks we found, and nothing else. I've spoken to Mossad, but they don't have much more than we know on Lebanon. They're all queuing up to recommend something be blown to shit.'

Harry understood. The Israelis always retaliated, in some manner. Retribution had to follow – in the ancient custom of the region. An eye for an eye. The perpetrators anticipated this, and factored the negative publicity of Israeli retaliation as a plus.

He hung up. There was a knock at the open door, and his mother entered. Although in her late sixties, Felice could pass for ten years younger. She was thin and wiry, with short black hair and a pale face partially hidden behind oversize glasses. Harry was her only child, having arrived like a miracle late in her married life. She embraced him fiercely, then sat him down and insisted upon a detailed account of what had happened. Surprisingly, he found it a relief and spared her none of the details. By the time he finished he was weeping profusely. She put her hand on his shoulder.

'Harry, the dead are dead, and we will grieve for them in our own time. You do what I cannot do, find my granddaughter. Let me look after the funeral.'

'Thank you mother, but you know my views. No *Shiva*. Keep it as simple as possible. None of us are religious, and you know Rachel's father isn't Jewish.'

'Simple yes, but I must insist on the *Seudat Havra'ah*. There has to be a meal.'

Harry relented, gave into her insistence that he rest and fell asleep almost immediately.

He awoke mid afternoon as his mother returned with bags of shopping. She busied herself with the domestic duties while he checked the phone. Among the many messages of sympathy and concern he found one from Brian Farrell, saying nobody at UNIFIL HQ had any idea who could be responsible. The Syrians were insisting they knew nothing at all and indeed were extremely angry about it.

The phone rang.

'Mr. Harry Katz?' a polite female voice.

'Yes.'

'One moment please.'

A couple of beeps, then a deep male voice Harry instantly recognised.

'Mr. Katz, this is Binyamin Netanyahu.'

The Prime Minister of Israel.

'I am calling to express the sincerest sympathy both of my government and myself with what has happened to your family. I have been informed about your daughter, and we hope and pray you will get news about her. While it may not be of any real consolation to you, their deaths are now being avenged. If I can be of any assistance please call my office.'

He sounded sincere, and Harry, who loathed him, thanked him and asked.

'Do we have any idea who is responsible?'

'Mr. Katz, I need you and your colleagues to tell me that.'

'Thank you. Shalom.'

'Easy for him to give sympathy,' said Felice, 'when all along he has been the

first one encouraging these settlers. Now somebody else is going to suffer too.'
Like Harry, she strongly disliked Netanyahu.

After supper his mother returned to Haifa. Harry poured himself a large
Scotch, and numbly watched the television news, dominated by scenes of the
settlement and reports of the Israeli Air Force's retaliatory bombing of
Hezbollah targets in Lebanon. He drank another Scotch, took some painkillers
and a sleeping tablet, and finally slept.

7

They buried Rachel and Beth together in an old cemetery on a hillside near
Tiberias, overlooking the calm waters of Lake Galilee. It was a quiet and digni-
fied ceremony, with no speeches, attended only by family.

No group had claimed responsibility for the killings.

8

Friday am: It had been late by the time the last guests had departed, but Harry
awoke before seven. Moving into the living room he found his father in law
already dressed and making breakfast. In his early fifties, with wispy grey hair
around a receding hairline, Roy was a distant and detached man, by career a
radiologist in New York. As Rachel had somewhat bitterly remarked, he had
always been more comfortable dealing with shadows than with human beings.

'Do you still want to go?' Harry asked.

'More than ever,' replied Roy. 'You don't have to come with us. I don't blame
you if you decide not to.'

'No, I'll go. It can't make this any worse.'

They ate, each in their own thoughts, until Anna walked in. A familiar face
on American television, Anna had her own news program on one of the major
networks. A slim woman in her late forties, she was of average height with short
curly blond hair. Her mother was Polish Jewish and her father Irish American

– a marriage that, she often joked, had pleased neither family. Today she wore spectacles, normally she used lenses. She barely spoke, helping herself to one of Harry's cigarettes and a cup of coffee before going off for a shower.

After an awkward breakfast they drove the same route as he and Eshan had driven in what now seemed another life. It was Roy and Anna's first time to see the settlement, Beth having moved there shortly after their last visit. On a crisp autumn day, it was a different journey. The section from Deganya to Hamat Gader was busy with tourist traffic, mostly buses visiting the hot springs of the resort. Anna slumped in the back, Roy and Harry quiet in the front as Harry drove. As the jeep ascended the tortuous bends up to the Golan summit, Harry broke the silence.

'This area is important to us,' he said, as he gestured around him. 'Before '67 it was Syria, but we captured it in that war. In the Yom Kippur war in '73 the Syrians attacked with over a thousand tanks. We pushed them back eventually, but it was close to a total disaster. Now it's only farms and the odd kibbutz. There are virtually no Arabs left in this part of the Southern Golan.'

When they reached the junction at Meitzar, Anna expressed her astonishment that a settlement could exist up such a terrible track, un-signposted and barely perceptible. The settlement itself presented another surprise. In a wilderness of scanty scrub, arid hillocks and boulders they came upon a compact cluster of neat buildings and caravans surrounded by the security fence and its obvious, prominent lights. Harry described how the militia members inside had been lured away by the diversion. Even then the intruders should have been spotted. Harry found it difficult to contain his anger.

An IDF guard of two young uniformed soldiers sat at the gate, sheltering under a gaudy multicoloured beach umbrella, sweating in the intense heat. An acne-faced corporal, having checked Harry's ID, told them they could do what they wanted. The only other people evident were two settlers loading animals into a truck. Both groups ignored the other.

Anna wanted to see where her daughters had died. From the outside Beth's caravan seemed undisturbed.Anna, weeping gently, spent some time alone in the hot caravan. Roy remained awkwardly outside while Harry conducted another fruitless search around the settlement. Anna emerged carrying a pullover, which she and Beth had knitted together. Her last reserves broke down, and she slumped against the wall. Roy embraced her for a few moments, and Harry moved over and enveloped both of them within his own arms. All three stood quietly together until Anna broke away, wiping her tears. She composed herself, and asked Harry to show her where Ami had been taken.

He led them along the path the police dog had followed, through the hole in the wire, and across the scrub towards the Syrian border. Cautiously they climbed down into the wadi, where Harry pointed out the place where Ami had been put on the ground, justifying his absolute faith in her survival by the certainty of the dog handler. They climbed up again, and slowly walked the last two hundred metres to the border.

There was no wind, and it was baking hot and painfully bright under a cloudless sky. Eerily calm, they seemed the only living beings in a whole vast burnt basin of barren dried scrubland and flattened white rocks. The only other evidence of human activity visible – the border fence – ran in an almost perfect straight line as far as the eye could see in each direction. There were no roads, except a barely visible track parallel to the fence on their side, and on the other side of the fence, in Syria, a dirt track which ran along the border for a short interval before turning east towards the hills in the distance.

A small eagle hovered high in a thermal on the other side of the fence. As they watched the bird dived to the ground and swooped up again, with what appeared to be a small rabbit in its claws. Nobody commented, but the parallels to their own situation seemed ominous. At the edge of the sand strip Harry described its twofold purpose. Guarded by mines planted along the whole length, the strip was under regular surveillance to spot any disturbance of the sand. Here there was no fixed observation; instead regular sweeps by orbiting satellites. As he detailed the significance of this, and its relevance to the attack on the settlement, he noticed Anna's glances of curiosity.

'You seem to know a lot about this sort of thing,' she said.

'I was here two days ago. I was told about it.'

'Yes, of course,' she said, turning and pointing. 'Ami could be just over there, but I can't go over and look for her.'

Harry walked over to the strip edge. It had been freshly raked, and the break in the fence repaired. 'She's not there; otherwise the Syrians would have found her body.' He indicated west. 'She's in Lebanon by now – it's less than two hours drive in that direction. We'll find her, I promise.'

All three stood in silence, looking across the empty plain, until Anna could bear no more. She made her way back towards the settlement and took one last look into the caravan before getting into Harry's car. At the gate the corporal informed them they had been seen by satellite.

'Men and their stupid toys!' Anna's eyes flashed. 'My whole family is murdered, and this idiot wants to impress me with how clever he is.'

The welcome cool of the car's air conditioning revived their energy, but Anna remained angry, an emotion Harry had never seen in her before, although Rachel had often warned him her mother's temper equaled her own.

'What is it about this place? There is nothing here worth a bloody cent, yet you are killing and murdering each other over it. Why?'

Roy turned around to pacify her, but Harry slowed the car to reply.

'You are right, we are killing each other, but not over nothing.' He pointed to a pile of rusting metal near the track. 'That used to be a tank, probably Syrian. As I said earlier, their tanks came right through here in the '73 war, nearly beat us. My uncle died somewhere near here – we never found his body. By international law this area is still Syria and recovering it is their national goal, but we need the Golan for our own defense. That's why this still goes on.'

'I'm sorry; I'm not blaming you, more humanity in general.' Anna had calmed slightly. 'It's just the big picture is used to justify everything. I've spent my life reporting about this type of thing, but it's the first time I have experienced the reality. My only children, my only grandchild gone, and for what? For a heap of useless stones?'

The loneliness of the empty apartment disturbed them, and they walked to an Italian restaurant situated down the hill, just at the edge of the old town. La Dolce Vita was unique among the restaurants of Tiberias, being virtually the only one open on a Friday night, Shabbat eve. Its owner ignored tourists and relied upon word of mouth among the residents to promote his business. This had succeeded, as many preferred a place where the staff remembered customers and treated them as friends. The manager said nothing about Rachel, as he greeted Harry warmly.

They had a surprisingly pleasant dinner, reminiscing about Rachel, the frustrations involved in having a daughter like Beth, and the grandparents contentedly let Harry give a long and detailed account of the past few months of Ami's life. He had just finished describing the mess she had made of the kitchen the week before when Anna put down her wineglass and looked sadly at him. In a measured voice she said she believed Ami was no longer alive. She knew the news business well, and the reason Ami had been taken away was the terrorists didn't want images of a murdered child all over the television screens of the world. Roy, looking down at the table, muttered his agreement.

Harry also stared at the table, at the remains of his meal.

'I refuse to believe she's dead, and I'm going to find her. There is one way you could help.'

'Of course, what is it?' Roy answered.

'Before I tell you, I must emphasise it will be illegal.'

'I'm listening.'

Harry told them about the arrangement he had made with the Irish officer.

'The paying of a ransom is against all policy,' he continued. 'While I'm fully prepared to take any consequences, I'm loath to involve anyone else. My problem is finance. I don't have enough for a ransom payment, nor does my mother. If a demand does come, could you lend me what I may need?'

'Yes.'

'I could need it at short notice,' Harry said, 'and it would have to be cash.'

'How much?'

'I'm not sure. Not too much and not too little. Probably something in the region of two hundred thousand dollars, but that's just a guess.'

'Not a problem,' Roy replied. 'I'll get my bank to wire it over Monday, but what then?' Roy, a businessman as well as doctor, was on more comfortable ground.

'Probably open a joint bank account, but I have no idea about any technicalities. You will be breaking the law in Israel. Are you prepared to do that?'

'Yes, we are.' Anna spoke for the two. 'Ami is our granddaughter, our only family now. The money is nothing, but you must think of yourself. Please be careful.'

Anna indicated to Harry she wanted to go outside for a cigarette. Roy, who did not smoke, preferred to remain inside in the cooler air. Outside was a veranda, overlooking a tiny crumbling floodlit synagogue. Anna and Harry moved to the restaurant edge, away from the tables, and as they lit their cigarettes she put her hand on his arm and looked straight into his eyes. 'There is one thing I must say, and I'm the most appropriate person to say it. You have been a wonderful husband to my daughter, and father to my grandchild.'

Harry muttered an embarrassed thanks.

'We are older,' she continued, 'and we may never recover from this, but we'll manage somehow. You are different – you are only twenty-eight, a young man. Yes, mourn for Rachel, but not forever.'

Harry attempted to interrupt.

'No,' she silenced him, 'let me finish. I am the only one who can say this, because our loss is the same as yours – perhaps even greater. Our life is not totally ruined – we still have each other – and yours must not be. The best thing you can do for us is to recover and not let this destroy you. Promise you will always keep in touch, no matter what.'

Harry threw away his cigarette and embraced her.

'I… I don't know what to say,' he stammered.

'Don't say anything. Come on, let's go back inside.'

'Thank you so much.' Harry eventually managed to speak. 'I appreciate all you have just said.'

They returned to their table but nobody wanted to go back to the apartment, so they decided to have coffees outside. They sat in silence as Harry struggled to make a decision. Finally he decided.

'There's something I need to tell you,' he said.

Anna nodded in encouragement as Harry framed his thoughts. From the first time Harry had met Rachel's parents he had maintained the pretense he worked in army procurement, which was why he avoided military service. He looked directly at Anna as he spoke quietly.

'I'm not strictly a civil servant, and I have some access to our intelligence services. Right now they are doing everything they can to find Ami, but in reality they believe she's dead and they'll soon stop. I'll keep on looking, but you can help.'

'Help? How?' asked Anna, genuine surprise in her eyes.

'You may hear things, even in America, which we don't. You're a journalist, you're in the loop.'

Anna exhaled softly, looking at Harry with the inquisitive gaze he had seen so many times on the video recordings Rachel had shown him of her television interviews.

'Okay Harry,' she stated with a cold intent. 'I've always guessed what you do.

No, Rachel told me nothing but she's my daughter – I've felt her worries. So, who really are you?'

'I'm a government employee.'

'Right,' she said. 'Not regular police. I've met so many over the years I can spot them from a mile. You don't work abroad so you can't be Mossad. Not army, that's for sure. You're so like those FBI people I've investigated, so it must be that. Your Shin Bet.'

'Shin Bet?' interrupted Roy. 'What's that?'

Harry remained silent until Anna had to reply.

'Maybe it's best you don't know, Roy. Would you agree, Harry?'

'I have no comment to make.'

Anna exhaled in a theatrical gesture of exacerbation. She turned towards her husband.

'Shin Bet is the nearest thing they have here to our FBI, Roy, only more secretive and far more ruthless. I'll drop the topic but I'll agree, Harry. We'll keep each other in touch, with one condition.'

'What?'

'That any information I provide will not under any circumstance lead to violence.'

Harry shook his head.'I can't promise that. It will not involve you, but revenge will happen if we do find who is responsible.'

Anna bit her lip to prevent replying. They finished their coffees and walked home.

9

___

Saturday am: When Roy and Anna drove off to visit Felice in Haifa, Harry was relieved to see them go – he wanted time on his own. He made his usual coffee and moved outside to the balcony, in the shade. He sat and brooded, but kept expecting Rachel or Ami to suddenly burst through the door. He tried to concentrate on the positives. Ami is still alive. He must find her, but sitting here he could only think about Rachel. He needed to be doing something.

He went inside and rang the office. Eshan answered.

'Can you spare an hour?'

'Yeah. Want to come here?'

'I'll come to Nazareth, but not to the office. Do you know Albasha's?'

'Café on CasaNova Street? With the blue shutters?'

'Yes. Ten thirty?'

The café was virtually empty. An Arab owned business, set up for tourists, it had suffered greatly since the virtual demise of the tourist trade in Nazareth caused by the first Palestinian Intifada. Even now, four years of relative peace later, business had not returned. Bright and modern, it had large glass windows and burnished steel tables and chairs. The owner was a young man whose disappointments and frustrations showed on his prematurely lined face. Harry had taken his Uzi, and ignoring the patent hostility of the owner and his few Arab customers hung it over the back of his chair, purposely selecting a seat with his back to a wall facing the door. He made no effort at greeting or conversation, but lit a cigarette and waited. He had not shaved, and wore an old sweatshirt and jeans. He felt in no mood for pleasantries, and the owner quickly picked up on this. Two men at the table nearest to him pointedly stood up and moved to the far end of the room.

Eshan also ignored the general hostility as he hung his own Uzi over the back of his chair. Harry ordered two cappuccinos as Eshan took out a cigarette, taking his time lighting it before leaning back and looking calculatingly at Harry.

'I got a call from Jerusalem on Thursday. The investigation was initially going to be a police job, but we took it over. They put me in charge.'

'Good. I'm glad it's you.'

'They wanted me to run it from Jerusalem, but I insisted on Nazareth. I'm using a spare office on the ground floor. I've read the forensics. Do you want me to tell you about them?'

'Go ahead,' Harry replied. 'I'll stop you if it's too much.'

Taking out a bunch of typed sheets Eshan summarised their contents. Four terrorists, one a woman. Two guns. One a .22, with a silencer, used to kill the twins. The other some sort of a .33. Neither gun had a history. No weapons were found, but fingerprints were everywhere. It would be a couple of days before these could be assessed. The group who created the diversion at Ramat Magshim had used the exact same technique to bypass the fence alarm.

Most surprisingly nobody had claimed responsibility – not even the usual braggers and liars. Jerusalem's view was the perpetrators were afraid of the Syrians, who were furious about the incursion, and were at pains to point out they were not involved. Headquarter's main concern seemed to be both groups knew the positions of the mines, a major security breach. While these mines had already been relocated, they needed to know how the perpetrators had found out.

Eshan stopped talking as the owner came over. The man pointedly removed Eshan's cup, but Eshan brusquely ordered two more coffees. The owner seemed about to say something, but stopped and walked away as the other customers continued to glare.

'That's about it with the facts,' Eshan continued. He stared down an old man on the other side of the café, who had caught his eye. The man stood up and shuffled out the door. 'The twins were killed by single shots – a classic execution. Clinical and painless. You don't need to know about the others, but no abuse. Professionals, in and out quickly. So why take a child? Doesn't make sense.'

'Have the analysts put it into a pattern?' Harry asked.

'No. It's totally new. They were good at their job, and that's worrying.'

'Could I look through those files?'

'Harry, you know the rules,' Eshan said, placing his hand over the sheets of paper. 'Victims or relatives are not allowed get involved. I shouldn't even be here with you.'

'Sorry, go on.' Harry apologised.

Eshan smiled suddenly, and then surprised Harry by admitting to a sense of blame that he himself had not acted faster once they had realised about the diversion.

'Not your fault.' Harry protested. 'I should have stopped them going there in the first place. I'll have to live with this forever, but I'm going to have to ignore it at the moment. I have to find Ami first.'

Harry was becoming more aware of the increasing hostility surrounding them. He stood up, not willing to create an incident. 'Let's leave, I'm not comfortable here. I'll go to the office if it's clear. Anyone there?'

'Only Pete, but I sent him to Jaffa on an errand. We'll be okay.'

The owner pointedly tried to ignore their bill, but Harry left a note on the table.

The litter-strewn town centre was almost deserted. At the office Harry relaxed slightly when he saw it empty. 'Let's get the rest over with. I haven't had the chance to analyse the facts with anyone yet, so tell me what you guys think.'

'The Syrians have too much at stake to upset their new American pals,' said Eshan, 'so that rules out any outfit based there. That eliminates Hezbollah and Amal, so it's most likely to be Palestinian. There are three or four groups who could be involved but there is a strong rumour that we and Arafat are just about to sign some agreement. If that's true then not even Arafat himself would sanction an operation, which excludes the mainstream Palestinians.'

'So what next?'

'Keep our ears and eyes open, and hope something turns up. It usually does. I have put it around that any whisper, even unlikely, is to come straight to me. That's all we can do, but you know that.'

Eshan pointedly looked at his watch. They got up and left the office together.

Something was bothering Harry that he could not pin down, and on the road home he realised what it was – a growing instinct not to trust his colleague. Eshan was far more motivated than Harry, and totally ruthless, never allowing anything to stand in his way, but up to now they had never had any conflict. Eshan's early insistence that he was the boss was correct, but he did not need to present it so starkly. Yes, he would help, but it would always be on his terms. Harry had no choice but accept. He trusted Eshan's ability, but would never forget his greater agenda. Every action he took, no matter how trivial, had one purpose. Eshan's gain.

At the roundabout entering Tiberias Harry made a full circle and headed back to Nazareth. He did not want to talk to Rachel's parents, and needed to continue doing something constructive. He parked and carefully looked around the office car park. Eshan's car was nowhere to be seen.

The complex was still busy – Shabbat meant little to the security services – but his own section was empty. He closed the office door, booted his computer and rummaged through his desk drawer. He exhaled a sigh of relief as he found the small notebook containing the passwords and entry codes, written in the strange encryption he had invented in school, which he had recorded when in the Haifa Active Service Unit. He had not needed them over the last eighteen months. Had the codes been changed?

First hurdle was easy. Virtually anyone in the Shin Bet could enter their

Intranet site, but after that it became progressively more difficult to access the more sensitive areas. Also an electronic trail was always left behind. This had been drilled into Harry and his colleagues on that course last year. You were always watched – remember that.

His passport worked, as did the codes.

First. Any information about incursions, both successful and aborted, into the Golan in the past two years.

Second. Incidents involving kidnapping of children from anywhere in the occupied territories, anytime. A list of four, which he was allowed to expand. All from years ago.

Third. Updates on all Shiite groups based in Syria, as of the last six months.

The computer began to display the requested information. Harry set it to "Print all twice", got up and strolled down to Current Status. He was told no, there was still nobody claiming responsibility for the massacre. Harry walked back to his office, picking up a coffee on the way.

Sixty sheets of printed paper awaited him, two sets of thirty. He scanned them quickly, but there was nothing of obvious use. He put one set of copies in his desk drawer, the second into his bag.

Next. Any outfits in the occupied territories which had threatened or planned child abductions. Go. This was a small list, which he expanded and looked at while he drank his coffee. When finished he closed it off, but did not print it out as it was useless.

Harry inputted details of the method used to bypass the security fence near the settlement, and then had to refine his search a number of times before getting a list of twelve incidents where the same bypass technique had been used. He swore in frustration as he inserted the code needed to expand farther, only to find his code was out of date. He was not allowed access this section, but he printed out what he had.

Now the crucial bit, what he had come here for. Palestinian splinter groups believed to be currently operating in Lebanon. He was given a list of nine. Four he immediately dismissed, and sighed in relief as he was allowed expand the other five. He opened each file and as swiftly as he could wrote the relevant names, aliases, last sightings and estimations of status on a sheet. He did not print. As soon as he finished he closed the site.

Last search. Execution type killings with a .22 anytime, anywhere, in the past two years. This was a surprisingly short list, only three, all believed to be criminal rather than terrorist. Harry closed this file without printing. About to shut down the computer, he made a request for killings or possible terrorist acts where no claims of responsibility were made. There were seven in the past year; again all believed to be criminal. Finally he turned off the computer.

Another coffee and a cigarette helped concentration as he looked through the list of the groups in Lebanon, then rewrote the same list more legibly. Pleased with his efforts he shredded his first handwritten list in the communal shredder. He left his desk drawer unlocked. Eshan could spend all tonight or tomorrow looking through it if he wished. Paranoia was healthy. He folded the handwritten list of the Lebanese based groups, put it into his pocket and signed out. Time to leave. He had told his in-laws he would be back by six.

10

Sunday: Harry couldn't sleep; his mind was in such a black despair that he was regarding his assertions that he would never forget Ami as pathetic attempts to atone for his guilt. It was his fault, all his fault. He had thrown their lives away for fear of a minor row with Rachel. He was worthless. He deeply regretted going to that Arab café. It had been immature and childish, a demonstration to the Palestinians, all Palestinians, who was the boss. The restaurant owner had done him no harm. He must keep his anger in check.

One sleeping tablet did not work, but a second one succeeded. He felt no better in the morning. Early television news gave only scant mention of the settlement massacre, and no reference to the searches for Ami. She had already been forgotten by the Israeli public, one minor statistic of tragedy among so many others. He knew why. Nobody in the media believed she was still alive. A kidnapped Israeli citizen – especially a toddler with an American mother – would be a major and ongoing news item, but a murdered child was only another name on a long list.

He phoned Eshan shortly after eight, but Eshan was short and terse. No, there had been no development. No, no group had claimed responsibility. Yes, he was still surprised, as it was so unusual. He would call or page Harry if he heard anything at all. Now he had to go to a meeting. Don't call his mobile again.

Harry had expected no less, but felt deflated by having allowed Eshan another opportunity to assert control. That would not be repeated. He heard sounds of his in-laws stirring in the bedroom and not wanting to talk to either, dressed quickly and went outside. Once there he cursed as he realised he had forgotten his cigarettes. He felt in his pocket. He had some money, so he walked into the woods below, down the hill and through the town to the lake's edge. In an empty tourist café he ordered coffee and cigarettes, and sat at a table smoking one cigarette after another, his mind numb and empty of any rational thought. He looked at a clock above him. Nearly ten. Better get back. He had barely enough time to have a shower and get changed.

He drove Anna and Roy to Ben Gurion Airport. It was a tense, unsatisfactory journey. Nobody knew what to say. His ID bypassed security at the airport gate, but he did not enter the building. Harry could never tolerate elaborate farewells. He removed their sparse luggage from the boot, gave Roy a firm handshake but then, in spite of himself, enveloped Anna in a long hug of mutual misery and hopelessness before getting back into the car and driving away.

His pager bleeped. A message from his mother. He phoned her from the car. Would he call to see her? Yes, would drive to Haifa, to her house.

Felice had considered selling her house when Harry's father had died twelve years ago, but could not bear to leave her garden and move to an apartment. Harry still considered the small house, in its tranquil setting, as his second home. Until he had met Rachel he regularly slept in his old room. At that time he had been based in Haifa and it was often easier to stay locally than drive home.

Ninety minutes later he pulled into the driveway, to be met by his mother waiting for him under the cypress tree.

'You look like shit,' she scolded like the teacher she used to be. 'At least you've shaved, but you look like you've slept in those clothes. Right, let's get those stitches out and make you half decent.'

Harry did not have the heart to protest as she led him inside, sat him down and efficiently removed six sutures from his forehead. She made him wait as she ran a bath, and then put out some old but freshly ironed clothes which had been left in his room. It worked, he did feel better. After a breakfast of toast, poached eggs and a strong coffee she indicated two seats outside in the garden.

'You may smoke,' Felice gave an ironic smile, 'but this time only – I'll make an exception under the circumstances. You need to talk.'

He did. He talked about Rachel. About his love for her, his loss, his devastation. His hopelessness. She would not let him discuss Ami. 'Ami is still alive. She needs you to look for her, to find her. But not today.' Harry talked and talked, cried and cried. Felice listened, sometimes supportively, sometimes critically, sometimes humorously, and always empathetically. She made lunch at one stage, and they continued talking until, by what seemed a simultaneous decision, both agreed they had talked enough. Harry was exhausted.

'Do you want to stay here tonight?' Felice asked. 'I'll make supper.'

'Thanks, but no. I need to go home sometime. I can cope with it now.'

She walked him to the car. As he sat inside and prepared to close the door, she stopped.

'This one is difficult, Harry,' she forced the words out.

'What?'

'Rachel's clothes. Her personal things. Someone needs to remove them. Do you want me to do it? Say no if you wish.'

Harry's face creased in a frown. He had not thought about this at all. He looked up.

'No, I would appreciate it. When?'

'Tomorrow, if you want. I'll give whatever seems appropriate to charity.'

'I'll go to the office – I'll be gone by eight. You have a key.'

At the roundabout outside Haifa he began to pull over to pick up two women hitch hikers in uniform, but changed his mind and kept on going as the news came on the radio. Nobody had claimed responsibility for the massacre. Harry rechecked his pager. A blank screen mocked him. He grimaced.

Six o'clock exactly as he entered his apartment. It was spotless – Anna and Roy had tidied it before they had left. He ate a bowl of cereal, made coffee and sat at the dining table with his handwritten notes from yesterday. He ranked the five terrorist groups or sub-groups in his own estimated order of importance, and wrote a list, in careful English, of their relevant details.

Satisfied, he picked up his phone and called the Farrells' house. Brian answered.

'Do you have any time free tonight?' asked Harry. 'I can't explain over the phone.'

Brian understood. It was common belief among UNIFIL officers living in Israel that their land phones were being listened to, and their mobiles always.

'Wait a minute, I'll check.'

Harry could hear a child crying in the background, then Brian's footsteps returning.

'Alice has an ear infection, but I can come over.'

Harry's bell rang ten minutes later. Brian, dressed in jeans and sweatshirt, carried a six-pack of Heineken. Harry fetched two glasses from the kitchen, and motioned Brian to the dining room table rather than the balcony.

'Don't want anyone listening,' said Harry.

Brian sat down and poured his own beer. Harry offered a cigarette. Brian declined.

'Thanks for coming. I need your help again,' said Harry.

'Go ahead.'

'You may not like this, but I am prepared to do anything at all, no matter what, to get Ami back.'

Brian nodded as Harry continued.

'You're in Lebanon all the time. You may have some idea of who is who up there, but I'm not sure you know the real people to ask about Ami.'

'And you do?'

'I do. I've a list of those that could be involved. It may be a bit inaccurate, but it's the best I can get.'

There was a sudden roar outside as two Israeli Air Force F15s screamed above the town, banked sharply over the lake then turned away to the north. Brian waited until the sound had died down before stabbing a finger at Harry.

'First tell me, Harry, who you work for.'

'I can't say. You know that.'

Brian shrugged. 'Okay, I'll accept it. So, what's this list?

Harry placed three folded sheets on the table, written sides downwards, and put his beer can on top.

'Details of the bad guys in Lebanon. If you accept you'll need to copy it and take it with you. I can't give you my list.'

Brian made no movement towards the paper.

'And how sure are you I don't know who to ask?'

'With respect, Brian, UNIFIL knows little. Hezbollah are everywhere and you guys are just sitting there looking at them. You can't enter the Palestinian camps; you can't go into the Bekka, but Ami's not there anyway. She's in Beirut or one of the cities. You can go there and ask questions, if you know the right people.'

Brian exhaled theatrically, reached across and picked up the sheets of paper.

'Not what I expected coming over. So, I presume what I have here is whatever you consider to be the opposition. Names, phone numbers, collar sizes and so on. What you are saying is if I open this I'm committed?'

'You can always leave, and we'll still remain friends.'

Brian made his decision. He turned the paper over and read the contents. Harry poured two more beers.

'Okay', said Brian eventually, 'I've heard of some of those groups, but the individuals are new to me. You're sure this is accurate?'

'Enough, and the names are true. Do you want to copy them?'

'Just pass the pen.'

Harry sat outside, on the balcony, until Brian slid open the door. He beckoned Harry inside and pointed to Harry's originals.

'They're yours now.'

Harry picked the sheets off the table, walked over to the waste bin and carefully shredded the pages into minute fragments. He removed the bin liner, took it outside to the refuse chute and disposed of it there.

'I think I'd have burnt it,' Brian said.

'Not that paranoid, but thanks. As of now, I never had that list, never saw or even heard of it. I'll deny it to the death. Also, assume from now both your phone and mine are being listened to.'

'You mean that, don't you?'

'You have no idea, Brian. And it's best we don't visit each other's apartments. You have my pager number and I have yours. Call me from a public phone and I'll do the same, unless it's something totally mundane. You're safe enough – they can't do much to a UNIFIL officer. The worst would be to expel you.'

'I've only six months more anyway. Can I check home that Alice's okay?'

Brian called, giving a mild sigh of relief.

'She's fast asleep. Another beer?'

'Sure.'

'Let's change the topic. I've no idea how you and Rachel met. Like to tell me?'

Harry smiled. Okay, he thought to himself, he would tell Brian about meeting Rachel, but certainly not the full story.

His name was Salim al Quto. Born and raised in Akko, an Arab town near to Haifa, he came from a prosperous business family and was a nineteen-year-old student in the technical college in Haifa. Although highly intelligent and from a privileged background he had always been a loner, quiet and introverted, whose main love in life was computer games. He would have seemed an unlikely candidate to be the driver of a car which had been parked outside a high school in Tsefat, a Jewish town in Upper Galilee. The car exploded five minutes later, miraculously killing nobody, although seven were seriously injured.

Salim had been seen on a security camera, and identified by Harry's section of the Haifa office of the Shin Bet. Harry insisted he personally would interrogate the suspect, but he would do it his own way. Salim was only small fry, a driver, a bit player. He wanted those behind Salim – the bomb manufacturer, the organisers, the recruiters. Harry succeeded beyond his wildest hopes.

They waited in a car near to the college and lifted Salim as he walked down a quiet street. They wanted no witnesses. They drove him to the car park of the Shin Bet compound, where they left him alone, chained by his hands and feet in the car in the hot sun. Harry drove to Salim's father's house in Akko and waited, without giving an explanation, until the father arrived.

Harry gave the father two choices. He could come with Harry, talk to his son, make Salim see reason and give Harry the information he required. Then his son could return home, could continue his career in college, and would have no criminal record. The alternative would be the Israelis interrogating Salim – and the father knew only too well what that meant – and Salim would go to prison for, maybe, thirty years. A life wasted. But that was not all. Everybody knew what happened to the families of bombers. The father's house and all his businesses would be razed to the ground the same day. His life's work destroyed, and for nothing. He must come with Harry and persuade his son.

The father, a man used to making decisions, followed Harry to Haifa. Salim lay huddled in the car, with the stench of urine and shit all too apparent as Harry opened the door. The father spoke to his terrified son for twenty minutes – a conversation not intelligible to Harry as he sat in the shade and waited – then he came over to Harry and, in a voice dripping with loathing, hissed yes. His son would talk, and talk he did. The terrified youth gave all the names. Harry kept his part of the bargain, releasing Salim without charge.

Harry was the office hero, but not to all. Sure, he had gotten the names, but he had let that little prick off. Most were on Harry's side, and a steady stream of agents called by to congratulate him. Harry, however, remained deeply unhappy. Yes, there were many positives. The ringleaders had been identified. A young life had been saved from a prison sentence, and many deaths and mutilations prevented, but Harry felt cheapened. He could not forget the father's query. How could Harry stoop so low as to do this thing?

Two agents interrupted Harry's thoughts. They were going for a beer in Karmiel, a town twenty minutes away where Harry was then living. Would Harry join them? Normally he would have politely refused, but he was still upset and agreed.

He had never been to this bar, a huge modern hangout popular with students, and as he entered he saw his two colleagues sitting at a table. He went to the counter to get a drink. As he waited he noticed a small pretty woman trying to balance five drinks on a tray. When Harry offered to help her carry them, she replied in English that she couldn't speak Hebrew, but if he were offering to assist she was grateful.

Harry took three of the drinks and followed her through the crowds of students to her table. She was sitting with four women, one of whom had served with Harry in the army. This woman immediately thought Harry knew her friend, and after some good-natured confusion introductions followed, the women insisting Harry join them.

He brought his colleagues over. All eight sat around the table talking, but Harry, sitting beside the woman from the bar, was interested only in her. The attraction seemed mutual

She was called Rachel, an American from New York. She had come to Israel only two weeks before, to spend a year in the technical college in Karmiel. Her family was half Jewish. The other women were work colleagues, and this was her first night out in the new country.

Gradually the others went their separate directions, until only Harry and Rachel remained. Both were moderately drunk as the bar began to close, and they walked hand in hand to Harry's small apartment, less than a kilometre away. It was not love at first sight, simply old-fashioned lust. They never made it to Harry's bedroom, and barely to the blue couch in his living room.

As Rachel remarked to Harry over a breakfast of cornflakes and coffee, she knew little about Harry except his name, how he liked his coffee and a good deal about his sexual preferences. He had to play a football match later that morning, and asked her if she would like to come and watch. Rachel knew nothing about soccer, and cared even less. She agreed to come and promised to dutifully cheer if Harry would take her for dinner afterwards.

And that was that. The telephone interrupted Harry's much-edited version. Alice was awake and crying. After Brian left Harry poured another beer as he continued to reminisce.

Over the years he had many girlfriends – "far too many" according to his mother – but this relationship was different. The initial interest, apart from the intense physical attraction, was cultural. He had never known an American before and there was a huge element of curiosity. Her tastes and hobbies were different to his. She quickly abandoned any pretense of an interest in football, but began to appreciate Arab art and music, two things which had been instilled into Harry from childhood by his father. Reciprocally, she introduced Harry to jazz and to modern art, her twin passions.

She was an accomplished flautist, and had already secured a place with the college orchestra. In all but name, she had moved into his apartment as the end of her year in Israel loomed. Rachel had all along expected to move back to America, to a junior professorship in Rochester, New York. She did not need to broach the topic, as Harry, who had by now realised he had fallen hopelessly in love with her, did not so much request her to marry him as ask where they would live afterwards.

One problem remained. Harry had told Rachel he worked as a civil servant, but now alarmed her by saying he must tell her something vitally important. He confided what work he really did. She had never heard of the Shin Bet but he stressed his work could be dangerous and unpleasant, and he could tell her no more. She needed only a moment to decide. Of course she would marry him.

Rachel managed to extend her contract in the college in Karmiel. They married within one month, the soonest possible in Israeli law. The wedding was the first time

Harry had met Rachel's parents and Beth, her twin sister. They went to Cyprus on honeymoon, and within six months Rachel was pregnant with Ami. Soon afterwards Harry was transferred to the Nazareth office, moving away from physical danger, but Rachel was never fully convinced this was a safer job.

Shortly before Ami's birth Rachel's twin Beth came over to an Israeli kibbutz, after the breakup of a relationship. She assisted Rachel in the first difficult weeks of Ami's life, staying for a month in their new apartment in Tiberias. Six months later she dropped her bombshell with news of her moving to the settlement in the Golan with a new boyfriend.

Harry's head jerked backward in the chair. The beers were working, and he realised he was very tired. He smiled ruefully. All this had happened because of Salim al Quto. The ultimate irony was the Shin Bet had recently executed Salim, after spending over a year on their list as the most dangerous and hunted of the many terrorist bombers.

11

Monday: Harry woke at six. He drove to the office, wanting to keep out of his mother's way as she removed Rachel's belongings. Eshan was not there. Harry tried to busy himself with some routine work, but gave up and walked aimlessly around Nazareth until his pager beeped with a message to call his apartment. Felice answered his call.

'Just checking there's nothing else for me to do here. I've taken only her clothes, makeup and so on.'

'Wait. There is one dress I want to keep. It's maroon. Did you find it?'

'Yes.'

'Leave that, and don't take anything of Ami's.'

'Of course not, and I'll hang the dress in your wardrobe.'

'Thank you. Just don't tell me what you do with the clothes.'

Tuesday: One week since Rachel was murdered. Seven days of silence about Ami's whereabouts. Eshan seemed to have disappeared. Harry waited impatiently until nine, pacing his apartment in frustration, and was about to call

Eshan when his doorbell rang. To his astonishment Eshan stood outside.

'I was just about to contact you,' said Harry, but stopped as he saw the grim look on Eshan's face. 'Come in. Coffee?'

Eshan declined the coffee, but sat down in the kitchen, looking coldly at Harry

'I have something to tell you I couldn't risk on the phone.' He spoke in a controlled voice. 'Firstly, I am being moved from Nazareth.'

'Moved?'

'Yes.'

Harry knew better than ask to where.

'It seems to be a promotion,' Eshan added, almost dryly, 'and I am back in the field. I have a replacement, but he apparently has only one arm.'

The bitterness was obvious. Eshan paced the floor in silent thought for a few moments. 'I have been told an Irish UN officer has been talking to certain people in Lebanon with the offer of a ransom for your daughter. I am annoyed you didn't tell me, and I hope I understand correctly. It has to be you and those Americans.'

'Yes, of course.'

'Good. I needed you to confirm it.' Eshan seemed to relax slightly. Harry's mind raced. If Brian's feelers had been passed on to the Israelis, then Shin Bet must have an operation working in Lebanon. Harry made a show about pouring a cup of coffee, to give him time to think. 'I would have preferred to have told you but I didn't want to get you involved. When are you leaving?'

'Now. They're winding down the investigation. Nobody believes Ami is alive.'

'Are you still prepared to help?'

'Of course,' Eshan replied, looking down at the table, 'you gave me the right answer. But there is something else.'

Eshan looked more agitated than Harry had ever seen, picking at non-existent hairs on his shirt.

'What is it?' asked Harry carefully.

'I'm going to give you something, but I need your absolute promise you will never show it to anyone unless I agree.'

Not sure whether to be angry or flattered, Harry nodded. Eshan picked up his briefcase, from which he took a brown envelope. He hesitated, and then removed a black and white A5 sized photograph which he passed to Harry.

'It came in two days ago,' Eshan said. 'I saw it purely by chance. This is the only copy; the original is still in Jerusalem.'

The photograph centred on the heads and shoulders of a man and a woman. Facing slightly to the side of the camera, they were outdoors, in a crowded place. The people in the background seemed Arab. The photo had been taken with a telephoto lens. The woman looked European, with fairish shoulder length hair, and seemed to be in her mid twenties. The man was slightly older, darker in complexion, and his face looked familiar. Harry waited for Eshan to speak.

'They took this last week,' Eshan said. 'You can guess where. We have no idea who she is.'

'I don't recognise her,' Harry mused, 'but I know him. It's the guy from those Islamic Hawks.'

'Correct, it's Hussam Farid,' Eshan replied abruptly, his voice altering. 'This is the first photo of him in some years.'

'Of course.' Harry looked carefully at Eshan as he spoke. 'He's the one in that fuckup in Jordan when our guy got caught trying to poison him.'

'Yes, he's responsible for me being transferred to Nazareth. It's personal. I'll get even with that bastard sometime.'

'I hope so,' Harry smiled in wry sympathy. 'So, Farid turns up in Lebanon. Someone snaps a photo of him with a woman; you are putting two and two together and getting – what?'

'We don't know.' Eshan seemed to be holding something back. 'I don't know.'

'You think she's involved? That the Hawks are involved?' Harry persisted. 'Is that why you gave it to me?'

'Look, I don't know,' Eshan replied, 'and that's the truth, but there's far too much coincidence. The Hawks have never had women involved. They would kill a child without hesitating, but this variable, what seems to be a European woman, may just account for a change in behavior. That's only a guess. I can't follow up the source, as I was never supposed to see the photo. I don't know any more.'

'So then why show it to me if you won't give me anything else?'

'Look, you know I'm way out on a limb already,' Eshan seemed to be getting annoyed, 'and I cannot over emphasise how dangerous that photo is. I'm one of only a very few aware of its existence, and the others don't know I even saw it, let alone copied it. To answer your question, the guy who took the photo reported that the Hawks seemed to be up to something, but he didn't know what. You may as well go up there and shoot him yourself if any news of this gets out – it would probably be a mercy compared to what else would happen.'

Harry understood the magnitude of Eshan's gesture, but still kept on trying.

'I appreciate that. I'm sorry, but it's still not enough. I thought the Hawks were inactive.'

Eshan thought this one out.

'We believed it also,' Eshan shrugged, 'and they have never operated inside Israel before, but I just feel it in my bones she's involved. Call it whatever you like, but I have been right before.'

This made sense, and Harry knew it was time to drop the topic. He was going to get nothing more.

'Eshan, I am truly grateful for what you have done, now and last week. I'll lock this away.'

Harry put the photo into his gun safe and came back into the kitchen to see Eshan letting himself out the apartment door. Neither man spoke.

Harry waited until early afternoon before driving to the office. It was empty. He had just sat down at his desk when he heard someone approach. Pete limped into the office, his bulky frame sweating and his face reddened from climbing the stairs. At fifty-seven years of age, he was near to retirement. In spite of a thirty-year age difference he and Harry had become close in their two years working together. Pete hugged Harry for what seemed an eternity before breaking down, ironically needing to be consoled by Harry. Somewhat recovered, he sat opposite and lit one of his customary cigars.

'Anything I can do to help?'

'Lots,' replied Harry. 'First, where's Eshan?'

'He was here earlier collecting some stuff. Rumour has it he's being moved.'

'Yes, he's gone. Now, what do you know of the Islamic Hawks?'

'Farid's outfit? Not much. Do you think they are involved?'

'Maybe. I'm going to sift through what we have here about them, but is your brother still with Aman?'

Aman, the intelligence section of the Israeli army, shared information with the Shin Bet but Harry would be unable to access it.

'No, he retired a couple of years ago.'

'Pity. Do you have any contacts there, or with Mossad?'

'None of any use, but I'll ferret around and see what I can find. I have to go to a meeting, but I'll keep in touch.'

Six o'clock: Harry's desk was littered with coffee cups, his ashtray heaped with half smoked cigarettes. He was getting nowhere, continually hitting brick walls as he attempted to retrieve updates on the Hawks. He needed the codes. He paged Eshan, to call him in the office. Two minutes later the phone rang.

'What do you want? I'm busy.'

'I need intranet access codes, and you have them. I can't get into anything of much use on Hussam Farid. It's there, but I can't enter.'

'And you want me to give you the codes?'

'You told me earlier, you have a score to settle with him. I promise I'll share anything I find with you.'

There was silence. Harry heard muffled voices in the background. He looked in surprise at the number on caller ID. Eshan had called on an unsecure line with a Jerusalem prefix.

'I'll have to think about it,' Eshan eventually replied. 'I'll send you an e-mail in the morning, with or without the codes.'

Next morning, Wednesday: The codes were there, with a stark warning that all of Harry's searches would be closely monitored, and the codes could become inactive at any moment of Eshan's choosing. Harry grinned – he had expected no less. When Pete arrived Harry gave him the codes and they began to work together.

The codes allowed farther degrees of entry to the Shin Bet database, but also access to the pooled information from both Mossad and Aman, their sister intelligence services. At Harry's insistence, neither man printed or downloaded any of the information on the screens. Harry was convinced either action would result in an immediate shutdown, so they wrote their notes by hand.

They worked through lunch, thick piles of paper mounting on their desks, until suddenly, just before three, their screens simultaneously blanked. The phone rang. Harry answered.

'Not my idea, Harry, but Mossad pulled the plug.' Eshan sounded apologetic. 'You tripped something there, but you should have had time enough.'

'Yeah, thanks. I'll keep in touch.'

Pete smiled as he listened.

'Well, we got about three hours longer than I thought that little shit would allow.' Pete pulled his sheets of paper together. 'I'll type this out – you'll never be able to read my writing.'

'Thanks. I'll do the same.'

By evening they had built a comprehensive file on the Hawks. At six Pete left. It was Erev Rosh Hashanah, the evening before Jewish New Year, a time when families traditionally congregate. Harry reviewed the files. He was in no hurry back to an empty apartment.

He had hundreds of pages, from mostly outdated and probably irrelevant sources. By nine o'clock he had assembled them chronologically, and condensed them into two pages he knew to be concrete facts. The rest was speculation, rumours, unconfirmed reports and copious pages of analysis.

In 1990 the Hawks had split from their parent organisation, the Popular Front for the Liberation of Palestine – General Command. This seemed to have been because of personal and political differences between the secretary-general of the PFLP-GC and the young Hussam Farid, his second in command. Farid apparently resented and mistrusted the influence the Syrian military maintained on the organisation. He preferred to seek backing elsewhere, confirmed to have been from the Saudis, who were becoming increasingly mistrustful of joint Syrian and Iranian influence in the region. Farid had also been forging links with European terrorist groups, mainly those based in Germany.

Only twenty-two years of age in 1990, Farid was already a seasoned terrorist.Born in a Palestinian refugee camp in Syria, he first came to the attention of the Israelis in 1988 when he was part of a group which hijacked a plane above Greece, destroying it at a remote airbase in Jordan. He had been linked to incidents in Lebanon, Jordan and Rome between then and 1990, when he had founded the Hawks.

Both Mossad and Shin Bet had made attempts to either capture or kill him, but none had succeeded. A Shin Bet agent had stuck a poisoned pellet into Farid's leg in Amman, but the Jordanians had captured the agent and the Israelis had to provide an antidote. This confirmed what Eshan had said. Shin Bet files on him since then were mainly suppositions and guesses, but Mossad had tracked him to Germany, where he was operating between Stuttgart and

Munich. In the summer of 1996 Mossad dispatched an action unit to Munich, preferably to capture Farid, but prepared to kill him if necessary. However the mission was abandoned at the last moment because German Intelligence, who had been co-operating with the Mossad team, belatedly realised their true intentions.

Harry grinned as he read that section, realising this was where Mossad had pulled the plug on him yesterday. He had obviously been stepping on someone's toes.

Farid left Germany in September 1996. There was a confirmed sighting in Tripoli in January 1997, but nothing since. All three Israeli intelligence agencies, at a joint meeting in June 1997, agreed Farid and the active members of his group were in Lebanon, probably based in one of the Palestinian refugee camps around Beirut. There were unconfirmed claims he had recruited a small number of Germans, believed to be specialists in various roles.

There were assessments, again speculative, that the Hawks numbered less than thirty active members. With the exception of the possible German guerillas, the rest were thought to be Palestinian, all from the refugee camps of either Syria or Lebanon. They were believed to have been responsible for at least three unsuccessful roadside bombing attacks on IDF soldiers in Southern Lebanon in the past six months. Three of the Hawks were reported to have been among those killed in a recent Israeli debacle on a Lebanese beach. This group was far from inactive.

Little was known of Farid's personal life. Both his parents had died in early middle age of natural causes, and he had one brother. Whereabouts unknown. He had never married, but was believed to have had relationships with a succession of women, all activists. He was not known to have any children.

Photographs were few, but there were two fairly good ones from the stakeout in Amman prior to the poisoning attempt. There were no images from Germany. So, Eshan had lied again – there were recent photographs. In these he had changed little from the photograph given to him by Eshan. Harry realised Farid looked quite like Harry himself. About the same height, the same build and colour of hair, although Farid's hair was always shorter. He could not make out the colour of Farid's eyes on the one colour photograph.

Harry drove home tired but satisfied. At the apartment he poured himself a Scotch and sat on the balcony, re-reading and re-editing his notes, all the while intermittently looking at two photographs. One, the family photo taken at Ami's birthday, the other the one given him by Eshan. Could these photos be linked?

12

Thursday and Friday: Rosh Hashanah. The Jewish New Year, when the country stops. When followed by Shabbat it makes for a three-day holiday. Harry spent both days with his mother's family in his old home in Haifa. No news from Eshan. He returned home Friday night along a deserted highway.

Saturday at seven he was in the office. The Jewish part of Nazareth was eerily quiet, the streets empty. The main office section was busy as usual, but Harry was alone in his department. Unique among the Shin Bet, his unit worked normal office hours. First he sent an e-mail to Eshan, enclosing his summary of the work he had done on the Hawks. He decided against phoning Eshan to tell him of this mail – he had done as he had promised. That was enough.

He walked over to Current Status. The same blond woman sat there. No sympathy with Harry's loss, and a continuing reluctance to assist anyone from the Department of the Misfits. Nothing on the child now officially classified as killed. No claims of involvement in the settlement massacre, downgraded to an item of little importance, except for the continuing concern over how they had known about the location of the mines. Islamic Hawks? Hussam Farid? No, nothing recent, but we'll keep you informed.

Back at his own desk his pager beeped. "Call me at home. Margaret". He went outside to a pay phone. Brian wanted to meet Harry urgently. Brian was in UNIFIL HQ in Naquora, in Southern Lebanon. Could Harry recommend somewhere?

He suggested the Pizza Hut in Nahariya, a holiday resort near the Lebanese border, much frequented by off-duty UN troops and open on Shabbat. Nahariya was about one hour's drive from both Nazareth and Naquora. When he called Margaret back five minutes later she confirmed it.

Three o'clock: Harry arrived ten minutes early. Brian was already making inroads into a large pizza. Dressed in his Irish army uniform of khaki shirt and trousers, he had placed a blue UN helmet on the empty seat beside him. Harry took a Coke from a vending machine and sat down opposite. Brian wiped his mouth before he began talking.

'All the stuff on your list was accurate, and one seems to have worked.'

'Have you heard something?'

'Maybe. This fella comes looking for me up at the Irish base in Tibili. Knows my name. I've never met him before, and he's a real piece of Lebanese scum. I mean the dregs. Dripping in jewellery; you're talking a pimp or a druggie. Anyway he talks a heap of bullshit and eventually comes to the point. Says he's heard I'm the person to talk to about a business arrangement – those are his exact words – about an Israeli child kidnapped two weeks ago. The gist of it is he wants to meet you, as soon as possible. He says it's strictly business, and nothing to do with politics.'

Brian took off his sunglasses and began to clean them. Harry waited silently, his heart pounding. 'This guy's a real shyster, and I wouldn't trust the bollox as far as I'd throw him.' He tapped the table in emphasis. 'It's up to you, but the bottom line is he wants to meet you face to face, and you have to bring ten thousand dollars in cash. Not exactly an equitable business arrangement, but he appears to hold all the cards.'

'Where and when?'

'Tomorrow, presumably to give you no time to organise a reception, and Cyprus, of course.'

Only United Nations troops could move freely between Israel and Lebanon, and Cyprus was adjacent to both. There were regular ferries and flights between Cyprus and Israel, and between Cyprus and Lebanon.

'No choice, but tell him I'll name the place. It must be somewhere open and public. Let's see. There's a tourist restaurant called Aphrodite's beside the old town in Limassol. Eight o'clock tomorrow evening? Make sure to tell him it's near the old town, the resort is huge.'

'Sounds okay.' Brian nodded in agreement, writing the name in a notebook. 'I offered to come as a mediator, but he wouldn't hear of it. It must be you alone.'

'I have a photo of myself here; can you give it to him.' Harry took it out of his pocket and handed it over. 'Don't worry about me; I have some experience of this type of thing.'

'I'm sure you do, but still, be careful.' Brian gave a wry smile. 'Can you get the money? If it's a problem I could loan you some.'

'Thanks, but I can get it.' Harry grinned in appreciation. 'It's probably about the correct amount for this sort of thing. Could you call me at home later to confirm it's on?'

Harry drove back, repeating to himself to treat this as just another operation. He could withdraw the money in cash in the morning. Getting to Cyprus would not be a problem, but where to get back up? He could involve neither Eshan nor anyone else from Shin Bet. His only advantages were choice of location, and the contact not knowing he worked for the Shin Bet.

Once inside his apartment he had an idea. He telephoned kibbutz Meitzar, and to his relief Rollie answered. Because he did not trust the phone, he asked Rollie if they could meet as soon as possible. Rollie suggested Hamat Gader in one hour.

Rollie's car stood parked outside the entrance, Rollie sprawled on a bench beside it, reading a newspaper. Harry pulled in behind. In spite of Shabbat a steady stream of cars and buses trundled out of the complex as dusk approached. Sitting inside Rollie's car to escape the noise and the dust, Harry gave an outline of the events to date.

'Shit, Harry, nothing surprises me now, so truly amaze me.' Rollie sounded intrigued. 'Why do you want me?'

'I'm going to meet this guy, no matter what, but...'

'Okay, you can stop there,' Rollie interrupted. 'You need back up. Before I agree to anything at all, you'll have to answer one question. And don't tell me you can't.'

Harry knew what was coming. 'What?'

'Don't act the fuckin' innocent.' Rollie was enjoying himself. 'Who are you? My guess is Aman, or maybe the shadows. Now stop fucking around or I promise you, I won't do it. I need to know who and what's stacked up against me.'

'I'm sorry Rollie, but I'm not allowed to tell you.'

Rollie relented, shrugging his shoulders.

'Then it has to be Shabak,' he said, using the older and more formal name for the Organisation. 'Now, make it easy for a simple kibbutz farmer. Why not get your own heavies to back you up? Why me?'

John O'Keeffe

69

Harry told about the ransom, and Rollie nodded.

'Okay, that makes sense. What do you want me to do?'

Harry began. Rollie will need to be in Cyprus tomorrow evening, but they cannot be seen together. He will give him eight hundred dollars for the airfare, and Rollie should be able to book a flight for tomorrow. If not he could take the night ferry. Harry will take the same ship from Haifa tonight anyway, as he'll be able to bring a gun with him. Harry will stay in the hotel where he spent his honeymoon, and Rollie should book into any other hotel, and then call Harry to let him know where he is. Rollie's job is to watch Harry's back and photograph Harry's contact, if possible.

'Do you have a camera?'

'No, but I can borrow one easily.'

'If you can get photos it would be perfect, but be careful. I'll leave the gun at your hotel.'

'Sounds better and better,' Rollie grinned hugely. 'Since it's your money, can I go first class?'

'Whatever. I don't know how to thank you sufficiently.'

'No need, this sounds like fun, and the kibbutz can manage without me for a few days. Also, do you have a mobile I can call you on if something hits the fan?'

'Yes, but don't call it. It'll be monitored. Use landlines.'

Harry's pager bleeped.

'That's Brian.' Harry exhaled a sigh of relief as he looked at the message. 'Great, it's definitely on, but at seven o'clock instead. You have the pager number – use it if you need me.'

Harry drove home, packed a suitcase – one with a small hidden compartment – and retrieved his revolver from the gun safe. Having cleaned and oiled the gun he put it into the case. He had a quick supper then drove to Haifa for the overnight ferry to Limassol.

13

Large waves crashed against the bow of the ferry as Cyprus gradually came into view. Sometime during the night the wind had risen, and by dawn it approached gale force. Harry awoke at six, as the ferry neared Limassol, and ordered breakfast in the restaurant. There was no sign of Rollie. In spite of the wind the huge ship barely rocked. The rising sun behind seemed to be guiding them into the port. He had just finished his meal as they docked

Customs at Limmasol ignored his bag, and he took a taxi to his hotel, memories of his honeymoon with Rachel flooding his mind. The Matalena, a modern ten storied building, stood on the seafront in a new section of the resort. Harry wanted a large and anonymous hotel, and this one suited perfectly. The tourist season being nearly over, he obtained a room without difficulty.

American Express presented his first problem. An Israeli national turning up unannounced at opening time and wishing to withdraw eleven thousand dollars in cash was unusual, even in that place. The tellers were polite and efficient, and after thirty minutes of telephone calls and bureaucracy Harry left with his money in a backpack. He returned to his hotel via the restaurant he had selected for the meeting. He checked with a sleepy cleaner that it would be open that evening, then walked around inspecting all the access routes. Although still breezy the cleaner assured him, in broken English, that the wind would die down soon. Back in the hotel he lay down and nervously waited for Rollie to call. At noon his phone rang.

'You won't believe it; I had no choice but fly first class,' Rollie chuckled. 'I got the last seat on the plane. Pity it's only a one-hour flight, but they serve excellent food. I'm in a hotel called the Ambassador; just down the road from yours. What now?'

'Don't come near this hotel or even phone me,' Harry replied. 'I'll find your hotel and leave the gun and some cash at reception. Any taxi will know Aphrodite's, but check it out first. I'll be there at seven. Keep my back covered – remember the goalkeeper is the last line of defense.'

'Don't I know that,' Rollie laughed. 'I'll have lunch in the restaurant, so keep out of my way. Then I think I'll have a leisurely swim in the sea before getting down to work. Shalom.'

Harry checked his notebook and called UNIFIL in Lebanon, leaving a message there with his hotel's phone number for Brian Farrell in case of a change of plan. He forced himself to think of this as just another service operation – to approach it as he had been taught. Know his goals and plan all aspects of his strategy. Consider and anticipate the hazards. He lay down, performed his formal relaxation exercises and succeeded in falling asleep for a few hours.

At six-thirty, showered and freshly dressed in jeans and a sweatshirt, he took a taxi to the restaurant. In spite of the gusty wind along the seafront this area remained calm and warm. It was almost dusk. He had been afraid the outside tables might be not in use because of the wind, but was reassured. The restaurant was quiet, with only a smattering of patrons, and he had no difficulty in getting the table he wanted. This was outside, in the centre but beside a partition wall. He told a waiter he was expecting friends, and would appreciate a favour. He had a surprise for one of his friends. Could the waiter look after an envelope, wrapped in colourful paper, until needed? A generous tip sealed this arrangement.

He had barely taken a sip of Coke when a tall thin young man came over to the table. Casually dressed in a navy leather jacket, he had long black hair in a ponytail and wore dark mirrored glasses. He looked Greek. He sat down uninvited and spoke to Harry in English.

'You are Mr. Katz?' His voice sounded unfriendly, almost mocking.

'Yes,' Harry replied, in Arabic.

'I'm sorry, but we must speak in English. Unless of course you can speak Greek.'

'English is fine.'

'A friend asked me to talk to you. Do you have something for him?'

'Yes.' Harry gestured down. 'It's in the shoulder bag at my feet.'

'Do you mind if I check it?'

'Go ahead.'

The Greek did, then sat back and looked at Harry.

'There is only five thousand dollars.' His voice was hostile. 'I expected ten.'

'The remainder is here,' Harry's voice hardened, 'but not in the bag. I will need to speak to your friend before it is paid. That is not negotiable.'

The Greek man slowly nodded his head, with a weak smile.

'My colleague wishes to be reassured your conversation is confidential, and with no risk to him. I am sure you appreciate that. Do you mind if I search you first, say in the toilets?'

'Yes, I do mind.' Harry looked at him disdainfully. 'I have no intention of being alone either with you or your colleague at any time. You know this table cannot be bugged. If you wish I will stand up and you can search me here.'

'There is no need, to offer is enough.' The Greek sounded friendlier. 'This table is fine; I will inform my colleague. I wish both of you well.'

He stood up, hung Harry's bag over his shoulder and left without another word. Harry looked around. The restaurant had been gradually filling up with tourists. As he drank another Coke a noisy group of Germans, four young women and three men, arrived and insisted that the two tables next to Harry's be placed together. A large man, wearing a Bayern Munich football shirt with contrasting shorts joined them. He loudly ordered champagne, in German. Harry's astonishment mingled with amusement. Rollie's disguise was inspirational, while insinuating himself with the Germans was a masterstroke. He intermittently took photographs of the group, continuing a loud commentary in German.

Harry kept looking around, but his trained eye spotted no signs of danger. It was now dark. Just as he was starting to get apprehensive that this might be a con and he had given away five thousand dollars for nothing, a man sat down opposite him. He did not offer to shake hands. Small and verging on fat, with heavily gelled straight black hair, he was about thirty years of age, expensively but casually dressed in a white suit with a black open necked shirt and much gold jewellry on his fingers, wrists and neck. He looked soft, certainly not like an activist.

'I know who you're supposed to be.' The man spoke Arabic, and had a soft lisping Lebanese accent. 'My name will do as Ahmed.'

'Are you the person I'm meeting,' Harry replied calmly, 'or another go-between?'

'I am the one.' Ahmed removed an emery board from his pocket and commenced filing his nails, looking down at them as he spoke. 'Your Arabic is perfect. Can you tell me how that is, and something about yourself?'

Harry told about his degree in Arabic, explained he was coach to a football team in Nazareth, and worked there as a minor civil servant in the Department of Trade. This led on to how he had met his wife, and the events of the day she died. In his version he drove alone to the settlement, having brooded at home and worried.

Harry knew the rituals involved in negotiations, but by suggesting ordering food offended the normal etiquette, which Ahmed ignored. They were interrupted by one of the Germans asking Ahmed to take their photograph. Ahmed rudely refused.

'One good thing about Lebanon,' he commented to Harry, 'there are none of these fucking Germans there.'

'Now, what do you have for me?' asked Harry.

'First, where is the remaining five thousand?'

'I can get it within one minute,' Harry's voice hardened, 'but only when I am satisfied you have something to offer.'

'That's all right, I would do the same myself.' Ahmed looked at Harry with increased respect. 'You must understand, I am a businessman. I have no sentiment except to make a profit, but also to preserve my own safety. I had nothing to do with your daughter's kidnapping, and came across where she is being hidden by chance.'

Ahmed carefully looked around before continuing.

'In my home village there is a woman who is politically connected. She has her own children, and on occasions she takes in others. I had been visiting my parents, and in these communities there is a lot of talk and gossip. My mother told me this woman had acquired a new female child, about fifteen months of age, and I have seen this child. Do you have a photograph of your daughter?'

Harry produced a selection.

'It is difficult to be sure, but the child in the village seems to be the child in the photograph.' Ahmed sounded definite.

'You are sure?' Harry's heart skipped a beat.

'Not by these photographs alone, of course, but the gossip on the street says she is the one.' Ahmed spread his hands to emphasise. 'All my colleagues are certain the group the woman is associated with carried out the action. I believe they are apprehensive of the Syrians, and that is why there has been no communication from them. Does she by any chance have anything, a scar or mark which would identify her for sure?'

'Yes, she has a thing called a strawberry naevus on the back of her left shoulder.' Harry could not conceal his eagerness. 'It's about three centimetres in diameter. You can see it in this photograph.'

'Yes, that is extremely helpful.'

'So what can you do for me?' Harry asked directly, never taking his eyes off Ahmed's.

'I cannot tell you where she is, or your army would come the next day and she would certainly die.' Ahmed again looked around. 'I propose my associates remove her from the woman. That part will be easy – when I visited there were no guards present. Then we will have to move quickly. I can bring her here, to Cyprus, to reunite her with you.' Ahmed moved his chair right up to the table, leaned forward and for the first time looked directly into Harry's eyes. Harry smelt a musky scent. 'Now, this will be extremely hazardous. Once we begin we will need to know any business arrangements will be honoured.'

The noise from the Germans was getting louder, and they began to sing, keeping rhythm by banging their glasses off their table. Ahmed looked around at them and turned back, his face creased with annoyance. 'Crowd of pigs! Will we move to another table?'

Harry pretended to consider, but shook his head.

'No. It's annoying, but I feel safer here. Don't take offence.'

Ahmed shrugged. 'Okay. It's your money. Now, talking about money, what is a stolen daughter worth to a grieving father? I myself have a young daughter, and I would be willing to beg, borrow or steal whatever was needed to get her back if she was missing. Are you that kind of father?'

The negotiations began, with Ahmed emphasising the danger to himself; not so much in the re-kidnap of the child, but in the retribution which would certainly follow if he were found out. Harry tried to stick to the figure he had decided upon, and only after an hour of theatrics and threatened walkouts, not to mention scorn on the fact a father would negotiate such a paltry price for his child's life, they agreed to a figure fifty thousand dollars higher that the amount he'd reckoned with Roy. In the end he knew he had no choice. Harry called over the waiter, who fetched the remainder of the ten thousand.

'I will remember that.' Ahmed seemed impressed. 'I would not try it in my country, or we would be scouring the streets looking for the waiter.'

Harry smiled, for the first time that day. They arranged communication channels. Harry gave Ahmed the details of his pager; assuring him he would carry it at all times, and that he was giving neither his mobile nor home phone. Ahmed suggested a paged message would give a phone number of a hotel or something similar here in Cyprus, which Harry could call. This seemed simple and effective.

Normally the termination of an interview between a Shin Bet agent and an Arab ended with a threat, either veiled or obvious, of the consequences of failure to complete an agreement, but Ahmed held all the trump cards. Harry could only go along with the arrangements.

'Realistically, when will this happen?' Harry asked.

'Next week, for sure.' Ahmed sounded convincing. 'If we delay too long they may move her. When can you have the money ready, and in cash?'

'Monday afternoon.'

'Good.' Ahmed smiled. 'Then we will try for Monday or Tuesday. Let us have one drink to toast our agreement, and the return of your beautiful daughter.'

With wildly conflicting emotions, they clinked glasses of ouzo and Ahmed departed into the dark street outside. Harry ordered moussaka and a salad – he had not eaten since breakfast on the ferry. He felt no threat or sense of danger, now that he had parted with the money. He finished eating, without making eye contact with Rollie, and took the precaution of taking a taxi back to his hotel. He had barely entered his room when his phone rang.

'That's some nasty looking piece of shit you were dealing with.' Rollie's Hebrew was a relief. 'I heard nothing. How did it go?'

Harry described the conversation.

'Looks like that's all we can do now,' Rollie said. 'I spotted nothing suspicious, and I don't think he was armed. The first guy definitely was. More good news, I must have ten or more photos of your pal and the other guy.'

'Thanks. I'll call you in the morning.'

'No. No, I'll call you. I've some unfinished business with my new German girlfriend. I'll leave the gun at my hotel's reception.'

'Enjoy yourself, you deserve it.'

14

Shortly after six, in the calm of the early morning, Harry walked across the road to a deserted beach. He stripped naked and swam far into the cold sea. On his return, still the only person on the beach, he dressed and strolled back to the hotel. Reception had booked him a flight to Tel Aviv. Next he walked to Rollie's hotel, where he found a package containing his gun, two rolls of film and a brief scribbled note. Rollie asked Harry not to disturb him unless it was imperative. Smiling broadly, he took the gun back to his own hotel, where he left it with his backpack in the care of the duty porter. If he did have to return, it might be by plane. Better to leave the weapon in Cyprus.

After an uneventful flight he took a bus to Haifa to collect his car. Back at his apartment there were no messages on his answering machine. He wrote a detailed report of the conversations and negotiations with Ahmed.

One o'clock – not too early to phone the United States. Roy answered almost immediately. Fifty thousand dollars more? No problem, he trusted Harry's judgment. As soon as the banks opened he would wire it over

Harry looked at the two rolls of film. He called the office in Nazareth and was given the number of the Organisation's technical department in Petah Tikvah. He phoned, drove straight there and one hour later handed over the rolls. He left the building with three copies of each photograph.

By five thirty he was sitting at the kitchen table with a coffee, looking through the photographs. There were five excellent images of Ahmed, head and shoulders perfectly framed, and two moderate ones of Ahmed's Greek colleague. The last five photos were of a partially clothed woman. Harry put these into an envelope, which he addressed to Rollie in Meitzar.

He paged Eshan, who rang back within minutes.

'You wanted me?'

'I need your help again. Something fairly important has come up. I can't tell you on the phone. Are you free anytime?'

'Call you back in ten minutes.'

Five minutes later Harry's phone rang.

'I take it you're free now,' Eshan asked.

'Yes.'

'Okay. Can you be at that army camp just north of Tiberias in twenty minutes?'

'Sure, I can, but why?'

'Just be there.'

Less than ten minutes later Harry pulled up at the barrier in front of the military camp. The corporal at the gate made a call on his radio, then came back to Harry to say he was expected, and to go to the administrative offices. Harry drove through and followed the signs. He parked the jeep, walked up some steps to an open door and entered. It was quiet, with a young woman in uniform sitting at a screen behind a desk. She looked at Harry's ID, asked him to wait in the reception area, and to leave his mobile phone with her. No, she had no idea what this was about, her only instruction had been to expect a Harry Katz.

His wait was short. He heard the sound of a helicopter and through the window saw a Bell 212 Anafa landing in the helicopter circle outside. Its door opened as the rotors slowed and Eshan emerged. Eshan discussed something with the pilot, turned and began to walk over towards the administration building. He entered and spoke to the receptionist, requesting the loan of an office. As she pointed Eshan to an open door he beckoned to Harry, who followed him.

'Don't flatter yourself,' Eshan said, smiling at Harry's obvious puzzlement. 'I was flying to Kiryat Shimona anyway and this is on the way. I have thirty minutes. What's up?'

The room had a table and two chairs. Eshan took the one in front of the window, the light behind him. Harry sat opposite.

'First, any progress your end?' Harry asked.

'No. I would have told you if anything had happened.'

'Okay. I've just come back from Cyprus this morning.'

'Cyprus! So your Irish friend turned up something. I'll bet it was expensive.'

'That's my business. Yes, a Lebanese guy calling himself Ahmed claims he knows where Ami is being held. I'm about ninety-nine percent sure it's all a heap of shit, but I'm going to run it by you. Do me a favour and listen before any smart-ass comments.'

He told Eshan the complete story, leaving out nothing. Eshan seemed impressed by the part of the German tourists, remarking that if Rollie were interested he should be sounded out about a position in the Shin Bet. He was less than amused with the whole scenario. A setup, plain and simple. Two crooks on the make, and Harry the sucker.

'It's obvious, Harry,' Eshan could not conceal the hint of a sneer. 'The Irish guy tells everybody there are dollars to be made. You'll get a call in a few days. "We have your daughter here in Cyprus", or something similar, and next morning the Americans have lost all their money.'

'That's the advice I'd give, and it's probably true.' Harry slowly took out and lit a cigarette, without offering one. 'But, maybe he is genuine. He's certainly a crook, but then again who else is going to come forward? Any Palestinian activist would be arranging his own suicide. I'm prepared to run with it.'

'Well, it's your money and your neck. What can I do?'

Harry took two copies of the photographs from an envelope and passed them across the table. Eshan looked at them with interest.

'I presume the small fat guy is Ahmed?'

'Yes. Do you recognise him?'

Eshan looked repeatedly at each image in turn before replying. 'No. Never seen him before, and I've no idea who the Greek is.'

'I didn't think you would. What I want from you is to circulate the photos and see if we can identify either. I'm not interested in the Greek, but then again he may be useful. I have one more favour to ask.'

'What?'

'If Ahmed contacts me, would you be prepared to supply any backup – I can't use Rollie again.'

'The photos, yes, I'll do that. I'll have to think about backup.'

'Well, look at it another way,' Harry pointed his cigarette to emphasise. 'Say he does come to Cyprus. One way or the other you can have a word with him; you know what I mean. We seem short of people in Lebanon at present – another asset there could be an unexpected bonus. The Greek might also be useful.'

Eshan's expression changed as he became more attentive.

'Harry, you're finally learning. I'll think about it, but promise me you won't go running off there on your own.'

'I'll think about it as well. One last question. Why do you seem so certain the Hawks are involved?There's nothing in the file I sent you that gives any indication.'

Eshan stroked his chin. Minutes passed in silence. He stood up, pointedly closed the door, sat down again and leaned forward.

'I always win,' he said, with a satisfied smile. 'All you need is logic – luck has nothing to do with it.'

'With what?'

'Okay. First, the fact they knew about the mines. Their mistake was to set their diversion in Ramat Magshim.'

'Why?'

'Not everybody knows this, but the Golan border with Syria is divided into four divisions. Meitzar and Ramat are in different ones.'

Harry nodded in gradual comprehension as Eshan continued.

'The mines are managed by the Border Guards. About thirty people in each division would know the mine locations, and maybe six would have access to both areas. They also inform the army. Twelve people there have access. So, now we have eighteen suspects. I concentrated on the army, and checked out who would have known about the change in satellite times. There were about forty, but now I'm down to the five who fitted into both groups,'

'Go on,' said Harry, unable to help a faint note of admiration in his voice.

'You don't know about the last piece. About three months ago in Lebanon we had a major scare. One of our patrols was lured into an ambush.'

'What's unusual about that?'

'This one was different. They were drawn in by someone using one of our distress codes, and went in thinking it was safe. Luckily nobody was killed, but there were some injuries. Our main cause for concern was how the terrorists had our code. Now, we know as a fact the Hawks were responsible for the ambush.'

'So where does this tally with my stuff?'

'Wait. I made a list of IDF people who would have known the code, and then cross referenced it with the five guys I mentioned earlier.'

'And they matched?'

'Two did. We hauled one guy in and interrogated him, but he's clean.'

'And the other?'

'Two of our people called to his house, but were not too subtle. He went into his bedroom, supposedly to get his keys, but shot himself dead.'

'What!'

'Turns out he was married with kids, but having an affair with a Palestinian woman. She grew up in a camp in Syria, and has a brother in the Hawks. She was blackmailing the guy.'

'A honey trap,' agreed Harry. 'Do we have her?'

'Yes, but she's trained. Denies everything. Says she was in love with him, and is so upset by what has happened etcetera. Probably have to let her go. So, you see – two definite links to the Hawks. It's enough.'

'I'm impressed. So why no claims of responsibility? They normally love to brag.'

'They're learning from us. Silence can be effective. These guys are good, but we'll get them. We always do.'

When Harry got home there was a message from Roy. The money had been transferred. He called Meitzar. Rollie had not returned – apparently he was on vacation in Cyprus. Not wanting to phone, Harry walked over to the Farrell's apartment, but it was empty. He scribbled a brief note to Brian requesting that he keep circulating about the ransom offer.

Tuesday and Wednesday: The days came and went. Nothing from Eshan. Nothing from Ahmed. Harry could not stay in one place. He constantly moved around, repeatedly checking that his pager still functioned, that he had not missed any messages. He spoke to nobody, bar fruitless twice-daily calls to Current Status. Hours of aimless driving. Numerous coffees in a late night café in Tiberias. Unable to sleep, waiting for the message which never arrived.

Thursday am: He awoke at five thirty when his doorbell rang. He went out to the balcony and looked down. A solitary figure stood outside – unmistakably Eshan. He barely grunted a greeting as Harry let him in, looking weary, unshaven with reddened eyes and disheveled clothes. There were what looked like blood stains on his shirt, and he wore his Glock revolver in its shoulder holster.

'Come on in,' Harry said. 'Coffee's made.'

'Thanks,' Eshan muttered as he sat down in the small kitchen, 'I need it.'

'You look like shit.' Harry poured the coffee. 'What's going on?'

'A lot.' Eshan looked tired. 'I'll get the hardest bit over first. Bad news.'

'Ami?' Harry gripped the table tightly for support. He sat down, dreading what Eshan would say.

'I'm sorry to be telling you this, but the whole thing with Ahmed was a setup.'

Harry slumped and put his head in his hands for a few minutes, then looked up and spoke. 'Okay. Tell me, but don't fuck around.'

Eshan poured himself another coffee. 'I've just come back from Lebanon.'

'Lebanon! You're joking.'

'I wish I were.' Eshan gave a thin smile. 'Mossad recognised Ahmed fairly quickly. Amazingly it's his real name. He's a small time crook – prostitutes in Tyre. Anyway, some of our people were going to Tyre to snatch a member of Hezbollah. I realised this would be right beside where Ahmed lives, so I went along for the ride.'

'Go on,' said Harry. 'I don't believe I'm hearing this.'

'We decided to call on Ahmed, and lucky for you we found him at home. He agreed to come with us, although he had a rather bumpy journey in the trunk. For once, it all went to plan. They snatched the Hezbollah objective without a shot fired. Drove back and were in SLA territory before dawn.'

The so-called South Lebanese Army, a Lebanese Christian militia and Israel's proxy army, controlled a narrow strip of Southern Lebanon. Ostensibly an independent Christian area, in reality the Israelis dictated everything that happened there.

'So what did you do with him?' Harry spat the words out.

'We couldn't bring him here, so we took him to Khiam.'

A prison in South Lebanon, Khiam was the subject of repeated condemnation by human rights organisations, both Israeli and international. Supposedly run and managed by the SLA, Israel had a major say in its control.

'I'll bet he enjoyed that,' Harry said furiously. 'What did you do? Pull out his toenails one by one, or maybe stick a cattle probe up his ass?'

'Calm down Harry. We never laid a finger on him. Turns out certain elements of the SLA were delighted to find out he was a guest of theirs. Anyway, when we mentioned that he suddenly became very co-operative, and in return for not releasing him to the SLA, told us all we needed, and more.'

'Go on, get it over with,' Harry sighed in resignation. 'I can guess.'

'As you knew deep down it was never true. He has no knowledge of Ami, and never had. They were planning to take the money and run, and while they never intended to kill you, they could have done so. The guy was scared shitless, and I know the truth when I hear it. He knows nothing – that's the bad news.'

'What have you done with him?' Harry asked, standing up and pacing around the kitchen.

'We gave him a few alternatives.' Eshan poured another coffee. 'He didn't seem too keen to stay in Khiam, and believe me it will be an extremely unpleasant job getting him out of there in one piece. The SLA guys don't like him.'

'That's unusually considerate of you,' Harry was getting increasingly annoyed.

'Not really.' Eshan ignored Harry's mood. 'We plan to let him remain in Khiam another day and contemplate things, and then move him to Cyprus. He'll be useful to us in Tyre when he returns there. That's your suggestion.'

'You're one devious son of a bitch,' Harry said, muted admiration mixed with abhorrence. 'Remind me never to get on the wrong side of you. And what about our Cypriot friend?'

'He could be a bonus.' Eshan gave a thin smile.

'Game set and match to you.' Harry gave a mock applause. 'One definite and one possible asset. I should be thanking you. You've saved my father-in-law a lot of money, but that's not what upsets me. It's Ami.' Harry paced around the room. 'I never believed his story, but it did give a glimmer of hope.'

'I'm sorry too, but you never know. One door closes, let's hope another opens.'

By now the morning sun had risen above the Golan Heights, on the other side of Lake Galilee, and shone on the front balcony. As Eshan reached for a cigarette Harry gestured towards the window, and they moved their coffees outside. In spite of the sun it was cool there. Eshan commented on the view over the lake, but Harry did not reply. He sat silently, deep in thought, and then interjected.

'That's it.' His eyes flashed with new eagerness. 'You just said it – it opens another door. I'm going to Khiam. I need to speak to Ahmed myself. Presumably that's all right with you?'

'I thought you might ask.' Eshan hesitated in his reply. 'On one condition – you don't show him the photograph.'

'That's taken for granted. Do you want to come, keep an eye on me?'

Eshan scowled and shrugged his shoulders. 'No, I need some sleep. Is it okay to stay here for a few hours?'

'Sure.'

'Something else. After Ahmed I assisted in the interrogation of the Hezbollah guy,' Eshan continued, glancing down at the bloodstains on his shirt. 'That went on all yesterday and most of last night. This guy was totally different from Ahmed and said nothing. I did manage to get a few moments alone, and asked him about Ami, making absolutely clear to him this would be a very separate agenda. I promised we would move him out of Khiam, in return for his cooperation, and he did talk a little. He says, and I believe him, Hezbollah were innocent, if such a word could ever be applied to that outfit. He himself knew or heard nothing.'

'Did he give an opinion?' Harry asked, again interested.

'Sort of.' Eshan chose his words carefully. 'He felt whoever did it must have come from Lebanon. Amal might have been implicated, but they are even more involved with the Syrians than his own movement. It can only be either a splinter group, or some new outfit. Certainly not the mainstream Palestinians – they can keep nothing a secret.'

'And why take Ami?'

'I'm sorry,' Eshan managed to look sympathetic, 'but the same as we all thought. No photos of a dead baby all over the news. He thinks they killed Ami, and buried her in Syria.'

'Did you show either of them the photograph?' Harry knew how Eshan's mind worked, and while Eshan could forbid another to use the photo, he would use it himself if he felt it justified.

'I did show it to Ahmed, very casually, among some other photos. He thought he knew Farid, but had no idea who the woman is. I didn't give him any other information, and he offered no suggestions. I couldn't show it to the Hezbollah guy, otherwise I would have had to terminate him.'

Harry looked carefully at him, and sighed slowly. 'You are one cold bastard. Do these things not bother you at all?'

'It's dog eats dog,' Eshan barely shrugged, 'and that guy knew it. He'd have done the same to me. If the kitchen's too hot, it's time to leave.'

15

At the border the IDF guards were reluctant to allow Harry to enter Lebanon. Although pleasant and polite, they remained unyielding until he phoned his apartment, waking an irritated Eshan, whose vitriolic orders to the troops to facilitate Harry were promptly obeyed. Beyond the border Harry carefully steered past disparate groups of ragtag militia, Israeli armoured vehicles and poverty stricken local people. On the thirty-minute drive to the town of Khiam he passed only local farmers with heavily laden donkeys.

Two hours separated the shopping malls and apartments of the late twentieth century from an almost medieval hell of suffering and deprivation. Al-Khiam Detention Centre, to give it its proper title, was a crumbling dirty grey two storey rectangular slab of a building. Perched on a barren windswept hill, it stood a few hundred metres away from the desolate Muslim town of Khiam, in the bitterly contested area of South Lebanon. The only near structure was a small but prominent United Nations military stockade. On his last visit Harry had been so shocked by the obvious brutalities carried out in this prison by his country's allies, the SLA, that he had seriously considered resigning his job. What had stopped him had been the attitude of his colleagues. Not only were they unmoved, but they were clearly prepared to commend the SLA on the "invaluable assistance" they provided to Israel. After consideration he had made the formal report which cost him his job.

At the filthy metal gate of the prison two dishevelled young guards, cigarettes in their mouths, stepped out of the shade into the blazing sun. Both had the wide-eyed nervousness of the amphetamine addicted. Harry stood out of his car and approached with an attitude of calm authority, showing them his ID. They searched the pack he was carrying, nodding satisfaction as they found only a flask and some papers, and opened the gate. He left his car outside.

It had been over two years since he had last visited Khiam, and the prison atmosphere was now even more evil and despairing – something he would not have thought possible. He realised why it disturbed him so – it vividly recalled the grainy old photographs from his childhood, shown to him by his grand-mother, detailing the fate of his mother's relatives. With the exception of this grandmother, all her family had perished in similar looking death camps in Silesia.

Inside the gate was a foul rectangular exercise yard, empty but for three men seated on green plastic seats around a small table on the other side. They looked disinterestedly at Harry as he walked over, then turned back to continue their game of cards, pretending to ignore him. There was one empty seat. Harry picked it up, moved it around towards the table and sat down. Harry lit a cigarette and waited. Eventually one of the men spoke.

'Nobody invited you to sit there.'

'Who's in charge here?'

'We all are. What do you want?'

'I'm looking for a Lebanese prisoner brought here yesterday. Name of Ahmed something. Where will I find him?'

'Never heard of him. There's lots of Ahmeds, or don't you know that?'

Harry leaned forward and swept the cards off the table onto the muddy ground. Two of the three jumped up, anger in their faces, but the third, sitting between them, grasped both of them by the arm, restraining them.

'Look, I don't have time for this,' Harry said. 'You know who I am, and I'll make it easy for you. Just tell me where to find the prisoner or the three of you will be up in the mountains fighting the Druze, instead of playing cards here.'

The seated man silently looked Harry up and down, and then turned to the man on his right.

'All right,' he said. 'Show our Jewish friend that Arab pig.'

The man walked across the yard. Harry followed him through a rusty grilled gate and along a series of increasingly fetid and badly lit passages, with a faint sound of distant screams. They stopped at a corner and the man grunted to Harry as he pointed. 'He's in number 14.'

An Israeli guard stood outside its door. Harry recognised him from the Haifa office, but had never spoken to him before. He warned Harry that he would have to move Ahmed to a nearby interrogation room if he wished to interview him, as it would be impossible in the cell.

Harry soon found out why.

Opening the door the stench of excrement greeted him. In a cell so narrow it was impossible to lie down and too low to stand upright, Ahmed crouched in his own waste, a look of terror on his face as the light temporarily blinded him. His fright changed to relief as he recognized Harry's voice, but Harry just stood aside as his Israeli colleague roughly tugged Ahmed out of the cell, barely giving him time to straighten his cramped limbs before dragging him barefoot along the corridor to an adjacent interrogation room. He was shoved into the room, which had two chairs and a small metal table. The guard locked the door behind as Harry entered. Ahmed wore a filthy T-shirt and a soiled striped pyjama bottom. His feet were swollen and covered in dried blood.

'It is you, my friend,' Ahmed spluttered. 'Tell them this is all a mistake. That I only wanted to help you.'

'Just shut up,' replied Harry coldly. 'I'm giving you one chance to save your miserable life. Here, take these.'

Harry removed a flask of coffee from his backpack and poured Ahmed a cup, at the same time putting cigarettes and matches on the table. Ahmed grasped the hot coffee in his shaking hands, gulping it down, and lit a cigarette.

'Just yes or no?' Harry asked. 'Do you know anything about my daughter?'

'It was business, only that,' Ahmed lisped. 'We meant you no harm.'

'Don't mess with me.' Harry moved towards the door. 'Yes or no? Answer now or I leave.'

'Stop. No. I know nothing about her.'

'Thank you,' replied Harry coldly, 'you just saved your life. Now, you owe me ten thousand dollars.'

'I will repay,' Ahmed babbled. 'I promise. I will repay it all.'

'There is no need. Consider it a payment for services rendered.'

'T-thank you,' stammered Ahmed in astonishment. 'But, there is a price?'

'Yes. Can you read Hebrew?'

'No, of course not.'

'No matter, it is in Arabic as well.'

Harry produced a folder. Inside were two sheets of typed paper. He put one on the table in front of Ahmed, a ballpoint pen beside.

'You can read the Arabic – the Hebrew is a direct translation. Just sign it and the other copy – that's all. It is a receipt for ten thousand dollars for services rendered to the Shin Bet.'

'I cannot sign this,' Ahmed's panic had returned. 'It's a death sentence.'

Harry said nothing, just sat watching. In the silence muffled screams could be heard from outside. Ahmed shrugged in resignation. He picked up the pen and signed the copy on the table, and then the second one Harry passed to him. 'So what do you want?'

'Nothing has changed. I want my daughter back, and as you know I am prepared to pay well for information. You work for me now. I'll get you out of here, and when you are back in Tyre I want you to keep your eyes and ears open. Always remember this bit of paper. The other one is your copy – you can do what you want with it.'

While Harry replaced his sheet into his backpack, Ahmed gazed open-mouthed in astonishment as he gradually assimilated his situation. He reached forward, tore the section of the paper with his signature from the rest and stuffed it in his mouth. The remainder he ripped into tiny shreds. As he threw them on the ground the door opened and the Israeli guard burst into the room, interrupting them.

'Trouble,' the guard spoke hurriedly. 'There's a bunch of militia heading this way. They want to lynch this piece of shit. Let's get the hell out of here.'

'What is he saying?' interrupted Ahmed in alarm, not understanding Hebrew.

'Just shut up,' hissed Harry, 'I'm trying to think.'

He turned to the Israeli. 'Why do they want him?'

'Apparently he raped someone's daughter. Her clan threw her out and he's using her as a prostitute. Just leave him here and let's scarper.'

'No. He's too valuable. I'll take him in my car.'

'On your own, pal.' The Israeli turned to leave. 'I'm off.'

'Like fuck you are,' Harry replied furiously. 'My rank is major, and this is a direct order. Cover me until we get in my car, then you can run away if you want.'

'Okay, but get moving.'

'Listen to me.' Harry turned to Ahmed. 'Come with us. Keep moving or you are a dead man.'

Ahmed nodded. The Israeli led the way down the gloomy corridor out into the exercise yard, his Uzi clasped menacingly in his hand. Ahmed, bare footed, shuffled behind and Harry took the rear. This part of the yard was empty, but there was a group of men the other end. Harry moved to the front, took out his ID and knocked at the gate. It opened; one of the young guards took a look at Harry's card and waved them through. They were outside before the other guard noticed.

'Stop, you can't take that man out of here,' shouted the second guard. Harry, tugging at Ahmed's sleeve, dragged him to the car and pushed him inside. He tore open the boot, took out and cocked his Uzi, and sat into the driver's seat.

'Jump in if you are coming.' The Israeli made a quick decision, did so and Harry sped away.

'Couldn't stay there,' the Israeli said in alarm, 'but what will we do? They'll catch us.'

'Not before we get to that UN post.' Harry looked in the mirror to see militiamen running towards their cars. 'We'll be okay there for a bit. Where's your radio?'

'Back there. They can have it, and my car belongs to the army. What can the UN do?'

'You'll see.'

Raising a large cloud of dust Harry drove across the sandy scrub towards the UN post, one kilometre away on a small mound. This housed a collection of three large wooden huts painted a brilliant white, with UN written in huge black letters on each wall, their roofs festooned with high aerials. Razor wire and sandbags surrounded them.

The car screeched to a halt. Harry and his two passengers emerged to the astonishment of four UN soldiers. Harry looked at their insignia – they were Irish. Behind this group more Irish soldiers hurried into an armoured car which swung its turret round, pointing its gun in their direction. Harry gave the Israeli his own gun and walked over to the soldiers, identifying a lieutenant.

'I need your help,' he said, in as friendly voice as he could manage. 'We are Israelis, and this man is a Muslim prisoner whom we have taken from the jail. The shit's about to hit the fan with those guys out there – they want to kill him.'

'You can't leave him here,' the Irish officer replied, 'he's your problem.'

'Look, we brought him here because he works for UNIFIL,' Harry spoke with calm authority. 'There's no time to argue. Could you radio Commandant Farrell and let me speak to him. He knows who I am. Please hurry.'

'You know Commandant Farrell? Okay. Come on in,' the lieutenant decided, 'but only you. The others stay outside.'

'Will you cover them?' Harry asked, pointing back towards three cars hurrying in their direction. The officer gave instructions and the turret of the armoured car swung around towards the approaching vehicles.

'That'll keep them away for a few minutes.'

Harry followed the Irish officer past the wire fence into the UN stockade to the unit's radio operator. Within minutes the lieutenant had made the connection and handed Harry the microphone.

'Brian,' Harry began, 'I need your help again, and badly.'

'Let me get this right,' said Brian. 'You're inside our base in Khiam with that Lebanese crook? Jesus Christ, I've heard it all.'

'I've got to get him out of here. I mean now. There's a bunch of SLA outside who want to lynch him.'

'What do you suppose I can do?'

'I need a chopper. Do you have access?'

'Maybe. I'm standing beside one, but it's small and unarmoured. There's no chance I could send it near Khiam without cover, and one armoured car isn't nearly enough.'

'How long would you take to get here?' Harry asked.

'Ten minutes. But I'm not coming without protection.'

'Trust me,' Harry replied. 'If I get our guys to provide cover, could you do it?'

'What can you guarantee?'

'I'll see if I can get an Apache.'

Brian whistled. 'Okay. If there's an Apache there, and if I decide it's safe, I'll take him.'

'Thanks,' sighed Harry in relief. 'I'll get working on it.'

'We'll see you on the ground, but I'm not coming anywhere near unless I see a gunship. Put me on to my guy again'

The officer spoke to Brian and hung up.

'He told me to help you,' the Irishman said, 'but I don't like what's happening.' He pointed towards the town of Khiam. At least five more vehicles were swiftly approaching, each in its cloud of dust.

'Can I use your radio?' Harry asked.

'Sure.'

Harry tuned to IDF Emergency channel, and was swiftly transferred to IDF headquarters. He explained his situation, stressing that Ahmed was the Shin Bet's most important agent in Lebanon. HQ promised a gunship as soon as feasible.

Harry thanked the officer and walked outside to a tense situation. Ahmed and the Israeli lay crouched in front of the UN sandbags. Confronting them stood a noisy ragtag of heavily armed SLA militia, becoming increasingly threatening as their numbers and confidence increased with each new arrival. The Irish soldiers looked nervous.

'We need more time,' Harry tried to reassure. 'I'll talk to them.'

He began to walk towards the militia.

'Keep your face hidden and say nothing,' he muttered to Ahmed as he passed.

He walked the forty metres to the SLA men, and as he neared them he heard the faint sound of a motor. A small white helicopter began to hover about a kilometre away. He turned back to the militia. 'What do you want?' Harry spoke to a man he estimated to be in authority. 'I am an Israeli officer – we are allies.'

'We have no argument with you,' replied the man, with unexpected politeness. 'Just give us that dog and we all go in peace.'

'Why do you want him?'

'It's not political – it's a family matter. He raped my cousin's daughter and he must pay. Stay out of it. Just hand him over and we will leave.'

'Are you sure he is the one?' Harry persisted. 'Can you prove it before we give him to you?'

Harry kept the argument going until he heard the low rumbling sound of powerful motors. He shrugged and turned towards the leader, pretending to agree.

'I'll tell the other guy to let Ahmed go,' Harry said. 'You wait here – the UN won't let you any closer.'

He turned and walked back, resisting the urge to run, all the time expecting to hear the sound of a shot. As he reached Ahmed and the Israeli he told them to jump behind the sandbags. All three leaped simultaneously, to the anger of the Irish soldiers, who did not understand the Arabic he had spoken.

There was an enormous roar as two tan Israeli Apache helicopter gunships swept into view, within seconds hovering in a cloud of grey dust in front of the UN stockade. The militias' cheering abruptly stopped as the gunships turned their weapons in their direction and a loudhailer ordered them to leave the area instantly. The leading gunship emitted a terrifying burst of fire from one of its Gatling guns into the scrub. As the militiamen halted their advance their vehicles turned and accelerated away. Those on foot hastily retreated a hundred metres or so farther back.

The white UN helicopter descended, landing in the space between the gunships and the stockade, and a grim looking Brian Farrell emerged. Harry and the Irish officer bundled a shaking Ahmed into the machine. The helicopter took off immediately. The Israeli gunships waited until the militia had cleared the area before heading away to the south.

Harry and the Israeli stood beside Harry's car, watching in silence, too overcome by this drama to speak. The Irish officer walked over, grinning as he pointed towards the prison, where a smoky fire had just appeared outside.

'I suppose that's your car in flames over there,' he chortled, a gesture that eased the tension.

'It's not mine,' Harry replied, relief in his voice. 'I'm sorry for all this, but I can assure you I didn't plan it.'

'That's okay,' the officer smiled. 'All seems to have ended fairly well. There'll be repercussions, but I suppose it's a life saved.'

Harry shook the captain's hand in relief and gratitude.

'Maybe more than one life.'

16

The coldest January in northern Israel for twelve years, and the hills of Lower Galilee were capped with mantles of clean white snow. On the uphill sections of his drive to work Harry had to slow to a near crawl behind the sparse traffic, barely moving along the icy road. Nazareth itself looked its bleakest. The dirty streets of the town centre were deserted, with wet litter blowing around in the violent gusts of freezing wind. Waiting at the coffee machine in the outer office Harry overheard two skiing enthusiasts gleefully discussing the snow conditions at Mount Hermon. In his own office Pete complained bitterly about the weather.

'Had to drive to HQ yesterday and between the roadblocks and the fog it was a bloody nightmare.' Pete huddled over the office radiator as he spoke. 'I bumped into Eshan. Have you seen him lately?'

'No, must be over three months.' Harry moved over to share the radiator. 'Things have been pretty distant since Khiam. He phones occasionally to tell me nothing has turned up.'

'Rumour has it he's taking over the whole Northern area,' Pete wheezed as he sat back at his desk. 'He'd be head honcho here. Could you cope with that?'

'I've heard that as well. Yeah, I'll manage. I mean, I respect Eshan's ability, but I don't like him as a person. I'm not scared of him, and he knows it, that's why he leaves me alone.'

'So you can work with him?'

'Have to. His problem is he hates Arabs. I don't, and he knows that as well. What I mean is that I distrust their leaders, and the radicals, but not the people. That's why he doesn't trust me. Anyway, you're okay. You have only what, six months or so?'

'Seven, and then Sydney,' Pete replied. Pete's two daughters had recently moved to Australia, and he planned to retire there. 'What about you long term?'

'I'd love to leave but can't. Have to stay to watch out for anything about Ami, but I'll sure as hell miss you.'

His pager beeped. "Phone me. Brian"

He put on his jacket and went out into the biting wind to a public call box, as he still did not trust the office phone.

'Your friend from the Greek restaurant wants to meet you,' Brian said. 'Today if possible – same time same place as before. Also you need to bring fifty thousand. I'll be seeing him in an hour. Can you do it?'

'I'll do my best to get a flight. Call you back when I know.'

'Margaret is here. Tell her.'

Harry had been praying for this message, but the urgency and the sum of money involved puzzled him. Fifty thousand seemed a strange amount. Not enough for a serious ransom demand and too much for an opening bid. He would find out soon enough. He hurried back to the office, and made a booking for the three o'clock flight. AMEX office in the airport would have the money ready in two hours. He called Margaret.

Before he left the office at ten he phoned Eshan who sounded nonchalant, almost dismissive, as he wished Harry an unenthusiastic "good luck" before hanging up.

The normally one-hour drive took two and a half. AMEX had his money, and he had time to buy toiletries, a couple of T-shirts and a bag. As he waited to board he took out a copy of his dossier, looking at the details of those whom the Israelis thought to be the core members of the Hawks. They believed Hussam Farid to be still in Lebanon, but there had been nothing of any concrete value since before the settlement massacre. They were now classified as being "probably" responsible for the massacre, and Farid upgraded to the highest "shoot on sight" category. The group itself had become quiet, and there were unconfirmed reports they might be disbanding.

Although there was no proven link to Ami, Harry knew he was on the right track. Surprisingly he did not feel nervous, more curious and in a strange way looking forward to seeing Ahmed.

In stark contrast to Northern Israel, Cyprus was warm and sunny. He took a taxi to his old hotel, and collected the bag he had left there four months previously. The gun was undisturbed. The porter had come in on his day off in response to Harry's phone call from Larnika Airport, and had expressed no surprise at Harry's request. He thanked him profusely for his generous tip, and offered his assistance, adding that before working in the hotel he had been in the Cypriot police force for twenty years.

Harry realised the porter must have seen the gun, but there was no hint of a threat, and he decided to ignore the approach. He went to his room, rested for an hour and at six left the hotel, picking up a taxi outside. He rode it to the other side of the town, from where he took a different taxi back to the restaurant, asking to be dropped off a few hundred metres away from Aphrodite's.

Although fifteen minutes early Ahmed was already seated outside. He wore a dark fleece, blue jeans and brown boots. He had grown a black beard, his hair was cut short and the ostentatious jewellery was absent. He stood up and embraced Harry with genuine affection, effusively thanking him for saving his life in Khiam, before cautioning that he had little time. He needed to take the last flight back to Beirut and they must get down to business immediately.

Harry ordered a beer, Ahmed wanting only water. Harry scanned the area. 'I'm alone. I presume you are the same?'

'Unfortunately yes.' Ahmed managed an ironic grin. 'Your people scared Yannis so much he has left Cyprus, but that is not important. Can you answer me one question?'

'Ask it first.'

'How did you know about me last time?'

Harry considered, but could think of no reason to refuse answering.

'The Germans – you remember them?'

'Of course, I should have known.' Ahmed sighed. 'Now to business. We know a Palestinian group attacked the settlement, and everybody thinks it had to be these so-called Hawks. Do you know of Hussam Farid?'

'Tell me about him.'

Ahmed gave a quizzical look then shrugged. 'Don't treat me as an idiot. You probably know what he eats for breakfast. Anyway, he's somewhere in Beirut and seems to be moving in different circles now. I'm not even sure if he is still in charge of the Hawks.'

'That's interesting. Do you know any more?"

'Let me explain. I have been trying for months to make a contact with these Hawks, but it is difficult. They are not interested in my business, and I don't deal in weapons, but we may have become lucky. They finance some of their income from selling gold, which they acquire in Iraq. I have made it known I wish to buy some, and we have arranged a meeting tomorrow night.'

'Go on.' Harry was interested. This made sense.

'For this I need money,' Ahmed smiled confidently, a far different Ahmed than Harry had previously experienced. There was no obvious manipulative behaviour, and he seemed almost relaxed. 'I would use my own if I had any, but my visit to Khiam became noticed and my business suffered badly. You won't get your money back, but I will give the Irishman any gold I buy. If you are interested you could make a lot of money selling it in your own country. I myself will need to keep only a small amount to finance these expensive flights.'

Harry could only grin at this nonsense. 'That can be discussed later, but how do I know I can trust you?'

'I'm afraid you will just have to.' Ahmed spread his hands. 'I trust you. You have more than proven it to me, and believe me there is nothing in it for me dealing with these savages. I am scared of your people, I am scared of the SLA, and now I will have to add another group who will probably scare me as well. I don't need this, but I owe you my life.'

'So, you buy the gold. What then?'

'I am not sure.' Ahmed nodded in acknowledgement. 'I only hope they drink alcohol. When I have some trust I will try and use that to loosen their tongues. Some men cannot resist the need to boast, and I will seek to find what I can about your daughter.'

'One question first,' said Harry. 'The SLA, they claim you raped one of their girls.'

Ahmed spread his palms.

'Yes, she was abused. Her brother raped her, and she fled her family in shame. Mine is a dirty business, and many girls who work for me come with the same story. I must train each girl myself. That part is not unpleasant, and yes, I trained her, but I never raped her.'

Out of habit, Harry did another scan. He stopped in alarm. In a café across the road, directly under a light, not looking in their direction sat a man whom he had not seen for some time. Insignificant looking, small, thin, middle-aged, nondescript, with short grey hair and glasses he was a sadistic torturer and killer. Seeing him sent a chill through Harry. His name was Chaim Duguid, one of Eshan's henchmen, a man loathed and feared in the occupied territories. Harry turned quickly away, but Ahmed had noticed his reaction and was about to look over when Harry grasped his arm.

'Look straight at me,' he hissed. 'Don't turn round. There is someone I know over there.'

He concentrated on pouring his beer as he decided what to do. 'You must leave.' He reached down to his bag and removed a thick envelope, which he rested on his thigh under the table. 'Keep looking at me and take the envelope from my knee. The money is there; you will have to trust me. Do you have a bag?'

'Yes, it's at my feet, but there is only a newspaper and some chocolate in it.'

'Good.' Harry ordered. 'Leave your bag there, take the money, go to the toilet, but don't come back. Go out the window if necessary, but get a taxi and go straight to the airport. When you are there stay in a public area until your flight. I'll remain here. Good luck, and keep in contact with the Irishman. Now order a beer and keep talking as if nothing has happened.'

Ahmed summoned the waiter and ordered. He casually stood up, gestured towards the toilets, and left the table. Harry watched Chaim, who at one point seemed to make a signal to another, but stayed at his table. Harry waited. At last he seemed to be on the right track. Did he believe Ahmed? Certainly not about the financial arrangements, Harry was on a loser there, but his gut feelings were yes, to believe him.

From the corner of his eye he observed the increasing agitation of the Israeli agent as Ahmed failed to return. Eventually Chaim motioned to someone out of Harry's vision, and almost immediately a furious looking Eshan burst into the restaurant area. He hurried past Harry in the direction of the toilet before reappearing again and taking Ahmed's empty chair, his face livid with anger.

'That little shit has gone,' Eshan snarled.

Harry sat unmoved. Eshan's arrival, after the sighting of Chaim, came as little surprise.

'Next time don't use that idiot.' Harry motioned towards Chaim, still sitting across the narrow road in the other café. 'So, now you tell me. What are you playing at?'

Eshan shrugged. 'Okay, I wanted Ahmed, but we'll get him again. He could have been useful to us in Tyre – but you know that, don't you. You win, but tell me what's going on.'

'First get rid of your gorilla – he gives me the creeps.'

'Order me a beer.' Eshan managed to grin. 'I'll tell Chaim to leave.'

Eshan walked away and on his return Harry filled him in on what had happened. Eshan accepted Ahmed's story and agreed to run with it, Harry promising to share any information. Eshan offered to take Harry home in the military plane he had flown over on, but Harry declined. 'One last thing,' Harry asked. 'Could you do something for me?'

'That depends.'

Harry picked up his bag.

'There's a gun here. I can't take it on my plane – could you bring it back for me?'

Eshan smiled.

'Even better, I'll get Chaim to carry it.'

17

Having waited all next morning for weather conditions in Tel Aviv Airport to improve, Harry arrived back in Israel at five. When he got home, he documented the sequence of events. If any gold did materialise from Ahmed he would register it with the relevant authorities – there would be no blackmailing. He could claim Brian knew nothing; Brian would be simply delivering a parcel. His notes made, he went for a short run. In spite of the cold it was a dry evening. Afterwards he watched television and fell into bed, too drained to do anything else.

The sounds of shouting followed by breaking glass awakened Harry from a troubled dream. He sat up in bed, startled, but then realised his neighbours were fighting again. As the row continued he got out of bed, turned on the light and went out into the corridor. He knocked on their door. The noise from within stopped and a red and tearful face appeared. In reply to Harry's expression of concern, his elderly neighbour apologised for any disturbance so early in the morning and said she felt fine. Harry shrugged his shoulders and returned to his own apartment.

As the seven o'clock news began on the radio he heard something which chilled him to the bone. He rushed over to get the end of a snippet telling of a missile strike by the air force the previous evening on a house in Tyre. The usual sound bites of justification and condemnation were rolled out, but he knew. He just knew.

In a panic he picked up the phone and called Nazareth. Current Status normally opened at seven and Harry cursed and then prayed as the phone rang and rang. Eventually someone answered.

'Current Status.' An unfamiliar voice.

Harry introduced himself, and waited for his ID to be verified. The operative came back on line.

'Okay, you're cleared.' She sounded sleepy.

'I'll need you to check a report for me.' Harry did his best to sound nonchalant. 'That hit in Tyre late last night. I've been involved in the planning and just want to know if it went off okay.'

'Should be able to find that,' she muttered. 'Let's see, you said Tyre, last night. I haven't heard about anything there. Wait, here it is.'

'A hit on a domestic,' Harry added, trying to sound as if it were a routine enquiry.

'Yes, that's it,' she said. 'Nine-thirty last night. Air force, one missile fired. A direct hit and they claim no collateral. I've no report of casualties. We've put out a statement to the media – it's the usual bullshit. Do you want me to read it?'

'No need, I could write it myself.' Harry had developed a headache as he forced himself to continue speaking in this vein. 'You say "we" put it out?'

'Yes, it was ours.'

'Can you tell who sanctioned it?' Harry asked, too rapidly.

'It came from Jerusalem.' There followed a silence, as the operative seemed to realise this might not be a routine enquiry. 'I'm afraid I can't say any more, you've called on an unsecure line.'

'No problem.' Harry backed off. 'Just wanted to check. Thanks for the info.'

Harry stood looking at the silent telephone, his shock changing to anguish and then to rage. He picked up the phone but put it down immediately. Instead he dressed quickly and hurried out of the apartment.

Outside was bitterly cold and grey. At the fork in the road outside Afula he took the decision to take the shorter route to Jerusalem through the Israeli occupied West Bank. Ten kilometres beyond Jenin the sleet changed to snow, driven by high winds. Traffic had slowed to a crawl because of the dismal visibility and the treacherous road surface. It took over two hours to get to the outskirts of Jerusalem. The snow was heavier, though the wind had eased.

Shin Bet HQ occupied a modern multi-storey glass building in West Jerusalem, similar to many others in its vicinity. Although Harry had been there many times, he had difficulty finding it because of the falling snow. Its car park looked virtually empty. He asked directions to Eshan's office and in a controlled fury walked straight in the door without knocking. Eshan sat at a large desk, with an older man who Harry did not recognise. Eshan, who seemed unsurprised at Harry's sudden arrival, asked the other man if he would excuse them. As soon as the door closed Harry confronted Eshan.

'You bastard,' Harry snarled. 'It was you.'

Eshan held both hands up in a gesture of attempted calm.

'That was quick,' Eshan replied. 'I expected you, but not so soon, and not in this weather.'

'Why?' Harry shouted. 'Why kill him?'

'Not my decision.' Eshan spread his hands wide. 'I voted against it but they overruled me.'

Eshan continued to coolly sit at his desk, Harry standing in front of him, face reddened in anger and prepared to strike his colleague. Instead he pulled back, walked over to the wall and hit it violently before turning around.

'Just let me hear you say it, you arrogant bastard.' Harry demanded. 'You authorised the killing of my only link to Ami. Go on, say it. Say it.'

'No. I neither recommended nor endorsed it.' Eshan remained calm. 'The decision came from above. Look, Harry, you know the story. They debriefed me on my return, and we considered lifting Ahmed and his Hawks contacts, but had no time to plan with any hope of success. Those guys have killed more of our people than those in the settlement, and it gave us a chance to get them.'

'So how did you manage it?'

'We followed Ahmed. He did meet with the three from the Hawks, as he told you, and they went to his house. Unfortunately Farid was not one of them. We got a positive ID and the decision was made in Jerusalem. Our guy highlighted the house with a laser and the missile did the rest. Look, I fully recognise what this means to you, but you have to remember something. You're not the only one who has had someone killed by these people. All the others are equally entitled to their vengeance. I'm sorry, but that's the way it is.'

Harry slumped, stunned. 'But you, Eshan.' Harry's voice sounded broken. 'You, you of all people. You were with me. I know Ami is alive, and you do this. You heard what he told me. Ahmed was going to find out, and then you went and killed him.'

Eshan stood up and walked to the window. He kept his back to Harry.

'I wish it had happened some other way,' Eshan spoke without showing his face. 'He could have been valuable. There is a small bit of good news, however.'

'Go fuck yourself from a height, and stuff your "good news" up your ass. You expect me to actually believe this bullshit? "They debriefed me on my return". Like fuck they did, and it's all my fault.'

'Don't push it, Harry.'

'I'm an idiot for trusting you. You came off the plane, drove straight to

Jerusalem and immediately set the whole thing going. You blame Farid for getting you scapegoated and demoted to Nazareth. I should have remembered. I handed you the chance to get him. Yes, there is good news. You didn't manage to murder him, so I still have a chance of finding what happened to Ami.'

'Just listen.' Eshan ignored Harry's outburst. 'We have some good sources in Lebanon now, and we have heard the Hawks have fallen out with the Syrians. They can no longer shelter in the Bekka, or in Beirut, and the group seems to be splintering. That is probably why those three were getting involved in gold smuggling. We may get another chance to get at them, who knows.'

'That's exactly what Ahmed told me,' interrupted Harry in exasperated fury. 'I had him set up to deliver, and then you decided to murder him. Don't give me this "good news" crap. You fucked it up, and you know it. And by the way, have you warned the Director General?'

'Warned?'

'Yes. To watch his back. That you are after his job. That you will climb over anyone to get there.'

Harry banged his fist on Eshan's desk and stormed out of the office, slamming the door after him. Eshan remained behind his desk drumming his fingers, his face an inscrutable mask.

18

It seemed just another routine interrogation of a Palestinian suspect. The man was well trained, and offered nothing; Pete and Harry were going through the motions like so many times before. They were about to terminate the session when Harry goaded the prisoner.

'Okay, I'll accept you know nothing,' Harry gave a wan smile, 'but tell me this. Have women taken over Hamas? Have they cut the balls off their fancy men? Are you so afraid of us you have to get your women to do the dangerous work? You guys sit and smoke in the café while she carries the bomb – is that how it works?'

This stung the prisoner. He glared at Harry.

'You talk of balls,' he hissed through clenched teeth. 'I'll tell you about balls.

Maybe I'll tell your wife. After I've shown her how a real man can satisfy her I'll do your daughter a favour too. She'll like that.'

Pete snorted in dismissal, but something snapped in Harry. He rushed around the desk and knocked the man to the floor with a savage blow, repeatedly kicking him in the head until Pete dragged him away. Harry's rage abated as quickly as it had arisen, and he sat in an almost catatonic state as Pete struck him on the face, to fake the injury needed.

Harry left the building and drove home. He spent the remainder of the day alone in a downward spiral of despair and self-loathing. His mood darkened farther over a sleepless night, and at dawn he went to the gun safe and removed his pistol. He looked at the photograph of Ami at her first birthday. Today he should be celebrating her second birthday. No, Rachel and he should. They all should. He stared at the photograph for some minutes, and then returned the gun to the safe.

He called his office and requested the number of the Organisation's stress counselling service. At ten o'clock he was shown into their clinic in Haifa. He had coped with Rachel's death, he told the counsellor; he had almost forgiven Eshan for his betrayal, and had accepted Ami was gone from his life forever. However this abuse of a defenceless prisoner had humiliated him to a degree that had shaken him to the core. For the first time since his talk with his mother shortly after Rachel's death he bared his naked soul to another. He made another appointment for two days time.

He went home and slept for six hours before walking over to the Farrells' house. Brian's term of duty in Israel was about to end and the family were having a farewell party before returning to Ireland. Harry spent a large part of the evening playing with their daughter Alice, who had shared her first birthday party with Ami. While he chased her around the room Brian walked over and put his hand in Harry's shoulder.

'Promise me one thing Harry. Never give up. She's out there. I know it as well as you. I can't do much from Ireland, but if you need any other help from our guys here then call me at home and I'll see what I can do. Don't abandon hope.'

Next morning: Although early June and barely seven o'clock the temperature was already a humid thirty. The final kilometre uphill was always the toughest, along a rough trail through the heavily wooded area below his apartment block. Harry forced his brain to ignore the pains in his limbs and chest. Body pain he could cope with. He had agreed with the counsellor he needed to regain physical as well as psychological fitness, and he was determined to complete the full twelve kilometres of this run.

He emerged from the trees onto the road leading to the block, grateful to be back on level ground, and saw a familiar figure seated on the steps. He summoned the energy for a sprint finish and stood panting and sweating in front of Eshan. Dressed formally by his usual standards, in spite of the heat Eshan wore a white shirt and a tie. He had a small attaché case at his feet and was smoking a thin black cigar.

'I need a shower, you can wait here.' Harry struggled to get his breath as he spoke.

Eshan nodded. Harry took his time. He made a cup of coffee, and brought it outside to where Eshan still waited.

'You know why I am here.' Eshan spoke first, casually flicking away his ash.

'Well, if this is an official visit you can look at this bruise here on my face,' Harry pointed. 'It backs up the report I filed, but you are as responsible as I am.' He jabbed his finger at Eshan. 'I had intended to submit a resignation, but I've changed my mind.'

'The report was bullshit. We all know that. But you, Harry? You of all people don't do that to prisoners, not even shits like that guy.' He threw away his cigar, stood up and stretched himself. 'Yes, I'm responsible as well. I realised it as soon as I saw the report.'

Harry relaxed slightly. 'Come on inside, this is not the best place.'

Eshan followed Harry and declined the offer of coffee. Harry hit the air conditioning and they sat in front of the window for a few moments in silence.

'It doesn't matter what you say to justify it,' said Harry eventually, 'you made a fundamental error killing Ahmed.'

'You're right. I made a big mistake. It also had repercussions for me personally.'

'Go on,' prodded Harry.

'Did you know my brother Benjamin was killed in Lebanon?'

'No. It's the first I heard. I'm very sorry.'

'They blew him up shortly after we terminated those three Hawks. The relevance is the Hawks were responsible. It was their last act. I'm sure there is some sort of a moral there.'

Harry was too numbed to think of a response.

'My point is,' Eshan continued, 'we should not have killed Ahmed. The others deserved to die, but we removed a source. While finding Farid had been a priority for me before, it's now even greater.'

'Thanks,' interjected Harry, his voice full of irony.

'I have some other news for you. We now have some information about the woman in the photo.'

'What?'

'We know for absolute certain the Hawks committed the settlement murders,' Eshan continued. 'The guy who provided them with that white taxi had met the woman.'

'Where? When?'

'Before the killings, and to answer your next question, he knows nothing about Ami. The woman is, he thinks, German, and is probably Farid's whore. This guy met her only once, very briefly. Her name is Baba, or something like that, but European names meant little to him.'

'Is he still around?'

'Yes, but he's Mossad's, not ours. He's back in Beirut and untouchable.'

'Do you think he knows more?'

'No. He knew little – he's only a car supplier. But there is something else.'

Eshan opened his case and removed a photograph. A poor quality black and white image of a man, wearing a cloth turban and what seemed a rough shawl draped over one shoulder. He had a black beard, and was carrying a rifle.

'Farid?' Harry asked.

'It's him, or we think it is. This came from our American "allies". Someone took it in Pakistan, of all places.'

'Pakistan!'

'Looks like he's moved there, and may even be working for Uncle Sam. All very murky who's in bed with who there now.'

Harry looked again at the photo of Farid and poured another coffee. He leaned back in his chair.

'So, the Americans are protecting Farid, which is why you aren't prowling around Islamabad waiting for your chance to waste him. Why show me this photograph – it's about as much use to me as the other one?'

Eshan ignored Harry's question. 'You're right,' he replied, almost casually. 'There are limits with what the Yanks will do for us. That's it, I must go. You can keep the photo. Stick with the counsellor. Shalom.'

Part Two

Davos Switzerland 2010

1

Harry glanced at the breakfast buffet and moved outside. The September sun, low in the hazy blue sky, was already shining on the hotel's wide empty balcony. He was first up. The air was cool, and he was comfortable in shorts and a polo shirt. He sat at a table and placed his phone in front of him, then decided against that and put it back into his pocket.

He ordered coffee from a waitress. He still drank at least six cups a day – his only aberration from an otherwise healthy diet. His physical appearance had changed little in thirteen years. A fit forty-one year old, he remained thin and boyish looking in spite of his shortened hair beginning to grey at the temples, although he had reluctantly acquired reading glasses. The previous intensity of his eyes had been replaced by an intangible vagueness, a sense of something missing.

Uri came out from the dining room, saw Harry, gave a wave and turned back towards the buffet. Harry waited, idly glancing through a Swiss newspaper. There was no hurry – they were not meeting the other hikers until nine, plenty of time for a leisurely breakfast. Uri sat down with a plate of cheese and ham slices and a bowl of yoghurt. Four years older than Harry he was a small, stocky, constantly moving man with receding rusty hair. He had been Harry's commanding officer in the Israeli Army, and had served in the Shin Bet before emigrating to Germany, where he had set up Weber GmbH, now a large business empire. Ten years ago, on a trip to Israel, he had met Harry and offered him a post as head of security for his company. Harry had accepted and moved to Munich.

'You look like you're ready to go.' Uri gestured towards the backpack on the ground beside Harry's chair. Harry grinned – he was looking forward to the weekend's activity, a planned two day hike. Then his phone vibrated. He took it from his pocket and stood up.

'Should have left it in my room,' he said as he moved away to take the call.

Eshan's voice hammered in Harry's ears as he hurried towards his room. Why this sudden call?"It's about Ami." Yes, that's what he had said. Those exact words. Eshan's voice had not changed. It was instantly recognisable, even after more than ten years, and it still had the power to send a chill through him. In his room he called the number showing on his caller ID. A Jerusalem prefix, but the rest meant nothing. A woman answered, in Hebrew.

'Bercovic office.'

'Harry Katz. I'm returning a call.'

'I was told to expect you. Mr Bercovic has just been called away, but he'll be back in a few moments. Can he phone you?'

Harry gave his hotel and room number, and the Swiss prefix. He paced up and down as he waited. What was Eshan up to? He picked up the photograph on the dressing table, the slightly fading image of his family taken on Ami's first birthday, looking at his missing daughter. She would be fifteen and three months old now. Yesterday was the anniversary of her disappearance.

The phone rang. Harry snatched it up.

'*Herr Katz?*' A woman's voice.

'*Ja.*'

'*Ein moment bitte.*'

'Harry.' Eshan wasted no time. 'Do you still have access to that photograph I gave you? Farid with the woman.'

'Yes,' Harry replied in astonishment. 'I have it on a website. Why?'

'Something's come up and it concerns her. I only heard an hour ago.'

'What's happened?'

'First, I must tell you the background.' Eshan took his time. 'When we put in a new system here I had a section created for her, where certain word combinations would trigger an alert. It happened for the first time this morning and they summoned me in.'

'Go on,' said Harry.

'It came from the Americans. You're probably aware we share intercepts of cellular phones. They were listening to some German outfit, but this linked into a Hawks connection. In the conversation the word "Bab" came up, which when associated with the word "Hawks" triggered my alert. Unfortunately it had to be translated from German, so we lost time.'

'Okay, I'm with you.'

'There's a meeting this weekend involving this woman as a go-between, with some sort of a transfer. She's representing the Hawks side. That much we know, but the Americans won't or can't give us anything about the other group.'

'Is that it?' Harry's mistrust had returned. 'The Hawks disbanded years ago, you told me yourself.'

'Agreed, but that's still the name they used in the intercept. Definitely the Hawks. The important part is we know the meeting is somewhere in Zurich Airport.'

'Zurich Airport!' Harry exclaimed. 'Where?'

'That's the problem; we don't have an exact location. I was surprised when you gave the Swiss prefix; I thought you were in Munich. Are you anywhere near Zurich?'

'I'm in a place called Davos. About two hours by car, maybe less.'

'Can you go to Zurich?'

'Of course. Only hope it's not too late. Do I have any backup?'

'No. The Americans are not interested. I contacted Mossad, but they politely told me to piss off. It's ancient history to them.'

'What about the Swiss?' Harry asked.

'Surprisingly we still get on fairly well with them, but by the time we go through a shitload of officialdom, it'll be too late. Use them if you have to. We're available here. I'm in the office and you can call anytime.'

'That's it?' Harry persisted. 'Zurich Airport? Possibly her? And even more possibly the Hawks? You must have more. Is it Saturday or Sunday – do you even know that?'

'Sorry Harry, but we don't.' Eshan sounded definite. 'I've a couple of hours free and I'll see if I can find any more. I'll call you if I hear anything. Remember, you have her photo – that's your ace.'

Harry backed off. 'Okay. I'll get going. I'll call you from the car.'

'I'll text you, so you'll have my cellphone number.'

'One other thing. How did you know my number?'

'Don't even ask.'

At the hotel reception the owner accessed Harry's website and arranged to have ten copies of a photograph printed. Harry returned to the veranda, where Uri waited, drumming his fingers on the table.

'So, what did that scheisster want?' Uri growled.

'Don't have time to tell you now, but I need to go to Zurich. Immediately. Sorry about mucking up the weekend, but I've no choice.'

'Is he sending you on some Shabak business?'

'No, it's personal. Something's turned up about Ami.'

'Ami? Your daughter?' Uri's face clouded as he spoke, sympathy in his voice. 'Harry, she's dead, you know that. Don't start all this again.'

'Not my idea. Look, I'll call you later, don't have time now.'

'Yes, you do, one minute makes no difference.'

Harry relented and told what had happened.

'Okay,' Uri agreed. 'It's worth checking out. Want me to come with you?'

Harry considered. Two would be better than one, but he declined the offer. The people they were hiking with were important business colleagues.

'Thanks, but no. I'll have time in the car to plan it.'

'Be careful, and don't trust Bercovic one bit. Keep me informed. Good luck.'

Harry scribbled a number on the menu sheet.

'You know Maxime, my assistant. Here's her mobile number. Could you call and ask her to find out who's who in Zurich Airport Security, and make an introduction for me?'

Harry hurried along the winding road downhill out of Davos. His was virtually the only car going that direction; all the others were weekenders heading up to the resort. He forced himself to keep just below the speed limit – the last thing he needed was a brush with the Swiss police.

Once on the AutoRoute, past the small town of Klosters, the road flattened and improved. He tailgated a speeding Porsche. He had no worries about speed cameras, only a police radar check, and the car in front blanketed him. Harry's phone beeped a text – Eshan's mobile number in Jerusalem. Harry glanced at it and began to make a quick mental list of his priorities.

Eshan had probably told the truth about the intercept, but why call Harry, especially after all this time? Eshan was now Director General of Shin Bet and must work hand in glove with Mossad. So had he asked Mossad for their help?

Probably yes, but as he had said Mossad would have considered this to be too minor a matter for them, especially with their problems in Gaza and Iran. So why phone Harry? The answer had to be in what Eshan had told Harry years ago. Hussam Farid had killed Eshan's brother in Lebanon. It had become personal. Eshan was using Harry to find the woman, and through her Farid. With what he knew of Eshan there could be no other explanation.

It all made sense, and Harry was prepared to run with it, but he needed help. On his own he would be useless; or even worse in great danger. He was unarmed. While the Israelis could provide information, that would be all. He would have to rely on the Swiss. Zurich Airport Security.

He needed more background. If the woman from the photograph was acting as a go-between, then it had to be one of three possible scenarios. She could be an intermediary, there could be the completion of a "sale", where some exchange would take place, or lastly there could be a simple one-way transfer. The implications of each were different, and it would be invaluable to know which it would be. He called the number Eshan had given him. Eshan answered.

'Do you have the actual report of the intercept with you? I'm calling from my car.'

'Yes, it's here. Just keep this vague.'

'I need to know the format of the meeting. Give me your opinion, I'll accept it.'

He could picture Eshan nodding in agreement.

'It's a transfer. I'm sure.' Eshan sounded definite.

'Thanks, I'll run with it. Also could you let Zurich know? It will strengthen my hand when I get there.'

'Done already.' Eshan replied, tersely.

'Anything new about the Hawks? Did they ever operate in Switzerland?'

'Not that we know of, and they don't seem to have been active in Germany since the mid '90s. Good luck.' Eshan obviously wanted to get off the phone as quickly as possible.

'One last thing,' Harry persisted. 'The man in the photo. Is he involved?'

'No, I'm as close to one hundred percent he's not there.'

'Doesn't answer my question.'

'He's disappeared. This one is about her and you, not him.'

'Okay,' answered Harry, not believing a single word. He disconnected the call.

Ten minutes later he pulled into the Maienfeld service station. He asked an attendant to fill the petrol tank, collected a coffee from the shop, and drove the car fifty metres to a picnic area. He sat at a wooden table with his coffee, took the phone from his pocket and called a number he knew by heart.

'Munich Airport Security.' A woman's voice.

'Harry Katz, head of security with Weber. Are you the duty officer?'

'Yes. How can I help?'

'I need to speak to Rainer Huttinger. Is he there today?'

'Herr Huttinger is not available. Can I assist you?'

'Is my number on your caller ID?'

'Yes.'

'Then ask Rainer to call me.'

'Herr Katz, I said he is not available.'

'My company put over fifteen million euro worth of business through your airport last year. A serious matter concerning Zurich Airport has come up. Tell your boss to call me; I don't have time to discuss this farther.'

Harry's phone went dead as she terminated the call, but three minutes later it rang.

'Herr Katz,' Rainer Huttinger spoke from the speaker, 'you need to talk to me?' There was ice in his voice. This was the first time in years he had called Harry by his surname, using the formal "sie" instead of his usual "du".

'Rainer, I have been working with you for what, ten years or so,' Harry said carefully. 'Have either I or my company ever abused that arrangement?'

'Look, I'm starting a tennis match and three people are waiting. What the fuck has Zurich Airport got to do with me?'

'Before I joined Weber you know I lived in Israel. Thirteen years ago my wife was murdered and my only daughter kidnapped.'

Rainer muttered a quick condolence, sounding puzzled.

'In that time absolutely nothing has turned up about my missing daughter until one hour ago,' Harry continued. 'It concerns Zurich Airport. I need your help, and badly.'

Harry heard Rainer shout something.

'All right, you have my attention.'

Harry filled him in as quickly as possible, adding he was on the autobahn about one hour from Zurich. His phone flashed he had missed a call.

'So you want me to phone my colleague in Zurich and let him know you are coming.' Rainer sounded friendlier. 'That's fair enough, I'll do it.'

'No, there's more. I need advice. I've never been to Zurich. Forget about who has the biggest dick here, but I presume both airports are fairly similar.'

'Pretty much so.'

'So procedures would be alike?'

'Yes, we work a lot with Zurich,' Rainer replied. 'I'm getting your drift.'

'The analysis from Israel is this woman is meeting one other person for a transfer. Because it's an airport we have to assume one of them flew in, so only one will be armed.I know how they would handle it in Israel, but how would you do it?'

'Shitty question, because the analysis is often wrong. Let's assume you are correct. Are they expecting trouble?'

'No.' Harry replied confidently.

'So two of them, and one armed. Nightmare scenario. The best option is to observe, let them transfer and grab them outside the airport. The Swiss have a big advantage here; their police have far more powers than we have. Does either have a record in Germany or Switzerland?'

'We don't know.'

'Pity. That's the best scenario. Lift, identify and question.'

'You haven't mentioned the more obvious option,' Harry prodded.

'You really don't want that, do you?' Rainer gave a hollow laugh. 'If I were in Zurich, I'd get you out of the way, allow them leave, go home and have a beer. Now I see why you called. You want me to tell you how to avoid that.'

'Exactly. I can't find the woman without them. So, what would persuade them to help?'

A silence followed. Four middle-aged bikers, with long hair, beards and studded black leathers sat down noisily at the next table to Harry. He stood up and began to walk back to his car.

'One problem,' Rainer eventually answered. 'I trust you but Zurich won't. With all that shit in Gaza you won't get the best welcome. They'll be afraid you just want their assistance in finding her, and then it's "thanks for the help" as Mossad wipes out their airport. No, this is my call. I'll reassure them.'

'Thank you – it was my main worry.'

'Something else. We had a circular from the Americans yesterday about al-Qaeda and a European airport. Zurich will have got the same. I'll remind them about it and they can draw their own conclusions. That's about all I can do.'

'More than enough.' Harry was satisfied, as he sat into his car. 'You have no idea how much this means to me.'

'I have some idea. I've only one son, and he nearly died in a car crash as a kid. He's wasting a year in Australia now. You don't have much time. I'll get on to Zurich.'

'Thanks again,' replied Harry. 'I owe you a beer.'

'You owe me more like half a fucking brewery. Good luck, and keep in touch. I'll text you my mobile number – call me if I can help.'

The intensity of his concentration while on the call had drained him. He started the car and pulled back onto the autobahn. "Call info" on his phone showed he had missed a call from Maxime. He phoned her back.

'You want to know about Zurich Airport Security?'

'Any luck?'

'Man called Thomas Reitz is on duty today, but they wouldn't let me speak to him. I left a message about who you are and that you will be arriving. That's about all I could manage, but I'll keep trying.'

'Thanks, Maxime.'

He called Jerusalem, but they had nothing else to add. Eshan had left the office. He kept his speed just below the limit. Within forty-five minutes he was approaching Zurich, and signs for the airport were appearing. Eighteen kilometres. He forced himself to relax and go over his mental checklist. Had he done all he could? Yes, he could think of nothing that needed changing.

A text message flashed, from Rainer Huttinger. "Thomas Reitz duty officer. Park area 4. *Viel Gluck*".

'I'll need it,' said Harry, out loud to himself.

2

As he drove into the car park his heart sank at the realisation that this was a huge modern airport. Everywhere enormous glass buildings, teeming with people. On his own he could do nothing. He locked his car and set off to find the security office, carrying only the folder with the photographs, his eyes scanning every woman. She could be here somewhere, but where? There was no sign of her, but he did notice a prominent police presence, passing scattered pairs of uniformed officers carrying Kockler machine guns.

The security offices were in an older section of the airport. A woman in a grey police uniform opened the door to him. Harry explained he had an appointment with Herr Reitz, and she ushered him into a tiny windowless room, two bare metal chairs its only furniture. He noticed a camera high on one wall.

'Please wait here,' she said, and closed the door behind him.

He looked at his watch. Ten-fifty. He waited in the silent room, forcing himself to remain calm and patient, repeatedly looking at the camera, as if this could convey some message. He decided to give it until eleven-fifteen but the door opened. The woman took him down a corridor to where a younger uniformed policeman asked Harry for his ID, and then motioned him through another door leading into a large much brighter room. Opposite was a shaded window, looking out onto rows of parked aircraft. The walls on either side had banks of flat screens and scattered through the room were metal desks, each topped with a white monitor. In the centre stood a rectangular table ringed by empty seats. The room was quiet, with no external noise. Harry counted six people there, all male.

A man in his late twenties, medium height with short spiky gelled blond hair, walked over and introduced himself as Thomas Reitz. He was formally dressed in dark trousers, white short-sleeved shirt and tie, and wore rimless glasses. He gave a polite handshake, and indicated two vacant chairs at the table. They sat down, and were joined by a slightly older man, briefly introduced as Otto, who was short, plump and untidy. He looked silently and intensely at Harry.

'Now, Herr Katz, I understand you are head of security for Weber.' Reitz's voice was polite and formal. 'I know of your company, but you don't use our airport. How can we be of assistance?'

'It's a long story. Have you been told anything already?'

'Perhaps it would be better if you yourself tell us,' the Swiss replied, with a trace of distain. 'Your accent. You are not German?'

'No.' Harry spread his hands in a gesture of acknowledgement. 'I'm originally from Israel, but now a German citizen. I have been with Weber for over ten years. Before I came here, I mean to Munich, I worked for the Israeli police.'

'Which section?' interjected Otto, only to be restrained by Reitz's hand.

'Let him continue.'

'I no longer work for them. Rainer Huttinger in Munich can confirm it. I have not heard from them, or vice-versa, since I left Israel. Until this morning, that is.'

He related the events of the morning.Reitz listened attentively, asking only the occasional question. When Harry finished he sat back.

'I am still not clear this has anything to do with us. You have my sincerest sympathy with what has happened to your family, but I must repeat. It is not a matter for us here in Zurich.'

Harry had been prepared for this. His eyes never left Reitz's. 'You are correct; the Hawks group is not a threat to your country. But they are here in Zurich.' He emphasised the word "here". 'It's only a matter of time before you become involved, and neutrality has little to do with al-Qaeda.'

At the mention of 'al-Qaeda' three others in the room drifted over to hear the conversation. Reitz remained nonplussed, scathing in his reply.

'Look, I get this crap all the time. Soon as someone wants our help they mention the magic two words and we're supposed to jump to attention. I don't buy it.'

'I never said they were al-Qaeda.' Harry cut in quickly. 'What I am sure about is they are here in your airport. It's far preferable to get them now rather than tidying up the mess afterwards.'

'Do you say this Hawks group is active in Switzerland?' Reitz sounded less sure of himself.

'I don't know.' Harry leaned forward. 'I'm no longer involved with my country's security services. You will have to ask Jerusalem, or your own people.'

Reitz's mood subtly changed, and he gave a barely perceptible gesture of acknowledgement. Harry gave a silent thanks to Eshan, who had obviously sent through some information. Harry had evidently said the right thing, but not enough.

'These meetings happen all the time,' Reitz persisted. 'We get daily warnings. So what's different about this one? Zurich is a busy airport, and while we might possibly be prepared to observe, there is little else we can do.'

Harry stood up and walked over to the window, turned and faced them. He gestured behind, almost theatrically.

'This is a clearly a major airport,' he said as he pointed. 'Even from here I can see two American planes. Unless I am mistaken, that is a Qantas 747 behind them. So, I have found three targets already within what – less than ten seconds?'

'I'll grant you that,' Reitz conceded, 'but it's not enough.'

It was time for Harry's bluff.

'On its own this meeting might seem insignificant, but we were informed, only this morning, there is an alert for an attack on a European airport.' He could see unconcealed glances between them. 'Jerusalem thinks this will be against a British airport, but in truth nobody seems to know.'

Again more looks of agreement.

'Jerusalem received the information about this meeting here only three hours ago, and they had to decide how to act on it. So why send me?'

'Yes, why you?' asked Reitz.

'Because they thought I was in Munich – it's pure chance I was in Switzerland. In addition I know this woman.'

'How?'

'When I was still active I was involved with her and the group she was part of. While I haven't seen her for many years I would still recognise her. Also this is low priority for Israeli security – they have more pressing matters.'

Harry had played his last card, and waited the response. Reitz considered until his demeanour changed.

'I will have to discuss this with my superiors. You are not offering us much, I'm afraid. A meeting somewhere here, but no time of this meeting. A woman with no name, and a group with no names. It could already have happened.'

'I agree, we don't have a time or a location but I do have something. A photograph of the woman.'

He opened his folder and removed the copies of the photograph. All the men in the room congregated around the table, passing the copies among themselves.

'It's an old photograph I took in 1997. She's now thirteen years older. Of course she will have changed, but it is a good shot of her face. Could you at the very least circulate it, as soon as possible? It's your decision what actions you will take if you do locate her, but please at least distribute the photograph. The man there is not involved.'

In Israel everyone would have had a loud opinion and would express it vociferously. Here the suggestions were made in a calmer manner. Reitz instructed a colleague to distribute the photograph, with the added order that nobody was to approach the woman if located. The photograph would be texted to the mobile phones of the security staff, and Reitz took Harry's number to include him. He would receive the same message.

Harry smiled with relief.

'One important question,' Reitz continued. 'Do you think they will be armed?'

'I don't know. In Israel we would assume them fully prepared to use weapons and have backup.'

Reitz nodded; then his face darkened momentarily. 'One thing you must remember. This is my airport, and I am in charge. If any of your colleagues are making their way here there will be major consequences.'

'No, there are none. They might have wanted to, but had no time.'

Reitz looked directly at Harry, then turned around and left the room. Harry did not know whether to be satisfied or frustrated, but realised there was nothing now except waiting and hoping. He had done all he could, and it had panned out as well as could be expected. They believed him, and they were distributing the photograph.

Harry followed a couple of the men out the door, held open for them by a man in the white uniform of the airport cleaners.

3

Harry looked at his watch. Twelve twenty-two. He had the beginning of a headache. He passed the policewoman at reception, and turned towards what seemed to be the main terminal. At an information desk he picked up a plan of the airport. Needing space to think and wanting coffee he headed towards the food area. This was a large open space with a semi-circle of fast food outlets fronting clusters of white tables and chairs. On both sides and opposite were glass-fronted shops, corridors, stairs and escalators, with large doors leading to the outside. The whole area hummed with activity.

Realising he had left his reading glasses in the car, he asked a policeman for directions to Parking Area 4. He was pointed to an escalator and told to follow the signs at the top. As he moved up the escalator he looked idly across to his right, at the crowds of people in the hall below him.

Suddenly he saw her!

The woman from the photograph!

Less than six metres away, she was hurrying from behind to in front of him, one among a mass of people. She turned her head momentarily in his direction and there she stood – framed for one fleeting instant in the same pose Harry had looked at a thousand times. She turned away and moved directly and purposefully towards the large doors leading outside.

Harry reacted immediately. He grasped the edge of the escalator, intending to jump, but he was too high up and a number of young children stood below. He turned farther to his right, to run down, but behind was a tightly packed group of people with large suitcases. He had no option but to run up the escalator. This was also crowded, but in a blind and uncaring panic he forced his way between protesting groups and reached the top. He turned to his left, quickly scanned the down escalator, and decided on the stairs. He ran down at full stretch, ignoring the angry outbursts of those he elbowed aside, reached the floor below and raced through the crowds.

Bursting through the outside door, which led into a short passage, he tripped over a suitcase on the ground and fell full length. He swore out loud, picked himself up, ran another five metres through another large door and stopped.

Outside, he stood panting at the edge of the nearest footpath of a three-lane traffic system, between the building he had left and one opposite, which had a large 'Terminal Two' sign above its entrance. There was no sign of the woman, and in contrast to the crowds inside, few people about.

He looked right. In the nearest lane were a couple of buses, but their doors were closed. A middle traffic lane had only an occasional car. On the far side he saw a long line of stationary white taxis. He ran straight across the three lanes and the walkways in between and through the door directly opposite into Terminal Two.

He had entered a vast area; about eighty metres long. This was a bustle of activity, but there was no sign of the woman. He ran thirty metres in one direction, then another, and then another, but he could not find her. Back near the door and gasping from the exertion he was about to try another direction when two uniformed policemen confronted him.

He had no option but to explain. As he took out his identity card the phones of all three beeped simultaneously. They reached for their mobiles and to Harry's relief the same photograph and accompanying text appeared on his and on theirs. One of the policemen told Harry to wait while he phoned his boss. Thomas Reitz answered, the policeman had a brief word in Swiss German and handed Harry his phone. Reitz sounded furious, ordering Harry to remain with the policemen. Harry was to do nothing on his own. Harry interjected that she had been wearing a beige jacket and a green shirt. Reitz agreed to text this information to his staff.

Harry asked the policemen to come outside with him.

'I assumed she came in here,' he said, 'but maybe she took a taxi. Let's ask if anyone outside saw her.'

There was still a line of taxis in the near lane, and now a couple of cars with drivers parked in the middle lane. The first taxi driver was of no assistance. He had seen no woman, and could not have been less interested. The second seemed keen to talk, and had plenty of suggestions, but had seen nothing. Harry went back to the policemen, who were talking to the car drivers, but they just shrugged.

What now? She had disappeared, but where? He looked around at the high glass buildings on each side, at the clear blue sky overhead, hoping for inspiration. He was on his own. He must decide. He had almost been within touching distance of her, this woman who might know something about Ami. Was it her? Could he be definite? Yes, he could. He was sure. He had memorised every detail of that photograph over thirteen years. He would never get this chance again, but what to do?

Of course. Cameras.

Escorted by the two policemen he hurried back to the security office. There were three people in the room; Reitz, Otto and another. Reitz dismissed the two policemen and almost grudgingly listened to Harry's description of events. He seemed skeptical that it had been a definite identification of the woman, but Harry refused to deviate. Reitz agreed to look back over the security cameras, but the one normally covering the area between the two buildings had been taken away for repair. Reitz looked over to Otto.

'Otto, can you rewind the unit inside the door of Terminal Two? Say ten minutes.'

'Sure.'

They watched as Otto halted the real time camera and rewound fifteen minutes. He ran it forwards at four times its normal speed until Harry suddenly appeared on screen, jerkily running in through the terminal door. Otto stopped the tape. He rewound it three minutes, and they watched in silence as he ran this portion at normal speed. Harry reappeared, but the woman did not precede him.

'Well, she didn't come in that door.' Reitz spoke first. 'Pity about the camera outside. Let's look at the ones inside the food hall.'

He had a brief discussion with Otto and they decided to run that camera backwards. They found Harry running in reverse from the door and disappearing out of the camera's view up the stairs. Now Otto slowed it, and with mounting excitement Harry clearly saw the woman hurrying in the door and apparently walking backward until out of the camera's vision. Otto replayed it forward slowly but swore, as none of the images were of sufficient clarity to give more than a partial facial view. He tweaked his controls, and quickly found her, again in reverse, as she backed towards a seat beside an empty table at the edge of the groups of tables in the food area. She sat down with her back to this camera.

'Can you get a frontal view?' Harry asked.

'Let's see.' He manipulated the images from two other cameras, only to curse in acceptance of defeat a few minutes later.

'No, that's the best I can do. None of the others are much help. That table is out of view of those cameras, and she has sat with her back to the one covering that area. She could not have picked a worse place for us.'

Harry caught a fleeting glance of a communication between the two Swiss. He turned to Reitz.

'Am I missing something?' Harry asked.

'No, no conspiracy,' Reitz replied hastily. 'It's just bad luck for us and good for her she sat at that particular table.' He switched the topic quickly. 'Go back to her, Otto.'

Otto rewound the images until she initially arrived at the table. He froze the image and then ran it forward at normal speed.

She wore a hat pulled low over her face and glasses. She carried a mug and had a large bag over her shoulder. She sat down, took off her hat and put it on one of the two free chairs at the table, moving the other chair slightly so it also faced away from the camera. Harry looked closely at Otto, but he did not seem to react to this. She put her shoulder bag on the table, and from it took a thick dark folder, which she laid on the free seat opposite. She put the hat into the bag, pulled the opposite seat forwards and tucked it under the table. The folder was now hidden. She removed her glasses and took a newspaper from the bag. Her preparations apparently complete, she seemed to settle down to wait, making no attempt to drink or to read.

'She's a pro,' Otto interjected enthusiastically. 'No doubt. Her bag came as hand luggage. All her preparation is standard. Look at the table she has chosen. See where it is – immediate access and perfect for a quick getaway, and although we can't see her too well she is fully in view from about twenty locations. Harry, you're right. This woman is dirty.'

Harry was becoming impatient as they continued watching her doing apparently nothing, but Otto waved him away as he asked him to speed it up, saying there was only ten minutes left. A teenage girl, cigarette in hand, briefly exchanged words before taking an ashtray from the woman's table and returning to her own. Otto zoomed in on the girl and followed her back to her table, where she joined a group of three others in animated conversation.

They agreed to dismiss the teenager as irrelevant.

The woman continued to wait, her only apparent action being an intermittent check of her makeup. Then, to their frustration, a group of six or seven tall athletic young men congregated near her table. They put bags on the ground and jostled around. Otto zoomed in on their kitbags, remarking they had the logo of an American basketball team. Two more joined the group, farther blocking their view, and they had only intermittent glimpses of the woman until she started to suddenly look around. In a quick, fluid movement she then crammed her belongings into her bag, reached forward and, taking the file from the chair, she hurried through the crowd to the door outside, passing the escalator from where Harry had seen her.

A cursing Otto repeatedly rewound the images of her before she had stood up, but he could not improve them. He eventually spread his hands in annoyance.

'Those bloody Americans,' Otto swore. 'We had her but for them. Okay, apart from the kid with the ashtray nobody came. All agree to dismiss the girl?'

Harry and Reitz assented.

'My analysis,' Otto continued. 'Her contact did not appear, and the most likely scenario is that she has an exact cutoff time point. She moved to her second meeting place. This must be outside the airport, since she didn't go into Terminal Two. She had a car waiting outside.'

Reitz agreed, but Harry was not convinced.

'Can you go back to just before she stood up?' Harry asked Otto.

Otto rewound, and then restarted.

'Thanks,' said Harry. 'Look, there it is. She starts to look all around her, when she had been so careful before. Why? Why suddenly change?'

'I just think her time was up,' Otto considered, 'and she couldn't help but have a quick look around before going – as simple as that. Perhaps she knew those guys were there behind her. No, she did. You saw how she kept pretending to check her makeup? She was using the mirror to look. She knew they were there, and they were blocking our view. See, she moved at exactly twelve thirty – not a coincidence.' Otto pointed to the corner of his screen. 'No, she's gone, and if the bloody camera outside worked we would see her get into a car.'

Reitz shuffled around in his seat. 'That's it. She was up to something, I'll give you that, but she's gone. I'm sorry, Herr Katz.' He spoke almost casually to Harry. 'You were right about her, but I'm afraid your woman has left my airport.'

'That's not it!' Harry rounded on him in frustration. 'First, Otto seems sure she knew about the cameras. Are you just going to ignore it?'

'I'm not. It's my biggest worry. It needs to be addressed urgently, but it's our problem, not yours.'

'How could she have known about the cameras?' Harry persisted.

'Two ways,' Otto replied. 'One is there is a leak from here, or else they have scanned our cameras. I don't know which is worse.'

'One last thing,' Harry asked. 'Can you track her backwards from when she arrived?'

'We could, but it would be a waste of time,' Otto said. 'This one is a pro – it's almost like she went to one of my training sessions. In fact, I'll use this tape for my next. I promise we'll check it over the next few days, but it is very laborious.'

Otto explained. They would find her coming in some door, but outside the door she would have changed her image. For instance wore no coat and hat. If she had arrived by air she could have taken the train one stop and then come back, as if arriving that way. The possibilities were endless, and the pros were near impossible to backtrack. Harry had to agree. Reitz had become visibly impatient. He stood up, edgily adding that he had much work to do, and could help no more. Otto could burn the images to a DVD for Harry.

Harry tensed with frustration. He had never felt so helpless and alone. So near. So very near. He had seen her, only metres away from him, but she had vanished. There must be something he could do, but he was not getting any assistance here. Something. Anything. He needed help. An idea came.

'I have one last favour.' He forced himself to remain polite. 'Could you recommend a private investigator I could contact immediately?'

'What about Veronika?' Otto asked Reitz. 'She'd be perfect.'

Harry turned to Otto.

'Who is that?' Harry asked, eagerly.

Reitz slowly nodded as in agreement.

'Would you know where to find her?' Reitz asked Otto.

'Think so,' Otto replied. 'I have her home number here somewhere.'

Reitz turned back to Harry.

'There are only a few so-called private investigators I have heard of in this city, and none I could recommend except Veronika Glass. She used to work here.'

'Not at home, but she has left her mobile number,' Otto called over from the other side of the room. 'Will I try it?'

Reitz raised his eyebrows at Harry. 'I am told she is expensive. Be prepared.'

Harry nodded. Otto dialed, and spoke for a couple of moments in rapid Swiss German. Otto put his hand over the phone.

'She'll speak to you, but she's really pissed off,' Otto whispered loudly. 'She's on a golf course.'

He handed the phone to Harry.

'Frau Glass,' Harry spoke as authoritatively as he could manage. 'My name is Harry Katz, and I need your services urgently. I am calling from Herr Reitz's office. I understand this is far from convenient, but I would not have called if it were not of the utmost importance.'

'Continue.'

'Can you be overheard?' Harry asked.

'No, but why?'

'Then can you tell me what your normal fee is?'

The woman laughed. 'Two hundred francs an hour, or one thousand two hundred a day. But I never work weekends.'

'I am prepared to offer you five times that amount, but only if you can come here immediately.'

A momentary silence followed. 'Allow me to speak to Thomas.'

Harry handed Reitz the phone and a brief exchange, unintelligible to Harry, took place. Reitz gave a wry smile and hung up.

'She said it would be my call,' Reitz looked at Harry, 'and I told her yes. She will come straight over – it will take about thirty minutes. By the way, how much is it five times of?'

'I am afraid you will have to ask her yourself.'

'Touché.' Reitz smiled.

Reitz showed Harry to an empty office, which he said used to be Veronika's old workplace, and they could use it until his own shift ended. Harry returned to the car to collect his glasses and his laptop. He bought a couple of filled bagels from the food hall, still scanning in case he saw the woman again. Back in the office he powered his laptop and was inserting the disc given to him by Otto as Veronika arrived.

4

Mid forties and slender, Veronika Glass was of average height. With vivid scarlet lipstick, she had very short red hair and dark rimmed glasses, framing a pale face. She still wore her golf outfit of blue polo neck, blue pullover and yellow trousers. She put her laptop on the desk, took a chair and looked at Harry.

'So, Herr Katz, why are you prepared to offer me so much money?'

Harry told his story quickly and she listened intently, with occasional questions and remarks. When he had concluded with the events of the afternoon she made him repeat some aspects again, focusing in on the appearance of the woman. Harry's initial memory of exact detail was hazy. She forced him to concentrate on the woman's face, her expression, her mood.

'Did she seem calm?' Veronika persisted. 'Was she annoyed, angry, happy?'

'No, agitated.' Harry felt more certain. 'She looked concerned. Yes, I'm sure.'

'Then maybe she did take a taxi.' Veronika said. 'Do you know the exact time you saw her?'

'Yes. She got up from the table at precisely twelve thirty. We saw that on the tape. A taxi would have been at most two minutes later.'

'That's what we need.' Veronika smiled. 'Right, let's get started.'

She connected broadband and picked up the phone, pushing her glasses up on her forehead. 'Money no object?'

'Within reason.'

'I'll offer five hundred to the controller and five hundred to the driver. That's one thousand. Okay?'

'Go ahead.'

'I'll try "Protaxi" first – they're the biggest.'

Harry listened as she persuaded the controller to help her, emphasising there was a sizeable reward. Veronika gave her own mobile number, and then repeated the same exercise with Graftaxi, MeierTaxi, and on through the other taxi companies of Zurich. She had just begun talking to 'ASA Taxi' when her mobile rang. She answered, punched the air, put her hand over the phone, and whispered they had it. Her call was from the taxi driver. They spoke for a few minutes, argued slightly, and she evidently concluded the exchange to her satisfaction. She finished the call with a contented smile.

'He's coming straight over. He has us over a barrel, and wants two hundred more, but we agreed on one hundred. I'll go tell reception to expect him.'

On her return she looked at Harry differently.

'You probably can't afford me, but now I'm here I'm interested. It's a change from the unfaithful partners. I'll do it for double my fee, which seems more than reasonable as it's the weekend. I must warn you I have an engagement later, but tomorrow I'm free. Now, tell me the complete story.'

The taxi driver had a close cut grey beard, short grey hair and a much-reddened face. He was about fifty, tall and heavily built, dressed in open necked checked shirt and casual trousers. He introduced himself as Martin Felder, and in reply to his query Veronika gave him permission to smoke, provided he stayed in that office.

'I have a photograph of a woman we are interested in,' she asked gently. 'Is she the one you took in your taxi?'

Martin needed only a brief look. 'She's changed, but this is the woman I picked up, no doubt.'

Harry slapped his thigh with delight.

'She's a good-looking woman,' Martin smirked. 'It's her.'

Veronika smiled weakly. 'So what happened? Start from before she got into the car.'

'It was unusual,' Martin said. 'She hurried in and ordered me to drive off immediately. I asked her where and she told me just to drive away, and then said she wanted to go to Oerkilon train station. We got there fairly quickly, as the traffic was light, but she stayed in the car and told me to take her to the Haupt-Bahnhof instead.'

'Did she say why?' asked Veronika.

'No. Anyway, at the main station she just grabbed her bag and rushed away. She gave me a fifty note but didn't ask for any change. I didn't object.'

'You are sure she went inside?' Veronika asked.

'Of course I'm sure,' Martin smirked. 'She was a stunner, and I appreciate a woman's ass. I took a good look.'

He gave Harry a wink and Veronika the beginnings of a leer, but he turned away when he saw the look of disgust on her face.

'Okay, you picked her up at shortly after twelve-thirty,' Harry interjected, 'so the station would have been what? One o'clock at the latest, probably just before that?'

'Yes. I picked up another fare almost immediately, and logged it. I checked on the way here, and it was twelve fifty-nine. I left her off at about twelve fifty-seven.'

'Describe what she wore.' Veronika asked.

'As I said, I like women, and notice clothes.' Martin replied. 'She wore a light khaki jacket, trousers the same colour, and light brown boots, probably suede or something similar. Her shirt looked wrong. It was a peculiar green, and didn't match. Little if any makeup, no glasses and no hat or scarf.'

'Did she have a bag?' Veronika attempted to smile as she spoke.

'Yes. A shoulder bag.'

'Could she have been carrying a gun?' Harry interjected.

Veronika and Martin turned towards Harry, surprise on their faces. Martin considered before replying.

'A gun? No, not carrying one.' He sounded definite. 'No shoulder holster, I am sure of it. If your politically correct colleague will allow me to say this, I do admit to having taken an occasional look at her in the mirror. It's not against the law here, at least not yet.'

'Stick to the point.' Veronika leant forwards, her face flushed with annoyance. 'Language? Accent?'

'She's not Swiss.' Martin spoke to Harry. 'Spoke Hoch Deutsch. Her German is perfect, but she's not a native speaker. Maybe Dutch, more likely English or American.'

'Her mood?' Harry asked. 'Her behaviour?'

'Agitated.' Martin closed his eyes momentarily as he considered. 'I told you what happened when she got into the car, and she remained like that for the whole journey. Hardly spoke, except for that bit at Oerkilon. She kept looking at something in her lap. When we arrived at the station she left her newspaper behind.'

'Which newspaper?' Veronika cut in.

'German crap. The Frankfurter Allgemeine. I threw it in the boot.'

Harry and Veronika reacted instantly.

'Is it still there?' Veronika spoke first.

'Sure.' Martin seemed puzzled. 'Why?'

'We will need it. Has anyone else touched it?'

'Ah, fingerprints.' Martin smiled in recognition. 'No, nobody except me.'

'Good. Anything else unusual?'

'Nothing I can think of.' Martin shrugged. 'The whole journey was unusual, but what's usual nowadays?'

'I presume she didn't say why she went to the station.'

'No, and I didn't ask.'

'You have been more than helpful.' Veronika forced another faint smile. 'I'm going to need one more favour. It will take about an hour, but could you help us create a fotofit of this woman?'

'No problem, but I have a lot of business on today.' Martin smirked as he sat back. 'It will cost you another, say, two hundred francs.'

Veronika looked at Harry.

'That's fine,' Harry replied in acceptance.

'Can you excuse me for a few minutes?' Veronika left the office and returned a few moments later, with a plastic bag and gloves. She asked Martin to collect the newspaper from his car, and not to touch it. As he left the office Veronika shook her head.

'What a creep! I have told Thomas the woman has left his precious airport. Now, we'll have to find a fotofit technician, easier said than done. I presume you can pay? It may be another five or six hundred.'

'No option.'

She scrolled her laptop, took the phone and started dialing. The third call was successful, and after a brief conversation she told Harry someone would arrive in about forty minutes. It would cost four hundred francs. Harry agreed.

'By the way,' Veronika added with a sheepish smile, 'I recorded our conversation with Herr Felder.'

'How did you do that?' Harry asked in surprise. 'I didn't notice anything?'

'The laptop had a few modifications. Don't worry; I didn't record us talking. There are few morals in my job, but recording a client unawares is just not done.'

While they were waiting Martin returned with the newspaper, safely in its plastic bag. The technician was announced at reception. Veronika went to let her in. As she closed the door Martin sniggered. 'That's one tough dyke. Thank God I don't work with her.'

'Leave it be, Martin, or I won't pay you. I mean it.'

The technician was named Kerstin. Early twenties and very pretty, she had short jet-black hair, multiple piercings and a long red snake tattooed on her bare right forearm. She was pale faced with Gothic black eyes, and purple lipstick. She was dressed in black, with a short skirt and fishnet tights. Martin could not keep his eyes off her legs, but she ignored him. She carried a pink laptop, which she put on the table.

While she dealt with Martin, Harry went to an automat and withdrew the money he needed with his company credit card. By the time he returned Martin had finished. Since they had no farther need for him Harry paid him his cash. Veronika asked Martin if he would give her the remainder of his cigarettes. He shrugged and threw the pack on to the table, gave Harry a wink, and left. Veronika smiled, produced a plastic glove, and with it put the packet into another plastic bag.

Fotofit technology had altered since Harry had last used it, and the process with the computer seemed easier and more intuitive than he remembered. He would be doing a frontal image only, as he had not seen a profile, and it took less than fifteen minutes to complete. There were now three images – Harry and Martin's frontal, and Martin's profile. This was the first time Harry had seen a profile of the woman, and he looked at it for a few moments. The frontal images both men had created were similar enough, but not identical. Kirsten next created a combined image, her computer mixing both and coming up with a composite. Now, with four images, Kerstin looked pleased.

'He's a total asshole,' Kerstin said, 'but he notices and remembers things well. I think these will be accurate. I'll burn them on to a CD and give it to you, and load them on to my website. The URL is on my business card, and you can access the photos by inserting a forward slash and your name, Harry.'

'That's clear enough. Thank you for your assistance, and I've included a further one hundred francs.'

Veronika took the CD, went to the main office, and returned in less than ten minutes with four copies of each image. She kept one set and gave Harry the remainder. She looked at her watch and apologised she would have to leave. She reminded Harry that she had Sunday free, and could meet him early. He said he would call her on her mobile next morning.

Harry drove the short distance to the Moevenpick Airport Hotel, a large modern glass building, and booked in. After a long shower, he placed the four fotofits on the spare bed and beside them laid the original photograph of the woman. Six o'clock, not too late to phone Eshan, but Eshan had his mobile on recording. Harry left a message. He next called Uri, who answered but was in noisy company. Harry gave a brief account, saying he would call again tomorrow.

He went to the largely empty restaurant for dinner, and was eating in silence when his phone rang, with Eshan's ID flashing. A waiter curtly pointed out to him a sign requesting phones to be turned off. Harry ignored him as he put the phone to his ear.

'I've just left a meeting with the PM.' Eshan's voice sounded strained. 'Have you not heard the news?'

'No. What's happened?'

'A bomb in Jerusalem – Ben Yehuda Street. I'm not sure how many are dead.'

'Are you all right?' Harry asked anxiously.

'Yes, thank God, but I saw the explosion. I have to go.'

'Do that. I'll phone you next week.'

Harry could not finish his meal. He went straight to his room and turned on CNN. Images of familiar Jerusalem streetscapes, with all too familiar sirens, ambulances and injured civilians followed one after another. He watched until he could look no more.

5

Seven thirty: Already showered and shaved, Harry phoned Veronika and arranged to meet her in the hotel restaurant for breakfast. Dressed more conventionally in blue jeans, T-shirt and black jacket, she had changed her glasses for contact lenses and looked considerably less conspicuous than yesterday. She had not heard about the bomb in Jerusalem and did not realise its significance until Harry explained that there would be little assistance from the Israelis. They sat in a quiet corner of the restaurant and began going back over the events of the previous day.

'We know our woman planned to meet someone,' Veronika began, 'and presumably either she or the other arrived by plane. Her newspaper was the Swiss edition, so she didn't buy it in Frankfurt. Let's assume she's the one who flew in, and planned to fly out again.'

'Okay.' Harry nodded. 'She waited for someone who didn't turn up, and then left in a hurry. Martin said she wanted to go to Oerkilon train station. Why there?'

'I think I know.' Veronika's eyes narrowed in concentration. 'She wanted the main station, but decided against the direct train from the airport. A taxi to Oerkilon and the commuter train would be the next quickest. So why change her mind? Wait, Martin said yesterday's traffic was unusually light. Maybe that's why.'

Veronika put down her coffee, and between mouthfuls of rye bread continued her flow of thought.

'So, now she's in the main station, and there are what, three possibilities? One is the meeting place changed to the station.'

'No. We decided she looked agitated,' Harry cut in. 'A pro would have been annoyed if the meeting had been changed, not agitated. Let's keep that as a possible, not a probable.'

'Option two,' Veronika continued. 'She went to the railway station, and as she spoke fluent German she went to Germany. We could go around the station with the fotofits, but who remembers a woman buying a railway ticket?'

'Only if we have to.' Harry took over. 'Option three. She originally planned to fly back to wherever she came from, but suddenly this changed. So, now she is in Zurich railway station. Where else could she fly from?'

'Two choices, Geneva or Basel. Geneva's much larger but it's four hours by train. Basel is only one hour. It depends where she's going. If it's a main airport then Basel would be fine, but if it's in the Middle East, Geneva would be better. Is this hotel wired for Internet?'

'They say it is.'

'Then let's go to somewhere quiet.' Veronika suggested.

They were shown a designated area near reception, with desks and booths. It took only moments to connect the laptops. Veronika opened the Swiss Railway site.

'Okay,' she said. 'Martin dropped her off just before one o'clock. Say five minutes to find a timetable, at least five more to buy a ticket, so that's one-ten.

Now, trains from Zurich to Basel.' Veronika tapped the table for emphasis. 'Yes, there it is. One twenty-one, that's perfect. There's a Geneva train at four minutes past one, but she'd never make it. The next one's an hour later, with a change in Bern. If I were undecided I'd go for Basel. So, she arrives in Basel at two twenty-six. Taxi to the airport. Not too far, max thirty minutes. Arrives at Basel airport about five to three. What are her options there?'

Harry opened the Basel Airport departure screen. 'Say four o'clock. Let's see. Swiss to London Heathrow at three forty-five, she might just have made that. Lufthansa to Frankfurt at four twenty. Easyjet to London at four fifty-seven, and five or six more within the next few hours.

'So, Basel it is. Let's go. It'll take about ninety minutes.'

They took Harry's Passat. The weather had changed to cooler and grey, but the Sunday traffic was light. On the way Veronika told Harry some of the story of her life. As Martin had guessed, she was gay. She had been in the regular police and had moved to the airport security section ten years before, where she had been advancing up the career ladder when she fell in love with a woman colleague, still her current partner. Unfortunately this woman was married to Veronika's immediate superior. When the woman decided to leave her husband she and Veronika moved into an apartment together, but there had been no option except for both women to resign from the service. Unable to obtain a transfer back to regular police, Veronika set up as a private investigator.

Cruising on the autobahn towards Basel she looked at Harry and spoke in carefully measured tones. She had some concerns. Normally the nature of her work was to find out something, and on completion her own task should be over. In contrast, her clients' involvement was not finished.

'Most have not thought through what they will feel or do once they get their information. I'm concerned for you if we manage to find this woman. What will you do?'

Harry kept his gaze firmly on the road ahead. 'I don't know. We, and by this I mean the Israeli intelligence agencies, don't know for sure if she is involved. If not then I'll tell Jerusalem and leave it to them. For me it will all be over.'

'And if she were involved?' Veronika persisted.

'I used to want revenge. Make her suffer like I'd suffered. But things have changed and now, now I just need to know what happened to Ami.'

'That's what I wanted to hear,' Veronika sounded relieved. 'But if she leads you to your daughter? What then?'

'That's something I've never stopped thinking about.' Harry's eyes narrowed. 'If she's in Lebanon she'll be an Arab girl, but I have no problem with that. When I see teenage girls I realise Ami would be like them, not a baby. I hope, if it does happen, I have someone like you to give me advice.'

Veronika gently squeezed Harry's hand.

'I could work this job for nothing, but I am not that sentimental. Let's find her.'

Harry parked outside the main terminal, a far smaller building than Zurich, and as Veronika told him, unique among airports. It was situated in France, but the road there from the city of Basel was Swiss territory. Switzerland, Germany and France shared the airport and had named it Basel-Mulhouse-Freiburg EuroAirport, although everybody referred to it simply as Basel.

It had begun raining, and as neither had coats they had to run to the entrance. In the reservation section the nearest counter was Lufthansa. The polite young man at the desk had been on duty the previous afternoon. They showed him the fotofit images. No, he had never seen this woman, nor had the woman at the nearby British Airways desk.The woman at Swiss Airways had not been on duty yesterday.

As they turned away a man appeared at the neighbouring Easyjet counter. He was not wearing a uniform, and appeared to be in a hurry. When Veronika approached him, he grunted that he was off duty – the desk would open in one hour. She moved to block him off, saying she and Harry were working in collaboration with Zurich Airport Security, and would prefer to keep it informal. They only needed one moment.

'All right,' he said, 'what do you want?'

'Were you working yesterday afternoon?'

'Yes. Why?'

'We are investigating a woman who may have taken a flight yesterday. We don't know her name, but we do have some photos.' Veronika passed over the batch of photographs. He looked at each in turn, then back at her.

'Yeah, I remember. She wanted to book the four fifty-seven to London Stansted, but arrived after the cut-off time. She tried to persuade me to let her take it, but it was too late. I had to turn her down.'

'You are absolutely sure?'

'Yes, I'm sure.'

'Did you get her name, or have any idea what she did next?'

'No, I was too busy.'

Harry and Veronika moved a short distance away, momentarily too excited for words. The woman had come here – they had guessed correctly. She had wanted to go to London. They were back in business. Harry allowed himself a brief moment of relief and then focused on his next task.

They checked the airport timetable on a large board. A Swiss Airways flight Saturday at five-sixteen to London Heathrow. Back to the Swiss counter, now empty of customers, with only the same woman they had spoken to previously. They introduced themselves as associated with Zurich Security. Yesterday's duty person? That was her colleague, Anneke. No, she was not rostered for duty today. While she did not know how to contact Anneke, her supervisor would.

The supervisor was a polite man in his mid twenties, who invited them into his office. Veronika gave him an edited version of what had happened and asked to speak to this Anneke. He called her at home, while Harry held his breath. The supervisor smiled. Anneke would be there in fifteen minutes.

Twenty minutes later Anneke, a young bubbly blonde woman, needed only a couple of seconds with the photos.

'Yes. She booked the five-sixteen to Heathrow. I could not possibly forget her, it was so unusual.'

'Unusual?' asked Veronika.

'She wanted to go to London urgently,' Anneke said, 'but economy was fully booked. There was some football match involving an English team. She took business class and paid in cash. Over six hundred euro, and that's why I remember her. She just took out a big wad of notes.'

'Do you have her details?' Harry tried to sound casual.

Anneke moved behind the desk and tapped into the computer. 'Here we are – she was the last to book in. Brigitte Maier. I have no other details, as she paid cash.'

'Maier. German?' Harry asked.

'Mmm. She had a German passport and spoke perfect German, not Swiss German, but I felt she was not a native speaker.'

'Did you record her passport number?'

'Yes, it's recorded at check-in.'

'Can we see?' Harry could not keep the trembling out of his voice, and Anneke gave a curious look before replying.

'I shall have to check with my supervisor.' Her voice acquired a formal tone. 'Could you wait a minute?'

She closed the programme and left the room.

'Smart woman,' interjected Veronika. 'Don't worry, Harry, Thomas can get it.'

The supervisor came back into the office and sat at the desk.

'Anneke is not permitted to disclose passport details,' he said, 'but I can.'

He sat at the computer and printed off a page, which he handed to Harry. A copy of the identity page of the passport, showing Brigitte Maier's name, date of birth and photograph. There she was, the same woman, no longer a mystery. The passport had been issued in 2000 and had only two months to run, but she was the woman from Beirut, almost identical to how she looked in Harry's old photograph. Harry put it in his pocket and they left the airport building.

Once outside, in spite of the wind and rain, Harry whooped and enveloped Veronika in a spontaneous embrace of happiness, only to pull back in embarrassment. Laughing loudly at this, Veronika grasped him around the waist and they performed a noisy dance of joy, to the amusement of passengers hurrying into the terminal.

6

Midday: It was still raining as Harry and Veronika entered the A3 autobahn heading back to Zurich. Traffic was heavy and he had to concentrate on the road ahead.

'One thing's bothering me,' said Harry.

'What?'

'We're assuming the passport was genuine,' he spoke cautiously, not wanting to accept this other possibility. 'What if it's not?'

'Why use a false passport? There's no way she could have anticipated we'd trace her to Basel. I'll bet my life it's genuine.'

'I hope you're right, but I'll feel better once we get it confirmed.'

Thomas Reitz's only reaction was one of obvious relief that the woman had left his airport. He would of course pass Harry's information onto the anti-terrorist police, and the Swiss authorities would assist them in chasing up this woman, but today was a busy Sunday and he had a lot of work to do. Tomorrow there will be a full staff on duty, and it will have to wait until then. He settled back in his chair, prepared to dismiss them.

Harry was about to make a reasoned argument, but noticed Veronika gripping the table until her knuckles were whitening, her lips drawing back. Eventually she let loose. She jumped up, and ignoring the grins on the faces of the other security staff in the room, not to mention Harry's embarrassed silence, began to yell at Thomas Reitz, her ex-trainee.

'You arrogant little shit. Have you no sympathy in your body. You know what this man has gone through and all you care about is your bloody protocols. I always knew you were the coldest shit I'd ever met, and now you've confirmed it.'

Reitz cowered in his seat as the onslaught continued.

'Think about it. How would you feel if in ten years time your only daughter was kidnapped and you asked Harry for help, only to be treated like this? Have you any bloody human emotion at all?'

Harry stood up and took her by the arm. 'Thanks for your concern, but perhaps that's enough.'

Veronika shrugged Harry's hand away, grasped a chair and sat back, noisily crossing her arms over her chest, looked up at the ceiling and emitted a loud grunt of distain. Thomas Reitz gave a wry smile as he shrugged his shoulders. He seemed totally unperturbed.

'I'd forgotten about that temper of yours,' he said to Veronika, then turned around to Harry. 'Okay. I'll contact Wiesbaden and chase up that passport, but I won't be able to do it for about half an hour.'

Harry accepted this face saving gesture. He thanked Reitz. Veronika grudgingly agreed, and decided they might as well go get some lunch. Harry was hungry and ordered a Chinese meal but Veronika just had coffee – she was the only person he knew who drank more coffee than he. He was showing her where he had seen the woman from the escalator when her phone rang. It was Reitz, asking them to return to his office.

Reitz and Otto looked grim. The Germans had traced the passport, but it had been stolen nine years ago, and had not been used since then. Frau Meier had been issued with a new passport, a copy of which had been faxed to Zurich. It was clearly not the same woman.

'Shit, shit, shit!' Harry sunk his head in his hands. 'Just when we thought we had her. A stolen passport! I was afraid of it all along.'

'Thomas, I appreciate your help,' Veronika said. 'Do you mind if we could use your other room to talk?'

'Sure,' Reitz replied, but Harry remained sitting.

'No. Let's try a bit of lateral thinking,' Harry said, looking at Otto. 'Let's accept she was originally going to fly out of here to London, so she may have come from there. Could we find if someone arrived, say yesterday morning, and had a booking back to London but didn't keep it?'

Otto gave a small grin but did not reply, instead looked quizzically at his boss. Reitz's indecision was obvious. Veronika was first to react.

'Thomas,' she said with a sweet smile, 'maybe you need a coffee?' She glanced at Otto. 'Ten minutes?'

'Make it fifteen,' replied Otto.

Reitz shrugged, formally informed Otto he was in charge of the office, and walked out. Harry was mystified.

'That smug prick would never allow it,' Otto said, 'but what he doesn't officially know can't harm him. I'm supposed to get his authority to hack into the airline details, but he'd never give it without passing the buck upstairs. Let's see. I'll try Swiss first, on one condition.'

'What's that?'

'Just keep quiet and let me get on with it. And don't let anyone in here.'

'I'll mind the door.'

Harry watched as Otto clicked away, giving a grunt of annoyance as he found nobody suitable on Swiss Airways. He tried Crossair next, again without success. British Airways was more difficult to access, but three minutes into their system Otto banged the table with his fist. 'Got one here. Sonya Klinnsman. Same name as that footballer. Came on their nine-twenty from London, booked back at twenty-thirty, but didn't turn up. Even better, it was Gatwick.'

'Why is that good?' interrupted Harry.

'Because they photograph them in Gatwick. This part's a little more difficult to get into. Yep, here's her photo. Crafty bitch, but it's her for sure.'

He pointed to his screen as Harry and Veronika moved behind him. The monitor showed an image of a woman as she checked in her ticket at a desk. She wore a light brown peaked cap, had large clear glasses with a heavy red frame, and brilliant red lipstick. She was wearing the same jacket and blouse as yesterday. They had found the right person.

'Who's the genius then?' beamed Otto. 'Okay. Now, let's find her ticket. Someone bought it in the Gatwick office on Friday, but paid for it in cash. Of course they would, they're not idiots. I'll get her passport details. Ha, another German! Let's see what Wiesbaden has to offer, but knowing this one's form I wouldn't bet on anything.'

'Just do it please,' interrupted Harry.

'Takes a few minutes, nothing we can do but wait. Doesn't matter if Thomas comes back, we're all legit now.'

Otto pushed back his chair and sat in silence. Veronika moved to the window and looked outside. Harry paced around the room. Thomas Reitz returned and Otto gave him a brief account. Reitz joined Veronika in her vigil at the window. Five minutes passed.

'Here it is.' Otto broke the silence. All four stared at the screen. 'Scheisse!' Otto exhaled in frustration. 'She's done it again. Another stolen passport. Sorry, Harry. Not what you wanted to hear.'

Harry felt as though he had been assaulted. He thought he had not allowed his hopes to rise, but of course he had, and now they had been comprehensively deflated. Just when he thought he had her! He slumped into a chair, dropping his head forward onto his chest while emitting a loud groan. Otto and Reitz muttered their sympathies, but Veronika took Harry by the elbow, pulled him upright and steered him out of the room, down the short corridor and back to her old office. She ordered him to wait while she got coffees.

When she returned Harry had recovered his composure. 'I'm fine now,' he said, without any show of embarrassment. 'How long more can you stay?'

'As long as I need to. I can't grasp this woman. She is like a damn ghost. Keeps coming into our reach and then disappears.'

'Okay. You know the routine; there's always something we missed.'

'You run it through first. First, though, I need a smoke. Don't open the door.' Veronika poured two coffees, lit a cigarette and opened the window.

'The positives are few,' Harry began. 'She was definitely here. She's guilty as hell of something. We have her fingerprints. Maybe the Germans can link the two passports. It's a lot better than nothing.'

Harry was chronologically recalling Saturday's events when he stopped talking. He stood up and paced around the room, then sat down with an enthusiastic expression.

'Of course,' he exclaimed. 'As always, it's there in front of us the whole time. Look! Look at the time patterns.'

He began writing.

'I arrived. Went to Thomas's office. Said my bit. Between him agreeing to circulate the photo and me spotting her was at the most fifteen minutes, in which time she panicked. Now two plus two equals four.'

'Yes, of course.' Veronika interjected. 'She was warned.'

'Someone tipped her off, but how?'

'Mobile?'

'Of course, but there is one thing in our favour.' Harry pointed his pencil to emphasise. 'Arab groups are very wary of mobiles. They are paranoid of the Americans listening, with good reason – that's how Eshan heard about her little meeting. What else could they use? How about a pager? There's something niggling at the back of my mind.' Harry was silent for a moment. 'Yes, I remember. You have the tape you made of Martin?Could you find the bit where we asked him about her mood?'

She powered her laptop, accessed the recording and found the section.

"She kept looking at something in her lap." Martin's voice was clear.

'That's the bit.' Harry interjected. 'We got so excited about the stupid newspaper we overlooked it. "Something in her lap". It could be a pager. Can you call Martin?'

The taxi driver answered immediately. Veronika handed the phone to Harry. Harry deflected his questions, and told him of their suspicion the woman might have been looking at a pager. Martin considered.

'Yes,' Martin said. 'It was a pager. Used have one myself. That's the way people always looked at them. I'm definite.'

'Thanks, Martin.' Harry wanted to get off the phone.

'How's that "friend" of yours?' Martin asked, with a faint chuckle.

'Very well, thanks.'

'Give her one from me.'

'What did he say?' interjected Veronika.

'He was inquiring about your health. It was a pager, he's sure about that. Right, let's work it out. She got up from her table at twelve-thirty exactly; we saw that on Otto's tape. So, can we trace paged messages sent out between twelve twenty-five and twelve thirty? How many paging services are there?'

'Only two, I think. Used be lots more. Money no object again?'

'Come on.'

'Just had to ask.'

The first call was straightforward, as the suggestion of three hundred francs empowered the man on the control to look back through the files and give the details of three messages paged out between those times. The second was more difficult, as the controller refused to cooperate. She was prepared to reveal there were six messages paged, but she would only talk to the police. What was of more interest to them was she said there was always a caller identification log kept, and it was on record where each call to the paging service had come from.

They needed Reitz again, and Harry knew he had the upper hand. If the woman had been warned, then the leak must have come from airport security. Veronika went back to the main office and returned shortly with Reitz. He started to go on about how busy he was, with not one but two Saudi princes expected that afternoon, when Harry interrupted.

'Thanks for coming. We can't use the main office, it's not secure. I didn't want to involve you, but Veronika persuaded me you're honest.'

'Honest! How dare you?'

'No, you are honest, but I suspect there is a leak in your department.'

'Don't be stupid.' Reitz turned around. 'Veronika, you can't be part of this nonsense.'

'Thomas, just listen. He is right.'

By the time Harry had finished talking Reitz had calmed. He spoke thoughtfully. 'You could just be correct. There were one or two things over the years I was more concerned about than my superiors. Otto and I set up a regular electronic sweeping, and feel if there is a leak it's not electronic. However, your conclusions are damning. We seem to have a major problem.'

Harry leaned forward.

'It must have been someone who was there yesterday.' Harry spoke supportively. 'Presumably Otto is kosher. Wait a minute. There's something on my mind.' Harry closed his eyes as he thought. 'The meeting broke up, and one, no two, guys left the room with me. I can't picture the faces. But there was someone else at the door. Someone in a white uniform. A man.'

Thomas went pale. 'That is Sayed,' he stuttered. 'He's the cleaner. He was here yesterday. But he's been working with us for years.'

'Sayed? Where's he from?' Harry asked.

'I'm not certain. Possibly Egyptian.'

'Is he here today?'

'No, I don't think so. You never really see him, or notice him.'

'Pity. I'd love a few minutes alone with him. You'll need to involve your superiors, but we've hit a dead end with the paged messages. Could you follow them up?'

A chastened Thomas Reitz promised to do what he could.

7

—

Next morning: At reception Harry booked in for another night. In the dining room, bustling with men and women in business clothes, he sat in front of a coffee and two croissants. Ignoring the sign about mobiles he placed his on the table but it lay silently, mocking his wishes for it to ring. Veronika would call him around midday, when she was free. He sent a text to Maxime, his assistant in Munich, to say he would not be at work today. He had no choice but to wait on Thomas Reitz.

After breakfast he walked to a nearby store to buy some clothes. The weather had yet again changed, and it was a warm morning, calm and with only an occasional cloud. Standing at the till, waiting for his credit card to clear, his phone rang. "Reitz" appeared on the screen. Harry moved away and answered.

'Herr Katz,' said Reitz, 'are you still in Zurich?'

'Of course.'

'Could you come to Stadtpolizei Headquarters at eleven o'clock?'

'Yes, but why, and where is it?'

'I can't say right now, and headquarters is right beside the HauptBahnhof on BahnhofQuai. Just ask anyone in the station and they'll show you. Reception will be expecting you.'

Harry was outside police headquarters at ten fifty. The building looked unimposing, a green roofed, four-storey white granite structure, similar to the offices on either side looking out on a river. Carrying his jacket over his arm, and wearing a new short sleeved white shirt, tie and dark trousers he strolled in the sunshine along the river quay until exactly eleven. The woman at reception found his name on a list, and a uniformed policewoman took him up a flight of stair and along a busy corridor. He was shown into a rectangular room, with bare white walls, three windows looking out on the quay and river, and a number of single wooden chairs along the walls. She said she would be back shortly and left, closing the door. He moved to the window, idly looking out.

Nothing happened. Nobody came. Eventually at eleven thirty Harry worried if there had been a mistake. He left the room and retraced his way back to reception. The same receptionist politely apologised to Harry for the delay, and asked him to return to the waiting room. He went back to his position at the window.

By twelve he had had enough. He was just about to go back to reception when he received a text to say Veronika was now free. He called her and told her what had happened. Unfortunately she could offer little. She had never worked in HQ and knew nobody there. Phone her back in thirty minutes if nothing had happened, and she would come over – she worked nearby. Also, would Harry join her and her partner for supper this evening? Harry muttered a distracted thank you.

Twenty minutes later the door opened and Thomas Reitz asked Harry to come with him. Harry said nothing – his patience was fast approaching meltdown. He silently followed Reitz down a series of corridors to a conference room, with a large table and scattered chairs. There were empty coffee cups on the table, and the deserted room smelt of cigarettes.

'I'm extremely sorry you were left there.' Reitz had the grace to seem apologetic as he gestured around. 'I thought you were invited to the meeting here, but my recommendations were ignored. I have also been instructed not to discuss in any way what transpired, but there is one thing I am able to do.'

'I'm doing my best to keep calm, so make it simple.'

'There is someone whom I feel you should meet. Ah, here he comes.'

Harry turned as Reitz looked past him. A door opened and a late middle aged man entered. He was medium sized, thin with receding silver hair and rimless glasses. Dressed in a dark suit, white shirt and dark tie, he seemed a stereotype in a city of bankers. He looked at Thomas Reitz.

'This is Herr Katz?' the man enquired. His was a quiet, confident voice.

'Yes.'

'Thank you, Herr Reitz. You may leave now.'

The newcomer waited until the door closed before proffering his hand to Harry. A firm handshake, but his face was grim.

'My name is Bruno Hartmann but please, call me Bruno. I am not a police officer, and I unreservedly apologise for the way they treated you. I have sat through a two-hour meeting discussing yesterday's events, and believe me I am as angry as you clearly are.'

'Go on.' Harry's exasperation had eased slightly.

'I am with Federal Internal Security, a similar service to that which you worked for in Israel. Our relationship with your people is good, and I have met a couple of your colleagues, including one I spoke to a few minutes ago. He has verified your account of yesterday.'

'So what did Eshan tell you?' Harry asked. He had begun to warm to this man.

'Unfortunately I am not at liberty to discuss whom I spoke to.'

They sat at the table and began a detailed discussion of the weekend's events. Bruno was well briefed, and his comments and questions were incisive and relevant. While Harry's doubts were gradually being replaced by growing trust, he was by now so wary of the Swiss that he forced himself to maintain a degree of skepticism. Still, he appreciated Bruno's obvious grasp of the situation. After he had given his own assessment he went on the offensive.

'Now you tell me a few things. What about this Egyptian cleaner? What about the paged messages?'

The Egyptian had disappeared. He was not at home, had not turned up for work this morning, and had not answered his mobile. Bruno was incredulous this man had ever been allowed into the security offices in the first place.

'And the paged messages?' Harry asked.

'We need a judicial order, but it should be ready by now. The Stadtpolitzei will be chasing them up as soon as the order is through.'

'Anything on the woman?'

'No, nobody has any idea who she is. We have checked the prints from the newspaper, but she is not on our files. Interestingly the taxi driver has a record for minor larceny.'

'What about Hussam Farid?' Harry asked, as casually as he could manage.

'His name crops up regularly. You should check with your colleague in Jerusalem – he knows far more than I do.'

Bruno looked expectantly at him, but Harry kept a consciously straight face as he deflected the suggestion, although this revelation had alerted him. Eshan was concealing something.

'What happens now?' He asked instead.

'They have suspended all the security staff that were on duty Saturday, but are concentrating on the cleaner. The police are following up the paged messages, and we have circulated the fingerprints and fotofits of the woman. Now we have to wait and see what happens. My own department is taking this extremely seriously; I can assure you of that.'

Harry stood up and walked around in silent thought before turning back to Bruno.

'Could I go with the police who are following up the messages, especially any with possible Arab connections? I won't get in their way.'

'I can certainly request it. Are you ready to go now?'

'Whenever.'

'Wait here and I'll see what I can do.'

Freudenbergstrasse is a long leafy street, winding uphill about two kilometres from Zurich city centre, lined with new and expensive apartment blocks interspersed with professional offices – doctors, lawyers and the like. The police car, driving slowly up the street as the occupants checked the numbers, seemed the only vehicle moving in the hot afternoon sun.

Harry slumped in the rear seat, thankful for the air conditioning, but it was about the only thing he appreciated. This would be the third call of the four that had been scheduled for them, and they were looking for building number 681. In the front of the car sat two uniformed policemen. Both Andre and Stefan were young, and clearly resented having a stranger imposed upon them, especially since he was presented as a civilian foreigner working for a German corporation.

The first two calls had been to shops near to the city centre. On both occasions Harry had to wait outside, looking in the window as the policemen made their enquiries – both times to their evident satisfaction. This third was different. It was to a residential apartment. A phone call had been sent from that apartment to the paging company, but also the pager to which the message had been sent was registered to a person in the same apartment. Harry listened in frustration as the policemen found the correct apartment block, and then discussed the message they were to investigate. At least they had the courtesy to speak in High German, which Harry could understand.

'That's the one,' said Andre, as the car slowed outside a small apartment block, set in a manicured and immaculate garden. 'Let's see, it's apartment number fourteen. Name is B. Salid – doesn't say if it's male or female.'

'What's the message this time?' enquired Stefan, barely suppressing a yawn.

'Wait for it. Earth shattering importance this one – the message is "Toothpaste forgotten". Wow. Big deal.'

'What a crock of shit. "Toothpaste forgotten".Come on, let's get it over with.'

'Salid is an Arab surname,' Harry interjected. 'It could be important. Do you want me to come with you?'

'Thanks, but no thanks.' Stefan smirked. 'I think we can manage ourselves. Stay here or go for a walk.'

Stefan turned off the engine. The car sat directly in the sun, and as the policemen left Harry realised he had no option but to get out, as its climate control had been turned off. He emerged, stretched his limbs and watched as the two young policemen walked up the steps to the front door. They rang a bell, waited a moment and entered as the door was unlocked, presumably from above.

It remained quiet on the nearly deserted street. At first Harry stood under a tree for shade, and then strolled slowly uphill for a hundred metres, glancing idly at the expensive houses and apartments. He turned and walked back to the car. There was no sign of the policemen. He continued past the car and downhill for about fifty metres. As he stopped to look at an unusual shrub in a garden he heard two faint pops, about one second apart, coming from the direction of the police car. He stiffened. He had heard this sound many times before – the sound of a low calibre gun. Then three lower pitched pops. He recognised these also, shots from a different gun. In a panic he ran at full speed back to the parked car, pausing to get his breath. All was silent, with only an occasional person on the road, walking without concern.

He rushed over and up the steps of the apartment block. The door was locked. He rang bell number fourteen, and as he waited he heard screaming from within. He began to ring each of the apartment bells in turn until a buzz indicated the door would open. As he began to push it a powerful black motor-cycle carrying two men emerged from the basement area. Both wore helmets, and the one on the back looked at Harry as they sped off in the direction of the city.

Harry ran into the lobby, cursing he was unarmed. The screaming from above grew louder. Looking around the plush lobby he saw a lift with a stairs beside it. He raced across and up the stairs. At the door to the first floor corridor he carefully opened the door. He looked to the left.

On the floor about six metres away lay the prostate body of Andre, the cadet policeman, his pistol in his unmoving right hand, and the front of his once blue shirt soaked in blood. His eyes gazed upward. He lay in front of an open apart-ment door, and standing behind him, cordless telephone in her hand, stood an elderly woman wearing a vivid green dressing gown. She stopped screaming as she noticed Harry, but remained rigid, her face a mask of fear and horror.

Harry crouched down beside Andre, who with faint gurgling sounds emanating from his gasping mouth was barely alive. At the entrance to the apartment Stefan's head was almost blown off. The pale carpet and walls of the lobby were splattered in blood.

Harry snatched the pistol from Andre's hand, flicked off its safety catch and entered the apartment. He crept from room to room, gun extended, but the place was empty. The only other person around was the hysterical woman, muttering to herself, still clutching the phone.

Harry walked across to her, held the pistol down and spoke slowly and clearly.

'Have they gone?'

She muttered incoherently.

'Have they gone?' Harry asked again, with as much authority as he could manage.

'Y-yes. Gone,' she stammered.

'Were there two of them, and do they have a motor bike?'

'Yes. Yes, Youssef has a black motor bike.'

'Are you on to emergency services?' Harry gestured to her telephone.

'Here. Take it.'

Harry put the phone to his ear. 'Is there someone there?'

'Police control,' a female voice replied. 'Who are you?'

'Has an ambulance been summoned?'

'Yes, it's on the way. Who are you please?'

'I'm a German policeman. I'm working with the officers who have been shot. The guys that did it have just left here on a black BMW 750 motorbike heading towards the city. Two men. Black helmets. The driver is wearing a red jacket. Passenger has a blue bag over his shoulder. That's all I can give you.'

'Thank you, I have it noted. What is the condition of the officers?'

'One dead, the other dying. I'll hand you back to the woman who called you.'

Without waiting for a reply Harry returned the phone to the woman. He could hear the sound of approaching sirens as he retraced his way out to the corridor, where he sat on the ground beside the dying Andre. He gently held both the young man's hands until a policeman came rushing in the door.

The next hours merged into a confused blur. Police, ambulance teams, forensic groups and a succession of increasingly senior ranking policemen arrived. Harry had been told to stay out of the way in the old woman's apartment, but all the new arrivals wanted to hear his version of the events. He had resisted, emphasising he had little to offer. The motorbike number needed to be found and circulated, and the woman witness was the most important person. When she had recovered enough to be interviewed they allowed Harry to be present.

The apartment next door had been rented to two young Iraqi men – such nice boys, always polite – and because her own door had been open she had heard everything. The two policemen were enquiring about a message sent by Youssef – one of the boys – to his flat mate Basir. Youssef had been speaking to the policemen, and they had seemed satisfied with his explanation the message had been sent as a joke. The policemen were leaving when Basir had arrived. After that it turned into confusion and horror.

She could see Basir as he came out of the lift, and he seemed to get a great shock when he saw the policemen. This had in turn alarmed one of the officers, who had been reaching for his weapon when Basir had taken out a gun and opened fire. Terrified, she had closed her door and phoned the police. She had heard the boys leaving and had emerged, just before Harry arrived.

Eventually a policewoman took the woman away. Harry remained in her apartment to avoid the hostile policemen, but then heard Bruno Hartmann's voice. He looked outside. Bruno acknowledged Harry's presence with a nod, and with a brief but authoritative motion of his hand indicated to Harry to remain where he was. Ten minutes later he came back.

'What's happening here?' Bruno's calmness had evaporated, and he looked furious. 'Those young officers murdered because of a stupid message about toothpaste. You saw the killers leave?'

'Yes, but I didn't know what had happened.' Harry replied.

Bruno changed the topic.

'Can you read Arabic?'

'Of course.'

'There are some documents in the apartment. They are looking for an interpreter, but you can do it. Come with me.'

Harry followed Bruno into the corridor, put on the gloves and mask given by a technician and entered the apartment. Three forensics teams were measuring, sweeping and photographing the interior. Bruno motioned Harry into the kitchen, large, spotless and ultramodern. On the table sat a small pile of papers.

'Have a look at these.' Bruno requested.

Harry read each in turn, only to look up in disappointment.

'Little here.' He shrugged. 'Notes on economics, a grocery list and some information on cultural events. Nothing of value. Who are these guys?'

'I was afraid of that,' Bruno said. 'This place is like a hotel room, there is nothing personal. They are supposedly Iraqi students in the Polyteknik. Their clothes have been bought locally, as has everything else in the apartment. Seems like they arrived in their underwear and got whatever else in Zurich.'

'Pros?'

'Looks like it. Lucky for you that you didn't come in.'

'No! I would have read it differently. What idiot sent a cadet – you knew who you were dealing with?'

'Herr Katz, it was not my decision.' Bruno seemed equally upset. 'My advice to you is to leave immediately. I promise I'll keep you in touch, and you do the same. I'll take you out the back – it's crawling with cameras out front.'

Harry followed Bruno down to the basement where both were allowed out a small door to the rear garden. Bruno showed Harry a way to the street and advised him to take a taxi to his hotel.

Six o'clock: Veronika's partner Mieke welcomed Harry with a badly needed gin and tonic. She was a pretty, overweight woman, with long blond hair and a radiant smile. She was forty years and two days old, she confided, as Saturday had been her birthday and that was why Veronika could not remain with Harry in the airport.

As Veronika smoked her cigarettes and Mieke enjoyed a small cigar they discussed the recent events, intermittently watching the television news, dominated by the shootings.

They saw the police chief being interviewed outside the apartment, claiming the Stadtpolizei were treating it as a drug related killing. One hour later, having analysed all the possible options but without any new suggestions, Veronika asked Harry to tell them about Rachel and his relationship with her.

As Harry reminisced he noticed Mieke seeming to lose interest. She lit another cigar, sat back in her chair, wine glass in hand, and almost casually inquired if she could change the subject.

'Go ahead,' he replied, a hint of puzzlement in his voice.

'I'm just a curious old gossip,' said Mieke. 'I assume you're not gay.'

'No, but why ask?'

'Well, although neither Veronika nor I am interested – or at least I hope Veronika isn't – you're a very attractive man. I can understand if you didn't get involved in Israel, but don't tell me you stay celibate in Munich.'

'No, of course not,' replied Harry with an embarrassed smile.

'And?' interrupted Veronika.

'Well yes, there was one relationship. We were together for three years.'

'Go on,' prodded Mieke.

'It's hard to describe, but it fell apart. She's a doctor, and all seemed to be going great until she began to complain there was a second female in our relationship.'

'And was there?' asked Veronika.

'You know the answer. I just couldn't let go of Ami, and eventually we split up. It was my fault, not hers. And no, I've no girlfriend at present.'

'Pity you don't live in Zurich,' laughed Mieke, 'we could easily fix that.'

8

Throughout the night he repeatedly checked his phone but it remained silent. At six o'clock, when he could bear it no longer, he called Bruno Hartmann's office. Bruno answered, and shared Harry's frustration – he in turn had been getting little co-operation from the Stadtpolizei. This was apparently usual; the cantonal police disliked and distrusted their federal colleagues. The Egyptian cleaner was still missing. The police had established that a call had been made to the Iraqis' apartment from the payphone beside the airport's security office at twelve-twenty Saturday. It all fitted. They had met a series of blanks in trying to identify the two Iraqis, who had disappeared. Bruno's own service had circulated the known details to sister agencies worldwide.

When Harry interrupted and asked why the police would not release the photographs of the woman to the media, Bruno hesitated. The police apparently claimed they were still not convinced of her involvement, and anyway she had left the country. They were also wary of the strict libel laws in Switzerland. Harry was initially speechless, then angrily vociferous.

'But it's the best way to identify her!' Harry said. 'Someone must recognise this woman. Do they not want to find out who killed their colleagues? Not involved? That's bullshit – she's totally involved.'

'Herr Katz, I agree with you, but it's out of my hands. I promise I will speak to the police commissioner, but I cannot make the decision.'

'So that's it. She kills two cops, walks away and your guys are scared of libel laws?'

'It's not that easy. She wasn't here when it happened, and there is no direct link, only circumstantial. We have circulated the photograph to all our allies.'

'I know it's not your fault,' Harry said, 'but it's probably the only way to get her. Can you keep me in touch?'

'I promise. You might as well return to Munich, but I'll let you know of any development.'

Leaving the hotel at six-thirty, Harry anticipated four hours for the drive home, but by nine twenty had already entered the A99 motorway circling Munich. His office was located in the company's headquarters on the opposite side of the city near Neufahren, a satellite town on the northern reaches. He stopped for petrol and coffee. In a motorway cafe he watched the television news. Even here in Germany it focussed on the police killings. Suddenly he saw what seemed to be fotofit photographs of the two Iraqi men. He moved over to catch the sound and heard an interview with a police spokesman. The man then released the text of the 'Toothpaste forgotten' message, and gave the usual appeals for any assistance from the public. Harry waited, but the photographs of the woman did not appear.

He sat alone, in this bright plastic service cafe, brooding. It had been so close. He had seen her, could almost have touched her, and he had no doubt that she was involved in Ami's disappearance. There remained nothing more he could do except hope, yet again, that something unexpected would happen.

Harry arrived back to his apartment at seven o'clock in the evening, poured himself a Scotch and turned on his television. While pacing up and down with the news in the background, an idea came to him. He looked up the telephone number of Anna, Rachel's mother, and called her at her new home in Florida.

She answered, sensed the urgency in his voice, and listened intently as he related what had happened. Her mind had lost nothing of its sharpness, and she correctly anticipated the purpose of his call.

'So, you want me to use whatever influence I have to get this woman's photograph shown in the British media?'

'Absolutely,' Harry replied. 'The Swiss won't, but it was London she went to. Someone there must recognise her.'

'I'm trying not to sound too negative,' Anna said, 'but I doubt any of their legal people will let them broadcast or print it, unless requested by the Swiss police. I'll try, I promise, but don't get too hopeful. Still, the story of two young policemen being murdered because of such a stupid message as "toothpaste forgotten", yes, they'll like that. Only hope it helps.'

'Can you do it?'

'For sure. The Telegraph newspaper owes me some favours, and my niece works in Sky News. I'll certainly get both of them to run it, and I'll see who else. Can you e-mail all that over to me?'

Wednesday: Harry went to work early, arriving in his office before seven o'clock, and checking through his e-mails, he found one from Anna.

"Success, of a sort. British Sky News has run with the story, but won't show the photographs. It's prominent in the Telegraph, and in all the tabloids. None of the serious channels here were interested, but Fox and CNN took it. Not sure what that says about me."

His previous month's work came to fruition later that afternoon, when he presented his annual security update to the company management team. Uri made a gracious speech, thanking Harry and his staff for their effort, and made a veiled reference to the fact it had been completed in spite of recent setbacks.

That evening he put the take-away Chinese meal he had collected on the way home into the microwave, and poured a glass of wine. After his meal he made a coffee, and on the kitchen worktop noticed his mobile phone, which was still on silent from that afternoon. He had missed two calls and a text, all from Bruno. "Call me", the text read.

Harry phoned immediately, but there was no reply and he left a message. He called repeatedly, and eventually put the phone on the pillow beside him as he went to bed.

Thursday: He was in work early again and he phoned Bruno in Zurich. Bruno himself answered.

'Harry, there's been a development.'

Harry waved away Maxime as she approached with some documents.

'It's a strange one. It's come from England, and thankfully directly to me. A colleague of mine in British security phoned. Some woman, and he will not say who she is, contacted him with the name of a friend she used to know as a child. Apparently they used to use the same "toothpaste forgotten" codeword for danger. She saw a report in a newspaper and decided to follow it up.'

'That's a bit tenuous, would you not think?' Harry moved over to the window, phone in hand. It was raining heavily, a strong wind lashing large drops against the glass, but the sky was largely blue. People scurried for shelter in the car park below, taken by surprise by the sudden shower.

'There's more. Reading between the lines, either the woman or her family are high profile, because this went straight to the top of MI5. What's important is her old childhood friend left England at thirteen years of age and moved. Guess where?'

'Alaska?'

'Ha! No, to Worms.'

'What? Our Worms, in Rhineland?'

'Yes. Do you know it?'

'Not only do I know it; we have a sizeable plant there. Is she sure about Worms?'

'It seems so. If you speak English, you will know why a child would remember that name.'

'Of course. Do you have any more details?'

'Her name is Barbara Fisher. Date of birth...'

'Say that again.' Harry interrupted excitedly. 'Her name is Barbara?'

'Yes, Barbara Fisher. You sound surprised.'

'No, I mean yes. This could be really important. Sorry, you were going to give me more details.'

'Date of birth, 30 July 1973. The woman was sure of that. This Barbara's birthday is two days later than her own, and they used to share parties. Left England sometime in October 1986 and went to a school in Worms. That's all. I'll e-mail you a summary. Can I take it your plant in Worms is due a visit?'

'For sure.' The shower had stopped as quickly as it had begun, and the sun shone brightly. Harry felt a corresponding lifting of his spirits. 'That Barbara name, it may be very relevant. I'll go to Worms as soon as possible and can do some checking out from here first. I'll keep in touch.'

He walked across the corridor to Maxime's office.

'Something's come up. I need to go to Worms today.'

'Worms? Today? I thought we were doing assessments.'

'Leave it to next week. See if you can you get me a flight, and I've another favour to ask. I need to track down a girl who moved to a school in Worms in 1986. If I give you her details could you get HR in Worms to phone around the schools and find which one she went to?'

'What's up, Harry?'

'I can't tell you now, but it's connected to what happened last weekend. Also if you find the school would you do your best to see if I can make an appointment there, preferably with the boss, as soon as possible?'

The company plane, which had been rostered to fly to Amsterdam at mid-day, dropped Harry off in Manheim Airport on route. He rented a car and arrived at the Worms factory before three o'clock. In the middle of a "security review" he was interrupted by a call from Maxime to say the school had been identified and a meeting arranged with the principal for seven-thirty the following morning.

9

On a grey stone pillar beside the wrought iron gates of Eleonoren Gymnasium Worms Harry noticed a blue metal plaque. He stopped the car to read its writing. Bold gothic script informed him the school had been founded in 1743. He followed the signs to the administrative department, in the oldest looking section of the school. Having parked in the visitors' parking space he walked to the office of the principal.

Frau Mohr arrived ten minutes late, in a fluster of apologies. A tall thin angular woman in her late thirties, she had short blond hair and a pale face, with no obvious make-up. Dressed casually in a shirt, jeans and trainers, she carried an orange plastic folder. Harry had opted for the conservative mode, and wore a dark jacket, casual shirt and tie, and dark trousers. She introduced herself as Helga Mohr, but wished to be called Helga. Harry reciprocated.

'So, Harry, you work for Weber, but wish to enquire about an ex-student of ours.' She sat behind her desk and motioned him to a seat opposite, pointedly placing the orange folder on the desk between them. 'First, you must tell me your purpose. We have always had an excellent relationship with Weber, but discussing students who have nothing whatsoever to do with your company is totally different.'

'Please do not interpret this as in any way a threat,' Harry continued to smile as he spoke, 'but I can get a legal order to obtain the information I require.

However, I would prefer to avoid that. You need only provide whatever you feel comfortable about. I can't tell you too many details, but this is part of an international search for the identity of a woman whom we know only from a photograph.'

'What has this to do with Weber and my school?'

'This woman is implicated in the murder of two policemen in Zurich, and I am assisting the Swiss authorities. I cannot say more. If you would prefer to speak to them instead, the Zurich police can make a formal visit.'

'Ah so, I saw that in the newspaper.' Helga thought silently for a moment. She moved the file, sat back and considered. Her frown deepened. 'So, what exactly do you want?'

'Only to identify her.' Harry leaned forward, more confidently. 'I have some photographs. All we want to know is whether she and your student is the same person. This is a photo of the woman, taken in 1997.'

He opened his briefcase, took out and passed over the Lebanese photograph. 'So that would have been, what, five years after she left here?' Helga asked.

'If she left in 1992 that would be correct.' He reached again into his case. 'These others are fotofits, done last week.'

'This woman has aged well.' Helga looked through the photographs. 'She would be, say, thirty-seven now. It does look like the same person.'

'That's what we think, and why I'm here,' Harry agreed. 'All we want to know, is this your ex-pupil? I must emphasise she is in extreme danger.'

'Then there is a quick way to find out.' Helga came to a decision. 'I don't know her myself, as I'm here only six years.' She opened the folder in front of her and removed some papers, which she shuffled into order. 'There is only a useless picture taken when she first arrived, but we have yearbooks with a photograph of each student in their Abitur year. It should be somewhere on this shelf.'

Helga crossed the room and rummaged through a set of books on a shelf, muttering the year of each as she did so. 'Ah so, 1992,' she exclaimed in satisfaction. 'Here it is. Let's see, Fisher. Yes Fisher, Barbara. She's here all right. This is her photograph.'

She moved back and laid the open yearbook on the table between herself and Harry, turned it around and there, in colour, was the woman from his old photograph. She had braces in her teeth, her hair looked longer and curlier and she was smiling, but he had no doubt.

Against all the odds, he had identified her.

He looked at the photograph, glanced up at Helga, and down again. He could not speak with the overwhelming emotion of the moment.

After all these years of pain, emptiness and frustration he finally knew who she was. He put the two photographs side by side and commenced blinking rapidly, managing to stop the tears that were attempting to appear. Helga Mohr said nothing as they looked at the images.

Eventually she spoke. 'This is more than a routine inquiry for you?'

'Yes it is.' Harry spoke softly. 'I have been looking for this woman for many years, and every time I got close to finding her, she disappeared again. Now I know her identity. That fact means everything in the world to me.'

'Maybe you should tell me about it.' Helga sat back, with the expectant air of one used to giving this suggestion.

'It's personal. My only daughter disappeared without trace thirteen years ago, and this Barbara Fisher is the one person who may know something about it. She's not responsible, but she may be able to tell me what happened. That's all I can say.'

Helga nodded and then smiled.

'I'll see what I can do to help.'

Helga rearranged the papers from the file on the desk to her satisfaction.

'Okay. Came here in October '86, and enrolled into seventh grade. After one day they reclassified her up to eighth grade.' Helga spoke almost to herself. 'She must have impressed my predecessor. Ah, so. Lives alone with her mother. Her father died and that's the reason why mother moved back to Germany. No problems in tenth grade, none in eleventh, none in twelfth, but missing some school as mother ill. This is interesting – she is attending the school counsellor. No notes about that here.'

Helga looked up to Harry, and then back to the file.

'This girl is bright, first or second in her class all the way. Her teachers like her, there are glowing reports. Involved in school activities, charity and third world projects. Seems too good to be true. Okay. Thirteenth grade, her last year. Tough one with her Abitur. Now this is interesting.'

Helga looked up at Harry, sitting immobile and patient. He smiled, encouraging her to continue.

'She missed school for a week in October, with a change of address.' Helga seemed somewhat concerned. 'Moved to live with her aunt. Ah, now I see what happened. Mother died in November. Attending the school counsellor regularly, but a brief summary in February says they felt no need for her to attend farther. Her Abitur in 1993.' Helga coughed as she continued through the file. 'Prima! These grades are fantastic, all firsts or near firsts. This girl could have gone anywhere. Yes, of course she got a scholarship. She went to LMU Munich. The Ludwig-Maximillian University.'

Harry exhaled in relief as he sat back.

'Munich,' he repeated, 'some luck at last. What happened to her mother? Does it say?'

She looked back at the file, and then shook her head.

'No, but to lose your only surviving parent in final year and still get those grades is astonishing. She's tough as well as clever.'

'Is there anything more?'

'A bit,' Helga muttered more to herself as she removed the last pages. 'She was accepted in LMU to study sociology and psychology, but wait – she applied for a deferral until the following year. Now that's a little bit unusual, as scholarships are usually concurrent, but there is an option to carry it over and they allowed her. That's about it. She left our school, and there is no more in our records.'

Helga put the last sheet back into the folder.

'Seemed a model student,' she said almost pensively, 'with a very sad final two years, reading between those lines. Doesn't sound at all like someone involved in shooting policemen.'

'Do you have the address of her aunt?' Harry asked.

'Yes, it's here. Hergantweg 21. It's near here, less than ten minutes walk. Her name is Frau Rosamund Braun.'

Harry wrote this down.

'Thank you, you have helped me so much. I am extremely grateful, believe me.'

Hergantweg was a narrow cobbled street of old terraced houses which opened directly onto the pavement, with no parking. Number twenty-one had an ancient clematis draped over the door, which was opened by an elderly woman, thin and neatly dressed, grey hair in a tight bun.

'Yes?' she asked, with a firm voice.

Harry had not decided upon a strategy, but guessed she would be more comfortable with formality.

'My name is Herr Harry Katz. I am a police officer. Are you Frau Braun, Frau Rosamund Braun?'

'Yes, I am she,' the woman replied.

'This is an unofficial inquiry, but if necessary I can return with official papers. I am trying to find out some information about your niece Fraulein, sorry, Frau Barbara Fisher.'

'I have neither seen nor heard from my niece for many years.' She moved past Harry as she spoke, looking up and down the narrow street. 'Please come inside, I do not wish to discuss this on the street.'

The house was spotlessly clean, neat and rather prim. She gestured Harry to a seat, and sat down rigidly opposite him.

'What do you wish to know?'

Harry attempted to calm the older woman with a smile.

'Barbara came here to live with you when her mother died. Have you kept in touch with her after she went to Munich?'

'No. She went away to Africa for a year to work with refugees, and only returned to collect her belongings before starting university.'

'Do you know what she did for that year?' Harry prodded carefully.

'In a vague way,' Frau Braun nodded. 'She worked here in a factory for the summer, to save money, and then went to this orphanage in Africa. I was against her going, but she never listened to me. We were never close, but she was always polite and courteous, I must grant her that. She was a hard worker, but had a wild streak, not surprising with parents like that.'

'What happened to her mother?'

'You don't know?' She seemed surprised. 'It was that father of hers – that pervert. He died first, and gave it to my sister. She took two years to die. I hear they can cure it now, but not then.'

'Was it AIDS?'

'Yes, of course.' Frau Braun's voice dripped with bitterness. 'Her father was a homosexual. I warned and warned my sister, but she was in love. And then she died. To this day I still curse that awful man. He did not deserve his lovely daughter.'

The old woman began to cry. Harry fetched a tissue from a box and gave it to her.

'She came to live with me,' she continued, dabbing her eyes, 'as I am the only relative on her mother's side, and I did my best for her. I hardly knew her when she moved in, and I do not blame her for not keeping in touch. It was my fault. She needed love and affection, which I should have provided, but did not. You harvest what you plant, and I deserted her emotionally when she needed someone.'

Harry saw the pain in her eyes and was tempted to tell her to stop, but he needed to know.

'I can only blame myself. She was not responsible for the evils of her father, or the foolishness of her mother.'

By now she was weeping despairingly, and Harry felt uncomfortable.

'You can help her,' he said. 'You are certain you have no idea where she lives now?'

'None,' the woman sobbed. 'She phoned a few times from Munich, and then the calls stopped coming. I have heard nothing since. I still cry myself to sleep at night thinking about it. She is my only relative in the world, as I never married.'

'I am very sorry.' Harry held her hand. 'Do you have any photographs of her?'

'Yes, over there, in that frame.' She pointed. 'I took it the time she came back from Africa.'

Harry went over to pick it up. There she was again. Barbara Fisher, the woman who had haunted him all these years. This time tanned, with a more mature face than the school photo, and with shorter hair. The emotional effect on Harry was less than seeing the one in the school yearbook.

'Thank you, and I am sorry for upsetting you. If I do manage to contact her I will tell her what you have told me. I promise you that.'

10

Harry took a commercial flight from Mannheim and arrived back in his Munich office at two o'clock. First he sent an e-mail to Bruno Hartmann, and then called in Maxime with an unexpected offer. In return for him treating her and her boyfriend to dinner in an exclusive Thai restaurant, would she find out whatever she could about a woman who came to Munich seventeen years ago to attend university? Maxime jumped at the offer. Her boyfriend played on Harry's soccer team and liked him, and they loved Thai food.

Harry was out of the office for some hours at a meeting. When he returned at five o'clock he found Maxime grinning.

'So, why so smug?'

'Seemed easy at first. The university people know us and were helpful. She started, as you said, in September '93, studying sociology and psychology. Came second in her class in sociology, first in psychology. Next year again great results, two seconds. But then she disappeared.'

'Disappeared?'

'Never came back for her third year.' She spread her hands to emphasise. 'Finished her second year but never returned. Simple as that.'

'Did she give any reason?' Harry asked, still in shock.

'No, nothing at all.' She also looked puzzled. 'The university people were very surprised. I mean, lots of students disappear, but not the summa cum lauda students.'

'How hard did they look?' Harry asked.

'Not very,' Maxime shrugged. 'What could they do? They have records of writing to her old apartment, but she had not been back there since leaving it in June. They contacted her tutors, but they had heard nothing.'

'So, did you turn up anything else?'

'Come on, Harry. Give me a break. All this was fifteen years ago, and LMU is huge. Nobody I spoke to knew or remembered her.'

'You mentioned her tutors.'

'Very good Harry.' She grinned hugely. 'That's why I'm smiling. She had three tutors. I'll start with psychology. In first year she had one tutor, who left

LMU and moved to Freiburg. They gave me her phone number and I managed to contact her. She vaguely remembers Barbara, but that's about it. Her second year psychology tutor is a professor in LMU, but is away in Vancouver.'

'So, why all the grins?'

'You may just be interested in her other tutor.' She gave a triumphant smile. 'She had the same one in sociology for two years. He's now a Professor in Ulm.'

'What's earth shattering about that?'

'Harry, have patience. His CV is on the Ulm website, and this is where I earned my dinner. He's a Palestinian, or so he describes himself. I printed this off for you. Short, but relevant.'

Harry scanned it. 'So,' he read out loud, 'Kamal Shamsoul. Born in Akko, in 1965. It's near where I come from. School in Akko, and I'll bet anything he went to Birzeit. Yes, here it is. Birzeit University 1986 to 1990. No military service for him, the lucky sod. First class degree in sociology – plenty of scope for that subject there.'

Harry took up a second sheet.

'1990 to 1996 here in Munich,' he continued. 'Assistant professorship in Frankfurt from 1996 to 1998. Then to Ulm as professor in their new department. Published works such and such, lectures etc. and so on. Well done. I'll have to pay him a visit.'

'Even better,' she beamed. 'I called his office. Wait for it; you have an appointment there tomorrow morning at eleven o'clock, supposedly about research grants.'

'Brilliant. Champagne with dinner.'

Saturday had turned wet and grey and the two-hour drive to Ulm passed uneventfully. On the front passenger seat were four pages of faxed paper, written in Hebrew. Three pages were copies of a file the Shin Bet had kept on the professor. In his student days a 'spotter' had identified him as being a potential intelligence source. He was gay, which would make him a possible subject for blackmail. While homosexuality had always been fairly well accepted by the Jewish Israeli public, it was frowned upon by the more conservative Palestinians. In the report, Shamsoul had been approached by an agent in the university, but had reacted strongly to the unsubtle attempts at recruitment and blackmail. He claimed he was proud to be gay, and not afraid of this fact being known. The agent had given up the attempt, and there had been no farther contact. They classified him as non-political, of no concern to the Shin Bet. The fourth faxed page was a scribbled handwritten note from Eshan, saying Mossad had no file on Shamsoul but would appreciate any feedback.

Following the signs to Ulm University, Harry arrived thirty minutes before his appointment. The security man at the gate pointed him towards the sociology department and he easily found Professor Shamsoul's office. Although fifteen minutes early, he knocked on the door. A medium height thin stooped man, with rimless glasses and short brown hair turning grey, answered. He was dressed in tweed jacket, polo neck shirt and brown trousers, with brown leather shoes.

'Professor Shamsoul?' Harry asked politely.

'You must be Herr Katz.' Shamsoul's accent sounded like Harry's. 'Come in. You have driven down from Munich?'

'Yes. Sorry I'm a bit early.'

'That's all right. Coffee?'

'Please.'

The formalities over, they sat down across the desk in the immaculately tidy office.

'Your accent? You are not German?' Shamsoul asked.

'No, not German as such.' Harry switched to Arabic. 'I am Israeli by birth, but I am now a German citizen. I hold a senior position with Weber, a large company in Munich.'

Shamsoul put down his cup, looked coldly at Harry then replied, also in Arabic. 'Ten years ago I would have pressed my alarm button, now I don't scare so easily. Who are you, and what do you want with me?'

'I do work with Weber,' Harry answered carefully, 'but I'm here on a purely personal matter.'

'Thank you at least for that.' Shamsoul gave a forced smile. 'Your accent is like mine – somewhere in the Galilee?'

'Nazareth.'

'Ah yes; now I recognize it.' Shamsoul nodded. 'I should have you thrown out, but I am intrigued. What do you want from me that you are prepared to go to these peculiar lengths?'

'I'll be as brief as possible.' Harry could scarcely conceal his relief. 'First, can you read Hebrew?'

'Yes, but with difficulty.'

'Take a look at these.' Harry passed over the three faxed sheets.

'Where did you get this?' Shamsoul paled as he read the reports. He stood up. 'This meeting is at an end.'

'No.' Harry remained seated, his eyes never leaving the professor's. 'I showed them to demonstrate my good faith. I never even knew you existed until yesterday. Most of what I found since then is from your own website. I haven't been in Israel for many years, but I have a cousin who has a position in one of the security services. I phoned to ask him if he knew anything about you, and he faxed this back. I feel ashamed this type of practice went on, and that's why I have shown this to you.'

'Perhaps.' The professor was silent for a few seconds as he reconsidered. 'Now tell me what you really want. At least you know threats don't work with me.'

'I used to work in Nazareth as a civil servant. In 1997 my wife was killed in an event, and my daughter disappeared. I buried my wife, but my daughter was never found. I felt angry and wanted revenge, but now I want to put a closure on it. To find where my daughter is buried, and finally say Kaddish for her.'

'By "event" you mean she was killed by my people?'

'Someone killed her,' Harry responded. 'I left Israel, moved here and accepted the past. However, I recently discovered the identity of a person who may be able to tell me where my daughter is buried.'

'And who is this?' Shamsoul interrupted.

'An old student of yours from Munich. Her name is Barbara Fisher.'

Harry watched Shamsoul's eyes. There was an instant spark of recognition. Then after what seemed an interminable silence, the professor spread his hands across the surface of the desk. 'Ah, Barbara Fisher. I knew she would come back to haunt me. In a way, I have always been waiting for this knock on the door. You seem well briefed, so you know something?'

Harry nodded. 'I have spoken to her old school teachers, and to the aunt who helped bring her up, but I know nothing about after she moved to Munich. That's why I'm here.'

'I don't mind telling you; it's all in the past.' Shamsoul spun his chair around, facing away from Harry. 'To save you wasting your time, I have not seen nor heard from her since those days, and I have no idea where she is now, or what she is doing.'

'A pity, since that's the main purpose of my visit.' Harry replied. 'But even if you knew you wouldn't tell.'

'That is true.' Shamsoul laughed coldly. 'Barbara was a remarkable girl – one of the brightest students I have ever known. If I were interested in women I could have been attracted to her. Besides being very bright, she was politically and socially aware. We shared an interest in the sufferings of my people, and I introduced her to comrades of mine involved in the same struggle. You may not believe this, but my political activities have been, and still are, non-violent. I have seen too much suffering.'

Harry remained silent as the professor continued.

'She became increasingly involved and in the summer after her first year I encouraged her to travel to Palestine. To stay with my family and to see for herself the suffering of my people.'

'You mean she visited Israel!' Harry interrupted. 'Must have been in what, the summer of '94?'

'Yes, 1994. She spent, if I recollect correctly, two weeks in Galilee, and another four with the so-called 'Peaceniks' in the occupied West Bank. The rest of the summer she worked in Gaza, with a German charity organisation. When she returned here she was even more committed to our cause.'

'Go on,' Harry prodded.

'We began to disagree with the methods that are necessary to help my people.' Professor Shamsoul sighed as he recollected. 'I have always opposed violence, and still feel strongly it has not and does not help our cause. Not many agree with me now, but that's that. While still coming to our meetings and helping in our activities, I became aware she had fallen under the influence of another organisation, with different political views than mine.'

Shamsoul leaned forward, clutching the edge of the table. Harry sat silently.

'We began to argue, but these disagreements were political, never personal, and we continued to have a good working relationship. I managed to make her keep up with her studies. She did fairly well in the second year exams, I remember that.'

'Second place,' Harry interjected.

'Was it second? She could have got first. I was not in Munich for the next summer, and when I returned she had disappeared.'

'Were you surprised?' Harry asked.

'Not really.' Shamsoul put his head in his hands. 'I blamed myself for not spotting this development and should have anticipated it. I probably could not have stopped her, but could have tried harder. She did telephone me later that year, I think in November. She would not tell me where she was, or what she had been doing; only she was now "fulfilled". She thanked me for showing her the way, and said she would remain in touch, but I never heard from her again.'

'Do you have any theories about what happened?' Harry asked softly.

'None I would disclose to you, I am afraid.' Shamsoul spoke firmly, looking directly at Harry.

'Then I will tell you. She joined the Islamic Hawks. I have a photograph of her from 1997. Would you be interested in seeing it?'

'Of course.' Shamsoul reached out his hand.

Harry gave him the one of the fotofits and watched closely for his reaction.

'That could not have been '97.' Shamsoul looked annoyed. 'She is far too old, and it looks like one of those police photographs you see in the papers.' He showed no sign of recognition of this image.

'It is a fotofit, done last week. This is the 1997 photo.'

He passed it over. The other man looked at it silently, then angrily at Harry.

'Yes, it is her, but you have been playing with me.' His voice was icy.

'I had hoped you could tell me how she knows Farid.' Harry never flinched. 'Did you introduce them? Are you responsible?'

The professor fiddled with the spoon of his coffee cup. 'Yes, it was me. I still blame myself, but it would probably have happened anyway.'

'Were they lovers?'

'Of course.' Shamsoul stared at the spoon. 'It was immediate, and reciprocal. That is all I am prepared to discuss, I have said too much. Now I must ask you to leave, but if you do locate her, ask her to contact me, especially if she needs any help. I cannot wish you well, but hope you can be happy in your own life. You must excuse me.'

Harry got up to leave.

'Never come here again or I will summon the police.'

Driving home Harry felt little satisfaction with the morning's events. Some gaps in his knowledge about Barbara had been filled, but were these of value? He already knew she and Farid were lovers, but finding they had spent over two years together before Lebanon made their relationship far deeper. Eshan must have known this. He would have to be more careful.

11

Three o'clock: Harry called Bruno from his apartment, but Bruno was in a meeting. Twenty minutes later he rang back.

'Sorry to have kept you, and thanks for that e-mail yesterday – we've been working on it. Has something happened?'

Harry detailed.

'That explains a lot. Could you create a file and mail it over, and can I send it to BND in Pullach?'

'BND? So you've been on to them?'

'Of course. Most of today.'

The Bundesnachrichterdienst, or BND, was the principal German federal counter-terrorism organisation. Previously headquartered in Munich-Pullach, it had been largely transferred to Berlin.

'Well, come on. Tell me.' Harry was unable to restrain himself.

'This Fisher woman is proving a real mystery.' Bruno's voice was puzzled. 'She has vanished off the face of the earth, assuming the details you sent me are correct.'

'They are, believe me.'

'It's a series of dead ends. They've checked through both Federal and Laender records. She has no German birth register, but then you told us she is English. She has a German social security number – I'll e-mail it to you – so yes, she exists. But that's all they know. Never had a German passport, has not married and has no criminal record. Never registered a car in Germany, never had a driving license, and paid no taxes. She has not existed in Germany by that name for thirteen years – simply vanished.'

'Not what I wanted to hear, but thanks anyway. Do they have any ideas, or anything positive?'

'Virtually nothing. They cross-referenced her with that Palestinian Farid, but it was only a brief summary. They can't access paper records until Monday.'

'And Farid himself? Anything there?'

'Nothing recent from the BND. Hasn't been in Germany for years, but the BND has been getting a lot of requests about him from both the Americans and the British lately. They have some speculative reports he may be in England. We're working on it here too.'

'Another dead end,' sighed Harry, 'but, as you say, she doesn't seem to be in Germany, so at least that's one area excluded. Any progress with the Iraqis?'

'Nothing concrete. I'm sorry but I have to rush off, I'm going to my goddaughter's wedding. Don't call me unless it's catastrophic.'

Harry made a case file of what he knew, reviewing what he had found out about Barbara Fisher. The more he discovered about her the more intrigued he became.

She fitted the classical psychological profile of German terrorism, where terrorists tended to be well-educated and middle class. Even if she was not personally involved in the settlement massacre, she must have known what had happened, provided of course the Hawks had done it. Israeli Intelligence had made mistakes before.

He emailed the file to Bruno, made a coffee and sat back to think, his brow furrowing. Then he got up and paced around the apartment before picking up his phone and calling Uri.

'I need to talk to you,' said Harry. 'Are you free anytime today?'

'Is it to do with the company, or your daughter?'

'Both.'

Harry heard a grunt.

'I'm playing a tennis match at five. Usually takes two hours. You know where the club is, I'll see you in the bar at seven.'

Harry moved to the window and scanned the car park. All seemed normal. There were only a few cars parked, and his Passat was in its usual place. A couple came down the steps and briskly walked towards the gate of the complex. A quiet Saturday afternoon.

He cursed, struck himself on his forehead in annoyance and moved to his bedroom, where he took his larger suitcase and filled it with clothes.

Seven o'clock: The sun was setting over the city on a warm and still autumn evening. Harry sat at a table on the veranda of Uri's club. He ordered two Weiss-biers. The perfectly manicured lawns below swept towards the club's boundary fence, beyond which clustered a swathe of houses belonging to the super rich of Bogenhausen. Next came the green areas of the Englischer Garten, sandwiched between Bogenhausen and the tall buildings of downtown Munich. Uri arrived just after the beers had been placed on the table. He picked up his drink and thirstily gulped a large draught before leaning forward and clinking glasses with Harry.

'Lechayim,' said Uri. 'To life.' Their conversations constantly switched between Hebrew and German. Harry responded in kind, looking around to check they were alone.

'We may have a big problem,' Harry said in Hebrew. 'I need your advice.'

'Spit it out.'

Harry handed the folder with his case file to Uri, who gave a weak smile.

'Don't have my glasses. Can I borrow yours?'

Harry passed them over, then excused himself as he went to the toilet. When he returned Uri was coming to the end of the report, a deepening scowl on his features. He re-read a few sections before slapping the report onto the table.

'Okay. The easy bit first. She's in England.'

'I agree.'

'How you'll find her – that's another matter.'

'My problem, not yours.'

'No, Harry, you're wrong.' Uri's face creased in annoyance. 'You've made it my problem, and a major one. You've fucked it up big time.'

'The Palestinian?'

'Of course. You may as well put the whole story on Al Jazeera. As soon as you closed his door he was on the phone to Farid. He knows you work for me, and it'll take them about ten seconds to figure out that Weber is Israeli owned. You saw what those Iraqis did in Zurich. They're probably gathering their Semtex right now and working out which factory to demolish. But you know that, don't you.'

'It's even worse,' Harry exhaled softly.

'Is it possible?'

'There was a security post with a video camera at the gate of Ulm University. I took my own car, so they've got my number. They'll call their pals in Cairo, liaise with Munich, and have my name and address by now.'

'Go on.'

'The other thing is that cleaner in Zurich. You saw in my report he had disappeared?'

'Yes, I was puzzled by that.' Uri scratched his ear as he spoke.

'I should have picked up on it. I mean, why disappear? He's done nothing wrong, but suddenly he takes off. Why run when you have spent years setting up an identity? Can only be one reason – they have another source in Swiss security. Now they know who stirred the whole thing up.'

'And they'll come after you?'

'You would. I would, and I'm going to assume they will. It's what you taught me on my first day.'

Uri grimly smiled in agreement, finished his drink and caught the eye of a waiter. He ordered another beer, but Harry declined.

'I've two choices,' said Harry. 'One is to assume I am being paranoid. Do nothing, but watch my back.'

'And the second?'

'Go after them. First, though, I recommend putting all our plants onto maximum security, as of tomorrow morning.'

'I was going to do it anyway.' Uri lifted his open hand to indicate silence as the waiter approached from behind Harry.

'I've left my apartment,' Harry said. 'I'll stay in a hotel tonight and go to London tomorrow.'

'What will you do there?'

'Bruno, that's the Swiss guy, has the answers. I'll ask him to get the British involved. If that fails I'll have no choice but to get Eshan's help.'

Uri took a draught from his glass, than put it down and wiped his lips.

'That bastard Bercovic again,' Uri swore. 'Right, you want my read on this?'

'That's why I'm here.'

'You mean nothing to Bercovic. He wound you up, pointed you and let you go. One phone call, and a week later he knows the identity of Farid's mistress. The Swiss guy will have forwarded your file to Jerusalem. Bercovic's not helping you, he's after Farid. But why? Between Gaza and Lebanon, not to mention the Iranians, he's got a shitload of problems, so why put all this energy into Farid? There has to be something else.'

'I thought I told you. Farid killed Eshan's brother in Lebanon. It's personal. In spite of that it's beginning to make more sense.'

'How?' Uri took a handful of nuts from a bowl as he asked.

'This is way too big for the Hawks – they were a small outfit. Put it all together. Farid in Pakistan, which means Afghanistan. Throw in an Egyptian in Zurich, two Iraqi thugs, another agent in Swiss security. Major league. Has to be al-Qaeda.'

'Agreed.' Uri nodded. 'So it's more than just a personal vendetta.'

'But if Farid's with them, then why does this Hawks stuff suddenly reappear after all this time? And why has Barbara Fisher returned?'

'She can't be al-Qaeda – they'd never use a woman. No, she's been reactivated from somewhere. Is she still Farid's mistress?'

'Eshan seems to think so.' Harry shrugged.

'That's it then. She's been lying low in England, still involved with Farid on a personal level, and he's reactivated her for some reason. Your guess is as good as mine. Then Bercovic gets lucky with that American intercept. He's not stupid. He acts quickly, calls you and hopes you will lead him to Farid. He's been right so far, and you've no option but let him run the show.'

'So, London it is.' Harry said.

'Where's your car?' Uri asked.

'In the car park below.'

'They'll never find it there. Leave it and take mine. Now, drive me home and we'll talk in the car.'

12

Seven o'clock: Harry's phone alarm beeped. After a swim in the hotel pool he drove to the office. At eight he called Maxime on her mobile. She answered sleepily.

'Could you come in to the office for a couple of hours?' Harry asked.

'Now?'

'Yes. It would help me a lot if you could.'

'Hang on.'

Harry heard her muttering to her boyfriend, and then she came back.

'Jorg is playing a match at ten. Nine-thirty okay?'

Harry texted Bruno's mobile, asking Bruno to call him as soon as possible, and sent him an e-mail. On the Lufthansa website he booked himself onto the two o'clock flight to London Heathrow, and on the same site arranged a room in the Hilton Hotel. Opening the wall safe he removed a heavy brown envelope, and from it took three thousand euro in fifty euro notes. Five hundred went into his pocket, the rest into his bag.

He bought four croissants and two coffees from the cafeteria, and had just walked back into the office when Maxime arrived. She looked tired. She picked up a croissant and took a bite. 'So, what's up?' she asked, flakes spilling from her mouth.

'I need to go to London, and don't know when I'll be back. You'll be in charge when I'm away, but there's a problem.'

'What?'

'You know the plan we drew up for a confirmed threat to the Weber complex? Now it's real – not a drill. We need to implement it.'

'Wow! You mean right now? Has Uri sanctioned this?'

'Yes. It's all set up, but you're better at running it. I'd prefer you to look after it.'

'How real is the threat?'

'It could be an over-reaction, but we can't take any chances.'

'And how long will we run it?'

'Not sure at present, but certainly for a few days.'

'You know I have to phone Uri to get his consent.'

'Do it now. I'll leave the room.'

He returned to find Maxime sitting at her computer.

'I did ring, you know.'

'No more than I would have expected.'

'He told me to go ahead.'

Harry steered the mouse over the box on the screen, typed his password and pressed "Go". The program swung into action. Maxime and he sat at their own desks, drinking their coffees as one by one the different security sections of the

Weber company replied. Each required a double authentication, which was duly provided, and by ten-fifteen all the units had responded.

'Prima,' exclaimed Maxime, her face lighting up with a wide smile. 'It works.'

'Thank goodness. You're in charge here now, but Uri's around, and you can call me on my mobile. I have to go.'

He finished his coffee and slid a key across the table.

'Tell Uri I've left his car in his usual space. I'll get a taxi to the airport.'

Passing a Vodafone store in Heathrow Airport Harry bought a throwaway mobile using a fictitious name and address, getting the agent to transfer the numbers on his own SIM card to the new phone. He took a taxi to the Hilton, booked in and sent texts to Maxime, Uri and Bruno, giving his new number. Strolling through a nearby park his phone rang.

'Sorry for taking so long to get back.' Bruno sounded apologetic. 'I've just got your messages. What's with the new number? Are you in England?'

'Yes.'

'Where?'

'Heathrow, in a hotel.' Harry sat on a bench. 'She's here somewhere, I know it. But there's another reason.'

'What?'

'That cleaner in Zurich. Why did he disappear?'

'I thought you might get to that. It's my biggest worry by far.'

'And mine. They'll know who I am, and I can't stay in Munich. I'll need to speak to your British colleague, the one who tipped you off about Barbara. Can you organise that?'

'I'll certainly ask, but can't do it until tomorrow morning. I've already sent him a file with all we know.'

Harry noticed curious glances from two teenage girls who were sitting on the same bench. They had noticed his use of German, and he moved away from them.

'Another thing,' Harry said, 'I'm as certain as I can be that Hussam Farid is up to his neck in this. Could you do me one other favour?'

'If I can.'

'Could you ask Mossad for any updates they have on Farid?'

'What? Why not ask them yourself?'

'My only contacts are with the Shin Bet.' Harry smiled to himself at Bruno's confusion. He sat down on another bench as he decided how to phrase his request. 'You know the Shin Bet deals with internal security. Mossad looks after the external stuff, but the two sometimes do not co-operate as they should. I have no authority to approach Mossad, but you could.'

There followed a long silence.

'It's probably better I don't know about your internal politics.' Bruno gave a low chuckle. 'Sure, I'll put an official request to Mossad. Can I give my British colleague your new phone number?'

'Of course.'

Monday: Harry was pacing around his hotel room when his mobile beeped. He looked at the screen. "Caller ID withheld". He answered.

'Hello.'

'Herr Katz?' A male voice.

'Yes.' Harry replied.

'My name is Bernard Kingston. I'm a British police officer. Bruno Hartmann requested me to call you.'

'Has Bruno told you why I am here, and why I asked for your assistance?'

'He has. I must admit I never thought my call to him would have had all these results.'

'I presume Bruno has sent you what we know about this Fisher woman. We all feel she is in England, and I will need assistance from the British authorities. Are you the correct person?'

'Depends. What are you requesting?'

'Two things. Firstly, whatever can be found about this woman from the information you now have.'

'And the second?'

Harry took a deep breath before replying.

'I need to meet the woman who told you about Barbara Fisher.'

'Why? She has told me all she knows.'

'I agree, but something that does not seem relevant to one person could help another.'

'Let me think about it,' Bernard said. 'I'll phone you back shortly.'

Harry relaxed slightly. His request had not been rejected out of hand. The return call came in fifteen minutes.

'Can you come to London tomorrow morning?'

'Yes.'

'Write this down. 144 Marsham Street. That's in central London, WC1 to be precise. Give my name at the door, and you will need to bring your passport for identification. Expect to be searched. Do you know London?'

'No, I've never been there.'

'Then train to Paddington and take a cab. Ten-twenty exactly. My phone number should be on your caller ID.'

'It is. Will I meet your source?'

'You will meet me.'

Tuesday: At the end of Marsham Street, a busy road lined with pre-war offices, stood a clock tower Harry recognised as Big Ben. His name was on a list at number 144. His passport was scrutinised and photographed and he had to pass through a metal detector before being allowed inside. An elderly orderly directed him to an office, where he waited a couple of minutes before the door opened and a tall young black man entered. With shaven head and piercing blue eyes, he looked like a professional footballer.

'Herr Katz, I am Bernard Kingston.' He sprawled on a chair across from Harry, took a small notebook out of his pocket and flipped it open.

'About this Barbara Fisher,' Bernard looked at his notes. 'Very interesting, but very strange. We know she was in school in Surrey, but otherwise she does not seem to have existed. Our usual enquiries – passport, birth certificate, social security and so on have come up with nothing. We are assuming the name and date of birth you gave the Swiss are correct.'

'Yes, they are correct.'

'Anyway, there is some good news.' He smiled weakly. 'You requested to speak to Ms Shaw.'

'Ms Shaw?' Harry asked, puzzled.

'Ms Shaw, my boss. She's the person who told us about this toothpaste message.'

'I see.' The name meant nothing to Harry. 'But I have no idea who Ms Shaw is.'

'You don't?' Bernard was now the one to be surprised. 'Helen Shaw is our Minister for European Co-operation. She is most interested in what has been happening, and is prepared to meet with you. I'll take you there now, as she has a few minutes free.'

The minister's office was bright and modern, with a large window overlooking a small square planted with grass and small shrubs. Helen Shaw was sitting on a red armchair, in front of a coffee table, holding a manila file. She was petite and slim with shoulder length black hair tied back. She wore an open neck white shirt and dark trousers and had rimless reading glasses on a thin gold chain around her neck. Her smile was friendly as she stood up.

'Hello. I'm Helen Shaw, but call me Helen.' She had an accent strange to Harry. They shook hands and she indicated a vacant armchair, and then looked over to Bernard, standing silently beside the door.

'Thank you Bernard,' she said, with a voice of authority. 'I think I will be safe here.'

Bernard shot her a disdainful glance as he left. Helen waited a few seconds before speaking.

'It's no disrespect to my security advisor, but some of what we may discuss could be personal, and I would prefer it kept that way. He doesn't fully agree.' She tapped the file, in front of her on the table. 'I have read all the reports and I must admit to being somewhat intrigued. Babs turned out like I would have predicted, up to a point. Bernard has told me your principal motive in looking for her is not, in fact, finding out who killed those poor Swiss policemen last week. Perhaps you can explain?'

Harry told about Rachel and Ami. Helen nodded sympathetically as Harry continued. 'I used to work for one of our intelligence services, and they believe a Palestinian group is responsible. I initially hoped my daughter could be alive, but have gradually accepted she is not.'

'So what on earth has Babs to do with this?'

'We know for certain she was in Lebanon at that time, and in the company of the group suspected of the killings. Even if she were not involved she may know something about my daughter.'

'So how do you think I can help?'

'By telling me what you remember about her. A repeat often throws up an item which may have been overlooked.'

'I read in that file you have a transcript of all I gave Bernard. I'm not sure I can add anything else.'

'What puzzles me most is where she came from.' Harry leaned forward. 'Your people have been unable to find a British birth certificate or passport, and we know she doesn't have a German one. So how did she ever get into school here?'

'Maybe her birth cert was Irish,' Helen replied.

'Irish?'

'I thought I told them that.' Helen paused for a moment as she considered. 'Yes, I'm sure of it. Her father was definitely Irish. I have no idea where she was born, but why not Ireland?'

Harry looked mystified.

'Would it be possible? I mean, I know nothing about Ireland.'

'I'm not too sure we do either,' Helen laughed lightly, 'but both our countries are closely connected. It would indeed be very possible. I can ask Bernard's people to chase it up, but it may take a few days.'

'Thank you, I appreciate that.' He could not wait a few days, but now was not the time to press this.

'One other thing to remember', said Helen, 'the Babs of today will not be the impressionable and vulnerable idealist of years ago. So, Harry, you are correct, it was worth your effort coming here. Now, if you can excuse me, I need to get on with my own work.'

Harry, still trying to assimilate this new development, managed to regain his perspective. He thanked her for her assistance, and she handed him her business card. They shook hands and she politely yet firmly led him to the door of her office, summoning her secretary to look after him.

Outside it was a warm and calm autumn day; the trees beside the nearby Thames River were already browning, and a scattering of leaves had fallen on the pavement. Harry decided to walk along the Embankment, to give him time to think. One thing was clear. He could not wait for the British authorities to act. He had no other reason to remain in England; if he were going to proceed he might have to go to Ireland. But Ireland was an unknown entity.

He sat in a cafe in the shadow of the London Eye, surrounded by tourists. He seemed to be the only person without a camera. A couple with two teenage children sat at the next table, and Harry listened in quiet amusement as the family vociferously argued in Hebrew. He gave no indication he understood, intermittently eavesdropping until they left.

As the waitress placed his second cappuccino on the table he slapped himself on the thigh in annoyance. Ireland. It was twelve years since he had seen him, but of course he knew an Irishman. Brian Farrell, from Tiberias. Was Brian still in the Irish army? He could find out in Dublin.

He took out the old mobile. He checked the settings, satisfied to see the phone gave his German prefix, and called Eshan, who answered on the third ring. Harry could hear muffled voices in the background as Eshan spoke. 'What do you want? I'm in a meeting.'

'Do we have an embassy in Dublin?' Harry asked.

'A what?'

'Is there an Israeli embassy in Dublin? Yes or no. Do you have any idea?'

Eshan swore violently in Hebrew, and Harry heard him asking the question, presumably to someone beside him. He heard the answer, in a woman's voice. "Yes, and I've been in it". Eshan came back on the line.

'There is one. Why?'

'I'm not going to repeat this. Call them and make an introduction for me. I'll be in Dublin tomorrow morning.'

'What the hell is going on, Harry?'

'Just do it.' Harry terminated the call, and turned the phone off. He knew Eshan would phone back, and did not want him to hear the distinctive British ringtone. With a smile of satisfaction he picked up his cappuccino, stirring his chocolate topping into the foam.

13

The last item Harry packed was the family photograph – the one from Ami's first birthday – kissing it gently before wrapping it into a sweater. He had booked the first flight to Dublin, and boarded at six-thirty. In Dublin one hour later he went straight to his hotel. The D4 Hotel was large and modern, set in a prosperous looking inner city suburb. The taxi driver pointed out the Israeli embassy as he dropped him off – in another modern building directly across the road from the hotel. He walked over. A small, barely visible sign on the door stated the embassy opened at nine.

Exactly at that time, having showered and eaten, he returned. As he approached he saw a man hoisting the Israeli flag outside. He entered the building through large glass doors into a lobby, with a young woman receptionist sitting behind a counter.

'Do you have an appointment?' she asked, in English.

'I'm an Israeli citizen, and I'm expected.'

'Could I please have your name, and I'll check.'

He gave the woman his details and waited, conscious of a watchful camera. Minutes later the lift door opened. A young man emerged, and walked over to Harry.

'You are Mr Katz?' he inquired in English, with an American accent.

'Yes,' Harry answered in Hebrew.

'I'm sorry,' the man said, 'but I can't speak Hebrew. I'm the security guard here.'

Harry noticed a pistol on his waist belt.

'My apologies, I thought you were Israeli. I need to speak to someone in the embassy.'

'Could you tell me what it's about?' the man asked in a polite voice.

'If I give you my identity card they will know,' Harry replied, 'and this is a telephone number in Jerusalem. If you call it they can vouch for me.'

He gave his Israeli passport, his old Shin Bet identity card, and a paper with Eshan's Jerusalem number. The security man returned to the lift. Harry waited for fifteen minutes until the man came back. He returned Harry's documents, and gestured towards the lift.

'Sorry about the wait. All seems in order.'

In the lift he described to Harry what would happen.

'When we come out there is a room on the right. Could you go in there and remove your shoes and jacket. Then empty your pockets, and place any items on the tray in the room. Put it on your side of the hatch, and when I have checked it I must come in and search you. All of this will be on close circuit television. Do you agree?'

'Sure.'

'Then could you sign this consent for a body search?'

'I'm not having any internal search.'

'Don't worry, we don't do those.'

Within five minutes a tall blonde haired woman, formally dressed in a pale blue suit, welcomed him into the embassy proper.

'Mr. Katz,' she spoke in Hebrew, 'I am Sonia Weismann, the First Secretary. Would you care to come into my office?'

'Your security is impressive.' Harry tried to sound relaxed. 'Does everyone get this reception?'

'If they turn up out of the blue, yes, even if they do have an identity card from one of our security services. I have never actually seen one of them before. Your organisation has requested us to assist you.'

Harry picked up a scintilla of distaste in her voice as she said "your organisation".

'Thank you.'

She did not reply, but motioned to Harry to follow her as she walked down a short corridor into a large office, with a floor to ceiling window looking down onto a busy road. She moved behind a desk and indicated a chair opposite.

'So Mr Katz, how can we help you?'

'It's a long story,' Harry replied, trying to decide what to make of his countrywoman, 'but I need to trace a person who may live here.'

'Could I make one thing very clear?' Her voice took on a cool edge. 'We try to keep our relationships with the Irish government cordial but occasionally, despite our best efforts, they do verge towards the hostile. We have learned to be extremely careful in our official dealings with them. On personal levels we get on very well, and hope to keep it that way. The ambassador would not under any circumstance approve of any sort of, of...,' she sought the correct word, 'of aggressive actions carried out in this country. I could not emphasise that point strongly enough. Have I made myself clear?'

'I understand.' Harry nodded in apparent agreement. 'Do you wish me to tell you why I am here?'

'No. I don't need to know.' Her voice was colder. 'I am not being discourteous, but if I don't know, then I am in no way condoning whatever it is you are up to.'

'Again I understand.' Harry kept his tone polite. 'Then let me ask you some questions, which you don't have to answer.'

'That seems fair enough.'

'I think the Irish police would be the best to help me. I presume you have some sort of liaison with them?'

'Of course.'

'Is it with a regional police department, or a federal one?'

'It's a bit different in Ireland. There is only one police service called the Guards. We liaise with their local station in Donnybrook.'

'Donnybrook?' This name meant nothing to Harry. He repeated it, to memorise it.

'It's the next suburb to here.' She gestured out the window.

'You presumably also have some relationship with federal anti-terrorist departments?' he asked again.

'Again yes, but that is less personal. We deal with many units and people, and are always careful to maintain our good relationship.'

'You seem to have a poor opinion of our security services.' Harry decided to pursue this.

She glared at him, but said nothing. Instead she walked over to a side table, where a newspaper lay. She picked it up and spread it on the desk in front of him. It was the 'Irish Times'. The banner headline read "Israeli army kills fifteen in Gaza" above a photograph of a crying Palestinian woman, holding a child's body in her arms.

'We have to deal with the fallout on an almost daily basis,' Sonia Weismann said, almost angrily. 'It does not make ours an easy job.'

Harry picked up the newspaper, looked at the photograph, and then put it back on the table. He stared her down.

'Would it be possible for you arrange a meeting for me with the Irish police?'

She stood up and walked over to the window before answering.

'I will need to ask the ambassador about it, but he's not here today. He is at a conference with some people from the Irish army. If you leave me your telephone number I will call you when I have discussed it, but that will be tomorrow.'

Harry had stopped listening but he noticed the first secretary's look of puzzlement.

'Sorry, but what you just said reminded me of something I meant to do. I had a friend in Israel who was in the Irish army there. How could I find out if he is still in the service?'

She shrugged.

'Easy enough. I have a sort of Who's Who of the Irish army somewhere.' She opened a desk drawer and removed a slim directory. 'What's his name?'

'Brian Farrell.' Harry replied. 'He was career army so he would probably be fairly high up by now.'

'No need to look. I've met him a few times. I can't remember his rank but he is near to the top. And I think he's based in Dublin.'

'Do you have any idea how I could contact him?'

Before she could reply her phone rang. She answered; a flash of annoyance crossed her face as she gave a terse reply. She glared at Harry, holding her hand over the speaker.

'That's RTE, the Irish television station, requesting a statement about those Gaza killings. I'm afraid you will have to excuse me. I will contact you after I have spoken to the ambassador – you can leave your number with my secretary outside. Good day, Mr Katz.'

She managed a dismissive smile as she spoke, gave a limp handshake and turned her back on him. Harry left the office and as instructed gave his phone number outside. He took the lift down to the lobby, quietly fuming. He could understand where the first secretary was coming from, but it was difficult to accept such treatment.

At his hotel reception he requested a Dublin telephone book. There were eleven Brian Farrells listed, but after the last one was a listing for a Brian and Margaret Farrell.

'These people here, the Farrells. Is this address in Dublin?' he asked the receptionist.

She turned the book around to see.

'Brian and Margaret Farrell?' she asked. Harry nodded. 'That's only round the corner. You'd walk it in ten minutes easily.'

'Can I use your phone?'

'Go ahead. Nine for an outside line.'

Harry dialled. Three rings and it answered.

'Farrell's.' A woman's voice.

'Is that Margaret?' Harry asked.

'Yes.'

'Margaret, it's Harry Katz. From Tiberias.'

'Good God. Harry Katz. I don't believe it. Are you in Dublin?'

'I'm in a place called the D4 Hotel. Just arrived.'

'It's great to hear from you. How long, is it twelve years?'

'About that.' Harry turned his back on the receptionist. 'I need to contact Brian urgently. Is it possible?'

'You're in luck; he only came back from Kosovo two days ago. He's dropping the twins to school, but he'll be back shortly. Are you free now?'

'Yes.'

'Then come on over. Do you have our address?'

'It's in the phone book.'

'Good. Reception can direct you. Still a coffee addict?'

'Afraid so.'

He took a taxi. Minutes later he stood outside the gates of a semi-detached redbrick house. Inside was a gravelled area with a silver VW Golf parked, the area ringed by a lawn and numerous rosebushes laden with red and orange blossoms. Margaret opened the door within seconds of him ringing the bell. Her hair was shorter and blonder, but otherwise she seemed unchanged from Tiberias.

'Harry Katz!' She smiled broadly as she shook his hand. 'Never thought I'd see you again. You look great. Come on in.'

He followed her down a wooden floored hall into an untidy kitchen, scattered with the remnants of breakfast. She apologised for the mess, and indicated a table in front of the window, with a pot of coffee and some cups. While waiting for Brian, Margaret brought him up to date. The twins, Katie and Rose, were now eight. Alice was fifteen, in school transition year, and currently on a school trip to the west of Ireland. Harry noticed her glancing at his left hand.

'And you?' she asked. 'Married? Girlfriend?'

'No, and not at present.'

'Pity.' She turned her head as she heard something. 'Great, here's Brian. I better catch him before he gets too much of a shock.'

Moments later Brian hurried into the kitchen, ignored Harry's outstretched hand and enveloped him in a hug. He too had scarcely altered. Possibly a bit heavier and jowlier, hair shorter and he was tanned. He was casually dressed in jeans and a sweater.

'I don't shaggin' believe it,' Brian grinned hugely. 'After all these years. Great

John O'Keeffe

to see you, Harry.'

'And you both,' replied Harry. 'My fault, I should have kept in touch.'

'Now, this may sound rude,' interrupted Brian, 'but I've only got about ten minutes. I have to go to a Kosovo debriefing, so tell me about it.'

Margaret stood up. 'I'll leave the pair of you. Can you come for dinner tonight, Harry?'

'I'd love to, but don't know where I'll be. Can I call you later?'

'Of course.' She left the kitchen.

Harry explained all to Brian as concisely as possible, Brian nodded in understanding.

'Jaysus, that's some story. So, what can I do? We have an Army Intelligence Section, but I'm not sure this is their area.'

'What I could really do with is an introduction to either the police or to a federal Intelligence service.' Harry took a scrap of paper from his pocket. 'The embassy said they deal with a Donnybrook department. Do you know anything about it?'

'No, but it's not far away. I'll give them a call and see what I can do. Hang on a few secs.'

Harry waited as Brian left the room, closing the door to the hall behind him. He heard his muffled voice speaking on a phone. Minutes later he returned.

'That went well. You're meeting a fella called Noel Murphy there at half eleven. I don't know him, but it doesn't matter. Now, I've got to rush off. Where are you staying?'

'The D4 Hotel.'

'I'm passing there. Do you want a lift?'

Brian stopped his Honda CRV across the road from the hotel. His smile was gone.

'The last time you asked me for a favour it all went pear shaped. What's the name of the Lebanese bloke?'

'Ahmed?'

'That's the guy. I'm told there was just about enough bits of him left to fill a matchbox after your air force blew him up. Still blame myself for it. I want a promise from you that you are out of this, or I'll call Donnybrook and cancel that meeting.'

'You blame yourself? How do you think I felt? He was my only hope to find

183

Ami. Do you think I wanted him killed?'

Brian drummed the steering wheel.

'Okay, I believe you, but you'll have me to deal with if there's any nastiness.'

'Brian,' Harry looked him straight in the eyes, 'I only want to find about Ami. This Fisher woman knows, but you have to trust me it's all over. I'm German, a civilian.'

'Just hope I'm not making a humungous mistake. Good luck with the coppers, and keep in touch. Hope to see you for dinner.'

Harry collected his file from his room. The directions given to him by the receptionist were clear. Less than a hundred metres away he passed the American Embassy, a four storey circular building surrounded by high black railings on the side of a broad road, lined on each side by large horse-chestnut trees. There was no sign of either police or army, apart from a single uniformed policeman standing at the gate. Around the corner was a park, and following his instructions he walked through the gate.

The police station lay on the other side of the park, and he located it easily. It was now only ten-fifty, too early to call in. He went back to the park, where he sat on an empty bench beside a pond, looking around at old men talking together or reading newspapers; mothers with children feeding ducks and swans; students wandering aimlessly, iPods in ears. He felt deeply saddened.

Nearly eleven twenty. Time to go.

Donnybrook Garda Station was a shabby grey granite three-storied building on the side of a busy street of prosperous looking shops and banks. After giving his name at reception he was taken around through a door, down a bright corridor and into a small office. Inside were two desks with computers, three chairs and a man slumped over one of the desks, his head lying on his crossed arms. He looked at Harry, stood up and offered his hand.

'Sorry, the auld brain's a bit slow to wake up today,' he said, in a thick accent Harry could barely understand. 'I'm Noel Murphy.'

'My name is Harry Katz.'

Noel looked about the same age as Harry and he was about the same height too but he was stockier with a ruddy jowly face and receding short hair starting to grey at the temples. Casually dressed in blue jeans and a blue T-shirt, he had a black fleece top draped over the back of his chair. He was clean-shaven, but had a couple of shaving cuts on his chin. He had a big friendly grin. Harry felt relaxed with him from the first moment.

'You're not Irish, and you look like a copper.'

'Nearly right,' Harry replied. 'I'm from Israel, but I live in Germany, and I used work for the Israeli police. Now I'm with a German company, in their security department. The Israeli embassy felt you might be able to help me.'

'In that case why did some army big shot call me?' Noel growled.

'It's personal. Brian Farrell and I were close friends in Israel, and I asked him for his assistance. He suggested you.'

'And the sky is full of flying pigs. Don't know the guy from Adam, but no matter.' Noel gave a grin of reassurance as he sat back in his chair. 'Take a seat. My daughter managed to break her arm last night, and I spent most of it in the hospital. Before you tell me what this is all about, I'm going to make a cup of coffee. Do you want one? I'm afraid it's instant, and pretty shite.'

'That would be fine.'

Harry waited, and Noel returned with the coffees. He produced a packet of biscuits from a desk drawer, gave one to Harry and sat back, dunking his own biscuit into his mug.

'So, what's the story, Rory?' He grinned at Harry's confusion.

'It's a long one, but basically I'm trying to trace a woman.'

'And you've come here all the way from Germany, just for that?'

'I have been looking for this woman for over thirteen years, and last week two Swiss policemen were shot dead in connection with her.'

Noel put his cup down, pulled his chair forward. His grin disappeared.

'Better start at the beginning. Go ahead.'

14

Noel listened without interruption, and then sat forward at his desk. 'That's livened up a dull Wednesday. Presume you have the photos?'

Harry reached into a folder. 'This is the original from Lebanon.' He passed the image over the desk to Noel. 'Ignore the guy; it's the woman I'm looking for.'

'Telephoto lens with no depth of field.' Noel glanced across at Harry, and then back to the photograph. 'Does seem Irish, if such a thing exists anymore. Looks anxious. The guy seems unconcerned. Pretty girl – we've had similar ones involved here.' Noel handed the photograph back to Harry. 'Is that all you had to go on?' Noel raised an eyebrow quizzically. 'Just one photo of an unknown woman? What made you so sure she was involved?'

'The man is Hussam Farid. He's the leader of the group that carried out the murders, and the photo was taken in Lebanon the day before. She's connected to him but yes, it was and still remains the slimmest hope. But it's my only one.'

Noel looked at Harry for a few moments, registering some realisation of the magnitude of Harry's task, and then held out his hand. 'Let's see the others.' He scanned them. 'You're correct, definitely the same bird, especially if the taxi driver had never seen her before.' Noel booted his computer. 'Give me those details and we'll find out if this yoke is going to do what it's supposed to. I'll try passport first, it's the easiest.'

'Can you access it directly?'

'Buggers are on a go slow, but it should work. Okay, I'm in. Fisher with or without a C?'

'Without.'

Noel looked at the screen, and then turned around with a disappointed look.

'Nothing there. There's two Fishers, but both are well over fifty. I'll come back to them if necessary. Let's try with the C. No, no joy there,' he sighed. 'Birth certs next. This is a bit slower. No luck with the C. Now without. Jesus, it's slow. Hang on. Bingo!'

Noel's face lit up.

'What?' Harry interrupted, trying to contain his excitement.

'She's here,' Noel exclaimed. 'There's a Barbara Katya Fisher, with that date of birth. So, she was born in Dublin. That's all I can get from the computer about her birth registration, but we can check the written stuff if necessary. But she doesn't have a passport – maybe she has it in a married name. Marriage registry is easy enough. Let's see. Shit, no luck, but then she could've married abroad.'

'Is there anything else you can check?'

'Criminal record is easy; it's this gadget's main function. I'll try Barbara and date of birth. No, nothing there, and it cross-references with the subversives.

Voting register next. Those two Fishers are there, but not her. Driving licence. No, not there. PPS, that's our social insurance number. No, she doesn't pay tax in Ireland – wish I could say the same for myself. Looks like she was born here and moved to England. That's it mate, sorry.'

Noel looked up in sympathy, but Harry remained focussed.

'I know I'm grasping at straws,' Harry placed his cup on the desk and stroked his chin, a gesture he had begun to use when stressed, 'but you said it's possible to check the original birth register.'

'Normally I wouldn't bother, but you've come so far, it's worth a go.' Noel picked up a phone as he spoke. 'I'll give them a call. They can photocopy that page of the register and fax it over – doesn't take too long. Stupid number's in the office outside. Back in a minute.'

Harry remained in the small room, gloomily sipping his coffee. He had thought the Irish connection unlikely, and what he had learned only backed up what he had known already. He would phone Margaret Farrell, visit them this evening, and fly back to Munich. He was rehearsing an anticipated row with Uri when Noel returned, a sheet of paper in his hand.

'Must be a record for that lot.' Noel's smile had returned. 'Now, this is interesting. The mother's name was Ulrike Fisher, but her father was a Malachy Elliott. Her parents weren't married.'

'Why is that relevant?' Harry's query sounded downbeat.

'It's only a hunch, but this woman probably knows how things work here. In Irish law she could take her father's surname and use that, it's easy to do. I'll try Social Security; it's the quickest today. Give me that date of birth again.'

Harry looked over Noel's shoulder, only to curse again as he drew a blank. Noel glanced again at the faxed printout.

'One last chance.' He turned back to his screen. 'Her second name is down there as Katya, so why not call herself Katya Elliott? Here we go. Holy shit! We've hit the jackpot.'

'What?' Harry exclaimed breathlessly.

'She's here,' Noel banged the desk, 'or at least a Katya Elliott with that date of birth exists in social security. Okay, back to birth registration. Yes, it's her. The crafty bitch – she changed it in 1999. Harry my boy, you're one lucky bugger.'

Harry sat slumped against the wall. For a moment he was too afraid to share Noel's enthusiasm. Then he stood up and punched the air.

'Got the wagon!' Noel's loud enthusiasm was infectious, and an older uniformed policeman looked in through the door. Noel waved him away. 'Right, criminal record first. No, she's clean. Passport. Ha, she has a passport, and here's her address. Lives in Glenageary – that's not too far away. What else? Okay. She's not married here, at least with this name. Unfortunately I can't get a photograph with their bloody work to rule. You need to go to the passport office for it, but we can do it if necessary.'

'Is all this current?' asked Harry, accustomed at this stage to so many frustrations.

'Yep, it's up to date.' Noel made a face of pretend hurt, and then laughed. 'Phone next. Yes, she has an Eircom landline in her name. I'll try the mobiles. Now that's interesting, she must be the only one in Ireland without a mobile. Wait, there's an O2 mobile registered at that address, but it's to a Julie Elliott. Even got the date of birth. It's the sixth of June, 1996.'

Harry's face drained of colour as the meaning of the date sank in. He forced himself to try and remain calm. 'Anything more on the girl?' he asked, almost in a whisper. 'Does she have a birth registration or passport?'

'Let's see. No, no birth registration here. Maybe she was born abroad. Yes. Passport info details her as being born in Munich, Germany. Father's name unlisted.'

'Can, can you get a photograph of her?' Harry stuttered.

'Not on the computer. I can request Passports to fax one over, but it'll take at least a day or so.'

'So, what do we do now?' Harry asked, as much to himself as to Noel.

'Lunch, that's what we'll do. One hour'll make no shaggin' difference.'

Noel took Harry to a pub across the road from the police station. They were the first lunchtime customers in the restaurant section, and sat at what seemed to be Noel's usual corner table. In spite of his profound emotional turmoil Harry was hungry, and chose a lasagne.

'Enjoy that, and tell me something about your own job,' muttered Noel as he noisily ate his meal. 'Give the auld brain a few minutes rest.'

Harry went along with Noel, realising the Irishman was assessing him. In turn he got Noel to briefly talk about his own job and family before returning across the road. They met the superintendent in charge on the way in and Noel briefly introduced Harry, but the man just muttered a greeting.

Back in his office Noel considered their three possible options. Assuming Katya and Barbara was the one person, they should get the Swiss involved – it would be the correct procedure. Harry strongly disagreed, for fear of another agent in the Swiss network. After hearing his explanation, Noel conceded to holding off for the time being.

The second option. To request and initiate a formal surveillance operation by the Irish police, to identify the woman and monitor her movements. Certainly his superintendent would prefer that decision, Noel had no doubt, but it would take some days to set it up. Also, because the woman was trained she might spot a surveillance, especially if she was already aware of someone pursuing her.

'So will you set it up?' Harry asked, with a pretence of innocence, but he had already made his mind up. He knew Barbara's new name and that she lived in a suburb called Glenageary. It was all he needed.

'Normally yes, we would,' Noel rubbed his forehead, 'but we have a loose cannon here, and that's you. I know the kind of bloke you are.'

Harry ignored that and asked. 'So, what's the last option?'

'Go check her out. You'd go anyway since I blurted out her bloody name and address. Also if we go now you won't have time to summon any of your pals.'

'Thank you very much.' Harry tried to appear hurt.

'Just so we fully understand each other. The other thing is you know her. If this Katya isn't your Barbara all we have to do is apologise and clear off. Let's think. It's Wednesday, and presumably the kid's in school. If she's anything like my daughter she'll get home about four. What's your read on the girl?'

Harry was unsuccessfully attempting to control a combination of nervousness and anticipation.

'Has to be Farid's kid,' Harry answered after a long pause. 'Another reason why Farid is still connected to the Fisher woman. Do you know where she lives?'

'I know the road. We'll call into the local station on the way and see if anyone there knows her. First, give me your ideas about what to expect.'

'She's a pro,' emphasised Harry. 'No doubt, after seeing what she was up to in Zurich. It's probably her family home, so it's totally different from calling to a rented apartment. She won't be prepared for us, but remember my agenda –

it's only information about my daughter I'm looking for.'

'Okay, let's go.' Noel stood up. 'We can talk in the car. I'll get my gear. Back in a few minutes.'

Noel returned wearing a leather jacket. Harry followed him to the rear of the police station, where he got into an unmarked Ford Focus.

'How far?' asked Harry.

'About twenty minutes if the traffic is light.'

They drove through prosperous looking suburban neighbourhoods, going away from the city. It was a bright autumn afternoon. Noel described the areas they were passing, but Harry barely listened. His mind had focussed solely on the girl. Could it, could it be Ami? The age was right. No, it had to be Farid's kid. The time patterns fitted, and it might explain why Barbara had left the university. But the baby had been born in Munich, not in Lebanon. Would she leave a fifteen-month baby behind and go on an active mission? No ordinary person would, but abnormal times breed abnormal people. But could it be Ami? His heart had begun pounding and beads of sweat had appeared on his brow. The end was in sight. If this Katya was Barbara, what then? No, leave it. Just concentrate on the here and now.

'Give me your suggestions for handling the approach.' Harry broke his nervous silence.

'Well, it's early afternoon, and they're probably out. If so I'll ask around the neighbours and see if we can get an ID from your photos. Then again a teenager has to be coming back from school sometime. It'll be the usual parking and watching. I'm sure you're used to that.'

'Not any more, thankfully.'

'Lucky bugger,' Noel muttered. 'It all depends on the layout of the house. They're single or double storey houses on that road. No apartments that I'm aware of. Let me do the talking; you can take over if we get in. I'm in two minds about getting a patrol car to hang around, just in case. I'll decide when I see the house.'

Soon they were driving beside the sea, visible on their left down a shallow incline, with a view across a wide bay. Next came a port, with a large marina full of yachts enclosed in a horseshoe sweep of old harbour walls.

'Nearly there,' Noel said. 'The cop shop's around the corner.'

They turned away from the harbour, up a road of what seemed to be hotels, and onto a shopping street at the top. One hundred metres farther Noel turned right and stopped the car outside a new redbrick police station.

'Wait here, and tell them I own this if one of those traffic gobshites appears,' Noel ordered.

He came out of the station after ten minutes.

'Good and bad news,' he said as he drove away. 'Nobody knows her, but they told me where the house is. The good news is I met an old pal in there. He's in Special Branch, that's an armed plainclothes unit. I didn't tell him much, but he's going to meet us. I'll feel a lot more reassured having him there.'

'So will I. By the way, what are you carrying?' asked Harry.

'Regular Smith and Wesson.' Noel took it out from his shoulder holster. 'Know them?'

'Yes, a lot of our guys used them. I had a Walther, but thankfully never fired it.'

'Wish I could say the same, but I missed the bugger.' Noel returned the gun to its holster. 'Right, this is Albert Road. We're looking for a house called Currane. Should ban people having only a house name. It's apparently half way up on your side. I'll go past and wait for Jack beyond, he said he would be at the bridge.'

Noel slowed and Harry looked out for the name of the house. He spotted it easily, in large letters on a small pedestrian gate. The house was first of a terrace of old two story houses, with small front gardens and low hedges. There was a narrow lane on the near side of the house. Noel continued on for another hundred metres. He crossed over a low railway bridge, turned into a small entrance on the opposite side, and reversed back onto Albert Road again, facing the direction they had come from. They were now hidden from the house by the bridge. 'This is where we're to wait for Jack. Pity about the bloody lane, we should have two people out back. Nice house, she can't be short of the few bob.'

'I'm sorry?' Harry asked, perplexed.

'I forgot,' Noel grinned again. 'Means the house is expensive. You can't get more middle class than here. Good place to hide yourself; nothing ever happens. We only need to visit places like this when they get broken into. Ah, here comes Jack.'

A battered Toyota Corolla pulled up behind them. A scruffy middle-aged man emerged and locked his car. He walked forward, opened the back door of Noel's car, and got inside. Noel introduced Harry. They shook hands.

'Harry's from Germany,' Noel spoke to Jack as he turned around to face him. 'He's not carrying. What I suggest is Harry and I take the front, and you take the lane and the back. The lane probably services the whole row.'

'How do you read it?' Jack asked.

'Probably nobody at home.' Noel considered. 'If there is, it's at minimum one female called either Barbara or Katya. This is her photo. She's weapons trained, and has been knockin' around with some dodgy types. One of her mates killed two Swiss coppers last week. But she won't be expecting us. There's also a kid; a girl called Julie, aged fourteen or so. No photos. That's all we know, but there could well be half of al-Qaeda in there too.'

Jack coughed nervously. 'That's more like Mary Poppins compared to some of my scumbags. I'll go first. I'll be down the lane. Bit of bad news, I forgot my bloody radio. Give me five minutes.'

'Didn't forget your weapon as well?' Noel asked.

'Not totally stupid.' Jack patted his armpit.

'And remember, this is Premier Division stuff, so be careful.'

'Don't worry. Just give me time.' Jack cuffed Noel on the shoulder as he got out the back door.

Five minutes passed.

'Let's do it, as the Yanks say,' said Noel.

He drove over the bridge, past the house and parked on the other side, about thirty metres beyond. Noel reached inside his jacket, took out his gun and slid the safety catch off before returning it.

'Don't lock the car,' he motioned to Harry as they emerged.

They crossed the narrow road and went up to the low gate, opening into a paved path through the grass to the front door. Sash windows with lace curtains prevented a view of the interior.

'Wait here and let me do the talking,' said Noel, as he checked inside his jacket again. He rang the doorbell as Harry waited out of sight behind the hedge.

The door was answered quickly by a young woman – definitely not Barbara – who had a conversation with Noel. After a couple of moments he heard Noel thanking her. She shut the door, and Noel emerged onto the road. He took

Harry's arm, steered him across the lane and stopped outside the neighbouring house, out of sight of the one they had just left.

'A bloody au pair!' Noel's face creased in annoyance. 'That went down like a lead balloon. I should have known – they all have those au pairs around here. Anyway, she told me where they are.'

'Where?'

'The kid goes to Glenvara Park School, and she's playing a hockey match this afternoon. Apparently mum's gone to watch, so they're both there. Let's get over to the school before that au pair warns her.'

'What about Jack?'

'Leave him.'

15

Noel sped off after a hasty three-point turn.

'It's not too far. The au pair looked bloody suspicious – I should have been more diplomatic. She'll call her.'

'Maybe she doesn't have a phone,' Harry said, more in hope than expectation.

'Of course she'll have a mobile, they all do. It'll be a throwaway in the name of Mary Murphy.'

There was a traffic signal ahead, with a line of cars waiting at the red light.

'There's a beacon in the glove compartment,' Noel instructed. 'Bang it up top.'

Harry reached out and placed the magnetic underside of the beacon on the roof. Noel started the siren and drove up the opposite side of the road, the line of cars waiting obediently until he had passed. He screamed around the corner onto a nearly deserted road, turning off the siren. Half way down the broad avenue was a sign on the left saying "Glenvara Park School". They drove through the gates onto a driveway, about fifty metres long, a row of elm trees on either side. At the end was the school building – a large old house, with a modern extension on its left hand side. A signpost pointed the way to the car park, around the original building counter clockwise. They drove carefully to the half empty car park, with playing fields up a small incline beyond. Noel parked the car, and both men stood out. Harry removed his jacket, left it in the car and turned to Noel.

'If she is playing hockey, presumably it's up there. I'll go first, as I know what she looks like. She'll see I'm not armed.'

'Go ahead, I'm right behind you,' Noel replied, once again checking his gun.

Harry walked up the shallow bank, and found himself at the corner of an all-weather hockey pitch. A match was in progress, with one girls' team wearing blue and white, and the other all green. Noel came up beside him.

'Wrong age,' Noel said. 'More like eighteen-year olds. Must be the other pitch.'

He gestured towards the second hockey pitch, farther away parallel to the one they were beside, separated by a gap of a few metres. There were a few spectators, adults and teenagers, in the space between the two pitches. The two men walked along the goal line, passed behind the goal, and reached the corner of the second pitch. A group of three teenagers, dressed in green school uniforms, stood watching the match. One team wore the same green colours as the older girls, the other team red. They were younger than the girls on the first pitch.

'This lot look about the right age,' said Noel.

Harry was staring at the players. Two teams in green, so she must be in green if this was her school. Which one was the girl they were looking for, this Julie Elliott? He turned towards the group of girls.

'Are you from this school?' Harry asked.

'Yes, why?' the nearest girl replied.

'Do you know Julie Elliott?'

'Sure, she's in my class.'

'Is she playing here?' Harry asked.

'Yes, she's one of our best players,' another girl answered.

'Could you point her out, I don't know her.'

'Sure. Let's see.' The teenager looked around. 'That's her, over there, facing away from us. The girl with brown hair in a ponytail. Can you see her?'

'The girl leaning on her stick?' Harry asked.

'Yeah, she's always doing that.'

The whole of Harry's being focussed upon his view of the girl leaning sideways on her hockey stick, facing away from him, and looking up the pitch. He kept his eyes peeled on her, as he moved slowly to his left along the goal line. Passing behind the goalpost, he took up the nearest position to her. He watched and watched, for what seemed an eternity, but she did not turn around. Then, suddenly, her team made an attack towards the goal beside Harry, and the girl was passed the ball. She trapped it, turned quickly, and passed it on to a team mate near her.

Harry grasped the goalpost, his sudden intake of breath almost explosive. There, only five metres away from him stood a girl – the image of her mother but slightly taller. She had Rachel's wild curly brown hair tied back in a ribbon; Rachel's chin, nose, and freckled skin. The way she stood and her intense concentration was the same. It was like looking at Rachel, but Rachel from the many photographs and videos she had shown Harry, of herself as a teenager.

He stood as still as a statue, taking long deep breaths. The girl gave a grimace of annoyance as her team mate missed the opportunity to score, but this changed quickly to a smile and a call of "tough luck" as she turned around and faced away. This was Rachel's smile. Harry saw nothing else, and heard nothing else. He was barely aware he was crying, wiping his eyes automatically without noticing.

His eyes followed Ami as she ran away from him towards the half way, and when she stopped he saw beyond her, standing on the touchline, a face he recognised. Barbara was taller than he had expected. She stood alone, wearing a black puffer jacket and blue jeans, a mobile phone to her ear. She was staring intently at Noel who was walking along the touchline towards her. Harry woke from his trance and started to move, first at normal pace and then quicker. He watched, as in slow motion, Noel stopping about five metres from Barbara. She said something that Harry could not hear, and then took a small gun from her bag. At the same time Noel removed his weapon from its shoulder holster. They stood in silence, each pointing their guns at each other.

Harry ran, and as he passed Noel he stopped.

'Leave this to me,' Harry commanded.

Without registering Noel's response he turned towards Barbara, raising his open palms to show he had no weapon. Slowly he advanced towards her, his eyes never leaving her face. He stopped less than two metres away from her. She stood impassive, betraying no visible alarm. Just, Harry computed, a terrifyingly cold determination. Her gaze remained unmoving, the small gun steady in her hand, pointing without a trace of tremor at Harry's chest. The standoff was broken as a figure in green rushed over and grasped the woman around the waist.

'Leave her alone. Leave my mum alone,' the girl screamed.

Harry did not respond to his daughter, but spoke assuredly and precisely to Barbara.

'*Wir sind Polizei.*' 'We are police.'

He advanced closer.

'*Wir sind Polizei. Gibst mir das.*' 'We are police. Give me that.' Harry repeated in a quieter voice, holding out his hand.

The colour drained from her face, and she replied with difficulty.

'*Wer sind sie?*' 'Who are you?' She asked again. '*Wer sind sie? Woher kommen sie?*' 'Who are you? Where are you from?'

'*Ich komme aus Israel.*' 'I am from Israel.' Harry replied clearly and slowly. Her eyes widened as he went on. '*Aus Israel. Ich bin ihr Vater.*' 'From Israel. I am her father.'

She seemed to visibly shrink.

'*Nein. Das kann sein nicht.*' 'No. That can't be,' she whispered.

'*Es ist wahr.*' 'It is true.' Harry held his hand out for the gun. '*Es ist alles fertig, Barbara.*' 'It's all over, Barbara.'

Slowly, in shock, she lowered the gun and let it drop to the ground. She stooped and hugged the girl fiercely, tears pouring down her face.

'What did he say, mummy? What did that man say?'

'Julie darling, you are going to have to be so brave.'

'Who is he, mummy? What's he saying?'

'We have to go with them,' Barbara replied, almost in a monotone.

Noel interrupted the shocked silence. First he picked up Barbara's gun from the ground and put it into his pocket. Only then did he speak.

'I'm a Detective Garda.' He showed Barbara a plastic card he had taken from his pocket. 'My car's over there. Take the girl and we'll walk over to it nice and slowly. And please, no heroics. Just get moving. I'm going to put my weapon out of sight, but remember it's there.'

Barbara nodded, and taking Julie's hand silently followed Noel, Harry bringing up the rear, carrying his daughter's hockey stick. They walked past hushed groups of teenagers, around and past the goalpost towards the car. A woman approached Barbara, who raised her hand and said something. The woman backed off.

Noel opened the passenger door and motioned Barbara into the front seat. She sat in and he closed the door. He opened the door behind her, showed Julie into the back seat, and walked around to Harry. As he indicated the door behind the driver he handed Harry his gun.

'You watch her,' Noel instructed.

'Where are we going?' Harry asked.

'Can't stay here, the shit's about to hit the fan. I'll decide in the car.'

Ami's terrified and uncomprehending eyes gazed at Harry, as he sat in the back seat and covered the gun loosely with his jacket. She shrank away from him towards her own door, grasping both of Barbara's arms around the side of the front seat. Up to then Barbara had been silent, slumped in her seat, staring out the passenger window. She turned around. Her tears had stopped but her eyes were vacant as she kept her own gaze fixed on Julie, behind her.

As Noel drove Harry stayed silent, unable to cope with a maelstrom of conflicting emotions. Suddenly, when all hope seemed gone, he had found his daughter. There was not the shadow of a doubt – Julie was Ami. She was almost a clone of her mother, except for her eyes, which were as green as his. He could not stop looking at her. He had never known what to expect when and if he discovered her, but not this. Not an Irish teenager who was terrified of him. Or was she? She was clasped to Barbara, but it was she who was protecting Barbara, and not the other way around. Her looks at Harry were changing from fear to hostility and anger. This girl was not cowed.

Noel pulled the car to the side of the road, and turned around to face Harry.

'If we go to the station I'll have to book her. You'll be shut out.'

'I need to talk to her. Could we take them to her house?'

'Her house?'

'It's not perfect, but we'll get some time there.'

Noel looked at Barbara and Julie in turn.

'Not sure it's a great idea, but okay.'

Minutes later Noel parked outside Barbara's house.

'Inside, miss. We need to talk to you,' he said to Barbara.

'Do you mind if I send Julie back to school with my au-pair?' Barbara asked as she stood out, helping her daughter from the back, her first words since leaving the touchline.

'I've no problem with that,' Harry said, 'but ring the doorbell and remain outside. Keep your hands where we can see them. The girl can go in, but you stay here until both of them have gone.' Harry could not bring himself to call his daughter Julie.

'By the bloody manual, I should have known,' Barbara said.

Her spirit was returning. She did exactly as Harry had instructed, and a tearfully reluctant girl was firmly ordered to return to the school in the company of the confused au-pair. 'Promise you won't harm my mum,' the girl pleaded as they set off up the road.

This was the first time Harry had heard his daughter speak, except for her scream to leave her mother alone. He wanted to take her into his arms, to hug her, to reassure her, to protect her forever.

'No, of course not,' he replied instead, and watched in silence as she walked away with the au-pair.

Realising he was still holding Noel's gun, Harry indicated to Barbara to go into the house, gesturing with the weapon. He ordered her to keep her hands on her head, followed her into a short hall and directed her through an open door leading into a large kitchen, with glass doors to other rooms and outside to a garden. At the far end was a large eating area containing a television, a sprawling bookshelf crammed with videos above a sideboard, a table and four chairs. On the sideboard were large silver framed photographs of Barbara and Julie.

'Sit over there,' Harry instructed Barbara, continuing to point the gun at her. He turned towards Noel. 'You have her gun. Is it loaded?'

'Sure is,' Noel replied as he checked. 'She was waiting for someone. You watch her while I check the house, but I'll secure her first.' Noel removed a length of grey cable tie from his pocket. 'Hands behind your back, on either side of the chair. Don't fuck around – you know the story.'

She glared at Noel, but followed his orders. Noel tightened the plastic strip until she winced. 'That'll do fine.' Noel left the room. Harry watched Barbara, who did not look up but sat quietly, her chin on her chest. He looked at each of the framed photos in turn. They seemed to have been taken roughly three years apart – all in the same place outdoors in a garden. Ami maybe five years old, her hair tied in two pigtails. Two others in between and one that seemed recent. In each photograph Barbara had her arm around his daughter's shoulder. Harry stiffened and brusquely turned over each photograph with a sharp rap. He looked back to Barbara, about to speak but was interrupted by Noel's return.

'Nobody here, it's clear,' Noel said. 'Seems it's just her, the kid and that au-pair.'

'So what do you want?' Barbara lifted her face and asked directly to Harry. 'Take this stupid thing off my wrist, it's hurting me.'

Harry looked to Noel, who shrugged his shoulders. Noticing a scissors on an adjacent worktop Harry picked it up and cut the plastic ties.

She stood up and removed her jacket. She was wearing a tight black top, with no sign of another weapon. Harry was about to reply but Noel walked over, took the magazine out of Barbara's gun and put the empty weapon on the table beside her.

'You can tell me later why you needed to take a gun to a hockey match, but I have a question for you.' Noel's face was grim, commanding authority. 'Two Swiss policemen were murdered in Zurich last week. Now think very hard before you reply. Did you have anything to do with it? It's a simple question and please, don't mess around with me.'

Barbara looked defiantly at Noel as she considered how to answer, and then made her decision. 'No,' she said boldly, confidently. 'The first I knew about it was hearing it on the German news. I had nothing to do with it, I swear.'

Harry returned his gun to Noel, then walked over and sat on a chair across the table from Barbara.

'We believe you about that, or at least I do,' Harry said as he glanced towards Noel. Noel gave a minute nod of agreement as Harry continued. 'I have many questions, but one above all. Like Noel just said, think very hard. Your future and Julie's will depend on how you answer. Did you kill Julie's mother? That's my question.'

This time Barbara's manner was less sure.

'I don't know what you are talking about.'

'No?' Harry barked. 'You don't know? Then I'll make it easy for you, Barbara or Katya or whatever you are calling yourself today. Rachel, that's Ami's real mother and not her pretend mother, was murdered thirteen years ago and you were there when she was killed. How do I know? Your fingerprints were there, that's how I know.'

'Bullshit.' Barbara replied, but her voice lacked the confidence to match her comment. 'My fingerprints were where? You're talking nonsense.'

'Am I?' Harry had regained control and his voice was steady. 'They were all over that caravan where you murdered Rachel and her sister. We got the prints from your own aunt's house.'

'My aunt?' interrupted Barbara, a new fear in her voice.

'Yes,' Harry replied firmly. 'Your aunt in Worms. Rosamund Braun in Hergantweg.' Barbara had begun to blink rapidly as Harry continued to mercilessly probe. 'Also your fingerprints were on the newspaper you left in the taxi you took from Zurich airport. That was a big mistake. The Zurich police are extremely interested in that paper, I can assure you.'

'What paper?' Barbara's voice sounded almost fearful, her defiance gone.

'Saturday's Frankfurter Allgemeine, but it's irrelevant. Now, answer my question. Did you kill Rachel? Did you murder my wife?'

Harry motioned to Noel to remain quiet as Barbara buried her face in her hands.

'It was so horrible,' she spoke through her fingers. 'I just couldn't do it. I couldn't shoot her, and then we found a little girl. There was never supposed to have been a child in that settlement.'

'What happened?' Harry interjected, encouraging her to continue.

'They were going to kill Julie,' Barbara continued, in a monotone, 'but instead decided to take her back to Lebanon and do it there. They gave her to me to mind but I dropped her when I fell down a ditch or something. That woke her, and when I heard her cry that was it. I wouldn't let them shoot her.'

'And then?' prodded Harry.

'None of your business.' Barbara's defiance was returning. 'She is mine. I saved her life. Without me she would have been killed – have no doubt about that. God, it was not easy. You have no idea what I went through, and I am not giving her up. No, to answer your question, I did not kill her mother, and I am not telling who did.'

Barbara attempted to stand but was roughly forced back into the seat by Noel. She gave a cry of pain.

'Hurt, did it?' Noel growled. 'Tough. Just stay sitting or I'll tie you up again.'

'You don't need to say who killed them.' Harry spoke again in the controlled voice he had used in so many interrogations. 'We know it anyway.

I just needed to be told it was not you who shot her.'

'Look,' Barbara glared at Harry with more confidence. 'Don't you get it? You know nothing about Julie. Do you know her friends? What she eats? What she wears? God, you know nothing at all. The best thing you can do is leave. Okay, big fucking deal. You have found your biological daughter, but she's not yours. If you really want to do the best for her then leave her alone. Go away, get out of our lives.'

'That's not an option.' Harry slapped the table loudly as he spoke. 'I have found my daughter after years of searching for her and I'm not walking away. Of course I don't know her, since you stole her from me. Ami is my daughter, not yours, and I will not abandon her. Ever'

Harry looked straight into Barbara's eyes, and she into his.

'We'll have to make a decision,' Noel broke the tense silence, sitting down and looking at each in turn. 'We've only a few more minutes at best before the guards arrive, so both of you need to concentrate on what I have to say. It looks to me like you need each other. She's right, Harry. You don't know the girl, and if Barbara goes to prison in Switzerland you'll win a battle but you could lose a war.' He turned towards Barbara. 'As for you, miss. You might convince me you'd nothing to do with Zurich, but the Swiss won't believe that. You need Harry, or else you're going to a Swiss prison.'

'You need a warrant to arrest me for that, and you obviously don't have one.' Barbara accused Noel defiantly.

'Don't talk shite!' responded Noel in annoyance. 'Of course I don't, but wait till we get to stolen passports, false identity, abducting a minor and whatever else. If you hadn't pulled that bloody gun on me then I probably couldn't arrest you, but I've more than enough justification under the Prevention of Terrorism Act. And you know it well. Even if you do have a licence for that gun.'

'No, of course not,' muttered Barbara, in resignation.

'So what do you suggest?' Harry asked Noel, haltingly.

'Agree to work together for now. Harry gets to share Julie, and in return keeps you from going to Zurich.' Noel looked at Barbara. 'That's all you're going to get from me. Social services will want explanations about her real identity, but that'll be another day's work. You're going to have a shitload of explaining to Julie and you'll need Harry for that as well. Do both of you agree?'

'So she gets away with what she has done?' Harry was furious.

'No.' Noel jabbed his finger at Harry as he spoke. 'As I said, she has a heap of explaining to do, firstly to us down in the station. More importantly, and she knows this, she will have to justify a lifetime of lying to Julie. She may avoid prison, but believe me she'll suffer. By God, she will.'

'If you can protect me, then I agree.' Barbara looked at Noel as she made her decision. 'There seems to be no option.'

'You don't like it?' Harry almost spat at Barbara. 'For thirteen years, up to thirty minutes ago, I thought Ami was dead, and I hoped if I found you, you could tell me where my daughter was buried. In my wildest dreams I never believed she could be alive. How do you suppose I feel, when I suddenly find her alive? Do you think you can just walk away? Are we supposed to feel sorry for you? Don't make me sick.'

Harry stood up. In impotent fury he looked out the window. The sun was shining on a neat rectangular lawn, surrounded by banks of flowers in full bloom. In the centre of the lawn was a large silver and blue trampoline. This is what he should have been looking at, with Rachel and their children, for the past thirteen years. This woman had stolen all this from him. But what she had said was true. She had saved Ami's life – that much he did believe. Barbara would never be extradited to Israel, there was no chance of that, and Noel was correct. If she went to Switzerland then Harry would win a hollow victory, but could lose his daughter. He slowly sat down again.

'I've no choice.' Harry looked down as he sighed in resignation. 'So what happens now?'

'I'll formally arrest her for having the gun, but we can do that in the station.' Noel became businesslike. He looked at Barbara. 'Agreed?'

'Yes.'

Noel turned to Harry.

'Yes,' answered Harry, this time with a new conviction.

'Come on, let's go.' Noel managed a wan smile. 'And Harry, I may very well be looking for a job in Munich next week.'

16

In Dun Laoghaire police station Noel gave Barbara two options. He could charge her with possession of an unlicensed weapon, but once this process began there was no going back. Alternatively she could voluntarily wait in a cell until a decision was made about what to do. She agreed to the latter and was led off to a holding cell, while Noel began a series of telephone calls. Within thirty minutes Noel's boss – the superintendent whom Harry had briefly met in Donnybrook station – bustled in the door, red of face and patently furious.

Harry was dispatched to an empty room. He sat in silence. There were two metal chairs and a table on the white tiled floor, and a small barred window that looked outside onto a featureless brick wall. Near the ceiling he noticed a tiny observation panel. He took out his phone, and texted. "Found Ami here in Dublin. Don't phone me". He sent the message to Brian Farrell, to Uri in Munich, and to Veronika in Zurich. Then, unsure if Veronika spoke English, he sent the message to her in German. He waited.

Brian was first to reply. A simple text. "Phone me". Two other messages arrived almost simultaneously. From Uri came "Congratulations. Call me". The third was from Veronika, in German. "My God Harry, I don't believe it". Resisting the temptation to call each, he paced around the room in a mixture of happiness and apprehension until the door opened. He was lead into an office where Noel, his superintendent and three uniformed policemen sat around a table littered with plastic cups and ashtrays. He was interrogated for nearly two hours, and replied truthfully to all their questions, with the exception of one. He repeatedly stressed that he had placed Noel in an impossible situation: he had told Noel he was going to go to Barbara's house to confront her alone, and Noel's reluctant decision to accompany him had been made solely for this reason.

Harry steadfastly refused to deviate. Noel, realising what Harry was doing, made a half-hearted plea in his defence, but Harry was fully prepared to shoulder the whole blame. Once he had signed a formal statement the tension eased. Harry was now prepared to discuss, but only off the record, all aspects of the situation. Finally the superintendent made the decision – to interview

Barbara, with the threat that at any time later she could be charged. Harry was given permission to observe, but not to participate.

The superintendent shook hands with Harry as he departed, giving what Harry interpreted as a wry smile of recognition of the bond which had clearly developed between Harry and Noel, and an appreciation of the loyalty Harry was showing to a fellow officer. Harry and two of the Irish police were shown into a stuffy observation room, as Noel and a female policewoman sat in an interview room with Barbara.

Barbara remained confidently defiant throughout her interrogation, refusing to admit to anything more than possession of a weapon. Initially she would not tell why she was carrying it, but eventually, in response to Noel's ceaseless prodding, conceded she was now in fear of her old comrades. She had no idea that either the Israelis or the Irish police knew of her whereabouts. When the au pair had phoned to warn her, she had assumed Noel was from a terrorist group and had come to harm her.

She claimed that she was tired, that she needed to see her daughter and either must be formally charged or let go. Noel snorted in derision, and gave her the option that either the police would search her house or she could show them where she had hidden any documents or weapons. She would have to also surrender hers and Julie's passports. He had the power to do all this under the Prevention of Terrorism Act – he did not need a judicial warrant. She relented, on condition that Noel alone accompanied her back to Albert Road.

Noel left the interview room and came into the room where Harry was listening. He was tired, and could not keep going much longer. He believed Barbara could be trusted, but only because of Julie. All agreed she had been surprised by their discovery of her, and would not have prepared a strategy in response. It was their call, and they made it. Noel would drive Barbara home, but this time he would take a police backup.

Harry felt sidelined. He too was exhausted, and sat in indecision. Noel strongly recommended that he return to Munich, get his affairs in order and come back to Dublin once things were settled. Harry agreed.

It was eight o'clock. A cool mist had descended while Harry had been in the station, and the road was lit by the eerie glow of bright orange streetlights. He put on his jacket and walked as advised down to the main street, where he had only a minute's wait before a taxi appeared. He rang Brian Farrell, asking if it was all right to call around to his house. Brian said yes.

Margaret came running to the gate, flinging her arms around Harry's neck and hugging him through tears of happiness. Brian waited at the door, and gave a formal, almost unfriendly handshake. Brian looked at Margaret.

'Sorry love, but I need five minutes with Harry. We'll go for a short walk.'

Margaret looked mystified, but nodded and went back inside. Harry gave Margaret his folders, and both men walked away from the house along the quiet road. There was a bench about thirty metres away, which Brian indicated.

'Do you know Alice was playing a match on that pitch last Saturday?' Brian asked, with a sudden intensity that took Harry by surprise. 'What the hell were you up to? It's a bloody miracle nobody was killed.'

Harry had been expecting some reaction from Brian. He turned and looked at him straight in the eyes.

'Brian, I'm sorry, but that's the way it panned out. If you give me the time I'll explain.'

'It better be bloody good.'

It was. Twenty minutes later they returned to the house. Margaret, waiting at the open door, noticed the sea change in the body language of both men. She looked towards her husband.

'Have you calmed down?'

'Yes. Sorry about earlier.' Brian gave his wife a kiss on the cheek.

'Thank goodness. Men!' She embraced Harry. 'My God, Harry, you have no idea how much this means to me. Come inside and meet the twins. I don't care what that grumpy husband of mine says, I'm opening a bottle of champagne.'

Two hours and almost two bottles of champagne later, the twins long gone to bed, Harry was leaving to walk back to the hotel.

'I can only guess how tired you must be,' Margaret said, 'but the offer is still open. If Ami wants to stay here she's welcome, you know that.'

'I'll have to see what happens. I can't thank you enough for your support. I better go.'

'I'll walk back with you,' said Brian. 'Have to do something to clear the head.'

As they approached the hotel Harry stopped. 'Look, it's all working out for me,' he said, 'but I'm afraid for Noel. Could I ask you another favour?'

'You can ask.'

'You must have connections. Could you put a word in the right ear? I don't want him to suffer because of me.'

Brian did not reply, and they walked in silence to the gates of the hotel. Brian stopped.

'I'll leave you here. Look, I'll phone the Garda Commissioner first thing tomorrow. Your man will get a rap on the knuckles but that's about it. Now would you go back to Germany for a while before asking me for any more favours.'

Harry requested a receptionist in the hotel to book him on a flight to Zurich in the morning. He went to his room and waited for the call, cradling the photograph of his family, trying to see a resemblance between Ami and Julie. They seemed like two different people, but Julie and Rachel were as one.

17

Harry arranged to meet Bruno Hartmann at four o'clock, but he was unable to contact Veronika. From Zurich Airport he took a train to the main railway station, deposited his bag in left luggage and walked to police HQ. Virtually at the door his phone rang. It was Veronika. Surprised and delighted to hear Harry was in Zurich, she suggested they meet later in the bar of the Schweitzerhof Hotel, directly across the street from the HauptBahnhof.

Inside HQ Harry was shown into the same conference room as before. He stood at the window looking down onto a narrow cobbled pedestrianised street, lined on both sides by small shops and cafes and busy with people, many buying flowers from a group of stalls. Dreading what was about to happen, he heard the door behind him open and turned around to see Bruno walking towards him, hand outstretched.

'May I offer my heartfelt congratulations. I couldn't believe it when I got your text.'

'I'm much the same. Still feel it's a dream. I could never have done it without your help, and I'm eternally grateful.'

'Perhaps that is not the reason why you have come to Zurich today, of all days. I feel you have something else to tell me.'

Harry moved from the window, sat at the table and stroked his chin. He took a deep breath and looked up at the Swiss man.

'I do. I had to tell you this in person. The woman in Dublin is the one we have been looking for, and has broken God knows how many laws in Switzerland, but she had nothing to do with the shootings.'

'Nothing? You are joking.'

'I wish I was. Yes, of course it was her who got the paged message, and yes, she fled using the false passports, but the shootings – no.'

Bruno pulled back a chair and slowly eased himself into it. He removed a thin black pipe from his jacket pocket, packed down its tobacco with his index finger and lit it with a gold lighter. He placed the lighter on the table, sat back in the chair and looked at Harry through the grey smoke. His eyes narrowed and his brow creased.

'I feel I am about to hear some bad news.' Disappointment clouded Bruno's face.

'Not really. Farid set the whole thing up, and he's the only person she had any contact with. He supplied the pager and the documents she was supposed to swap. Barbara has absolutely no idea who the Iraqis are. We didn't ask her about the cleaner, but I know the answer.'

'And you swallowed all this? In Israel, would you have believed it?'

'Bruno, I have interrogated many suspects and can tell a liar when I meet one. Also, I know fairly quickly who will give you nothing. She won't talk – take my word for it. You want the Iraqis and the other agent in your network, but she can't assist you there.'

Bruno continued to puff at his pipe.

'This does not help me much. Are you telling me you want to allow her walk away?'

'No.' Harry stood up, moved back to the window and turned around. 'You had two of your officers shot, but I had my wife and her sister murdered, and my daughter stolen for thirteen years. She was involved in all of this, but she did not pull any triggers. Do you think I like her? That I admire her? That I want to protect her?'

'So give her to us.'

'Give her to an Israeli court, yes, if that were possible, but here, no. I am extremely sorry about it, but I have to consider my daughter and this Fisher woman is the person she regards as her mother. I'll need time to think about it, but for the moment I'm unable to assist you. That's about all I have to say, except an unreserved thank you for your assistance.'

Bruno stood up and without another word walked out of the room.

There was one free table in the bar of the Schweitzerhof Hotel. Harry ordered a beer. He paid for it when it arrived but left it sitting on the beer mat and sat slumped forward, his head resting on his arms. He felt a tap on his shoulder and Veronika's voice. 'Harry, is it you?'

She was looking anxiously at him. He stood, smiled and embraced her warmly.

'Beer! Should be champagne,' she said.

'Maybe later.'

She took the chair opposite and lit a cigarette while catching the eye of a waiter. She ordered a glass of champagne and turned back to Harry.

'So, what's up? Why that look on your face?'

Harry explained about his meeting with Bruno. He needed to unburden his guilt about how shabbily he had treated him. She listened patiently. When he finished she put it into context, emphasising that while it was without doubt unfair to Bruno, none of this was of Harry's making and he had been left with no choice in the matter. Also he had the considerable courage to come to Zurich and tell Bruno to his face. Harry cheered up a little, but returned to despondency as he described his feelings of anti-climax at finding Ami. She reminded him that she had discussed this with him in the car on the way to Basel.

'That's exactly what I expected. You have to accept she's no longer Ami, she's Julie. An Irish girl who's a stranger to you, but she's still your daughter. From the sound of it she seems like a normal teenager. Now it's up to you to get to know her as she is, not who or what you expected her to be. Do you have a photo?'

'No. Last thing on my mind.'

'Pity, I'd love to have seen her. Does she look like Rachel?'

'I couldn't believe it. They are so alike, except she has green eyes. And you are absolutely right; she is Julie, not Ami. But it's difficult.'

'I agree. It's tough, but the only way. You have to look it at from her side. She has never heard the name Ami, and has been Julie all her conscious life. And Barbara has been her mother. You can't change that now.'

'Yes,' Harry sighed in resignation, 'I'll get used to it. Have to.'

'Consider your glass half full, not empty.' Veronika grasped Harry by the elbow to emphasise. 'You have thirteen years of catching up with Julie, and I'm sure she has so much to tell you. Look forward to it. I would.'

Veronika took a sip from her champagne, put the glass in front of Harry, removed his beer and ordered another glass of champagne for herself.

'Now, no beer. Back to the beginning and tell me the whole story, starting from when you left our apartment last week.'

Veronika was a tower of strength. Her final words, three hours later after dinner, were that Harry was to concentrate on getting to know his daughter. To be there for her now – as without doubt her world had been shattered – and to suspend judgment on Barbara until he knew more. Yes, Barbara could well be a seasoned terrorist – don't get taken in by any first impression – but from Veronika's reading on it the woman had changed. Harry was, however, never to underestimate how determined Barbara would be to keep her "adopted, for want of a better word" daughter.

Harry left to catch the nine o'clock train to Munich, and Veronika came with him to the station. They embraced on the platform. Harry slept on the train, and by two-thirty he was back at his Munich apartment.

Next day Uri insisted Harry take indefinite leave from work, on full pay, and return to Dublin. They decided to continue their maximum security status for another week. Harry tidied up loose ends in Munich, both in work and at home, and booked a flight back to Dublin for early Monday morning. He spoke to an emotional Anna in Florida, and had difficulty in dissuading her from flying immediately to Dublin.

Noel phoned Sunday evening. Barbara had contacted him, and she wanted to speak to Harry urgently. When he called the number Barbara was brief and to the point. She had told Julie the truth, leaving nothing out. Julie had been devastated, but was now demanding to meet Harry. Barbara felt this was too early, but Julie was refusing to back down. Barbara had agreed. Yes, tomorrow would be fine. Barbara wanted to meet somewhere public, and suggested a local hotel, the Killiney Castle. In the hotel lounge at four o'clock.

Having negotiated the Golf into the only free space in the car park of the Killiney Castle Hotel, Harry emitted a sigh of relief. The receptionist at his hotel had correctly estimated that the drive to Killiney would take about thirty minutes. What he had not anticipated was the stress of driving on the left-hand side of the road for the first time, compounded by the erratic and unpredictable behaviour of the Irish motorists. He was pleased to get there safely, without physical damage either to himself or the hired car.

Harry arrived at three-thirty. He was sure Barbara's suggestion that they meet in a neutral hotel was genuine, but he was taking no chances. Any rendezvous with an activist, even one supposedly no longer involved, carried a degree of danger. He was unarmed, and had no backup. If she was not there by four-fifteen he was leaving. If she came without his daughter he was leaving. If she did not turn up he would abandon the car until checked by the police for a bomb.

He waited until a group of three men approached, going towards the hotel entrance. As they passed he joined them and walked to the door as if in their company. The meeting place seemed acceptable. The hotel was a four-story building which looked like a converted manor house with modern extensions. Inside the entrance a reception lobby opened on the left to a lounge area, with large windows and clusters of armchairs grouped around coffee tables. Most of the tables were occupied by groups of men and women, expensively but casually dressed. A notice beside reception gave the explanation. In German and Italian it welcomed delegates to a conference on Dental Surgery, and moving into the lounge area Harry heard conversations in those languages. As a group of three vacated a table he sat down.

It was perfect. A crowded area. Back to a wall, but with a clear view. He asked a waiter for a mineral water, and requested the two chairs opposite be kept for his guests. The waiter put a "reserved" sign on the table. Harry left his jacket on his seat and checked around the room but felt no threat or any danger signals. He located two other exits, one close to his table, and sat down. It was three forty-five.

An overwhelming apprehension replaced his safety concerns. All his working life he had been trained to anticipate problems. To access risks and prepare strategies for both expected and unexpected hazards, but now he was about to face what could be the most crucial meeting of his life. He felt he was ready, but was he? Sitting in the comfortable chair, nervously sipping water, he did not know what to expect.

Four o'clock. He looked towards the entrance and exactly at that time Barbara and Julie entered. His daughter was wearing her green school uniform, and Barbara was dressed in a long brown skirt and white blouse. She carried no bag. Both were stony faced. While Julie walked into the lounge with a fixed stare, Barbara spotted him immediately but proceeded to scan the whole room, much as he had done. Apparently satisfied she said something to Julie, and she looked in his direction.

Harry stood up and waited as they crossed the lounge to his table. Julie stopped mid way but Barbara continued until she was standing in front of Harry. Neither offered a handshake, and Barbara was the first to speak.

'*Nur dreizig Minuten. Geht das?*' 'Thirty minutes only. Is that acceptable?' Barbara's voice was cold, formal, and unfriendly.

'*Stimmt.*' 'Okay.' Harry was surprised by her use of German, but replied in the same language.

'No German!' An angry Julie interrupted. 'Talk English in front of me.' She looked between both adults as she spoke.

'I'm sorry,' Barbara sighed. 'It's time for formal introductions. Julie, this is Harry Katz, your birth father. Harry, you of course know who Julie is.'

Politely, almost formally, Julie stretched out her hand and smiled. She had braces on her teeth. He shook her hand warmly.

'Let's sit down,' Harry said with an attempted grin. 'This is like a funeral.'

It worked. Both females relaxed slightly. Julie sat opposite Harry on his right, Barbara on his left. Harry took unconscious command of the situation. He looked only at his daughter. 'I don't know how much you've been told,' Harry spoke carefully, directly to her, 'and I don't know where to begin.'

She looked down at the floor, crossing and uncrossing her legs, her hands firmly clasped together. Eventually she looked up.

'I've dreamt all my life of having a father. You have no idea what it's like to be the only one in my class without a dad.'

Harry met her gaze without blinking, almost overcome with the emotion of the moment.

'I can only begin to imagine what it has been like for you,' he said, 'but I must tell you this. You were ours; I mean you were your mother's and my daughter for a very short but wonderful fifteen months. Then your mother was killed and you were stolen. Yes, stolen. We loved you very much, you must realise that. My heart was broken when you disappeared, and I have spent every second of the past thirteen years thinking about you. You had a father all these years, only you did not know it.'

Julie began to cry, at first quietly and then loudly and incoherently. She stood up abruptly, looked around and rushed off in the direction of the Ladies. Barbara jumped up and glared at Harry.

'You bloody idiot. What did you say that for?' she hissed.

'It's the truth – face up to it,' Harry shot back. She did not reply but hurried away after Julie.

Five minutes later they returned, both their faces reddened from crying. Julie was still dabbling at her eyes with a tissue, but Barbara appeared to have recovered, although she looked furious. They sat back into the same chairs.

'So, what do I call you?' Julie asked. 'Is it Dad, or Harry? What do you call me?' Her expression was pained; she was clearly under strain.

'Harry is fine with me,' Harry replied in as comforting a manner as he was able, 'and you are Julie, not Ami.' Harry leaned forward and touched Julie's hand as he spoke. Julie did not recoil from his touch. 'Did you know your name was Ami?'

'No, of course, I didn't. Ami? Is that with a y or an i?' Julie asked with interest.

'With an i,' Harry answered. 'Your second name is Anna, the same name as your grandmother, your mum's mum. She is the only one of your birth grandparents still alive.' He looked at Barbara, a flicker of something crossing her features. 'Your family name is Katz. With a z. It's a German name.'

'My grandmother Anna, the one still alive.' Julie's expression was innocent, inquiring. 'What's she like? Is she Israeli?'

'She's great.' Harry was eager to continue this topic. 'She's not Israeli, and has only been there a few times. She's American, and lives in Florida. Still works as a journalist. I spoke to her last night, and she wants to come over and meet you.'

'You know,' Julie sighed. 'That's the first nice thing I've heard in all this random yukkiness. I've always wanted a granny.'

'One bit of advice. Don't call her granny; she would kill you if she heard that.'

The three of them smiled at this, and were silent for a couple of moments, nobody sure how to proceed until Julie stood up.

'Have to go to the bathroom again,' she announced, and without waiting for a reaction walked away.

'I'm not going to go into it,' Barbara was first to speak, 'but it has been total hell for both of us. I don't want sympathy from you. I know I'm not going to get it, but bear with her.'

'How much of the truth have you told her?' There was a touch of menace in Harry's voice.

'I've told her all I could.' Barbara picked up on this immediately. 'I had to play down the details about what happened to her mother.'

'And what "happened" to her aunt. Did you play down her murder too, or was she airbrushed out as well?' He stopped. He shouldn't allow bitterness to creep in. He held up his hands in surrender. 'No, this is not the place. Go ahead.'

'I've told her what I can.' Barbara replied in a steady monotone. 'When she comes back we'll leave. Do you want to see her again?'

'Of course I do. First I want to give her something. She's right behind you.'

Barbara turned around but said nothing as Julie sat down.

'Julie,' Harry took charge again. 'I'll have to leave in a few moments, but I'd like to see you again soon. Could I give you something first?'

Julie looked to Barbara for guidance, and Barbara nodded her consent. Harry reached for his shoulder bag and removed Ami's old teddy bear. He handed it to Julie. She took it from him and looked at it in surprise.

'It's yours,' Harry said. 'You used to play with it as a baby. I've carried it for thirteen years hoping to return it to you.' Harry stuttered as he spoke, and his eyes misted. Julie cradled the battered teddy, then leaned forward and kissed Harry on the cheek.

'Thanks, dad.' She was crying again. She stood up abruptly and without a backwards glance made for the exit with Barbara hurrying after her.

Noel and Harry were in the virtually empty bar of his hotel. It was seven o'clock, less than three hours since Harry had met Barbara and Julie. Noel and he had met by arrangement, the corner of the dark wooded bar ideal for their purpose.

'Was that not bloody stupid, meeting her alone?' asked Noel.

'I didn't care,' Harry replied, his face registering a surprise at the taste of his first Guinness. He put it down as he continued. 'I mean, I took the usual precautions but then something snapped. It didn't matter anymore. I had done what I was driven to do, I found Ami. I found a normal girl. She's devastated but she'll get over it.' Harry looked into his drink as he continued. 'No, either we all, and by that I mean myself, Barbara and Julie will have to work this through together or not at all.'

'Your choice, mate,' replied Noel, 'but I think I can see where you are coming from. Now, are you free tomorrow morning, at eleven?'

'Why?'

'Got a call on the way here from a fella called Ray Culliton. He's head of our anti-terrorist section, and he's a total bollox. Ordered me to be in Donnybrook tomorrow at ten, and then asked where you were.'

'What did you tell him?'

'That I was meeting you for a drink. He didn't seem to like it, but tough shit. Anyway, told me to ask you to come to Donnybrook for eleven.'

'What's going on?' Harry asked.

'Don't know, but might be better if you turn up.'

'I'll be there. One other thing has puzzled me. How come the media never picked up on all this?'

'More luck than anything else,' said Noel. 'One paper was tipped off, and I was given the job of damage control. Said Barbara and me were coppers, and it was a monumental cock up. Told the school the same story. Had to give the reporter a sweetener about a drugs haul and she backed off.'

'And what's happening with the Swiss?' Harry asked, this time with more concern.

'I'm being kept in the dark there,' Noel shook his head. 'I'm not the Super's favourite boy at the moment, but he did order me to assist you so he's stuck with the consequences. Tomorrow may well be to do with that.'

'And the gun possession? What's happening about that?'

'Nothing I know of.' Noel took a large draught of his Guinness. 'It's being kept on ice and can be used to threaten her, but it will have to be soon. She's told us virtually nothing– she's one cool operator.' There was a note of admiration in Noel's voice. 'We confiscated hers and Julie's passports, but she probably has twenty more lying around.'

'You know she cannot be extradited to Israel, as what she did was technically committed in Syria,' Harry changed the subject, with a degree of resignation. 'I mean, if we could lift her and take her to Israel like we used to do then she could be tried and sentenced, but those days are over. It would never get approval now.'

'You know more about that than I do. We officially informed the Israelis about her, but there's been no reply, to the best of my knowledge.'

In the end they decided time would reveal what the policeman's call had been about, and after a second pint Noel left for home.

18

It was just coming up to eleven and Harry was outside the now familiar entrance to Donnybrook Garda Station. It was a cool clear morning. Noel, standing just inside the station door, noticed Harry, muttered something to a man beside him and gestured Harry back towards the street.

'Don't know what's going on,' Noel said. 'I've been told to keep you out of the way for half an hour then take you back to the Super's office. We'll walk around the block.'

When they arrived back Harry was asked to remain in the corridor as Noel was shown into the superintendent's office. Ten minutes later Harry was ushered in. It was a large room – desk, five or six chairs and a scattering of monitors. There were two people standing by a window. One was Noel; his shoulders slightly forward, looking down at the carpet. The second man was heavily built with clipped black hair and a beery reddened face. He wore a short-sleeved blue shirt and tie, and had an air of authority. His smile was forced as he greeted Harry.

'I'm Commissioner Ray Culliton.' His handshake was firm.

'Harry Katz.'

'Let's keep it informal. Call me Ray. Okay. Why are you here? Firstly, to tell you what we have found out about this Fisher woman. Seems a model citizen.' Culliton's mouth smiled, but his eyes were hard. 'Runs her own business – a small public relations company. Interestingly has never used the Katya name; everybody calls her Babs, which she claims is a nickname.' Harry nodded. 'The whole business about getting a birth certificate and a new identity was a total disgrace. Wouldn't happen now, thank God. Claims that apart from having the gun she committed no offence in Ireland, which seems true, but we can always hammer her for the weapon. Can't touch her here for the kid's false identity – it was a forged German birth cert.'

'That's all very interesting,' Harry said, 'but you haven't summoned me here just to tell me this.'

Culliton moved over to a desk and sat down. He opened a drawer and removed some sheets of paper, which he placed in front of him. His attempted smile had gone.

'We have received two requests for extradition.' His voice was clinically cold.

'Two?'

'The first came from Israel, but will be automatically discounted as being politically unacceptable.' He looked at Harry for his reaction. Harry refused to reply, keeping his face impassive. 'Our problem is with the request from the Swiss.'

Culliton moved one of the sheets of paper and turned it towards Harry. Harry ignored it and kept looking up. 'You were a police officer yourself,' Culliton continued, 'and you will appreciate that extradition requests relating to the murder of fellow officers are always, and I mean always, treated with extreme seriousness. The Swiss request has been considered at the highest levels, and this is what I need to discuss with you. Sorry, excuse me.' He held up his hand as a phone buzzed beside him. He picked it up. 'Thank you. Show him in,' he said down the phone.

Harry turned as the door behind him opened. All along he had been waiting for an involvement by Eshan, and his reaction was annoyance at the ridiculous charade they were enacting. Eshan was dressed in a dark suit, with a white shirt and a dark tie. He looked tired, slightly stooped and visibly aged since Harry had last seen him, but he had lost none of his intensity.

'Harry,' Eshan was effusive, 'congratulations on your success. The girl is Ami? No doubt?'

'No doubt at all sir, thank you,' Harry responded in Hebrew.

'How is she?'

'Grown up a bit.'

'Great.' Eshan turned towards Ray Culliton, walked over and the pair mutually backslapped. It was obvious they knew each other well. The Irishman introduced Eshan to Noel, and they exchanged guarded greetings.

'Now gentlemen, work to do,' Culliton said.

He indicated the chairs but sat behind his desk. The other three, distanced from each other, sat in front of him. Harry was seething. All his suspicions were confirmed by Eshan's dramatic appearance. Avoiding Eshan's gaze he looked at the Irish commissioner, determined to speak first.

'I feel responsible for those Swiss guys getting killed,' Harry gritted his teeth as he spoke, 'but Barbara Fisher had nothing to do with the shootings.'

Noel muttered a "yes" of agreement.

'I will do whatever to help the Swiss find who killed those guys, but I will not assist in her extradition.' Harry noticed the barest flicker of support from Noel. 'If she could be sent to Israel it would be another matter. I'm sorry.'

Harry pushed back his chair, nodded to Noel and turned towards the door. As he put his hand on the handle he heard a slow, mocking clap of applause from Eshan.

'Very noble of you, Harry, but please, stop wasting our time.' Eshan spoke in Hebrew. 'Sit down and listen to me, and then go away if you wish.'

There was a steely edge to Eshan's voice which invited compliance. Harry turned around.

'I know your agenda,' Harry replied in Hebrew. 'I've known it all along. Okay, I'll stay, but speak English.'

He sat back down, with a minor feeling of triumph. Eshan's English was poor.

'Thank you, Mr. Katz.' Ray Culliton seemed unperturbed. 'Now, I must inform you we have provisionally agreed to the Swiss application for her extradition.'

He held up his hand to silence Harry, as Harry attempted to interrupt.

'A warrant has been issued for her arrest,' Culliton picked up a sheet of printed paper, 'signed by me, and all I need to do is to order its implementation. However, your Israeli colleague has something to say to you first.'

Harry knew what was coming, but refused to give Eshan the satisfaction. He turned around and spoke before Eshan could begin.

'It's Farid. It's Farid you wanted all along,' Harry rasped in fury. 'You never cared a shit about Ami. Okay, go ahead and give me your agenda.'

'I'm not going to argue,' Eshan managed to look hurt, 'I want Farid, but so does most of the civilised world. This man is a great danger to our country.

None of us knows where he is, but the Fisher woman does.'

'So what do you want?' asked Harry, already knowing the reply.

'She gives us Farid,' Eshan replied, 'and she stays in Ireland. No extradition and no charges against her. It's Farid or her. She can choose freedom or twenty years prison in Switzerland.' He spread his hands to emphasise his point.

'You don't have enough for an extradition!' Harry exclaimed, turning towards the commissioner.

Culliton shrugged and picked up a thick file on the table in front of him.

'I've been through this file so often I know it by heart,' he said emphatically. 'The irony is you gave the Swiss virtually all of it. The videos in the airport, the time of the paged message, the teenage girl getting the ashtray from her table. Yes, they traced that girl and she saw the pager. Fingerprints on the newspaper, the taxi driver's story, the false passports and so on and so on. They have more than enough to link her to the shootings.'

Harry knew he was right, but decided on another tack. He shrugged.

'Okay then, send her to Zurich. It's not my problem – I've found Ami. Do what you like with Miss Fisher. Of course I'd like to get even with Farid, but I'm out of that game now.'

Culliton shook his head.

'It's not so easy,' he said. 'What about the girl?'

'She's my daughter. I'll look after her.'

'No, you won't, at least not in the short term. You will first have to prove paternity to an Irish court, and satisfy Social Services you would be a suitable parent. It all takes time – far longer than you can imagine.'

'Okay,' Harry persisted, 'I can do that.'

'Maybe so,' Culliton said, 'but think about the reality. She will go straight into a care centre, and believe me, I would not like my own daughter going anywhere near one of those. Explain it to him, Sergeant Murphy.'

Noel coughed in embarrassment.

'He's right, Harry. If she's not a junkie going in, she could be by the time she leaves. You don't want Julie going there.'

Realising he was beaten, Harry turned back to Eshan.

'How sure are you she can give you Farid?' Harry asked, in English.

'They have a history,' Eshan spoke in a matter of fact voice. 'We've known about her for years, but we always thought she was German. I had no idea she was Irish.'

'If she co-operates, what guarantee can I give her?' Harry asked Culliton, ignoring Eshan. 'I'll need it in writing, black and white.'

'I can give you that. Now, you must understand I have been placed in a difficult position. The Swiss need to arrest some guilty person and she will do, but if we get him he goes to Zurich instead of her.'

'It's a tough game Harry,' added Eshan unnecessarily. 'She knew the rules when she got into it.'

Realising he had been backed into a corner, Harry paced around the room in silent thought. As he looked over he saw Noel silently mouthing the words 'Do it.' Harry turned back towards Culliton.

'Okay, but I don't know if she'll cooperate.' Harry conceded.

He took out his mobile and looked up Barbara's number, the others watching as he rang, Eshan's face changed to an angry scowl as Harry and Barbara conversed in rapid German.Harry told her she had no option but to agree. He had to meet her now, no matter what she was doing. She agreed to see him in one hour, but would have Julie and a school friend of Julie's with her. She gave a location, telling Harry that if Noel were driving then Noel would find the place easily. Harry said nothing to Eshan, but requested and was granted Noel's assistance. They left the office together.

Harry and Noel were deep in silent thought as they drove to Sandycove, near to Barbara's house. Harry was sceptical of Eshan's conviction that Barbara would be able to influence Hussam Farid. Still, if he could persuade her to assist even in some small way it might be enough to avoid her extradition. If not it could buy time for negotiation. She would have to give the Swiss something, that much was clear.

It was another cloudless and still autumn day. As they approached Sandycove, driving around the margin of a bay which Noel said was called Scotsman's Bay, the water looked like a sheet of blue glass extending to a low headland in the distance. An occasional yacht floated motionless with empty sails. Sandycove was a tiny harbour, almost a toy harbour, with a narrow entrance opening into a small beach. Noel told a disbelieving Harry that fishing boats had once used it. It was tidal, but the tide was now nearly full in and young children were paddling in its shallow water.

There was nowhere nearby to park, so Noel left Harry at the top of a small slipway and drove off to find parking. On the other side of the beach Harry saw Barbara, Julie and another teenage girl sitting on a grey stone bench. He moved along the narrow strip of sand and up a few steps. Julie and her friend were wearing their green school uniforms, and Barbara wore jeans, a loose black top and sandals. She was smoking a cigarette and glared as Harry approached. They were many people on the pier, mostly mothers with small children enjoying the sunshine.

Julie's smile moved him to the core.

'Hello Harry. This is my friend Deirdre. Deirdre, this is my dad.'

'Hello Deirdre.' Harry gave the girl his best smile, but then turned towards his daughter. 'It's great to see you, Julie, but I need to speak to your mum alone. Can you excuse us for a moment?'

'Sure.' Julie shrugged.

Harry indicated to Barbara that they move away. At the end of the pier, only ten metres farther but nearly empty, Barbara took a pack of cigarettes from her bag and lit another from the one she held. She threw the old one into the water, ignoring the disapproving look of a woman walking past.

'I hope that "Hello Harry" crap didn't fool you,' Barbara muttered, cigarette in her mouth. 'That was a cheap dig at me. I can smell a problem, so tell me.'

Harry looked out towards the sea. There were a number of canoes paddling slowly through the bay.

'There's trouble.' He turned back to Barbara. 'Big trouble. They're going to arrest you.'

'Me?' Barbara's face changed to surprise. 'For what? When?'

'Now, if you go home,' Harry tried to keep his voice as calm as possible, 'and it's not for the gun. They're going to send you to Zurich.'

'Zurich!' Barbara spat out. 'But you promised me.' She turned to leave but Harry grabbed her firmly by the elbow, stopping her.

'It's not my doing. I only found out just before I phoned you.'

'But they can't send me to Zurich. I did nothing there.'

'You did.' Harry sat down and Barbara almost reflexively slumped down beside him. 'They can link you directly to that pager. The airport monitors have you sitting in the food hall at the exact time of the message. Do you remember a teenage girl asking you for the ashtray on your table?'

'A teenage girl?' Barbara tried to remember. 'Yes, I vaguely do. But what about her?'

'They traced her,' Harry continued, his hand on her arm. 'The girl saw you get the message on the pager. They have the time on their video and it's damning evidence, as no other messages were paged in Zurich at that exact time. It links you directly to the shootings. Then there's the taxi driver, your prints on the newspaper, you leaving Basel with the false passport and so on. It's fairly watertight if they want to pursue it, and they claim the best you could hope for would be ten years.'

Barbara stood up, threw her cigarette into the water and turned on Harry. 'So why haven't they come with the handcuffs? Why are you here?'

'Before I tell you, look back there,' Harry ordered, not reacting to her anger.

'Where?' asked Barbara as she turned. 'What's there?'

'I see my Ami there. Not your Julie.' Harry's voice was cold and harsh as he pointed. 'If you go to Zurich I keep her. I can and will move to Dublin, but there's an alternative.'

Barbara turned back to him, a new uncertainty in her demeanour. She seemed about to speak but instead stood up and lit yet another cigarette. She drew heavily on it.

'What?'

Harry reached into the inside pocket of his jacket and removed the photograph. Silently he handed it to her. In surprise she turned it over.

Her face drained of colour as she looked at the photo. Her knees seemed to give and she staggered slightly before sitting down on a small capstan, still staring at the photograph.

'So, this is the photo of me that appeared in Zurich?' she asked haltingly.

'So you knew?'

'I was told a Zionist agent had appeared with a photo, but I wasn't prepared for this. I don't need to ask, it's from Lebanon.'

'Yes. It's what led me to you.'

'It's a shock seeing it.' She gave a hollow, mocking laugh. 'Not a bad photo of me if it's going to be all over the papers.'

'There's your answer, Barbara.' He kept his voice authoritative. Still seated, his face was fixed with intense concentration. 'Farid. They know about you and him. It's a trade-off. Give them Farid, and you won't be charged. Do nothing, and you go to prison. It's your call.'

'No, I won't do that.' Barbara's eyes flashed. 'I can't do it.'

'I can only possibly guess how much he means to you,' Harry's voice continued calm, reassuring. 'Kamil Shamsoul told me.'

'What! You've met Kamil?'

'And others.' Harry lowered his voice and moved closer to her. 'I know a lot about you, but one thing makes absolutely no sense. Why Zurich? You had walked away from this business. After all these years, why? Why did you do it?'

'Do you think I have thought about anything else the past two weeks?' Barbara snapped. 'It should have been so easy. It was only a simple swap. The woman I was meeting knew me from the old days. Just hand over some papers and leave. I even thought the false passports a bit unnecessary, but wasn't taking any chances, and they had nearly expired anyway. I insisted on the pager as a doomsday backup, but I used that stupid toothpaste message.'

'Yes,' Harry replied gently, 'it was that message.'

'So it had to be Helen,' Barbara sighed in resignation as Harry nodded. 'I just prayed she wouldn't make the connection.'

'But you still haven't answered. Why Zurich?'

'For him.' Barbara looked down at the ground as she spoke, not wanting to meet Harry's gaze. 'For Hussam. He asked me. He's still in love with me, but all I feel is guilt. I still see him, but I don't love him anymore. In spite of that he's the only man in my life. He half-heartedly tried to blackmail me, but I knew he would never follow through. That's why I had the gun, I was afraid of them.'

'And who is "them"?'

She shot a look of utter contempt. 'Don't act the idiot.'

Harry shrugged in acceptance. 'You will have to do it, Barbara,' he persisted. 'Not for me, but for Julie. Do it for her.'

Barbara looked back at the two teenagers, huddled together in conversation, and then turned back to Harry, her face flushed with rage.

'Fuck you!' she shouted, uncaring of the people around her. 'Fuck all of you. I will never forgive you for this. Do you have any idea what this means? You know I have no choice, no bloody choice.'

Barbara stormed off towards the two hushed girls and strode past them in silence. Julie shot a puzzled look at Harry. He indicated to her to follow

Barbara. She took her friend by the arm and they hurried away.

19

Thursday pm: The official go ahead was given. Harry was called with a message to go directly to Harcourt Square, headquarters of the Garda Special Units. Noel was waiting at reception and took Harry to the planning office, a long shabby room with a rectangular table in the centre. Commissioner Culliton was seated there with Eshan, along with two men from the Irish Army's elite Ranger division. No names were exchanged. The Rangers' role would be to secure the street outside; inside would be left to Harry and a policewoman called Susan. Culliton apologised that Susan would be a bit late.

The atmosphere remained tense. Eshan prowled around the room in scowling silence. Harry had insisted if Eshan were to be allowed to attend, he must not speak. Culliton had reluctantly accepted, but in turn insisted he, Culliton, must chair the meeting. They waited until seven fifteen and decided to commence without Susan.

First, Culliton summarised their plan. Barbara had agreed to stay in a hotel, where she would be guarded around the clock and have her mobile monitored until her meeting with Farid. Culliton, with Eshan's backing, made it clear he did not trust Barbara, and they were going to sit on her until the very last moment. He appreciated that she had pressurised Farid to agree to meet her on Friday, but there were still far too many variables.

Their plan predicated on Farid arranging to meet Barbara in their usual place, a cafe called Biba in Ranelagh, an old inner city suburb near to the main city mosque. For this reason it attracted a regular Muslim clientele. Their main problem was that Farid never committed to a time and place until just before he and Barbara were due to meet, when he would text her. At such short notice they had no backup plan for another venue.

All going well, Barbara would meet Farid in the café, apologise for her hostility at their last meeting, but tell him she was irrevocably finished with all activism. She would still continue seeing him, but all else would be over. They would leave together and outside the café the Rangers would seize Farid.

Nobody suggested any intervention inside the café – it would be too hazardous.

Harry had insisted he be inside. While he knew Farid, Farid did not know him. Harry could of course speak Arabic, and, even Eshan had to admit, had been trained for such a scenario. Most importantly, he was fluent in German and could listen in to whatever Barbara and Farid discussed in that language. However, no matter how hard Harry pressed, Culliton would not let him carry a gun.

Their discussion was interrupted by the arrival of the policewoman who would accompany Harry in the café. She was unlike anyone's stereotype of a police officer. In her late twenties, she was petite, with wild curly red hair and a scattering of freckles. She wore a black denim jacket, black jeans, white sneakers and a white top with a huge red letter P on the front. She had a green stud in her nose. Culliton introduced her to all, except the Rangers. She took a chair and sat forward to join the discussion.

Five o'clock next day. The group nervously waited in an apartment in Ranelagh, just around the corner from the Biba Café. They were four – Harry, Noel, Susan and Barbara. Harry's concern was Barbara. She was too quiet, and looked deathly pale as she sat in the corner of the room, smoking one cigarette after another, looking at the floor.

Noel received a text and gave a grunt of satisfaction. All was in place. For the third time Harry repeated the anticipated procedure. Barbara would go in first, and as she entered a woman sitting at the nearest table to the door would get up to leave, allowing Barbara to take that table. Harry and Susan would go in five minutes later and join two "friends", who would be sitting at the next table. The friends would depart shortly after, leaving Harry and Susan in position. There would be other armed police already in the café, but they would be unknown to the others.

Five-fifteen. Barbara's phone beeped a text.

"Biba. 5.30"

Apart from a perfunctory "yes" Barbara never spoke. She texted "OK" in reply and left the apartment without looking at the others. They waited as the police radio reported her progress. Harry and Susan counted down the five minutes, and then hand in hand walked to the café.

The café entrance opened into a corner of a bright square room. On the right of the door, viewed from inside, was a large plate glass window looking onto the street. On the left side was a yellow wall with a magazine rack and pictures. The floor was tiled in black and white squares, and there were about fifteen tables, a mixture of circular and square. Most were occupied by couples or people sitting alone. The background music was easy listening rock. The counter stood along the wall farthest from the door, and there was only the one entrance from the street.

As Harry went in he passed Barbara, sitting at the arranged table, staring at a cup of tea on the table in front of her. She was on the chair closest to the door with the chair opposite her, facing the door, empty. Behind the free seat was a table for four, with two women seated there. One of the women called to Susan, and she pretended surprise. She introduced Harry as a new boyfriend, and Susan accepted the invitation to take the two free seats. Harry sat on the arranged chair, with his back to the seat opposite Barbara. It seemed perfect. On the wall opposite hung a huge mirror, giving a clear view of behind.

After ten minutes of animated conversation the two women at their table expressed their annoyance that they had to go, and after much hugging and promising to meet soon they departed. In the mirror Harry could see Barbara as she pretended to read a newspaper. Susan sat on Harry's right, and she took out a crossword and began to complete this, insisting on Harry's help. Harry could not help smiling, it all seemed so banal.

Still, he needed reassurance.

'Your gun,' he leaned forward to whisper to Susan. 'Which side is it?'

'Why?'

'I can't see it, and just want to be certain you have it.'

'Good,' she smiled and patted under her right armpit. 'It's here. I'm left handed.'

'You're definite you are ready for this?' he asked unnecessarily. She nodded. 'It could get nasty. Make sure the holster is open and the safety off, and for God's sake don't shoot me.'

'I'll do my best,' she replied with a cheeky grin. To Harry's relief she reached inside her jacket and adjusted her holster as he had advised. Their mobiles lay on the table among the coffee cups. Their preparations made, they continued the crossword.

Farid arrived three minutes early.

At 5.27 a young Arab man opened the door and scanned the café. Harry noticed Barbara take her bag from the floor and put it on the table. The young man went out and closed the door. Harry softly pressed on Susan's foot.

'It's on.' Leaning forward he whispered in her ear. 'Bag on table means the coast is clear. He's coming.'

Susan was cool. She never even blinked; just put down the pen she was holding and in an apparent search around her pockets for a tissue re-checked her gun. She blew her nose and picked up the pen again.

Still pretending to check the crossword Harry, in the mirror, saw the door open and Hussam Farid enter. Had he not been expecting him Harry would never have recognised Farid. He looked like a prosperous businessman, with small briefcase, expensive looking navy suit, light blue shirt and dark tie. His hair was short and gelled, and he wore gold-rimmed glasses. He did not look around the room, but pushed back the chair opposite Barbara and sat down, back to back with Harry. Harry sat upright to hear better, his eyes fixed on the mirror. He was totally focused, only concentrating on what was happening behind him. Susan had ceased to exist. If only he had a gun!

Farid pulled his chair towards the table slightly and their chair backs no longer touched. Harry could see only Barbara's head as she leaned forward. Presumably Farid could not see her face either. Farid said nothing and the only thing Harry heard was the sound of Barbara deeply breathing until Farid spoke to her, in heavily accented German.

'What is it?' Farid's voice sounded caring. 'What's wrong?'

Barbara continued looking down at the table, and Harry barely heard her as she spoke.

'I'm sorry,' she whispered. 'I'm so very sorry.'

Harry tensed. This was going badly wrong. From behind him Harry could hear Farid ask again what was wrong, and in the mirror could see only the top of Barbara's lowered head. He could sense Farid beginning to worriedly look around the café. Harry saw his eyes stop at a door beside the counter, factoring it as a possible exit point. Then he looked in Harry's direction, and in the mirror their eyes met for an instant. It was enough. Harry knew he had been made – Farid had intuitively recognised Harry for what he was.

It was now or never! Harry lunged across and reached inside Susan's jacket. Before she had time to respond he grasped the handle of her Walther automatic and in one movement jerked it out. He jumped up, turned around and violently rammed the muzzle of the gun to the side of Farid's head, just as Farid had begun to get to his feet.

'Don't move!' Harry barked in Arabic as he clicked the gun's safety catch. 'I'll blow your fucking head if you move.'

There were terrified screams all around. From the corner of his eye Harry saw Susan stand up, take out a card and shout that she was a police officer. To Harry's right two punks with green Mohican hair jumped up, guns in hand, yelling they were police. Everybody must leave the café immediately, out the back door. Harry was aware of Susan shouting down her radio to get the guy outside. In a few moments of confusion and terror the café emptied. Harry remained standing, his gun still firmly pressed to Farid's head.

Farid did not panic. He did not even look towards Harry; instead he tried to lift his hand off the table to touch Barbara, only to stop as Harry barked he would shoot unless Farid put his hand down immediately. Farid let his hand drop and seemingly ignoring Harry spoke to Barbara, again in German.

'So that's it?' Farid's voice held an edge of sadness. 'You, Babs, of all people. You betray me! I don't know who this joker with the gun is, but I'm going to stand up and leave.'

Barbara finally looked up. She was agonised, her lips trembling.

'Hussam. I'm so sorry.' Her voice was barely audible as she stammered. 'He is Julie's father.'

'What?' Farid now seemed to accept Harry's presence, turning slowly around.

'You killed his wife,' Barbara stressed. 'He'll shoot you, believe me.'

Harry's knuckles whitened as he gripped the gun, but he remained focused. Somewhere in his head he heard a voice telling him to shoot. This creature had killed Rachel. Killed Beth. Ruined my life. Took my daughter. Kill him. But his finger did not tighten. Farid looked at him, and Harry stared back. Neither moved until the café door opened and Noel rushed in, gun in hand. Harry never took his eyes off Farid as he sensed Noel's approach, and he held the gun steady as Noel roughly handcuffed Farid. He barely heard Noel's official notification to Farid that he was arresting him on foot of an extradition request.

Farid turned away from Harry towards Noel, and then looked past Noel as Ray Culliton entered the café, closely followed by Eshan. A bead of sweat appeared on Farid's brow as his face changed to a look of hatred.

'You!' Farid hissed in Arabic, anger clear in his voice as he recognised Eshan. 'You cannot extradite me to your shithole country. Tell this pig to take the gun away.'

'Mr Hussam Farid,' Culliton interjected, 'I have a warrant for your arrest as an accessory to the murder of two policemen in Switzerland.'

'Two Swiss police killed, and you want to arrest me?' Farid shouted and pointed towards Eshan. 'Why? I am not a criminal. That Jew is. He is the great terrorist. Arrest him, not me.'

Farid leaned forward and Harry let the gun fall to his own side. He watched as Farid turned to Barbara, still sitting slumped, her face in her hands.

'I'm not afraid of these people,' Farid spoke to her. 'My work will continue anyway, but you. Of all people, you are the one who betrays me. After all we have done together. This is the biggest hurt.'

Barbara never moved. Noel grasped Farid's arm and roughly forced him upright, turning him towards the door. Harry stood back, but as they passed him Farid turned towards Harry.

'I made only one mistake,' he snarled, in Arabic. 'I should have killed that Jew child, like I killed her mother. This is the thanks I get for my mercy.'

Something in Harry snapped. He brushed Noel aside, raised the gun to Farid's head, and was about to squeeze the trigger when something stopped him. He dropped the gun to the ground and slumped back in a chair, silently watching as Farid was led out of the café, followed by Culliton. Harry sat still, emptied of emotion. Eventually Barbara stood up and glared at him.

'I hope you're bloody happy now,' she hissed. She seemed about to say something else but instead turned and ran out the door, leaving her bag on the table. Eshan watched her leave, and leaned towards Harry. He was smiling.

'Well done Harry.' He spoke in Hebrew. 'We got him. Congratulations.'

Harry ignored Eshan. He picked up Barbara's bag and hurried out the door, past the cordon of heavily armed police. Through the curious crowd and down the pavement he hastened after her fleeing figure.

20

Monday am: Harry walked to Spar and bought an Irish Times. He sat on a bench nearby and scanned the news section. The front page was dominated by a political scandal, and there was a six-line snippet, well inside the paper, about the events of Friday. The police claimed they were still questioning two foreign nationals, believed to be about a drugs shipment. He walked back to the bed and breakfast he had moved to, which was one block away from the Farrell's house, and owned by a friend of Margaret's. He looked at his watch. Eight-thirty. One hour before his meeting in the Israeli embassy.

Harry's phone rang. It was Eshan on caller ID, the fifth time he had called. As with the previous calls, Harry let it ring out. A text followed – the same as the others. "Call me". Once again Harry ignored it. He wanted no further communication with Eshan. He smiled as he looked at his previous received message, this one very different. "Seven o'clock Dad. xxx Julie". She had invited him to dinner on Monday evening.

It was warm but cloudy as he walked to the embassy. He arrived ten minutes early but stood a distance away scanning the street. There was no visible media presence. Still not prepared to take any chances, he waited for a group of men dressed like him to appear, and as he had done in Killiney he walked to the embassy as if with them. Just as he reached it a car pulled up and Ray Culliton, in civilian clothes, emerged and hurried to the entrance, reaching it simultaneously with Harry. He ushered Harry through the door, but once inside gave a warm smile. His attitude was different from Saturday's debriefing, when he had been openly hostile.

'Just in case you're wondering what I'm doing here,' Culliton said. 'I called this meeting, and it was my suggestion to ask you. Can't tell you what's going to happen, but would you have a word with me afterwards? Strictly off the record.'

'Sure.'

The receptionist took them over to the lift. Neither spoke in the short ascent, and on entering the embassy proper were met by Sonia Weismann, who formally welcomed the Irishman but gave Harry an even colder greeting than before. They followed her into her office.

Weismann apologised for the absence of the ambassador, and formally asked Commissioner Culliton why he had requested the meeting. It was clear Harry was not present at her invitation. Culliton removed some papers from a folder, passed them to her, and stated that their contents were the response of the Irish authorities to the formal Israeli request for the extradition of a Mr. Hussam Farid. Unfortunately, for the reasons contained therein, the request was refused. Weismann nodded in acceptance. She would of course pass this information on to Jerusalem. She seemed not the slightest bit upset, unlike Harry. He had expected no less but still felt an enormous grievance. Weismann politely thanked Culliton for his assistance, and enquired if there was anything more. The Irishman glanced at his watch, and took a Blackberry from his pocket. He scrolled, found what he was looking for, gave a grimace of annoyance and turned towards Harry.

'First, I must emphasise in the strongest possible manner that this situation is not my wish.' He raised his eyes theatrically. 'As of ten minutes ago Mr. Farid is on a plane to Sweden. Apparently there are virtually no extradition agreements between Sweden and Switzerland. I argued all weekend to send him to Zurich, but the Attorney General made the decision to refuse the Swiss request. We had no farther grounds to detain him.'

A silence followed. Harry looked at the First Secretary, and she at him. Her face betrayed no emotion, but to his immense surprise Harry felt little disappointment. It was as if Zurich did not matter. Farid had not been there. He had not killed the policemen, but he had certainly killed Rachel. Although Harry knew all along Farid would never be sent to Israel, it still was a body blow to actually hear the reality. No, there was unfinished business between himself and Farid. Had he made a mistake in ignoring Eshan's attempts at communication?

The meeting was over. Weismann stood up, thanked the Irishman for his assistance, ignored Harry and showed them to the lift. In the lobby Culliton recommended they go by a rear exit, as he did not want anyone seeing them together. They needed somewhere to talk. Harry suggested Herbert Park. Culliton ushered Harry into his waiting car and within five minutes they were strolling through the gates. Culliton was the first to speak. He offered Harry a cigarette. Harry declined.

'I'll get the hardest bit over first,' Culliton began. 'In that cafe, I thought I had made the biggest mistake of my life. I was sure you were going to shoot that bastard!'

'I nearly did. If we meet again I will kill him, I promise you that, but it will be at a time and place of my choosing. That's unless Eshan gets there first. So, where is he? Where's Eshan?'

'Gone. Left early Saturday – you saw he wasn't at the debriefing.'

'I presumed he went back, but wasn't sure. Did he talk to Farid?'

Culliton walked to a litterbin, extinguished his cigarette and put it inside.

'Yes, chaperoned by two of our officers. Unfortunately we couldn't find anyone who spoke Arabic, and promised we wouldn't record the meeting. Farid never spoke a single word, just looked at the floor for two solid hours. I don't think Mr Bercovic expected otherwise. I can't possibly over stress how angry I am that he was released. Why do we bother? All that shaggin' work and they fly him first bloody class to Stockholm.'

Harry grunted an agreement, and both were silent as a group of women wearing Islamic veils passed by. Harry was beginning to change his assessment of the Irishman, but he waited for him to continue. Culliton stopped walking and looked directly at Harry.

'Now, this bit is strictly off the record, off all records. Do you agree?'

'That's okay with me.'

'I sincerely hope everything works out with your daughter. So, if things pan out well, you might make a move to Dublin?'

'That depends on many things.'

'I understand. I've two teenage daughters, and they're more than a handful. Now, you'll need a job if you stay here. I have discussed this with my own boss, and you may be the answer to one of our problems. We need an advisor on Islamic related subversives. There is no way on earth we would consider using an Israeli, but we could come to an arrangement with a German national. On a purely consultancy basis, of course. Think about it.'

Harry blinked in surprise, then gave a wry smile.

'Now that is unexpected,' he said. 'Yes, I'll think about it, but I'm not too sure. I have a meeting later this week with a friend of Brian Farrell's, and there may be a possibility of a job offer there. What's happening with Barbara Fisher?'

'Nothing. She kept her part of the arrangement, and we have notified the Swiss we have to refuse their request. I discussed the status of your daughter with our social services, and they decided not to take her into care. She's better at home than in a grotty hostel. There is some good news.'

'What?'

'Miss Fisher has agreed to your formal registration as the girl's biological father. We can prove it by DNA analysis, but nobody is contesting it. It's considered to be in the girl's best interests.'

Culliton looked at his watch and apologised. He must go. Harry sat at the same bench where he had sat a week previously, once again looking at mothers with young children feeding the ducks. He gazed up. The sun had broken through the clouds and shone brightly on him. For the first time in years he felt a sense of happiness.

Barbara answered the door. Harry had brought a bottle of wine, unsure about the protocol. She gestured him inside. Julie stood in the kitchen, putting what seemed the finishing touches to the spaghetti Bolognese she had cooked. The previous times he had met Julie she had been wearing her school uniform, but seeing her in her normal clothes brought a sudden realisation this was a beautiful young woman, not a girl. Her hair was tied up and she wore makeup. "Too much makeup," as Barbara muttered in an aside. Julie gave Harry a kiss on the cheek, and indicated Harry and Barbara to their seats.

She fussed elaborately over dinner, her nervousness clearly evident, but after they had finished eating she seemed more relaxed. They sat at the table where Barbara, Harry and Noel had talked and argued on the first day, but now it had two lighted candles. Outside it was dusk and raining heavily, the drops loud against the window. When they had finished eating Barbara cleared the table, leaving only Harry's wineglass, and took a seat at the other end of the kitchen. She lit a cigarette and sat back with her own glass of wine.

Harry picked up an envelope he had left on a chair. 'I only brought three photos,' he began. 'I have hundreds more, but in Munich. This one is Rachel when she was sixteen, only a bit older than you are now.'

He passed the first photograph to Julie, who took a couple of deep breaths before turning it around. It was an un-posed head and shoulders image of Rachel. The resemblance to Julie was striking. Julie gripped the edges of the photo tightly, intermittently looking down at the image and up at her father before handing it over to Barbara, who looked at the photo in silence.

'That could be me.' Julie spoke, haltingly. 'Now I can see why you spotted me on the hockey pitch – we are so similar. What was she like at my age?'

'I didn't know her then, but Rachel and her mother always said she was interested only in dancing and playing the flute. She went to university in Boston after high school, and then moved to Israel. That's where I met her.'

'And she had a twin sister. Lucky girl.'

'I'm not too sure about that,' Harry smiled. 'They were very different from each other, and used to squabble all the time.'

'Still, it would be nice,' Julie sighed, almost theatrically. 'You have other photographs of her?'

'Hundreds, as I said, but not here. Now, the second photo. This was taken at our wedding.'

He passed it to her, but this time she remained seated.

'She is so beautiful.' Julie was silent for a few moments as she scanned around the photograph. 'That's you there, but who are the others?'

'That's my mother,' Harry pointed, 'but she has passed away. The other two are Rachel's parents. His name is Roy, and he died a few years ago. Her mum there, Anna, is still very much alive. I told you about her. She's on the phone all the time wanting to meet her granddaughter. You'll like her.'

'She looks nice.'

Harry showed her the third photo.

'This is your first birthday party. It was on a beach near Tiberias – that's the town in Israel where we used to live. It's beside Lake Galilee.'

'Which one is me?' Julie asked.

'The one with the curly hair.' Harry pointed. 'The other baby is Alice, and those are her parents. They're Irish. They live near here and would love to meet you. Alice and you are the same age.'

'Can I keep these?'

'Of course you can, it's why I brought them.'

Julie put the photographs together, stood up and said she wanted to leave them in her bedroom. Harry and Barbara waited in silence. He sipped his wine until she returned. Julie sat down again at the table, and played with her glass for a moment.

'I've got to get this over with,' she looked serious, 'so here goes. You're not going to like it.'

233

'Go ahead.' Harry met her gaze.

'You know this has all been terrible for me,' Julie spoke confidently, 'but there are some things I must say. Apparently I'm Jewish, and have no choice in the matter as my birth mother was Jewish. I don't mind that, but I'm not and never will be Israeli. I'm Irish and I'm going to remain Irish. Also mum said you worked for the Israeli secret police against those poor Palestinians. Is that true?'

Harry looked over to Barbara, who looked coldly back, a thin smile of defiance on her lips.

'Yes, you were born Jewish,' Harry conceded, 'and I agree with you, you are Irish. And yes, I did work for the Israeli police.'

'And how could you possibly justify Gaza, and what they are doing to the Palestinians? Yes, I know a lot about it. Mum discusses it with me all the time.'

'It's a long story, but I'll try and explain.'

Julie glanced over to Barbara, looking for backup, and Barbara moved over to the table. She sat down, wineglass in one hand, Julie's hand in her other.

'I'm looking forward to hearing this part.' Barbara smiled sweetly at Harry.

'Well,' Harry began, ignoring Barbara, 'it depends when you want to start. It could be two thousand years ago, when we were expelled from Judea, or 1949 when the Palestinian Arabs left.'

'Left!' Julie interrupted. 'Bullshit. They didn't leave, they were driven out.'

The argument intensified......

Ends

John O'Keeffe

.

John O'Keeffe

John O'Keeffe